THE DEVIL RIDES OUT

*

The Devil Rides Out is a Black Magic story by Dennis Wheatley, who writes: 'I, personally, have never assisted at, or participated in, any ceremony connected with Magic—Black or White. Should any of my readers incline to a serious study of the subject and thus come into contact with a man or woman of Power, I feel that it is only right to urge them, most strongly, to refrain from being drawn into the practice of the Secret Art in any way. My own observations have led me to an absolute conviction that to do so would bring them into dangers of a very real and concrete nature.'

BY DENNIS WHEATLEY

NOVELS

The Launching of Roger Brook
The Shadow of Tyburn Tree
The Rising Storm
The Man Who Killed the King
The Dark Secret of Josephine
The Rape of Venice
The Sultan's Daughter
The Wanton Princess
Evil in a Mask

The Scarlet Impostor
Faked Passports
The Black Baroness
V for Vengeance
Come Into My Parlour
Traitors' Gate
They Used Dark Forces

The Prisoner in the Mask
The Second Seal
Vendetta in Spain
Three Inquisitive People
The Forbidden Territory
The Devil Rides Out
The Golden Spaniard
Strange Conflict
Codeword—Golden Fleece
Dangerous Inheritance

The Quest of Julian Day
The Sword of Fate
Bill for the Use of a Body

Black August
Contraband
The Island Where Time Stands
   Still
The White Witch of the South
   Seas
To the Devil—A Daughter
The Satanist

The Eunuch of Stamboul
The Secret War
The Fabulous Valley
Sixty Days to Live
Such Power is Dangerous
Uncharted Seas
The Man Who Missed the War
The Haunting of Toby Jugg
Star of Ill-Omen
They Found Atlantis
The Ka of Gifford Hillary
Curtain of Fear
Mayhem in Greece
Unholy Crusade

SHORT STORIES
Mediterranean Nights
Gunmen, Gallants and Ghosts

HISTORICAL
'Old Rowley'
(*A Private Life of Charles II*)
Red Eagle
(*The Story of the Russian Revolution*)

AUTOBIOGRAPHICAL
Stranger than Fiction
(*War Papers for the Joint Planning Staff*)
Saturdays with Bricks

Dennis Wheatley

The Devil Rides Out

ARROW BOOKS

ARROW BOOKS LTD
3 Fitzroy Square, London W1

AN IMPRINT OF THE HUTCHINSON GROUP

London Melbourne Sydney Auckland
Wellington Johannesburg Cape Town
and agencies throughout the world

*

First published by
Hutchinson & Co (*Publishers*) Ltd 1934
First Arrow edition 1954
Second impression 1958
Third impression 1958
Fourth impression 1959
Fifth impression 1963
Sixth impression 1964
Seventh impression 1965
Eighth impression 1966
Ninth impression 1968
This new edition June 1969
Second impression November 1969
Third impression September 1970
Fourth impression May 1971
Fifth impression November 1972
Sixth impression June 1973

*Made and printed in Great Britain
by The Anchor Press Ltd,
Tiptree, Essex*

ISBN 0 09 907240 8

Contents

To my old friend

MERVYN BARON

of whom, in these days, I see far too little but
whose companionship, both in good times and in
bad, has been to me a never-failing joy.

D.W.

Author's Note

I desire to state that I, personally, have never assisted at, or
participated in, any ceremony connected with Magic—Black or
White.

The literature of occultism is so immense that any conscientious
writer can obtain from it abundant material for the background
of a romance such as this.

In the present case I have spared no pains to secure accuracy
of detail from existing accounts when describing magical rites or
formulas for protection against evil, and these have been verified
in conversation with certain persons, sought out for that purpose
who are actual practitioners of the Art.

All the characters and situations in this book are entirely
imaginary but, in the inquiry necessary to the writing of it, I
found ample evidence that Black Magic is still practised in
London, and other cities, at the present day.

Should any of my readers incline to a serious study of the
subject, and thus come into contact with a man or woman of
Power, I feel that it is only right to urge them, most strongly, to
refrain from being drawn into the practice of the Secret Art in
any way. My own observations have led me to an absolute
conviction that to do so would bring them into dangers of a
very real and concrete nature.

DENNIS WHEATLEY

1

The Incomplete Reunion

The Duke de Richleau and Rex Van had gone in to dinner at eight o'clock, but coffee was not served till after ten.

An appetite in keeping with his mighty frame had enabled Van Ryn to do ample justice to each well-chosen course and, as was his custom each time the young American arrived in England, the Duke had produced his finest wines for this, their reunion dinner at his flat.

A casual observer might well have considered it a strange friendship, but despite their difference in age and race, appearance and tradition, a real devotion existed between the two.

Some few years earlier Rex's foolhardiness had landed him in a Soviet prison, and the elderly French exile had put aside his peaceful existence as art connoisseur and dilettante to search for him in Russia. Together they had learned the dangerous secret of 'The Forbidden Territory' and travelled many thousand verts pursued by the merciless agents of the Ogpu.

There had been others too in that strange adventure; young Richard Eaton, and the little Princess Marie Lou whom he had brought out of Russia as his bride; but as Rex accepted a long Hoyo de Monterrey from the cedar cabinet which the Duke's man presented to him his thoughts were not of the Eatons, living now so happily with their little daughter Fleur in their lovely old country home near Kidderminster. He was thinking of that third companion whose subtle brain and shy, nervous courage had proved so great an aid when they were hunted like hares through the length and breadth of Russia, the frail narrow-shouldered English Jew—Simon Aron.

'What could possibly have kept Simon from being with them tonight,' Rex was wondering. He had never failed before to make a third at these reunion dinners, and why had the Duke brushed aside his inquiries about him in such an offhand manner. There was something queer behind De Richleau's reticence, and Rex had a feeling that for all his host's easy charm and bland, witty conversation something had gone seriously wrong.

He slowly revolved some of the Duke's wonderful old brandy in a bowl-shaped glass, while he watched the servant preparing to leave the room. Then, as the door closed, he set it down and addressed De Richleau almost abruptly.

'Well, I'm thinking it's about time for you to spill the beans.'

The Duke inhaled the first cloud of fragrant smoke from another of those long Hoyos which were his especial pride, and answered guardedly. 'Had you not better tell me Rex, to what particular beans you refer?'

'Simon of course! For years now the three of us have dined together on my first night, each time I've come across, and you were too mighty casual to be natural when I asked about him before dinner. Why isn't he here?'

'Why, indeed, my friend?' the Duke repeated, running the tips of his fingers down his lean handsome face. 'I asked him, and told him that your ship docked this morning, but he declined to honour us tonight.'

'Is he ill then?'

'No, as far as I know he's perfectly well—at all events he was at his office today.'

'He must have had a date then that he couldn't scrap, or some mighty urgent work. Nothing less could induce him to let us down on one of these occasions. They've become—well, in a way, almost sacred to our friendship.'

'On the contrary he is at home alone tonight. He made his apologies of course, something about resting for a Bridge Tournament that starts . . .'

'Bridge Tournament my foot!' exclaimed Rex angrily. 'He'd never let that interfere between us three—it sounds mighty fishy to me. When did you see him last?'

'About three months ago.'

'What! But that's incredible. Now look here!' Rex thrust the

8

onyx ash-tray from in front of him, and leaned across the table. 'You haven't quarrelled—have you?'

De Richleau shook his head. 'If you were my age, Rex, and had no children, then met two younger men who gave you their affection, and had all the attributes you could wish for in your sons, how would it be possible for you to quarrel with either of them?'

'That's so, but three months is a whale of a while for friends who are accustomed to meet two or three times a week. I just don't get this thing at all, and you're being a sight too reticent about it. Come on now—what do you know?'

The grey eyes of almost piercing brilliance which gave such character to De Richleau's face, lit up. 'That,' he said suddenly, 'is just the trouble. I don't *know* anything.'

'But you fear that, to use his own phrase, Simon's "in a muddle—a really nasty muddle" eh? And you're a little hurt that he hasn't brought his worry to you.'

'To whom else should he turn if not to one of us—and you were in the States.'

'Richard maybe, he's an even older friend of Simon's than we are.'

'No. I spent last week-end at Cardinals Folly and neither Richard nor Marie Lou could tell me anything. They haven't seen him since he went down to stay last Christmas and arrived with a dozen crates of toys for Fleur.'

'How like him!' Rex's gargantuan laugh rang suddenly through the room. 'I might have known the trunkful I brought over would be small fry if you and Simon have been busy on that child.'

'Well I can only conclude that poor Simon is "in a muddle" as you say, or he would never treat us all like this.'

'But what sort of a muddle?' Rex brought his leg-of mutton fist crashing down on the table angrily. 'I can't think of a thing where he wouldn't turn to us.'

'Money,' suggested the Duke, 'is the one thing that with his queer sensitive nature he might not care to discuss with even his closest friends.'

'I doubt it being that. My old man has a wonderful opinion of Simon's financial ability and he handles a big portion of our interests on this side. I'm pretty sure we'd be wise to it if he'd burned his fingers on the market. It sounds as if he'd gone bats about some woman to me.'

De Richleau's face was lit by his faintly cynical smile for a moment. 'No,' he said slowly. 'A man in love turns naturally to his friends for congratulation or sympathy as his fortune with a woman proves good or ill. It can't be that.'

For a little the two friends sat staring at each other in silence across the low jade bowl with its trailing sprays of orchids: Rex, giant shouldered, virile and powerful, his ugly, attractive, humorous young face clouded with anxiety, the Duke, a slim, delicate-looking man, somewhat about middle height, with slender, fragile hands and greying hair, but with no trace of weakness in his fine, distinguished face. His aquiline nose, broad forehead and grey 'devil's' eyebrows might well have replaced those of the cavalier in the Van Dyck that gazed down from the opposite wall. Instead of the conventional black, he wore a claret coloured vicuna smoking suit, with silk lapels and braided fastenings; this touch of colour increased his likeness to the portrait. He broke the silence suddenly.

'Have you by any chance ever heard of a Mr. Mocata, Rex?'

'Nope. Who is he anyway?'

'A new friend of Simon's who has been staying with him these last few months.'

'What—at his Club?'

'No—no, Simon no longer lives at his Club. I thought you knew. He bought a house last February, a big, rambling old place tucked away at the end of a cul-de-sac off one of those quiet residential streets in St. John's Wood.'

'Why, that's right out past Regent's Park—isn't it? What's he want with a place out there when there are any number of nice little houses to let in Mayfair?'

'Another mystery, my friend.' The Duke's thin lips creased into a smile. 'He *said* he wanted a garden, that's all I can tell you.'

'Simon! A garden!' Rex chuckled. 'That's a good story I'll say. Simon doesn't know a geranium from a fuchsia. His botany is limited to an outsized florist's bill for bunching his women friends from shops, and why should a bachelor like Simon start running a big house at all?'

'Perhaps Mr. Mocata could tell you,' murmured De Richleau mildly, 'or the queer servant that he has imported.'

'Have you ever seen this bird—Mocata I mean?'

'Yes, I called one evening about six weeks ago. Simon was out so Mocata received me.'

'And what did you make of him?'

'I disliked him intensely. He's a pot-bellied, bald-headed person of about sixty, with large, protuberant, fishy eyes, limp hands, and a most unattractive lisp. He reminded me of a large white slug.'

'What about this servant that you mention?'

'I only saw him for a moment when he crossed the hall, but he reminded me in a most unpleasant way of the Bogey Man with whom I used to be threatened in my infancy.'

'Why, is he a black?'

'Yes. A Malagasy I should think.'

Rex frowned. 'Now what in heck is that?'

'A native of Madagascar. They are a curious people, half-Negro and half-Polynesian. This great brute stands about six foot eight, and the one glimpse I had of his eyes made me want to shoot him on sight. He's a "bad black" if ever I saw one, and I've travelled, as you know, in my time.'

'Do you know any more about these people?' asked Rex grimly.

'Not a thing.'

'Well, I'm not given to worry, but I've heard quite enough to get me scared for Simon. He's in some jam or he'd never be housing people like that.'

The Duke gently laid the long, blue-grey ash of his cigar in the onyx ash-tray. 'There is not a doubt,' he said slowly, 'that Simon is involved in some very queer business, but I have been stifling my anxiety until your arrival. You see I wanted to hear your views before taking the very exceptional step of —yes *butting in*—is the expression, on the private affairs of even so intimate a friend. The question is now—what are we to do?'

'Do!' Rex thrust back his chair and drew himself up to his full magnificent height. 'We're going up to that house to have a little heart-to-heart talk with Simon—right now!'

'I'm glad,' said De Richleau quietly, 'you feel like that, because I ordered the car for half past ten. Shall we go?'

2

The Curious Guests of Mr. Simon Aron

As De Richleau's Hispano drew up at the dead end of the dark cul-de-sac in St. John's Wood, Rex slipped out of the car and looked about him. They were shut in by the high walls of neighbouring gardens and, above a blank expanse of brick in which a single, narrow door was visible, the upper stories of Simon's house showed vague and mysterious among whispering trees.

'Ugh!' he exclaimed with a little shudder as a few drops splashed upon his face from the dark branches overhead. 'What a dismal hole—we might be in a graveyard.'

The Duke pressed the bell, and turning up the sable collar of his coat against a slight drizzle which made the April night seem chill and friendless, stepped back to get a better view of the premises. 'Hello! Simon's got an observatory here,' he remarked. 'I didn't notice that on my previous visit.'

'So he has.' Rex followed De Richleau's glance to a dome that crowned the house, but at that moment an electric globe suddenly flared into life about their heads, and the door in the wall swung open disclosing a sallow-faced manservant in dark livery.

'Mr. Simon Aron?' inquired De Richleau, but the man was already motioning them to enter, so they followed him up a short covered path and the door in the wall clanged to behind them.

The vestibule of the house was dimly lit, but Rex, who never wore a coat or hat in the evening, noticed that two sets of outdoor apparel lay, neatly folded, on a long console table as the silent footman relieved De Richleau of his wraps. Evidently friend Simon had other visitors.

'Maybe Mr. Aron's in conference and won't want to be disturbed,' he said to the sallow-faced servant with a sudden feeling of guilt at their intrusion. Perhaps, after all, their fears for Simon were quite groundless and his neglect only due to a prolonged period of intense activity on the markets, but the man only bowed and led them across the hall.

'The fellow's a mute,' whispered the Duke. 'Deaf and dumb I'm certain.' As he spoke the servant flung open a couple of large double doors and stood waiting for them to enter.

A long, narrow room, opening into a wide *salon,* stretched before them. Both were decorated in the lavish magnificence of the Louis Seize period, but for the moment the dazzling brilliance of the lighting prevented them taking in the details of the parquet floors, the crystal mirrors, the gilded furniture and beautifully wrought tapestries.

Rex was the first to recover and with a quick intake of breath he clutched De Richleau's arm. 'By Jove she's here!' he muttered almost inaudibly, his eyes riveted on a tall, graceful girl who stood some yards away at the entrance of the *salon* talking to Simon.

Three times in the last eighteen months he had chanced upon that strange, wise, beautiful face, with the deep eyes beneath heavy lids that seemed so full of secrets and gave the lovely face a curiously ageless look—so that despite her apparent youth she was as old as—'Yes, as old as sin,' Rex caught himself thinking.

He had seen her first in a restaurant in Budapest; months later again, in a traffic jam when his car was wedged beside hers in New York, and then, strangely enough, riding along a road with three men, in the country ten miles outside Buenos Aires. How extraordinary that he should find her here—and what luck. He smiled quickly at the thought that Simon could not fail to introduce him.

De Richleau's glance was riveted upon their friend. With an abrupt movement Simon turned towards them. For a second he seemed completely at a loss, his full, sensual mouth hung open to twice its normal extent and his receding jaw almost disappeared behind his white tie, while his dark eyes were filled with amazement and something suspiciously like fear, but he recovered almost instantly and his old smile flashed out as he came forward to greet them.

'My dear Simon,' the Duke's voice was a silken purr. 'How can we apologise for breaking in on you like this?'

'Sure, we hadn't a notion you were throwing a party,' boomed Rex, his glance following the girl who had moved off to join another woman and three men who were talking together in the inner room.

'But I'm delighted,' murmured Simon genially. 'Delighted to see you both—only got a few friends—meeting of a little society I belong to—that's all.'

'Then we couldn't dream of interrupting you, could we Rex?' De Richleau demurred with well-assumed innocence.

'Why, certainly not, we wouldn't even have come in if that servant of yours hadn't taken us for some other folks you're expecting.' But despite their apparent unwillingness to intrude, neither of the two made any gesture of withdrawal and, mentally, De Richleau gave Simon full marks for the way in which he accepted their obviously unwelcome presence.

'I'm most terribly sorry about dinner to-night,' he was proclaiming earnestly. 'Meant to rest for my bridge, I simply have to these days, to be any good—even forgot till six o'clock that I had these people coming.'

'How fortunate for you Simon that your larder is so well stocked.' The Duke could not resist the gentle dig as his glance fell on a long buffet spread with a collation which would have rivalled the cold table in any great hotel.

'I 'phoned Ferraro,' parried Simon glibly. 'The Berkeley never lets me down. Would have asked you to drop in, but er—with this meeting on I felt you'd be bored.'

'Bored! Not a bit, but we are keeping you from your other guests.' With an airy gesture De Richleau waved his hand in the direction of the inner room.

'Sure,' agreed Rex heartily, as he laid a large hand on Simon's arm and gently propelled him towards the *salon*. 'Don't you worry about us, we'll just take a glass of wine off you and fade away.' His eyes were fixed again on the pale oval face of the girl.

Simon's glance flickered swiftly towards the Duke, who ignored, with a guileless smile, his obvious reluctance for them to meet his other friends, and noted with amusement that he avoided any proper introduction.

'Er—er—two very old friends of mine,' he said, with his little nervous cough as he interchanged a swift look with a fleshy, moon-faced man whom De Richleau knew to be Mocata.

'Well, well, how nice,' the bald man lisped with unsmiling eyes. 'It is a pleasure always to welcome any friends of Simon's.'

De Richleau gave him a frigid bow and thought of reminding him coldly that Simon's welcome was sufficient in his own house, but for the moment it was policy to hide his antagonism so he replied politely that Mocata was most kind, then, with the ease which characterised all his movements, he turned his attention to an elderly lady who was seated near by.

She was a woman of advanced age but fine presence, richly dressed and almost weighed down with heavy jewellery. Between her fingers she held the stub of a fat cigar at which she was puffing vigorously.

'Madame.' The Duke drew a case containing the long Hoyos from his pocket and bent towards her. 'Your cigar is almost finished, permit me to offer you one of mine.'

She regarded him for a moment with piercingly bright eyes, then stretched out a fat, beringed hand. 'Sank you, Monsieur, I see you are a connoisseur.' With her beaked, parrot nose she sniffed at the cigar appreciatively. 'But I 'ave not seen you at our other meetings, what ees your name?'

'De Richleau, Madame, and yours?'

'De Richleau! a *maestro* indeed.' She nodded heavily. '*Je suis* Madame D'Urfé, you will 'ave heard of me.'

'But certainly.' The Duke bowed again. 'Do you think we shall have a good meeting tonight?'

'If the sky clears we should learn much,' answered the old lady cryptically.

'Ho! Ho!' thought the Duke. 'We are about to make use of Simon's observatory it seems. Good, let us learn more.' But before he could pump the elderly Frenchwoman further, Simon deftly interrupted the conversation and drew him away.

'So you have taken up the study of the stars, my friend,' remarked the Duke as his host led him to the buffet.

'Oh, er—yes. Find astronomy very interesting, you know. Have some caviare?' Simon's eyes flickered anxiously towards Rex, who was deep in conversation with the girl.

As he admired her burnished hair and slumbrous eyes, for a moment the Duke was reminded of a Botticelli painting. She had, he thought, that angel look with nothing Christian in it peculiar to women born out of their time, the golden virgin to the outward eye whose veins were filled with unlit fire. A rare *cinquecento* type who should have lived in the Italy of the Borgias. Then he turned again to Simon. 'It was because of the observatory then that you acquired this house, I suppose?'

15

'Yes. You must come up one night and we'll watch a few stars together.' Something of the old warmth had crept into Simon's tone and he was obviously in earnest as he offered the invitation, but the Duke was not deceived into believing that he was welcome on the present occasion.

'Thank you, I should enjoy that,' he said promptly, while over Simon's shoulder he studied the other two men who made up the party. One, a tall, fair fellow, stood talking to Mocata. His thin, flaxen hair brushed flatly back, and whose queer, light eyes proclaimed him an Albino; the other, a stout man dressed in a green plaid and ginger kilt, was walking softly up and down with his hands clasped behind his back, muttering to himself inaudibly. His wild, flowing white hair and curious costume suggested an Irish bard.

'Altogether a most unprepossessing lot,' thought the Duke, and his opinion was not improved by three new arrivals. A grave-faced Chinaman wearing the robes of a Mandarin, whose slit eyes betrayed a cold, merciless nature: a Eurasian with only one arm, the left, and a tall, thin woman with a scraggy throat and beetling eyebrows which met across the bridge of her nose.

Mocata received them as though he were the host, but as the tall woman bore down on Simon he promptly left the Duke, who guessed that the move was to get out of earshot. However, the lady's greeting in a high-pitched Middle Western accent came clearly to him.

'Waal, Simon, all excitement about what we'll learn tonight? It should help a heap, this being your natal conjunction.'

'Ha! Ha!' said De Richleau to himself. 'Now I begin to understand a little and I like this party even less.' Then, with the idea of trying to verify his surmise, he turned towards the one-armed Eurasian, but Simon—apparently guessing his intention—quickly excused himself to the American woman, and cut off the Duke's advance.

'So, my young friend,' thought De Richleau, 'you mean to prevent me from obtaining any further information about this strange gathering, do you? All right! I'll twist your tail a little,' and he remarked sweetly:

'Did you say that you were interested in Astronomy or Astrology, Simon? There is a distinct difference you know.'

'Oh, Astronomy, of course.' Simon ran a finger down his

16

long, beak-like nose. 'It *is* nice to see you again—have some more champagne?'

'Thank you, no, later perhaps.' The Duke smothered a smile as he caught Mocata, who had overheard him, exchange a quick look with Simon.

'Wish this were an ordinary meeting,' Simon said, a moment later, with an uneasy frown. 'Then I'd ask you to stay, but we're going through the Society's annual balance-sheet tonight —and you and Rex not being members you know . ; .'

'Quite, quite, my dear fellow, of course,' De Richleau agreed amicably, while to himself he thought. 'That's a nasty fence young sly-boots has put up for me, but I'll be damned if I go before I find out for certain what I came for.' Then he added in a cheerful whisper: 'I should have gone before but Rex seems so interested in the young woman in green, I want to give him as long as possible.'

'My dear chap,' Simon protested, 'I feel horribly embarrassed at having to ask you to go at all.'

A fat, oily-looking Babu in a salmon-pink turban and gown had just arrived and was shaking hands with Mocata; behind him came a red-faced Teuton, who suffered the deformity of a hare lip.

Simon stepped quickly forward again as the two advanced, but De Richleau once more caught the first words which were snuffled out by the hare-lipped man.

'Well, Abraham, *wie geht es*?' then there came the fulsome chuckle of the fleshy Indian. 'You must not call him that, it is unlucky to do so before the great night.'

'The devil it is!' muttered the Duke to himself, but Simon had left the other two with almost indecent haste in order to rejoin him, so he said with a smile: 'I gather you are about to execute Deed Poll, my friend?'

'Eh!' Simon exclaimed with a slight start.

'To change your name,' De Richleau supplemented.

'Ner.' He shook his head rapidly as he uttered the curious negative that he often used. It came of his saying 'No' without troubling to close the lips of his full mouth. 'Ner—that's only a sort of joke we have between us—a sort of initiation cere-mony—I'm not a full member yet.'

'I see, then you have ceremonies in your Astronomical Society—how interesting!'

As he spoke De Richleau, out of the corner of his eye, saw Mocata make a quick sign to Simon and then glance at the ormolu clock on the mantelpiece; so to save his host the awkwardness of having actually to request his departure, he exclaimed: 'Dear me! Twenty past eleven, I had no idea it was so late. I must drag Rex away from that lovely lady after all, I fear.'

'Well, if you must go.' Simon looked embarrassed and worried, but catching Mocata's eye again, he promptly led the way over to his other unwelcome guest.

Rex gave a happy grin as they came up. 'This is marvellous Simon. I've been getting glimpses of this lady in different continents these two years past, and she seems to recall having seen me too. It's just great that we should become acquainted at last through you.' Then he smiled quickly at the girl: 'May I present my friend De Richleau? Duke, this is Miss Tanith.'

De Richleau bent over her long, almost transparent hand and raised it to his lips. 'How unfortunate I am,' he said with old-fashioned gallantry, 'to be presented to you only in time to say good-bye, and perhaps gain your displeasure by taking your new friend with me as well.'

'But,' she regarded him steadily out of large, clear, amber eyes. Surely you do not depart before the ceremony?'

'I fear we must. We are not members of your er—Circle you see, only old friends of Simon's.'

A strange look of annoyance and uncertainty crept into her glance, and the Duke guessed that she was searching her mind for any indiscretions she might have committed in her conversation with Rex. Then she shrugged lightly and, with a brief inclination of the head which dismissed them both, turned coldly away.

The Duke took Simon's arm affectionately, as the three friends left the *salon*. 'I wonder,' he said persuasively, 'if you could spare me just two minutes before we go—no more I promise you.'

'Rather, of course.' Simon seemed now to have regained his old joviality. 'I'll never forgive myself for missing your dinner tonight—this wretched meeting—and I've seen nothing of you for weeks. Now Rex is over we must throw a party together.'

'We will, we will,' De Richleau agreed heartily, 'but listen; is not Mars in conjunction with Venus tonight?'

18

'Ner,' Simon replied promptly, 'With Saturn, that's what they've all come to see.'

'Ah, Saturn! My Astronomy is so rusty, but I saw some mention of it in the paper yesterday, and at one time I was a keen student of the Stars. Would it be asking too much my dear fellow, to have just one peep at it through your telescope? We should hardly delay your meeting for five minutes.'

Simon's hesitation was barely perceptible before he nodded his bird-like head with vigorous assent. 'Um, that's all right—they haven't all arrived yet—let's go up.' Then, with his hands thrust deep in the trouser pockets of his exceedingly well-cut dress suit, he led them hurriedly through the hall and up three flights of stairs.'

De Richleau followed more slowly. Stairs were the one thing which ruffled his otherwise equable temper and he had no desire to lose it now. By the time he arrived in the lofty chamber, with Rex behind him, Simon had all the lights switched on.

'Well you've certainly gone in for it properly,' Rex remarked as he surveyed the powerful telescope slanting to the roof and a whole arsenal of sextants, spheres and other astrological impedimenta ranged about the room.

'It's rather an exact science you see,' Simon volunteered.

'Quite,' agreed the Duke briefly. 'But I wonder, a little, that you should consider charts of the Macrocosm necessary to your studies.

'Oh, those!' Simon shrugged his narrow shoulders as he glanced around the walls. 'They're only for fun—relics of the Alchemistic nonsense in the Middle Ages, but quite suitable for decoration.'

'How clever of you to carry out your scheme of decoration on the floor as well.' The Duke was thoughtfully regarding a five-pointed star enclosed within two circles between which numerous mystic characters in Greek and Hebrew had been carefully drawn.

'Yes, good idea, wasn't it?' Simon tittered into his hand. It was the familiar gesture which both his friends knew so well, yet somehow his chuckle had not quite its usual ring.

The silence that followed was a little awkward and in it, all three plainly heard a muffled scratching noise that seemed to come from a large wicker basket placed against the wall.

'You've got mice here, Simon,' said Rex casually, but De Richleau had stiffened where he stood. Then, before Simon could bar his way, he leapt towards the hamper and ripped open the lid.

'Stop that!' cried Simon angrily, and dashing forward he forced it shut again, but too late, for within the basket the Duke had seen two living piniioned fowls—a black cock and a white hen.

With a sudden access of bitter fury he turned on Simon, and seizing him by his silk lapels, shook him as a terrier shakes a rat. 'You fool,' he thundered. 'I'd rather see you dead than monkeying with Black Magic.'

3

The Esoteric Doctrine

'Take—take your hands off me,' Simon gasped.

His dark eyes blazed in a face that had gone deathly white and only a superhuman effort enabled him to keep his clenched fists pressed to his sides.

In another second he would have hit the Duke, but Rex, a head taller than either of them, laid a mighty hand on the shoulder of each and forced them apart.

'Have a heart now, just what is all this?' His quiet, familiar voice, with its faint American intonation, sobered the others immediately and De Richleau, swinging on his heel, strode to the other side of the observatory, where he stood for a moment, with his back towards them, regaining control of his emotions.

Simon, panting a little, gave a quick, nervous wriggle of his bird-like head and smoothed out the lapels of his evening coat.

'Now—I'll tell you,' he said jerkily, 'I never asked either of you to come here tonight, and even my oldest friends have no right to butt in on my private affairs. I think you'd better go.'

The Duke turned, passing one hand over his greying hair. All trace of his astonishing outburst had disappeared and he was once more the handsome, distinguished figure that they knew so well.

'I'm sorry, Simon,' he said gravely. 'But I felt as a father might who sees his child trying to pick live coals out of the fire.'

'I'm not a child,' muttered Simon, sullenly.

'No, but I could not have more affection for you if you were actually my son, and it is useless now to deny that you are playing the most dangerous game which has ever been known to mankind throughout the ages.'

'Oh, come,' a quick smile spread over Rex's ugly, attractive face. 'That's a gross exaggeration. What's the harm if Simon wants to try out a few old parlour games?'

'Parlour games!' De Richleau took him up sharply. 'My dear Rex, I fear your prowess in aeroplanes and racing cars hardly qualifies you to judge the soul destroying powers of these ancient cults.'

'Thanks. I'm not quite a half-wit, and plenty of spiritualistic séances take place in the States, but I've never heard of any-one as sane as Simon going bats because of them yet.'

Simon nodded his narrow head slowly up and down. 'Of course—Rex is right, and you're only making a mountain out of a molehill.'

'As you like,' De Richleau shrugged. 'In that case will you permit us to stay and participate in your operations tonight?'

'Ner—I'm sorry, but you're not a member of our Circle.'

'No matter. We have already met most of your friends down-stairs, surely they will not object to our presence on just this one occasion?'

'Ner.' Simon shook his head again. 'Our number is made up.'

'I see, you are already thirteen, is that it? Now listen, Simon.' The Duke laid his hands gently on the young Jew's shoulders. 'One of the reasons why my friendship with Rex and yourself has developed into such a splendid intimacy, is because I have always refrained from stressing my age and greater experience, but tonight I break the rule. My conscious life, since we both left our schools, has been nearly three times as long as yours and, in addition, although I have never told you of it, I made a deep study of these esoteric doctrines years ago when I lived in the East. I beg of you, as I have never begged for anything in my life before, that you should give up whatever quest you are engaged upon and leave this house with us immediately.'

For a moment Simon seemed to waver. All his faith in De Richleau's judgment, knowledge, and love for him, urged him to agree, but at that moment Mocata's musical lisping voice cut in upon the silence, calling from the landing just below:

'Simon, the others have come. It is time.'

'Coming,' called Simon, then he looked at the two friends with whom he had risked his life in the 'Forbidden Territory,' 'I can't,' he said with an effort, 'You heard—it's too late to back out now.'

'Then let us remain—please,' begged the Duke.

'No, I'm sorry.' A new firmness had crept into Simon's tone, 'but I must ask you to go now.'

'Very well.'

De Richleau stepped forward as though to shake hands then, with almost incredible swiftness, his arm flew back and next second his fist caught Simon a smashing blow full beneath the jaw.

The action was so sudden, so unexpected, that Simon was caught completely off his guard. For a fraction of time he was lifted from his feet, then he crashed senseless on his back and slid spread-eagled across the polished floor.

'Have you gone crazy?' ejaculated Rex.

'No—we've got to get him out of here—save him from himself—don't argue! Quick!' Already De Richleau was kneeling by the crumpled body of his friend.

Rex needed no further urging. He had been in too many tight corners with the Duke to doubt the wisdom of his decisions however strange his actions might appear. In one quick heave he dragged Simon's limp form across his shoulders and started for the stairs.

'Steady!' ordered the Duke. 'I'll go first and tackle anyone who tries to stop us. You get him to the car—Understooood?'

'What if they raise the house? You'll never be able to tackle the whole bunch on your own?'

'In that case drop him, I'll get him out somehow, while you protect my rear. Come on!'

With De Richleau leading they crept down the first flight of stairs. On the landing he paused and peered cautiously over the banisters. No sound came from below. 'Rex,' he whispered.

'Yep.'

'If that black servant I told you of appears, for God's sake don't look at his eyes. Watch his hands and hit him in the belly.'

'O.K.'

A moment later they were down the second flight. The hall was empty and only a vague murmur of conversation came to them from behind the double doors that led to the *salon*.

'Quick!' urged the Duke. 'Mocata may come out to look for him any moment.'

'Right.' Rex, bent double beneath his burden, plunged down the last stairs, and De Richleau was already halfway across the hall when the dumb servant suddenly appeared from the vestibule.

For a second he stood there, his sallow face a mask of blank surprise then, side-stepping the Duke with the agility of a rugby forward, he lowered his bullet head and charged Rex with silent animal ferocity.

'Got you,' snapped De Richleau, for although the man had dodged with lightning speed he had caught his wrist in passing. Then flinging his whole weight upon it as he turned, he jerked the fellow clean off his feet and sent him spinning head foremost against the wall.

As his head hit the panelling the mute gave an uncouth grunt, and rolled over on the floor, but he staggered up again and dashed towards the *salon*. Rex and the Duke were already pounding down the tiled path and in another second they had flung themselves into the lane through the entrance in the garden wall.

'Thank God,' gasped the Duke as he wrenched open the door of the Hispano. 'I believe that hellish crew would have killed us rather than let us get Simon out of there alive.'

'Well, I suppose you do know what you're at,' Rex muttered as he propped Simon up on the back seat of the car. 'But I'm not certain you're safe to be with.'

'Home,' ordered De Richleau curtly to the footman, who was hiding his astonishment at their sudden exit by hastily tucking the rug over their knees. Then he smiled at Rex a trifle grimly. 'I suppose I do seem a little mad to you, but you can't possibly be expected to appreciate what a horribly serious business this is. I'll explain later.'

In a few moments they had left the gloom of the quiet streets behind and were once more running through well-lit ways towards Mayfair, but Simon was still unconscious when they pulled up in Curzon Street before Errol House.

'I'll take him,' volunteered Rex. 'The less the servants have to do with this the better,' and picking up Simon in his strong arms as though he had been a baby, he carried him straight upstairs to the first floor where De Richleau's flat was situated.

'Put him in the library,' said the Duke, who had paused to murmur something about a sudden illness to the porter, when he arrived on the landing a moment later. 'I'll get something to bring him round from the bathroom.'

Rex nodded obediently, and carried Simon into that room in the Curzon Street flat which was so memorable for those who had been privileged to visit it, not so much on account of its size and decorations, but for the unique collection of rare and beautiful objects which it contained. A Tibetan Buddha seated upon the Lotus; bronze figurines from ancient Greece; beautifully chased rapiers of Toledo steel, and Moorish pistols inlaid with turquoise and gold; ikons from Holy Russia set with semi-precious stones and curiously carved ivories from the East.

As Rex laid Simon upon the wide sofa he glanced round him with an interest unappeased by a hundred visits, at the walls lined shoulder high with beautifully bound books, and at the lovely old colour prints, interspersed with priceless historical documents and maps, which hung above them.

De Richleau, when he joined him, produced a small crystal bottle which he held beneath Simon's beak-like nose. 'No good trying to talk to him tonight,' he remarked, 'but I want to bring him round sufficiently to put him to sleep again.

Rex grunted. 'That sounds like double-dutch to me.'

'No. I mean to fight these devils with their own weapons, as you will see.'

Simon groaned a little, and as his eyes flickered open the Duke took a small round mirror from his pocket. 'Simon,' he said softly, moving the lamp a little nearer, 'look upward at my hand.'

As he spoke De Richleau held the mirror about eighteen inches from Simon's forehead and a little above the level of his eyes, so that it caught and reflected the light of the lamp on to his lids.

'Hold it lower,' suggested Rex. 'He'll strain his eyes turning them upwards like that.'

'Quiet,' said the Duke sharply. 'Simon, look up and listen to

24

me. You have been hurt and have a troubled mind, but your friends are with you and you have no need to worry any more.'

Simon opened his eyes again and turned them upwards to the mirror, where they remained fixed.

'I am going to send you to sleep, Simon,' De Richleau went on softly. 'You need rest and you will awake free from pain. In a moment your eyes will close and then your head will feel better.'

For another half-minute he held the mirror steadily reflecting the light upon Simon's retina, then he placed the first and second fingers of his free hand upon the glass with his palm turned outward and made a slow pass from it towards the staring eyes, which closed at once before he touched them.

'You will sleep now,' he continued quietly, 'and you will not wake until ten o'clock tomorrow morning. Directly you awake you will come straight to me either here or in my bed-room and you will speak to no one, nor will you open any letter or message which may be brought to you, until you have seen me.'

De Richleau paused for a moment, put down the mirror and lifted one of Simon's arms until it stood straight above his head. When he released it the arm did not drop but remained stiff and rigid in the air.

'Most satisfactory,' he murmured cheerfully to Rex. 'He is in the second stage of hypnosis already and will do exactly what he is told. The induction was amazingly easy, but of course, his half-conscious state simplified it a lot.'

Rex shook his head in disapproval. 'I don't like to see you monkey with him like this. I wouldn't allow it if it was anyone but you.'

'A prejudice based upon lack of understanding, my friend. Hypnotism in proper hands is the greatest healing power in the world.' With a quick shrug the Duke moved over to his desk and, unlocking one of the lower drawers, took something from it, then he returned to Simon and addressed him in the same low voice.

'Open your eyes now and sit up.'

Simon obeyed at once and Rex was surprised to see that he looked quite wide awake and normal. Only a certain blankness about the face betrayed his abnormal state, and he displayed no aversion as De Richleau extended the thing he had taken from the drawer. It was a small golden swastika set with precious stones and threaded on a silken ribbon.

'Simon Aron,' the Duke spoke again. 'With this symbol I am about to place you under the protection of the power of Light. No being or force of Earth, or Air, of Fire, or Water can harm you while you wear it.'

With quick fingers he knotted the talisman round Simon's neck and went on evenly: 'Now you will go to the spare bedroom. Ring for my man Max and tell him that you are staying here tonight. He will provide you with everything you need and, if your throat is parched from your recent coma, ask him for any soft drink you wish, but no alcohol remember. Peace be upon you and about you. Now go.'

Simon stood up at once and looked from one to the other of them. 'Good night,' he said cheerfully, with his quick natural smile. 'See you both in the morning,' then he promptly walked out of the room.

'He—he's not really asleep is he?' asked Rex, looking a little scared.

'Certainly, but he will remember everything that has taken place tomorrow because he is not in the deep somnambulistic state where I could order him to forget. To achieve that usually takes a little practice with a new subject.'

'Then he'll be pretty livid I'll promise you. Fancy hanging a Nazi swastika round the neck of a professing Jew.'

'My dear Rex! Do please try and broaden your outlook a little. The swastika is the oldest symbol of wisdom and right thinking in the world. It has been used by every race and in every country at some time or other. You might just as well regard the Cross as purely Christian, when we all know it was venerated in early Egypt, thousands of years before the birth of Christ. The Nazis have only adopted the swastika because it is supposed to be of Aryan origin and part of their programme aims at welding together a large section of the Aryan race. The vast majority of them have no conception of its esoteric significance and even if they bring discredit upon it, as the Spanish Inquisition did upon the Cross, that could have no effect upon its true meaning.'

'Yes, I get that, though I doubt if it'll make any difference to Simon's resentment when he finds it round his neck tomorrow. Still, that's a minor point. What worries me is this whole box of tricks this evening. I've got a feeling you ought to be locked up as downright insane, unless it's me.'

De Richleau smiled. 'A strange business to be happening in modern London, isn't it? But let's mix a drink and talk it over quietly.'

'Strange! Why, if it were true it would be utterly fantastic, but it's not. All this hooha about Black Magic and talking hocus-pocus while you hang silly charms round Simon's neck is utter bunk.'

'It is?' The Duke smiled again as he tipped a lump of ice into Rex's glass and handed it to him. 'Well, let's hear *your* explanation of Simon's queer behaviour. I suppose you do consider that it is queer by the way?'

'Of course, but nothing like as queer as you're trying to make out. As I see it Simon's taken up spiritualism or something of the kind and plenty of normal earnest people believe in that, but you know what he is when he gets keen on a thing, everything else goes to the wall and that's why he has neglected you a bit.

'Then this evening he was probably sick as mud to miss our dinner, but had a séance all fixed that he couldn't shelve at the last moment. We butt in on his party, and naturally he doesn't care to admit what he's up to entertaining all those queer, odd-looking women and men, so he spins a yarn about it being an astronomical society. So you—who've read a sight too many books—and seem to have stored up all the old wives' tales your nurse told you in your cradle—get a bee in your bonnet and slog the poor mut under the jaw.'

De Richleau nodded. 'I can hardly expect you to see it any other way at the moment, but let's start at the beginning. Do you agree that after knocking him out I called into play a supernormal power in order to send him cheerfully off to bed without a single protest?'

'Yes, even the doctors admit hypnotic influence now, and Simon would never have stood for you tying that swastika under his chin if he'd been conscious.'

'Good. Then at least we are at one on the fact that certain forces can be called into play which the average person does not understand. Now, if instead of practising that comparatively simple exercise in front of you, I had done it before ignorant natives, who had never heard of hypnotism, they would term it magic, would they not?'

'Sure.'

'Then to go a step further. If, by a greater exertion of the same power, I levitated, that is to say, lifted myself to a height of several inches from this floor, you might not use the word *magic* but you would class that feat in the same category as the ignorant native would place the easier one, because it is something which you have always thought impossible.'

'That's true.'

'Well, I am not sufficient of an adept to perform the feat, but will you accept my assurances that I've seen it done, not once, but a number of times?'

'If you say so, but from all I've heard about such things, the fellows you saw didn't leave the ground at all. It is just mass hypnotism exercised upon the whole audience—like the rope trick.'

'As you wish, but that explanation does not rob me of my point. If you admit that I can tap an unknown power to make Simon obey my will, and that an Eastern mystic can tap that power to the far greater extent of making a hundred people's eyes deceive them into believing that he is standing on thin air, you admit that there *is* a power and that it can be tapped in greater degrees according to the knowledge and proficiency of the man who uses it.'

'Yes, within limits.'

'Why within limits? You apparently consider levitation impossible, but wouldn't you have considered wireless impossible if you had been living fifty years ago and somebody had endeavoured to convince you of it?'

'Maybe.' Rex sat forward suddenly. 'But I don't get what you're driving at. Hypnotism is only a demonstration of the power of the human will.'

'Ah! There you have it. The *will to good* and the *will to evil*. That is the whole matter in a nutshell. The human will is like a wireless set and properly adjusted—trained that is—it can tune in with the invisible influence which is all about us.'

'The *Invisible Influence*. I've certainly heard that phrase somewhere before.'

'No doubt. A very eminent mental specialist who holds a high position in our asylums wrote a book with that title and I have

28

not yet asked you to believe one tenth of what he vouches for.'

'Then I wonder they haven't locked him up.'

'Rex! Rex!' De Richleau smiled a little sadly. 'Try and open your mind, my friend. Do you believe in the miracles performed by Jesus Christ?'

'Yes.'

'And of His Disciples and certain of the Saints?'

'Sure, but they had some special power granted to them from on high.'

'Exactly! *Some Special Power*. But I suppose you would deny that Gautama Buddha and his disciples performed miracles of a similar nature?'

'Not at all. Most people agree now that Buddha was a sort of Indian Christ, a Holy Man, and no doubt he had some sort of power granted to him too.'

The Duke sat back with a heavy sigh. 'At last my friend we seem to be getting somewhere. If you admit that miracles, as you call them although you object to the word magic, have been performed by two men living in different countries hundreds of years apart, and that even their disciples were able to tap a similar power through their holiness, you cannot reasonably deny that other mystics have also performed similar acts in many portions of the globe—and therefore, that there is a power existing outside us which is not *peculiar to any religion*, but can be utilised if one can get into communication with it.'

Rex laughed. 'That's so, I can't deny it.'

'Thank God! Let's mix ourselves another drink shall we, I need it?'

'Don't move, I'll fix it.' Rex good-naturedly scrambled to his feet. 'All the same,' he added slowly, 'it doesn't follow that because a number of good men have been granted supernatural powers that there is anything in Black Magic.'

'Then you do not believe in Witchcraft?'

'Of course not, nobody does in these days.'

'Really! How long do you think it is since the last trial for Witchcraft took place?'

'I'll say it was all of a hundred and fifty years ago.'

'No, it was in January, 1926, at Melun near Paris.'

'Oh! You're fooling!' Rex exclaimed angrily.

'I'm not,' De Richleau assured him solemnly. 'The records of the court will prove my statement, so you see you are hardly

29

accurate when you say that *nobody* believes in Witchcraft in these days, and many many thousands still believe in a personal devil.'

'Yes, simple folk maybe, but not educated people.'

'Possibly not, yet every thinking man must admit that there is still such a thing as the power of Evil.'

'Why?'

'My dear fellow, all qualities have their opposites, like love and hate, pleasure and pain, generosity and avarice. How could we recognise the goodness of Jesus Christ, Lao Tze, Ashoka, Marcus Aurelius, Francis of Assisi, Florence Nightingale and a thousand others if it were not for the evil lives of Herod, Caesar Borgia, Rasputin, Landru, Ivan Kreuger and the rest?'

'That's true,' Rex admitted slowly.

'Then if an intensive cultivation of good can beget strange powers is there any reason why an intensive cultivation of evil should not beget them also?'

'I think I begin to get what you're driving at.'

'Good! Now listen, Rex.' The Duke leaned forward earnestly. 'And I will try and expound what little I know of the Esoteric Doctrine which has come down to us through the ages. You will have heard of the Persian myth of Ozamund and Ahriman, the eternal powers of Light and Darkness, said to be co-equal and warring without cessation for the good or ill of mankind. All ancient sun and nature worship—festivals of spring and so on, were only an outward expression of that myth, for Light typifies Health and Wisdom, Growth and Life; while Darkness means Disease and Ignorance, Decay and Death.

'In its highest sense Light symbolises the growth of the Spirit towards that perfection in which it can throw off the body and become light itself; but the road to perfection is long and arduous, too much to hope for in one short human life, hence the widespread belief in re-incarnation; that we are born again and again until we begin to despise the pleasures of the flesh. This doctrine is so old that no man can trace its origin, yet it is the inner core of truth common to all religions at their inception. Consider the teaching of Jesus Christ with that in mind and you will be amazed that you have not realised before the true purport of His message. Did He not say that the 'Kingdom of God was within us,' and, when He walked upon the waters declared: 'These things that I do ye shall do also; and greater things than these shall ye do, for I go unto my Father which is in Heaven,' meaning most certainly that He had achieved perfection but that others had the same power within each one of them to do likewise.'

De Richleau paused for a moment and then went on more slowly. 'Unfortunately the hours of the night are still equal to the hours of the day, and so the power of Darkness is no less active than when the world was young, and no sooner does a fresh Master appear to reveal the light than ignorance, greed, and lust for power cloud the minds of his followers. The message becomes distorted and the simplicity of the truth submerged and forgotten in the pomp of ceremonies and the meticulous performance of rituals which have lost their meaning. Yet the real truth is never entirely lost, and through the centuries new Masters are continually arising either to proclaim it or, if the time is not propitious, to pass it on in secret to the chosen few.

'Apollonius of Tyana learned it in the East. The so-called Heretics whom we know as the Albigenses preached it in the twelfth century through Southern France until they were exterminated. Christian Rosenkreutz had it in the Middle Ages. It was the innermost secret of the Order of the Templars who were suppressed because of it by the Church of Rome. The Alchemists, too, searched for and practised it. Only the ignorant take literally their struggle to find the Elixir of Life. Behind such phrases, designed to protect them from the persecution of their enemies, they sought Eternal Life, and their efforts to transmute base metals into gold were only symbolical of their transfusion of matter into light. And still to-day while the night life of London goes on about us there are mystics and adepts who are seeking the Eightfold Way to perfection in many corners of the Earth.'

'You really believe that?' asked Rex seriously.

'I do.' De Richleau's answer held no trace of doubt. 'I give you my word Rex, that I have talked with men whose sanity you would never question, an Englishman, an Italian, and a Hindu, all three of whom have been taken by guides sent to fetch them to the hidden valley in the uplands of Tibet, where some of the Lamas have reached such a high degree of enlightenment that they can prolong their lives at will, and perform today all the miracles which you have read of in the Bible. It is there that the sacred fire of truth has been preserved for centuries, safe from the brutal mercenary folly of our modern world.'

'That sounds a pretty tall story to me, but granted there are mystics who have achieved such amazing powers through their holiness I still don't see where your Black Magic comes in?'

'Let's not talk of Black Magic, which is associated with the preposterous in our day, but of the order of the Left Hand Path. That, too, has its adepts and, just as the Yoga of Tibet are the preservers of the Way of Light, the Way of Darkness is exemplified in the horrible Voodoo cult which had its origin in Madagascar and has held Africa in its grip for centuries, spreading even with the slave trade to the West Indies and your own country.'

'Yes, I know quite a piece about that, the Negroes monkey with it still back home in the Southern States, despite their apparent Christianity. Still I can't think that an educated man like Simon would take serious notice of that Mumbo Jumbo stuff.'

'Not in its crude form perhaps, but others have cultivated the power of Evil, and among whites it is generally the wealthy and intellectual, who are avaricious for greater riches or power, to whom it appeals. In the Paris of Louis XIV, long after the Middle Ages were forgotten, it was still particularly rampant. The poisoner, La Voisin, was proved to have procured over fifteen hundred children for the infamous Abbé Guibourg to sacrifice at Black Masses. He used to cut their throats, drain the blood into a chalice, and then pour it over the naked body of the inquirer who lay stretched upon the altar. I speak of actual history, Rex, and you can read the records of the trial that followed in which two hundred and forty-six men and women were indicted for these hellish practices.'

'Maybe. It sounds ghastly enough but that's a mighty long time ago.'

'Then, if you need more modern evidence of its continuance hidden in our midst there is the well authenticated case of Prince Borghese. He let his Venetian Palazzo on a long lease, expiring as late as 1895. The tenants had not realised that the lease had run out until he notified them of his intention to resume possession. They protested, but Borghese's agents forced an entry. What do you think they found?'

'Lord knows.' Rex shook his head.

'That the principal *salon* had been redecorated at enormous cost and converted into a Satanic Temple. The walls were hung from ceiling to floor with heavy curtains of silk damask, scarlet and black to exclude the light; at the farther end there stretched a large tapestry upon which was woven a colossal figure of Lucifer dominating the whole. Beneath, an altar had been built and amply furnished with the whole liturgy of Hell; black candles, vessels, rituals, nothing was lacking. Cushioned prie-dieus and luxurious chairs, crimson and gold, were set in order for the assistants, and the chamber lit with electricity fantas-tically arranged so that it should glare through an enormous human eye.'

De Richleau hammered the desk with his clenched fist. 'These are facts I'm giving you Rex—facts, d'you hear, things I can prove by eye-witnesses still living. Despite our electricity, our aeroplanes, our modern scepticism, the power of Darkness is still a living force, worshipped by depraved human beings for their unholy ends in the great cities of Europe and America to this very day.'

Rex's face had suddenly paled under its tan. 'And you really think poor Simon has got mixed up in this beastliness?'

'I know it man! Could you have been so intrigued with the girl that you did not notice the rest of that foul crew? The Albino, the man with the hare-lip, the Eurasian who only possessed a *left* arm. They're Devil Worshippers all of them.'

'Not the girl! Not Tanith!' cried Rex, springing to his feet, 'She must have been drawn into it like Simon.'

'Perhaps, but the final proof lay in that basket. They were about to practise the age-old sacrifice to their infernal master just as your Voodoo-ridden Negroes do. The slaughter of a black cock and a white hen—Yes. What is it?' De Richleau swung round as a soft knock came on the door.

'Excellency.' His man Max stood bowing in the doorway. 'I thought I had better bring this to you.' In his open palm he displayed the jewelled swastika.

With one panther-like spring the Duke thrust him aside and bounded from the room. 'Simon,' he shouted as he dashed down the corridor. 'Simon! I command you to stay still.' But when he reached the bedroom the only signs that Simon had ever occupied it were the tumbled bed and his underclothes left scattered on the floor.

4

The Silent House

De Richleau strode back into the sitting-room. His grey eyes glittered dangerously but his voice was gentle as he picked the jewelled swastika from his servant's palm. 'How did you come by this Max?'

'I removed it from Mr. Aron's neck Excellency.'

'What!'

'He rang for me Excellency and said that he would like a cup of bouillon and when I returned with it he was sleeping, but so strangely that I was alarmed. His tongue was protruding from between his teeth and his face was nearly black; then I saw that his neck was terribly swollen and that a ribbon was cutting deeply into his flesh. I cut the ribbon, fearing that he would choke—the jewel dropped off, so I brought it straight to you.'

'All right! you may go—and it is unnecessary to wait up—I may be late.' As the door closed the Duke swung round towards Rex. 'Simon must have woken the moment Max's back was turned, pulled on a few clothes, then slipped out of the window and down the fire-escape.'

'Sure,' Rex agreed. 'He's well on his way back to St. John's Wood by now.'

'Come on—we'll follow. We've got to save him from those devils somehow. I don't know what they're after but there must be something pretty big and very nasty behind all this. It can't have been easy to involve a man like Simon to the extent they obviously have, and they would never have gone to all that trouble to recruit an ordinary dabbler in the occult. They are after really big stakes of some kind, and they need him as a pawn in their devilish game.'

'Think we can beat him to it?' Rex asked as they ran down the staircase of the block and out into Curzon Street.

'I doubt it—Hi, taxi!' De Richleau waved an arm.

'He can't have more than five minutes' start.'

'Too much in a fifteen minutes' run.' The Duke's voice was grim as they climbed into the cab.

'What d'you figure went amiss?'

'I don't know for certain, but there is no doubt that our poor friend is completely under Mocata's influence—has been for months I expect. In such a case Mocata's power over him would be far stronger than my own which was only exercised, in the hope of protecting him, for the first time tonight. It was because I feared that Mocata might countermand my orders, even from a distance, and compel Simon to return that I placed the symbol of Light round his neck.'

'And when Max took it off Mocata got busy on him eh?'

'I think Mocata was at work before that. He probably witnessed everything that took place in a crystal or through a medium and exerted all his powers to cause Simon's neck to swell the moment he got into bed, hoping to break the ribbon that held the charm.'

Rex had not yet quite recovered from the shock of learning that so sane a man as De Richleau could seriously believe in all this gibberish about the Occult. He was very far from being convinced himself, but he refrained from airing his scepticism and instead, as the taxi rattled north through Baker Street, he began to consider the practical side of their expedition. There had been eight men at least in Simon's house when they left it. He glanced towards the Duke. 'Are you carrying a gun?'

'No, and if I were it would be useless.'

'Holy Smoke! You are bats or else I am.' Rex shrugged his broad shoulders and began to wonder if he was not living through some particularly vivid and horrible dream. Soon he would wake perhaps; sweating a little from the nightmare picture which De Richleau had drawn for him of age-old evil, tireless and vigilant, cloaked from the masses by modern scepticism yet still a potent force stalking the dark ways of the night, conjured into new life by strange delvers into ancient secrets for their unhallowed ends; but wake he must, to the bright, clear day and Simon's chuckle—over a tankard of Pim's cup at luncheon—that such fantastic nonsense should centre about him even in a dream. Yet there was Tanith, so strange and wise and beautiful, looking as though she had just stepped out of a painting by some great master of the Italian Renaissance. It was no dream that he had at last actually met and spoken with her that evening at Simon's house, among all

35

those queer people whom the Duke declared so positively to be Satan worshippers; and if she was flesh and blood they must be too.

On the north side of Lord's cricket ground, De Richleau stopped the taxi. 'Better walk the rest of the way,' he murmured as he paid off the man. 'Simon's arrived by now and it would be foolish to warn them of our coming.'

'Thought you said Mocata was overlooking us with the evil eye?' Rex replied as they hurried along Circus Road.

'He may be. I can't say, but possibly he thinks we would never dare risk a second visit to the house tonight. If we exercise every precaution we may catch him off his guard. He's just as vulnerable as any other human being except when he is actually employing his special powers.'

Side by side they passed through two streets where the low roofs of the old-fashioned houses were only faintly visible above the walls that kept them immune from the eyes of the curious, each set, silent and vaguely mysterious, among its whispering trees; then they entered the narrow, unlit cul-de-sac.

Treading carefully now, they covered the two hundred yards to its end and halted, gazing up at the darkened mass of the upper stories which loomed above the high wall. Not a chink of light betrayed that the house was tenanted, although they knew that, apart from the servants, thirteen people had congregated there to perform some strange midnight ceremony little over an hour before.

'Think they've cleared out?' Rex whispered.

'I doubt it.' The Duke stepped forward and tried the narrow door. It was fast locked.

'Can't we call the police in to raid the place?'

De Richleau shrugged impatiently. 'What could we charge them with that a modern station-sergeant would understand?'

'Kidnapping!' Rex urged below his breath. 'If I were back home I'd have the strong arm squad here in under half an hour. Get the whole bunch pinched and gaoled pending trial. They'd be out of the way then for a bit, even if I had to pay up heavy damages afterwards—and meantime we'd pop Simon in a mental home till he got his wits back.'

'Rex! Rex!' The Duke gave a low, delighted chuckle. 'It's an enchanting idea, and if we *were* in the States I really believe we might pull it off—but here it's impossible.'

'What do you figure to do then?'

'Go in and see if Simon has returned.'

'I'm game, but the odds are pretty heavy.'

'If we're caught we must run for it.'

'O.K., but if we fail to make our get-away they'll call the police and have *us* gaoled for housebreaking.'

'No—no,' De Richleau muttered. 'They won't want to draw the attention of the police to their activities, and the one thing that matters is to get Simon out of here.'

'All right.' Rex placed his hands on his knees, and stooping his great shoulders, leaned his head against the wall. 'Up you go.'

The Duke bent towards him. 'Listen!' he whispered. 'Once we're inside we've got to stick together whatever happens. God knows what they've used this house of Simon's for, but the whole place reeks of evil.'

'Oh shucks!' Rex muttered contemptuously.

'I mean it,' De Richleau insisted. 'If you take that attitude I'd rather go in alone. This is the most dangerous business I've ever been up against, and if it wasn't for the thought of Simon nothing on earth would tempt me to go over this wall in the middle of the night.'

'Oh—all right. Have it your own way.'

'You'll obey me implicitly—every word I say?'

'Yes, don't fret yourself . . .'

'Good, and remember you are to bolt for it the instant I give the word, because the little knowledge that I possess may only protect us for a very fleeting space of time.' The Duke clambered on to Rex's shoulders and heaved himself up on to the coping. Rex stepped back a few yards and took a flying leap; next second he had scrambled up beside De Richleau. For a moment they both sat astride the wall peering down into the shadows of the garden, then they dropped silently into a flower-border on the other side.

'The first thing is to find a good line of retreat in case we have to get out in a hurry,' breathed the Duke.

'What about this?' Rex whispered back, slapping the trunk of a well-grown laburnum tree.

De Richleau nodded silently. One glance assured him that with the aid of the lower branches two springs would bring them to the top of the wall. Then he moved at a quick, stealthy run across a small open space of lawn to the shelter of some bushes that ran round the side of the house.

From their new cover Rex surveyed the side windows. No glimmer of light broke the expanse of the rambling old mansion. As the Duke moved on, he followed, until the bushes ended at the entrance of a back yard, evidently giving on to the kitchen quarters.

'Have a care,' he whispered, jerking De Richleau's sleeve. 'They may have a dog.'

'They couldn't,' replied the Duke positively. 'Dogs are simple, friendly creatures but highly psychic. The vibrations in a place where Black Magic was practised would cause any dog to bolt for a certainty.' With light, quick, padding steps he crossed the yard and came out into the garden on the far side of the house.

Here too every window was shrouded in darkness and an uncanny stillness brooded over the place.

'I don't like it,' whispered De Richleau. 'Simon can't have been back more than a quarter of an hour at the outside—so there ought still to be lights in the upper rooms. Anyhow, it looks at if the others have gone home, which is something—we must chance an ambush.'

He pointed to a narrow, ground floor window. 'That's probably the lavatory, and most people forget to close their lavatory windows—come on!'

Silently Rex followed him across the grass, then gripping him by the knees, heaved him up until he was well above the level of the sill.

The sash creaked, the upper half of the window slid down, and the Duke's head and shoulders disappeared inside.

For a moment Rex watched his wriggling legs, heard a bump, followed by a muffled oath, and then clambered up on to the sill.

'Hurt yourself?' he whispered, as De Richleau's face appeared, a pale blot in the darkness.

'Not much—though this sort of thing is not amusing for a man of my age. The door here is unlocked, thank goodness.'

Immediately Rex was inside, the Duke squatted down on the floor. 'Take off your shoes,' he ordered. 'And your socks.'

'Shoes if you like, though we'll hurt our feet if we have to run—but why the socks?'

'Don't argue—we waste time.'

'Well—what now?' Rex muttered after a moment.

'Put your shoes on again and the socks over them—then you can run as fast as you like.' As Rex obeyed the Duke went on in a low voice. 'Not a sound now. I really believe the others have gone, and if Mocata is not lying in wait for us, we may be able to get hold of Simon. If we come up against that black servant, for God's sake remember not to look at his eyes.'

With infinite care he opened the door and peered out into the darkened hall. A faint light from an upper window showed the double doors that led to the *salon* standing wide open. He listened intently for a moment, then slipping out stood aside for Rex to follow, and gently closed the door behind them.

Their footsteps, now muffled by the socks, were barely audible as they stole across the stretch of parquet. When they reached the *salon* De Richleau carefully drew aside a blind. The dim starlight was just sufficient to show the outlines of the gilded furniture, and they could make out plates and glasses left scattered upon the buhl and marquetry tables.

Rex picked up a goblet two-thirds full of champagne and held it so that the Duke could see the wine still in it.

De Richleau nodded. The Irish Bard, the Albino, the one-armed Eurasian, the hare-lipped man and the rest of that devilish company must have taken fright when he and Rex had forcibly abducted Simon, and fled, abandoning their unholy operations for the night. He gently replaced the blind and they crept back into the hall.

One other door opened off it besides those to the servants' quarters and the vestibule. De Richleau slowly turned the knob and pressed. The room was a small library, and at the far end a pair of uncurtained french-windows showed the garden, ghostly and mysterious in the starlight. Leaving Rex by the door, the Duke tiptoed across the room, drew the bolts, opened the windows and propped them wide. From where he stood he could just make out the laburnum by the wall. A clear retreat was open to them now. He turned, then halted with a sharp intake of breath. Rex had disappeared.

'Rex!' he hissed in a loud whisper, gripped by a sudden nameless fear. 'Rex!' But there was no reply.

5

Embodied Evil

De Richleau had been involved in so many strange adventures in his long and chequered career, that instinctively his hand flew to the pocket where he kept his automatic at such times, but it was flat—and in a fraction of time it had come back to him that this was no affair of shootings and escapes, but a grim struggle against the Power of Darkness—in which their only protection must be an utter faith in the ultimate triumph of good, and the use of such little power as he possessed to bring into play the great forces of the Power of Light.

In two strides he had reached the door, grabbed the electric switch, and pressed it as he cried in ringing tones: *'Fundamenta ejus in montibus sanctis!'*

'What the hell!' exclaimed Rex as the light flashed on. He was at the far side of the hall, carefully constructing a booby trap of chairs and china in front of the door that led to the servants' quarters.

'You've done it now,' he added, with his eyes riveted upon the upper landing, but nothing stirred and the pall of silence descended upon the place again until they could hear each other's quickened breathing.

'The house is empty,' Rex declared after a moment. 'If there were anyone here they'd have been bound to hear you about. It echoed from the cellars to the attics.'

De Richleau was regarding him with an angry stare. 'You madman,' he snapped. 'Don't you understand what we're up against? We must not separate for an instant in this unholy place—even now that the lights are on.'

Rex smiled. He had always considered the Duke as the most fearless man he knew, and to see him in such a state of nerves was a revelation. 'I'm not scared of bogeys, but I am of being shot up from behind,' he said simply. 'I was fixing this so we'd hear the servants if there was trouble upstairs and they came up to help Mocata.'

'Yes, but honestly, Rex, it is imperative that we should keep as near each other as possible every second we remain in this ghastly house. It may sound childish, but I ought to have told you before that if anything queer does happen we must actually hold hands. That will quadruple our resistance to evil by attuning our vibrations towards good. Now let's go upstairs and see if they have really gone—though I can hardly doubt it.'

Rex followed marvelling. This man who was frightened of shadows and talked of holding hands at a time of danger was so utterly different to the De Richleau that he knew. Yet as he watched the Duke mounting the stairs in swift, panther-like, noiseless strides he felt that since he was so scared this midnight visitation was a fresh demonstration of his courage.

On the floor above they made a quick examination of the bedrooms, but all of them were unoccupied and none of the beds had been slept in.

'Mocata must have sent the rest of them away and been waiting here with a car to whisk Simon off immediately he got back,' De Richleau declared as they came out of the last room.

'That's about it, so we may as well clear out.' Rex shivered slightly as he added: 'It's beastly cold up here.'

'I was wondering whether you'd notice that, but we're not going home yet. This is a God-given opportunity to search the house at our leisure. We may discover all sorts of interesting things. Leave all the lights on here, the more the better, and come downstairs.'

In the *salon* the great buffet table still lay spread with the excellent collation which they had seen there on their first visit. The Duke walked over to it and poured himself a glass of wine. 'I see Simon has taken to Cliquot again,' he observed. 'He alternates between that and Bollinger with remarkable consistency, though in certain years I prefer Pol Roger to either when it has a little age on it.'

As Rex spooned a slab of Duck *à la Montmorency* on to a plate, helping himself liberally to the *foie gras mousse* and cherries, he wondered if De Richleau had really recovered from the extraordinary agitation that he had displayed a quarter of an hour before, or if he was talking so casually to cover his secret apprehensions. He hated to admit it even to himself, but there *was* something queer about the house, a chill seemed to be spreading up his legs from beneath the heavily-laden table, and the silence was strangely oppressive. Anxious to get on with the business and out of the place now, he said quickly. 'I don't give two hoots what he drinks, but where has Mocata gone—and why?'

'The last question is simple.' De Richleau set down his glass and drew out the case containing the famous Hoyo de Monterrey's. 'There are virtually no laws against the practice of Black Magic in this country now. Only that of 1842, called the Rogues and Vagabonds Act, under which a person may be prosecuted for "pretending or professing to tell Fortunes, by using any subtle Craft, Means or Device!" But since the practitioners of it are universally evil, the Drug Traffic, Blackmail, Criminal Assault and even Murder are often mixed up with it, and for one of those reasons Mocata, having learnt that we were on our way here through his occult powers, feared a brawl might attract the attention of the police to his activities. Evidently he considered discretion the better part of valour on this occasion and temporarily abandoned the place to us— taking Simon with him.'

'Not very logical—are you?' Rex commented. 'One moment it's you who're scared that he may do all sorts of strange things to us, and the next you tell me that he's bolted for fear of being slogged under the jaw.'

'My dear fellow, I can only theorise. I'm completely in the dark myself. Some of these followers of the Left Hand Path are mere neophytes who can do little more than *wish* evil in minor matters on people they dislike. Others are adepts and can set in motion the most violent destructive forces which are not yet even suspected by our modern scientists.

'If Mocata only occupies a low place in the hierarchy we can deal with him as we would any other crook with little risk of any serious danger to ourselves, but if he is a Master he may be able to strike us blind or dead. Unfortunately I know little enough of this horrible business, only the minor rituals of the Right Hand Path, or White Magic as people call it, which may protect us in an emergency. If only I knew more I might be able to find out where he has taken Simon.'

'Cheer up—we'll find him.' Rex laughed as he set down his plate, but the sound echoed eerily through the deserted house, causing him to glance swiftly over his shoulder in the direction of the still darkened inner room. 'What's the next move?' he asked more soberly.

'We've got to try and find Simon's papers. If we can, we may be able to get the real names and addresses of some of those people who were here tonight. Let's try the Library first—bring the bottle with you. I'll take the glasses.'

'What d'you mean—real names?' Rex questioned as he followed De Richleau across the hall.

'Why, you don't suppose that incredible old woman with the parrot beak was really called Madame D'Urfé—do you? That's only a nom-du-Diable, taken when she was re-baptised, and adopted from the Countess of that name, who was a notorious witch in Louis XV's time. All the others are the same. Didn't you realise the meaning of the name your lovely lady calls herself by—Tanith?'

'No.' Rex hesitated. 'I thought she was just a foreigner—that's all.'

'Dear me. Well, Tanith was the Moon Goddess of the Carthaginians. Thousands of years earlier the Egyptians called her Isis, and in the intervening stage she was known to the Phœnicians as the Lady Astoroth. They worshipped her in sacred groves where doves were sacrificed and unmentionable scenes of licentiousness took place. The God Adonis was her lover, and the people wept for his mythical death each year, believing upon him as a Redeemer of Mankind. As they went in processions to her shrines they wrought themselves into the wildest frenzy, and to slake the thwarted passion of the widowed goddess, gashed themselves with knives. Sir George Frazer's *Golden Bough* will tell you all about it, but the blood that was shed still lives, Rex, and she has been thirsty through these Christian centuries for more. Eleven words of power, each having eleven letters, twice pronounced in a fitting time and place after due preparation, and she would stand before you, terrible in her beauty, demanding a new sacrifice.'

Even Rex's gay modernity was not proof against that sinister declaration. De Richleau's voice held no trace of the gentle cynicism which was so characteristic of him, but seemed to ring with the positiveness of some horrible secret truth. He shuddered slightly as the Duke began to pull open the drawers of Simon's desk.

All except one, which was locked, held letter files, and a brief examination of these showed that they contained nothing but accounts, receipts, and correspondence of a normal nature. Rex forced the remaining drawer with a heavy steel paper knife,

43

but it only held cheque book counterfoils and bundles of dividend warrants, so they turned their attention to the long shelves of books. It was possible that Simon might have concealed certain private papers behind his treasured collection of modern first editions, but after ten minutes' careful search they assured themselves that nothing of interest was hidden at the back of the neat rows of volumes.

Having drawn a blank in the library, they proceeded to the other downstairs rooms, going systematically through every drawer and cabinet, but without result. Then they moved upstairs and tried the bedrooms, yet here again they could discover nothing which might not have been found in any normal house, nor was there any safe in which important documents might have been placed.

During the search De Richleau kept Rex constantly beside him, and Rex was not altogether sorry. Little by little the atmosphere of the place was getting him down, and more than once he had the unpleasant sensation that somebody was watching him covertly from behind, although he told himself that it was pure imagination, due entirely to De Richleau's evident belief in the supernatural, of which they had been talking all the evening.

'These people must have left traces of their doings in this house somewhere,' declared the Duke angrily as they came out of the last bedroom on to the landing, 'and I'm determined to find them.'

'We haven't done the Observatory yet, and I'd say that's the most likely spot of all,' Rex suggested.

'Yes—let's do that next.' De Richleau turned towards the upper flight of stairs.

The great domed room was just as they had left it a few hours before. The big telescope pointing in the same direction, the astrolabes and sextants still in the same places. The five-pointed pentacle enclosed in the double circle with its Cabalistic figures stood out white and clear on the polished floor in the glare of the electric lights. Evidently no ceremony had taken place after their departure. To verify his impression the Duke threw up the lid of the wicker hamper that stood beside the wall.

A scraping sound came from the basket, and he nodded. 'See Rex! The Black Cock and the White Hen destined for sacrifice, but we spoilt their game for tonight at all events. We'll take them down and free them in the garden when we go.'

'What did they really mean to do—d'you think?' Rex asked gravely.

'Utilise the conjunction of certain stars which occurred at Simon's birth, and again tonight, to work some invocation through him. To raise some dark familiar perhaps, an elemental or an earthbound spirit—or even some terrible intelligence from what we know as Hell, in order to obtain certain information they require from it.'

'Oh, nuts!' Rex exclaimed impatiently. 'I don't believe such things. Simon's been got hold of by a gang of blackmailing kidnappers and hypnotised if you like. They've probably used this Black Magic stuff to impose on him just as it imposes on you—but in every other way it's sheer, preposterous nonsense.'

'I only hope that you may continue to think so, Rex, but I fear you may have reason to alter your views before we're through. Let's continue our search—shall we?'

'Fine—though I've a hunch it's a pity we didn't call in the cops at the beginning.'

They examined the instruments, but all of them were beyond suspicion of any secret purpose, and then a square revolving bookcase, but it held only trigonometry tables and charts of the heavens.

'Damn it, there must be something in this place!' De Richleau muttered. 'Swords or cups or devils' bibles. They couldn't perform their rituals without them.'

'Maybe they took their impedimenta with them when they quit.'

'Perhaps, but I'd like even to see the place in which they kept it. You never know what they may have left behind. Try tapping all round the walls, Rex, and I'll do the floor. There's almost certain to be a secret cache somewhere.'

For some minutes they pursued their search in silence, only their repeated knockings breaking the stillness of the empty house. Then Rex gave a sudden joyful shout.

'Here, quick—it's hollow under here!'

Together they pulled aside an early seventeenth-century chart of the Macrocosm by Robert Fludd, and after fumbling for a moment found the secret spring. The panel slid back with a click.

In the recess some four feet deep reposed a strange collection of articles: a wand of hazelwood, a crystal set in gold, a torch with a pointed end so that it could be stuck upright in the ground, candle-sticks, a short sword, two great books, a dagger with a blade curved like a sickle moon, a ring, a chalice and an old bronze lamp, formed out of twisted human figures, which had nine wicks. All had pentacles, planetary signs, and other strange symbols engraved upon them, and each had the polish which is a sign of great age coupled with frequent usage.

'Got them!' snapped the Duke. 'By Jove, I'm glad we stayed, Rex! These things are incredibly rare, and each a power in itself through association with past mysteries. It is a thousand to one against their having others, and without them their claws will be clipped from working any serious evil against us.'

As he spoke De Richleau lifted out the two ancient volumes. One had a binding of worked copper on which were chased designs and characters. Its leaves, which were made from the bark of young trees, were covered with very clear writing done with an iron point. The text of the other was painted on vellum yellowed by time, and its binding supported by great scrolled silver clasps.

'Wonderful copies,' the Duke murmured, with all the enthusiasm of a bibliophile. 'The Clavicule of Solomon and The Grimoire of Pope Honorius. They are not the muddled recast versions of the seventeenth century either, but far, far older. This Clavicule on cork may be of almost any age, and is to the Black Art what the Codex Sinaiticus and such early versions are to Christianity.'

'Well, maybe Mocata didn't figure we'd stay to search this place when we found Simon wasn't here, but it doesn't say much for all his clairvoyant powers you make such a song about for him to let us get away with his whole magician's box of tricks. Say! where's that draught coming from?' Rex suddenly clapped a hand on the back of his neck.

The Duke thrust the two books back and swung round as if he had been stung. He had felt it at the same instant—a sudden chill wind which increased to a rushing icy blast, so cold that it stung his hands and face like burning fire. The electric lights flickered and went dim, so that only the faint red glow of the wires showed in the globes. The great room was plunged in shadow and a violet mist began to rise out of the middle of the pentacle, swirling with incredible rapidity like some dust devil of the desert. It gathered height and bulk, spread and took form.

The lights flickered again and then went out, but the violet mist had a queer phosphorescent glow of its own. By it they could see the cabalistic bookcase, like a dark shadow beyond it, through the luminous mist. An awful stench of decay, which yet had something sweet and cloying about it, filled their nostrils as they gazed, sick and almost retching with repulsion, at a grey face that was taking shape about seven feet from the floor. The eyes were fixed upon them, malicious and intent. The eyeballs whitened but the face went dark. Under it the mist was gathering into shoulders, torso, hips.

Before they could choke for breath the materialisation had completed. Clad in flowing robes of white, Mocata's black servant towered above them. His astral body was just as the Duke had seen it in the flesh, from tip to toe a full six foot eight, and the eyes, slanting inward, burned upon them like live coals of fire.

6

The Secret Art

Rex was not frightened in the ordinary meaning of the word. He was past the state in which he could have ducked, or screamed, or run. He stood there rigid, numbered by the icy chill that radiated from the figure in the pentagram, a tiny pulse throbbed in his forehead, and his knees seemed to grow weak beneath him. A clear, silvery voice beat in his ears: 'Do not look at his eyes!—do not look at his eyes!—do not look at his eyes!'—an urgent repetition of De Richleau's warning to him, but try as he would, he could not drag his gaze from the malignant yellow pupils which burned in the black face.

Unable to stir hand or foot, he watched the ab-human figure grow in breadth and height, its white draperies billowing with a strange silent motion as they rose from the violet mist that

47

obscured the feet, until it overflowed the circles that ringed the pentagram and seemed to fill the lofty chamber like a veritable Djin. The room reeked with the sickly, cloying stench which he had heard of but never thought to know—the abominable affluvium of embodied evil.

Suddenly red rays began to glint from the baleful slanting eyes, and Rex found himself quivering from head to foot. He tried desperately to pray: 'Our Father which art in Heaven—hallowed—hallowed—hallowed . . .' but the words which he had not used for so long would not come; the vibrations, surging through his body, as though he were holding the terminals of a powerful electric battery, seemed to cut them off. His left knee began to jerk. His foot lifted. He strove to raise his arms to cover his face, but they remained fixed to his sides as though held by invisible steel bands. He tried to cry out, to throw himself backwards, but, despite every atom of will which he could muster, a relentless force was drawing him towards the silent, menacing figure. Almost before he realised it he had taken a pace forward.

Through that timeless interval of seconds, days or weeks, after the violet mist first appeared, De Richleau stood within a foot of Rex, his eyes riveted upon the ground. He would not even allow himself to ascertain in what form the apparition had taken shape. The sudden deathly cold, the flicker of the lights as the room was plunged in darkness, the noisome odour, were enough to tell him that an entity of supreme evil was abroad.

With racing thoughts, he cursed his foolhardiness in ever entering the accursed house without doing all things proper for their protection. It was so many years since he had had any dealings with the occult that his acute anxiety for Simon had caused him to minimise the appalling risk they would run. What folly could have possessed him, he wondered miserably, to allow Rex, whose ignorance and scepticism would make him doubly vulnerable, to accompany him. Despite his advancing age, the Duke would have given five precious years of his life for an assurance that Rex was staring at the parquet floor, momentarily riveted by fear perhaps, yet still free from the malevolent influence which was streaming in pulsing waves from the circle; but Rex was not—instinctively De Richleau knew that his eyes were fixed on the Thing—and a ghastly

48

dread caused little beads of icy perspiration to break out on his forehead.

Then he felt, rather than saw, Rex move. Next second he heard his footfall and *knew* that he was walking towards the pentagram. With trembling lips he began to mutter strange sentences of Persian, Greek and Hebrew, dimly remembered from his studies of the past—calling—calling—urgently—imperatively, upon the Power of Light for guidance and protection. Almost instantly the memory that he had slipped the jewelled swastika into his waistcoat pocket when Max returned it, flashed into his mind—and he knew that his prayer was answered. His fingers closed on the jewel. His arms shot out. It glittered for a second in the violet light, then came to rest in the centre of the circle.

A piercing scream, desperate with anger, fear, and pain, like that of a beast seared with a white-hot iron, blasted the silence. The lights flickered again so that the wires showed red—came on—went out—and flickered once more, as though two mighty forces were struggling for possession of the current.

The chill wind died so suddenly that it seemed as if a blanket of warm air had descended on their faces—but even while that hideous screech was still ringing through the chamber De Richleau grabbed Rex by the arm and dragged him towards the door. Next second the control of both had snapped and they were plunging down the stairs with an utter recklessness born of sheer terror.

Rex slipped on the lower landing and sprawled down the last flight on his back. The Duke came bounding after, six stairs at a time, and fell beside him. Together they scrambled to their feet—dashed through the library—out of the french-windows—and across the lawn.

With the agility of lemurs they swung up the branches of the laburnum—on to the wall—and dropped to the far side. Then they pelted down the lane as fast as their legs could carry them, and on until a full street away they paused, breathless and panting, to face each other under the friendly glow of a street lamp.

De Richleau's breath came in choking gasps. It was years since he had subjected himself to such physical exertion, and his face was grey from the strain which it had put upon him. Rex found his evening collar limp from the sweat which had streamed from him in his terror, but his lungs were easing rapidly, and he was the first to recover.

'God! we're mighty lucky to be out of that!'

The Duke nodded, still unable to speak.

'I take back every word I said,' Rex went on hurriedly. 'I don't think I've ever been real scared of anything in my life before—but that was hellish!'

'I panicked too—towards the end—couldn't help it, but I should never have taken you into that place—never,' De Richleau muttered repentantly as they set off down the street.

'Since we've got out safe it's all to the good. I've a real idea what we're up against now.'

The Duke drew Rex's arm through his own with a friendly gesture. Far from desiring to say 'I told you so!' he was regretting that he had been so impatient with Rex's previous unbelief. Most people he knew regarded devil worship and the cultivation of mystic powers as sheer superstitions due to the ignorance of the Middle Ages. It had been too much to expect Rex to accept his contention that their sane and sober friend Simon was mixed up in such practices, but now he had actually witnessed a true instance of Saiitii De Richleau felt that his co-operation would be ten times as valuable as before.

In the St. John's Wood Road they picked up a belated taxi, and on the way back to Curzon Street he questioned Rex carefully as to the form the Thing had taken. When he had heard the description he nodded. 'It was Mocata's black servant, undoubtedly.'

'What did you say he was?'

'A Malagasy. They are a strange people. Half Negro and half Polynesian. A great migration took place many centuries ago from the South Seas to the East African Coast by way of the Malay Peninsula and Ceylon. Incredible though it may seem, they covered fifteen thousand miles of open ocean in their canoes, and most of them settled in Madagascar, where they intermarried with the aborigines and produced this half-breed type, which often has the worst characteristics of both races.'

'And Madagascar is the home of Voodoo—isn't it?'

'Yes. Perhaps he is a Witch doctor himself . . . and yet I wonder . . .' The Duke broke off as the taxi drew up before Errol House.

50

As they entered the big library Rex glanced at the clock and saw that it was a little after three. Not a particularly late hour for him, since he often danced until the night clubs emptied, nor for De Richleau, who believed that the one time when men opened their minds and conversation became really interesting was in the quiet hours before the dawn. Yet both were so exhausted by their ordeal that they felt as though a month had passed since they sat down to dinner.

Rex remade the remnants of the fire while the Duke mixed the drinks and uncovered the sandwiches which Max always left for him. Then they both sank into armchairs and renewed the discussion, for despite their weariness, neither had any thought of bed. The peril in which Simon stood was far too urgent.

'You were postulating that he might be a Madagascar Witch doctor,' Rex began. 'But I've a hunch I've read some place that such fellows have no power over whites, and surely that is so, else how could settlers in Africa and places keep the blacks under?'

'Broadly speaking, you are right, and the explanation is simple. What we call Magic—Black or White—is *the Science and Art of Causing Change to occur in conformity with Will*. Any required Change may be effected by the application of the proper kind and degree of Force in the proper manner and through the proper medium. Naturally, for causing any Change it is requisite to have the practical ability to set the necessary Forces in right motion, but it is even more important to have a thorough qualitative and quantitative understanding of the conditions. Very few white men can really get inside a Negro's mind and know exactly what he is thinking—and even fewer blacks can appreciate a white's mentality. In consequence, it is infinitely harder for the Wills of either to work on the other than on men of their own kind.

'Another factor which adds to the difficulty of a Negroid or Mongolian Sorcerer working his spells upon a European is the question of vibrations. Their variation in human beings is governed largely by the part of the earth's surface in which birth took place. To use a simple analogy, some races have long wave lengths and others short—and the greater the variation the more difficult it is for a malignant will to influence that of an intended victim. Were it otherwise, you may be certain that

51

the white races, who have neglected spiritual growth for material achievement, would never have come to dominate the world as they do today.'

'Yet that devil of Mocata's got me down all right. Ugh!' Rex shuddered slightly at the recollection.

'True—but I was only speaking generally. There are exceptions, and in the highest grades—the Ipsissimus, the Magus and the Magister Templi—those who have passed the Abyss, colour and race no longer remain a bar, so such Masters can work their will upon any lesser human unless he is protected by a power of equal strength. This associate of Mocata's may be one of the great Adepts of the Left Hand Path. However, what I was really wondering was—is he a human being at all?'

'But you said you saw him yourself—when you paid a call on Simon weeks back.'

'I *thought* I saw him—so at first I assumed that the Thing you saw tonight was his astral body, sent by Mocata to prevent our removing his collection of Devil's baubles; but perhaps what we both saw was a disembodied entity, an actual Satanic power which is not governed by Mocata, but has gained entry to our world from the other side through his evil practices.'

'Oh Lord!' Rex groaned. 'All this stuff is so new, so fantastic, so utterly impossible to me—I just can't grasp it; though don't think I'm doubting now. Whether it was an astral body or what you say, I saw it all right, and it wasn't a case of any stupid parlour tricks—I'll swear to that. It was so evil that my bones just turned to water on me in sheer blue funk—and there's poor Simon all mixed up in this. Say, now—what the hell are we to do?'

De Richleau sat forward suddenly. 'I wish to God I knew what was at the bottom of this business. I am certain that it is something pretty foul for them to have gone to the lengths of getting hold of a normal man like Simon but, if it is the last thing we ever do, we've got to find him and get him away from these people.'

'But how?' Rex flung wide his arms. 'Where can we even start in on the hope of picking up the trail? Simon's a lone wolf—always has been. He's got no father; his mother lives abroad; unlike so many Jews, he hasn't even got a heap of relatives who we can dig out and question?'

'Yes, that is the trouble. Of course he is almost certain to be

52

with Mocata, but I don't see how we are to set about finding somebody who knows Mocata either. If only we had the address of any of those people who were there this evening we might . . .'

'I've got it!' cried Rex, leaping to his feet. 'We'll trace him through Tanith.'

7

De Richleau Plans a Campaign

'Tanith,' the Duke repeated; 'but you don't know where she is, do you?'

'Sure.' Rex laughed, for the first time in several hours. 'Having got acquainted with her after all this while, I wouldn't be such a fool as to quit that party without nailing her address.'

'I must confess that I'm surprised she gave it to you.'

'She hadn't fallen to it that I wasn't one of their bunch— then! She's staying at Claridges.'

'Do you think you can get hold of her?'

'Don't you worry—I meant to, anyhow.'

'You must be careful, Rex. This woman is very lovely, I know—but she's probably damnably dangerous.'

'I've never been scared of a female yet, and surely these people can't do me much harm in broad daylight?'

'No, except for ordinary human trickery they are almost powerless between sunrise and sunset.'

'Fine. Then I'll go right round to Claridges as soon as she is likely to be awake tomorrow—today, rather.'

'You don't know her real name though, do you?'

'I should worry. There aren't two girls like her staying at Claridges—there aren't two like her in all London.'

De Richleau stood up and began to pace the floor like some huge cat. 'What do you intend to say to her?' he asked at length.

'Why, that we're just worried stiff about Simon—and that it's absolutely imperative that she should help us out. I'll give her a frank undertaking not to do anything against Mocata or any of her pals if she'll come clean with me—though Heaven knows I can't think she's got any real friends in a crowd like that.'

'Rex! Rex!' The Duke smiled affectionately down into the honest attractive, ugly face of the young giant stretched in the armchair. 'And what, may I ask, do you intend to do should this lovely lady refuse to tell you anything?'

'I can threaten to call in the cops, I suppose, though I'd just hate to do anything like that on her.'

De Richleau gave his eloquent expressive shrug. 'My dear fellow, unless we can get some actual evidence of ordinary criminal activities against Mocata and his friends, the police are absolutely ruled out of this affair—and she would know it.'

'I don't see why,' Rex protested stubbornly. 'These people have kidnapped Simon, that's what it boils down to, and that's as much a crime as running a dope joint or white slaving.'

'Perhaps, and if they had hit him on the head our problem would be easy. The difficulty is that to all outward appearances he has joined them willingly and in his right mind. Only *we* know that he is acting under some powerful and evil influence which has been brought to bear on him, and how in the world are you going to charge anyone with raising the devil—or its equivalent—in a modern police court?'

'Well, what do you suggest?'

'Listen.' The Duke perched himself on the arm of Rex's chair. 'Even if this girl is an innocent party like Simon, she will not tell you anything willingly—she will be too frightened. As a matter of fact, now that she knows you are not a member of their infernal circle it is doubtful if she will even see you, but if she does—well, you've got to get hold of her somehow.'

'I'll certainly have a try—but it's not all that easy to kidnap people in a city like London.'

'I don't mean that exactly, but rather that you should induce her, by fair means or foul, to accompany you to some place where I can talk to her at my leisure. If she is only a neophyte I know enough of this dangerous business to frighten her out of her wits. If she is something more there will be a mental tussle, and I may learn something from the cards which she is forced to throw on the table.'

'O.K. I'll pull every gun I know to persuade her into coming here with me for a cocktail.'

De Richleau shook his head. 'No, I'm afraid that won't do,

immediately she realised the reason she had been brought here she would insist on leaving, and we couldn't stop her. If we tried she would break a window and yell Murder! We have got to get her to a place where she will see at once the futility of trying to call for outside help. I have it! Do you think you could get her down to Pangbourne?'

'What? To that river place of yours?'

'Yes; I haven't been down there yet this year, but I can send Max down first thing in the morning to open it up and give it an airing.'

'You talk as though I were falling off a log to get a girl to come boating on the Thames at what's practically a first meeting—can't you weigh in and lend a hand yourself?'

'No. I shall be at the British Museum most of the day. It is so many years since I studied the occult that there are a thousand things I have forgotten. It is absolutely imperative that I should immerse myself in some of the old key works for a few hours and rub up my knowledge of protective measures. I must leave you to handle the girl, Rex, and remember, Simon's safety will depend almost wholly on your success. Get her there somehow, and I'll join you in the late afternoon—say about six.'

Rex grinned. 'It's about as stiff a proposition as sending me in your place to study the Cabbala, but I'll do my best.'

'Of course you will.' The Duke began to pace hurriedly up and down again. 'But go gently with her—I beg you. Avoid any questions about this horrible business as you would the plague. Play the lover. Be just the nice young man who has fallen in love with a beautiful girl. If she asks you about our having abducted Simon from the party, say you were completely in the dark about it. That you have known me for years—and that I sprung some story on you about his having fallen into the hands of a gang of blackmailers, so you just blindly followed my lead without a second thought. Not a word to her about the supernatural—you know nothing of that. You must be as incredulous as you were with me when I first talked to you of it. And, above all, if you can get her to Pangbourne, don't let her know that I am coming down.'

'Surely—I get the line you want me to play all right.'

'Good. You see, if I can only squeeze some information out of her which will enable us to find out where Mocata is living, we will go down and keep the place under observation for a day or two. He is almost certain to have Simon with him. We will note the times that Mocata leaves the house and plan our raid accordingly. If we can get Simon into our hands again I swear Mocata shan't get him back a second time.'

'That's certainly the idea.'

'There is only one thing I am really frightened of.'

'What's that?'

De Richleau paused opposite Rex's chair. 'What I heard this evening of Simon's approaching change of name—to Abraham, you remember. That, of course, would be after Abraham the Jew, a very famous and learned mystic of the early centuries. He wrote a book which is said to be the most informative ever compiled concerning the Great Work. It was lost sight of for several hundred years, but early in the fifteenth century came into the possession of a Parisian bookseller named Nicolas Flamel who, by its aid, performed many curious rites. Flamel was buried in some magnificence, and a few years later certain persons who were anxious to obtain his secrets opened his grave to find the book which was supposed to have been buried with him. Neither Flamel nor the book was there, and there is even some evidence to show that he was still living a hundred years later in Turkey, which is by no means unbelievable to those who have any real knowledge of the strange powers acquired by the true initiate such as those in the higher orders of the Yoga sects. That is the last we know of the Book of Abraham the Jew, but it seems that Simon is about to take his name in the service of the Invisible.'

'Well—what'll happen then?'

'That he will be given over entirely to the Power of Evil, because he will renounce his early teaching and receive his re-baptism at the hands of a high adept of the Left Hand Path. Until that is done we can still save him, because all the invisible powers of Good will be fighting on our side, but after—they will withdraw, and what we call the Soul of Simon Aron will be dragged down into the Pit.'

'Are you sure of that? Baptism into the Christian Faith doesn't ensure one going to Heaven, why should this other sprinkling be a guarantee of anyone going to Hell?'

'It's such a big question, Rex, but briefly it is like this. Heaven and Hell are only symbolical of growth to Light or

56

disintegration to Darkness. By Christian—or any other *true* religious baptism, we renounce the Devil and all his Works, thereby erecting a barrier which it is difficult for Evil forces to surmount, but anyone who accepts Satanic baptism does exactly the reverse. They wilfully destroy the barrier of astral Light which is our natural protection and offer themselves as a medium through which the powers of Darkness may operate on mankind.

'They are tempted to it, of course, by the belief that it will give them supernatural powers over their fellow-men, but few of them realise the appalling danger. There is no such person as the Devil, but there are vast numbers of Earthbound spirits, Elementals, and Evil Intelligences of the Outer Circle floating in our midst. Nobody who has even the most elementary knowledge of the Occult can doubt that. They are blind and ignorant, and except for the last, under comparatively rare circumstances, not in the least dangerous to any normal man or woman who leads a reasonably upright life, but they never cease to search in a fumbling way for some gateway back into existence as we know it. The surrender of one's own volition gives it to them, and, if you need an example, you only have to think of the many terrible crimes which are perpetrated when reason and will are entirely absent owing to excess of alcohol. An Elemental seizes upon the unresisting intelligence of the human and forces them to some appalling deed which is utterly against their natural instincts.

'That, then, is the danger. While apparently only passing through an ancient barbarous and disgusting ritual, the Satanist, by accepting baptism, surrenders his will to the domination of powers which he believes he will be able to use for his own ends, but in actual fact he becomes the spiritual slave of an Elemental, and for ever after is nothing but the instrument of its evil purposes.'

'When do you figure they'll try to do this thing?'

'Not for a week or so, I trust. It is essential that it should take place at a real Sabbat, when at least one Coven of thirteen is present, and after our having broken up their gathering to-night I hardly think they will risk meeting again for some little time, unless there is some extraordinary reason why they should.'

'That gives us a breathing space then; but what's worrying

me is that it's so early in the year to ask a young woman to go picnicking on the river.'

'Why? The sunshine for the last few days has been magnificent.'

'Still, it's only April 29th—the 30th, I mean.'

'What!' De Richleau stood there with a new and terrible anxiety burning in his eyes. 'Good God! I never realised!'

'What's the trouble?'

'Why, that was only one Coven we saw tonight, and there are probably a dozen scattered over England. The whole pack are probably on their way by now to the great annual gathering. It's a certainty they will take Simon with them. They'd never miss the chance of giving him his Devil's Christening at the Grand Sabbat of the year.'

'What in the world are you talking about?' Rex hoisted himself swiftly out of his chair.

'Don't you understand, man?' De Richleau gripped him by the shoulder. 'On the last night of April every peasant in Europe still double-locks his doors. Every latent force for Evil in the world is abroad. We've got to get hold of Simon in the next twenty hours. This coming night—April 30th—is Saint Walburga's Eve.'

8

Rex Van Ryn Opens the Attack

Six hours later, Rex, still drowsy with sleep, lowered himself into the Duke's sunken bath. It was a very handsome bathroom some fifteen feet by twelve; black glass, crystal mirrors, and chromium-plated fittings made up the scheme of decoration.

Some people might have considered it a little too striking to be in perfect taste, but De Richleau did not subscribe to the canon which has branded ostentation as vulgarity in the last few generations, and robbed nobility of any glamour which it may have possessed in more spacious days.

His forbears had ridden with thirty-two footmen before them, and it caused him considerable regret that modern conditions made it impossible for him to drive in his Hispano with no more than one seated beside his chauffeur on the box. Fortunately his resources were considerable and his brain sufficiently astute to make good, in most years, the inroads which the tax gatherers made upon them. 'After him,' of course 'the Deluge' as he very fully recognised, but with reasonable good fortune he considered that private ownership would last out his time, at least in England where he had made his home; and so he continued to do all things on a scale suitable to a De Richleau, with the additional lavishness of one who had had a Russian mother, as far as the restrictions of twentieth-century democracy would allow.

Rex, however, had used the Duke's £1,000 bathroom a number of times before, and his only concern at the moment was to wonder vaguely what he was doing there on this occasion and why he had such an appalling hangover. Never, since he had been given two glasses of bad liquor in the old days when his country laboured under prohibition, had he felt so desperately ill.

A giant sponge placed on the top of his curly head brought him temporary relief and full consciousness of the events which had taken place the night before. Of course it was that ghastly experience he had been through in Simon's empty house that had sapped him of his vitality and left him in this wretched state. He remembered that he had kept up all right until they got back to Curzon Street, and even after, during a long conversation with the Duke; then, he supposed, he must have petered out from sheer nervous exhaustion.

He lay back in the warm, faintly scented water, and gave himself a mental shaking. The thought that he must have fainted shocked him profoundly. He had driven racing cars at 200 miles an hour, had his colours for the Cresta run, had flown a plane 1,500 miles, right out of the Forbidden Territory down to Kiev in one hop. He had shot men and been shot at in return both in Russia and in Cuba, where he had found himself mixed up with the Revolution, but never before had he been in a real funk about anything, much less collapsed like a spineless fool.

He recalled with sickening vividness, that loathsome, striking manifestation of embodied evil that had come upon them—and his thoughts flew to Simon. How could their shy nervous,

59

charming friend have got himself mixed up in all this devilry? For Rex had no doubts now that, incredible as it might seem, the Duke was right, and Satan worship still a living force in modern cities, just as the infernal Voodoo cult was still secretly practised by the Negroes in the Southern States of his own country. He thought again of their first visit to Simon's house as unwelcome guests at that strange party. Of the Albino, the old Countess D'Urfé, the sinister Chinaman, and then of Tanith, except for Simon the only normal person present, and felt convinced that, but for the intervention of De Richleau some abominable ceremony would certainly have taken place, although he had laughed at the suggestion at the time.

Sitting up he began to soap himself vigorously while he restated the situation briefly in his mind. One: Mocata was an adept of what De Richleau called the Left Hand Path, and for some reason unknown he had gained control over Simon. Two: owing to their intervention the Satanists had abandoned Simon's house—taking him with them. Three: Simon was shortly to be baptised into the Black Brotherhood, after which, according to the Duke, he would be past all help. Four: today was May Day Eve when, according to the Duke, the Grand Sabbat of the year took place. Five: following from four, it was almost a certainty that Mocata would seize this opportunity of the Walpurgis Nacht celebrations to have Simon rechristened. Six: in the next twelve hours therefore, Mocata had to be traced and Simon taken from him. Seven: the only possibility of getting on Mocata's trail lay in obtaining information by prayers, cajolery, or threats from Tanith.

Rex stopped soaping and groaned aloud at the thought that the one woman he had been wanting to meet for years should be mixed up in this revolting business. He loathed deception in any form and resented intensely the necessity for practising it on her, but De Richleau's last instructions to him were still clear in his mind, and the one thing which stood out above all others, was the fact of his old and clear friend being in some intangible but terrible peril.

Feeling slightly better by the time he had shaved and dressed, he noted from the windows of the flat that at least they had been blessed with a glorious day. Summer was in the air and there seemed a promise of that lovely fortnight which sometimes graces England in early May.

To his surprise he found that De Richleau, who habitually was not visible before twelve, had left the flat at half-past eight. Evidently he meant to put in a long day among the ancient manuscripts at the British Museum, rubbing up his knowledge of strange cults and protective measures against what he termed the Ab-human monsters of the Outer Circle.

Max proffered breakfast, but Rex declined it until, with a hurt expression, the servant produced his favourite omelet.

'The chef will be so disappointed, sir,' he said.

Reluctantly Rex sat down to eat while Max, busy with the coffee-pot, permitted himself a hidden smile. He had had orders from the Duke, and His Excellency was a wily man. None knew that better than his personal servitor, the faithful Max.

Noting that Rex had finished, he produced a wine-glass full of some frothy mixture on a salver. 'His Excellency said, sir,' he stated blandly, 'that he finds this uncommon good for his neuralgia. I was distressed to hear that you are sometimes a sufferer too, and if you'd try it the taste is, if I may say so, not unpleasant—somewhat resembling that of granadillas I believe.'

With a suspicious look Rex drank the quite palatable potion while Max added suavely: 'Some gentleman prefer prairie-oysters I am told, but I've a feeling, sir, that His Excellency knows best.'

'You old humbug.' Rex grinned as he replaced the glass. 'Anyhow last night wasn't the sort of party you think—I wish to God it had been.'

'No, sir! Well, that's most regrettable I'm sure, but I had a feeling that Mr. Aron was not quite in his usual form, if I may so express it—when he er—joined us after dinner.'

'Yes—of course you put Simon to bed—I'd forgotten that.'

Max quickly lowered his eyes. He was quite certain that his innocent action the night before had been connected in some way with Simon Aron's sudden disappearance from the bed-room later, and felt that for once he had done the wrong thing, so he deftly turned the conversation. 'His Excellency instructed me to tell you, sir, that the touring Rolls is entirely at your disposal and the second chauffeur if you wish to use him.'

'No—I'll drive myself; have it brought round right away—will you?'

'Very good, sir, and now if you will excuse me I must leave at once in order to get down to Pangbourne and prepare the house for your reception.'

'O.K., Max—See-yer-later—I hope.' Rex picked up a cigarette. He was feeling better already. 'A whole heap better,' he thought, as he wondered what potent corpse-reviver lay hidden in the creamy depths of De Richleau's so-called neuralgia tonic. Then he sat down to plan out his line of attack on the lady at Claridges.

If he could only talk to her he felt that he would be able to intrigue her into a friendly attitude. He could, of course, easily find out her real name from the bureau of the hotel, but the snag was that if he sent up his name and asked to see her the chances were all against her granting him an interview. After all, by kidnapping Simon, he and the Duke had wrecked the meeting of her Circle the night before, and if she was at all intimately associated with Mocata, she probably regarded him with considerable hostility. Only personal contact could overcome that, so he must not risk any rebuff through the medium of bell-hops, but accept it only if given by her after he had managed to see her face to face.

His plan, therefore, eventually boiled down to marching on Claridges, planting himself in a comfortable chair within view of the lifts and sitting there until Tanith made her appearance. He admitted to himself that his proposed campaign was conspicuously lacking in brilliance but, he argued, few women staying in a London hotel would remain in their rooms all day, so if he sat there long enough it was almost certain that an opportunity would occur for him to tackle her direct. If she did turn him down—well, De Richleau wasn't the only person in the world who had ideas—and Rex flattered himself that he would think of something.

Immediately the Rolls was reported at the door, he left the flat and drove round to Claridges in it. A short conversation with a friendly commissionaire ensured that there would be no trouble if the car was left parked outside, even for a considerable time, for Rex thought it necessary to have it close at hand since he might need it at any moment.

As he entered the hotel from the Davies Street entrance he noted with relief that it was only a little after ten. It was unlikely that Tanith would have gone out for the day so early, and he settled himself to wait for an indefinite period with cheerful optimism in the almost empty lounge. After a moment it occurred to him that somebody might come up to him and inquire his business if he was forced to stay there for any length of time, but an underporter, passing at the moment, gave him a swift smile and little bow of recognition, so he trusted that having been identified as an occasional client of the place he would not be unduly molested.

He began to consider what words he should use if, and when, Tanith did step out of the lifts, and had just decided on a formula which contained the requisite proportions of respect, subtle admiration, and gaiety when a small boy in buttons came marching with a carefree swing down the corridor.

'Mister Vine Rine—Mister Vine Rine,' he chanted in a monotonous treble.

Rex looked at the boy suspiciously. The sound had a queer resemblance to the parody of his own name as he had often heard it shrilled out by bell-hops in clubs and hotel lounges. Yet no one could possibly be aware of his presence at Claridges that morning—except, of course, the Duke. At the thought that De Richleau might be endeavouring to get in touch with him for some urgent reason he turned, and at the same moment the page side-tracked towards him.

'Mr. Van Ryn, sir?' he inquired, dropping into normal speech.

'Yes,' Rex nodded.

Then to his utter astonishment the boy announced: 'The lady you've called to see sent down to say she's sorry to keep you waiting, but she'll join you in about fifteen minutes.'

With his mouth slightly open Rex stared stupidly at the page until that infant turned and strutted away. He did not doubt that the message came from Tanith—who else could have sent it, yet how the deuce did she know that he was there? Perhaps she had seen him drive up from her window—that seemed the only reasonable explanation. Anyhow that 'she was sorry to keep him waiting' sounded almost too good to be true.

Recovering a little he stood up, marched out into Brook

Street and purchased a great sheaf of lilac from a florist's a few doors down. Returning with it to the hotel he suddenly realised that he still did not know Tanith's real name, but catching sight of the boy who had paged him, he beckoned him over.

'Here boy—take these up to the lady's room with Mr. Van Ryn's compliments.' Then he resumed his seat near the lift with happy confidence.

Five minutes later the lift opened. An elderly woman leaning upon a tall ebony cane stepped out. At the first glance Rex recognised the parrot-peaked nose, the nut-cracker chin and the piercing black eyes of the old Countess D'Urfé. Before he had time to collect his wits she had advanced upon him and extended a plump, beringed hand.

'Monsieur Van Ryn,' she croaked. 'It is charming that you should call upon me—sank you a thousand times for those lovely flowers.'

9

The Countess D'Urfé
Talks of Many Curious Things

'Ha! ha!—not a bit of it—it's great to see you again.'

Rex gave a weak imitation of a laugh. He had only spoken to the old crone for two minutes on the previous evening and that, when he had first arrived at Simon's party, for the purpose of detaching Tanith from her. Even if she had seen him drive up to Claridges what in the world could have made her imagine that he had come to visit *her*? If only he hadn't sent up that lilac he might have politely excused himself—but he could hardly tell her now that he had meant it for someone else.

'And how is *Monseigneur le Duc* this morning?' the old lady inquired, sinking into a chair he placed for her.

'He asked me to present his homage, Madame,' Rex lied quickly, instinctively picking a phrase which De Richleau might have used himself.

'*Ça, c'est très gentille.* 'E is a charming man—charming an' 'is cigars they are superb.' The Countess D'Urfé produced a square case from her bag and drew out a fat, dark Havana. As Rex applied a match she went on slowly: 'But it ees not right that one Circle should make interference with the operations of another. What 'ave you to say of your be'aviour lars' night my young frien'?'

'My hat,' thought Rex, 'the old beldame fancies we're an opposing faction in the same line of business—I'll have to use this if I can;' so he answered slowly: 'We were mighty sorry to have to do what we did, but we needed Simon Aron for our own purposes.'

'So!—you also make search for the Talisman then?'

'Sure—that is, the Duke's taking a big interest in it.'

'Which of us are not—and 'oo but *le petit Juif* shall lead us to it.'

'That's true.'

''Ave you yet attempted the Rite to Saturn?'

'Yes, but things didn't pan out quite as we thought they would,' Rex replied cautiously, not having the faintest idea what they were talking about.

'You 'ave satisfy yourselves that the aloes and mastic were fresh, eh?' The wicked old eyes bored into his.

'Yes, I'm certain of that,' he assured her.

'You choose a time when the planet was in the 'ouse of Capricorn, of course?'

'Oh, surely!'

'An' you 'ave not neglect to make Libation to Our Lady Babalon before'and?'

'Oh, no, we wouldn't do that!'

'Then per'aps your periods of silence were not long enough?'

'Maybe that's so,' he admitted hurriedly, hoping to close this madhatter's conversation before he completely put his foot into it.

Countess D'Urfé nodded, then after drawing thoughtfully at her cigar she looked at him intently. 'Silence,' she murmured. 'Silence, that ees always essential in the Ritual of Saturn—but you 'ave much courage to thwart Mocata—'e is powerful, that one.'

'Oh, we're not afraid of him,' Rex declared and, recalling the highest grade of operator from his conversation with De Richleau, he added: 'You see the Duke knows all about this thing —he's an Ipsissimus.'

The old lady's eyes almost popped out of their sockets at this announcement, and Rex feared that he had gone too far, but she leaned forward and placed one of her jewelled claws upon his arm. 'An Ipsissimus!—an' I 'av studied the Great Work for forty years, yet I 'ave reached only the degree of Practicus. But no, 'e cannot be, or 'ow could 'e fail with the Rite to Saturn?'

'I only said that it didn't pan out quite as we expected,' Rex hastened to remind her, 'and for the full dress business he'd need Simon Aron anyway.'

'Of course,' she nodded again and continued in an awestruck whisper, 'an' De Richleau is then a real Master. You must be far advanced for one so young—that 'e allow you to work with 'im.'

He flicked the ash off his cigarette but maintained a cautious silence.

'I am not—'ow you say—associated with Mocata long—since I 'ave arrive only recently in England, but De Richleau will cast 'im down into the Abyss—for 'ow shall 'e prevail against one who is of ten circles and a single square?'

Rex nodded gravely.

'Could I not—' her dark eyes filled with a new eagerness, 'would it not be possible for me to prostrate before your frien'? If you spoke for me also, per'aps 'e would allow that I should occupy a minor place when 'e proceeds again to the invocation?'

'Ho! Ho!' said Rex to himself, 'so the old rat wants to scuttle from the sinking ship, does she. I ought to be able to turn this to our advantage,' while aloud he said with a lordly air: 'All things are possible—but there would be certain conditions.'

'Tell me,' she muttered swiftly.

'Well, there is this question of Simon Aron.'

'What question?—Now that you 'ave 'im with you—you can do with 'im as you will.'

Rex quickly averted his gaze from the piercing black eyes. Evidently Mocata had turned the whole party out after they had got away with Simon. The old witch obviously had no idea that Mocata had regained possession of him later. In another second he would have given away their whole position by demanding Simon's whereabouts. Instead—searching his

66

mind desperately for the right bits of gibberish he said: 'When De Richleau again proceeds to the invocation it is necessary that the vibrations of all present should be attuned to those of Simon Aron.'

'No matter—willingly I will place myself in your 'ands for preparation.'

'Then I'll put it up to him, but first I must obey his order and say a word to the lady who was with you at Aron's house last night—Tanith.' Having at last manœuvred the conversation to this critical point, Rex mentally crossed his thumbs and offered up a prayer that he was right in assuming that they were staying at the hotel together.

She smiled, showing two rows of white false teeth. 'I know it, and you must pardon, I beg, that we 'ave our little joke with you.'

'Oh, don't worry about that,' he shrugged, wondering anxiously to what new mystery she was alluding, but to his relief she hurried on.

'Each morning we look into the crystal an' when she see you walk into the 'otel she exclaim, "It is for me 'e comes—the tall American," but we 'ave no knowledge that you are more than a Neophyte or a Zelator at the most, so when you send up the flowers she say to me, "You shall go down to 'im instead an' after we will laugh at the discomfiture of this would-be lover." '

The smile broadened on Rex's full mouth as he listened to the explanation of much that had been troubling him in the last hour, but it faded suddenly as he realised that, natural as it seemed compared to all this meaningless drivel which he had been exchanging with the old woman, it was in reality one more demonstration of the occult. These two women had *actually seen him* walk into the hotel lounge when they were sitting upstairs in their room peering into a piece of glass.

'In some ways I suffer the disappointment,' said the old Countess suddenly, and Rex found her studying him with a strange, disconcerting look. 'I know well that promiscuity gives a greaty power for all 'oo follow the Path an' that 'uman love 'inders our development, but nevair 'ave I been able to free myself from a so stupid sentimentality—an' you would, I think, 'ave made a good lover for 'er.'

Rex stared in astonished silence, then looked quickly away,

as she added: 'No matter—the other ees of real importance. I will send for 'er that you may give your message.'

With a little jerk she stood up and gripping her ebony cane stumped across to the hall porter's desk while he relaxed, unutterably glad that this extraordinary interview was over.

However, he felt a glow of satisfaction in the thought that he had duped her into the belief that De Richleau and himself were even more powerful adepts than Mocata, and at having played his cards sufficiently well to secure a meeting with Tanith under such favourable circumstances. If only he could get into his car, he was determined to inveigle her into giving him any information she possessed which might lead to the discovery of Simon's whereabouts, although, since Madame D'Urfé was ignorant of the fact that he was no longer with the Duke, it was hardly likely that Tanith would actually be able to take them to him.

With new anxiety Rex realised the gravity of the check. They had practically counted on Tanith having the knowledge, if only they could get it out of her, and even if he could persuade her to talk about Mocata the man might have a dozen haunts. If so it would be no easy task to visit all before sundown and the urgency of the Duke's instructions still rang in his ears.

Today was May Day Eve. The Great Sabbat of the year would be held tonight. It was absolutely imperative that they should trace and secure Simon before dusk or else, under the evil influence which now dominated his mentality, he would be taken to participate in those unholy rites and jeopardise for ever the flame of goodness, wisdom and right thinking which men term the soul.

After a moment Madame D'Urfé rejoined him. 'For tonight at least,' she whispered, 'things in dispute between the followers of the Path will be in abeyance—is it not?—for all must make their 'omage to the One.'

He nodded and she bent towards him, lowering her voice still further: 'If I could but see De Richleau for one moment—as Ipsissimus 'e must possess the unguent?'

'That's so,' Rex agreed, but he was horribly uncertain of his ground again as he added cryptically: 'But what of the Moon?'

'Ah, fatality,' she sighed. 'I 'ad forgotten that we are in the dark quarter.'

He blessed the providence which had guided his tongue as

she went on sadly: 'I 'ave try so often but nevair yet 'ave I succeeded. I know all things necessary to its preparation, an' 'ave gathered every 'erb at the right period. I 'ave even rendered down the fat, but they must 'ave cheated me. It was from a mortuary per'aps—but not from a graveyard as it should 'ave been.'

Rex felt the hair bristle on the back of his neck and his whole body stiffened slightly as he heard this gruesome confession. Surely it was inconceivable that people still practised these medieval barbarities—yet he recalled the terrible manifestation that he had witnessed with the Duke on the previous night. After that he could no longer employ modern standards of belief or unbelief to the possibilities which might result from the strange and horrible doings of these people who had given themselves over to ancient cults.

The old Countess was regarding him again with that queer disconcerting look. 'It matters not,' she murmured. 'We shall get there just the same, Tanith and I—an' it should be interesting—for nevair before 'as she attended the Great Sabbat.'

The lift gates clicked at that moment and Tanith stepped out into the corridor. For a fleeting instant Rex caught a glimpse of her wise, beautiful face, over the old woman's shoulder, but the Countess was speaking again in a husky whisper, so he was forced to look back at her.

'Nevair before,' she repeated with unholy glee, 'and after the One 'as done that which there is to do, 'oo knows but you may be the next—if you are quick.'

Forcing himself out of his chair Rex shut his ears to the infernal implication. His general reading had been enough for him to be aware that in the old days the most incredible orgies took place as the climax to every Sabbat, and his whole body crept at the thought of Tanith being subjected to such abominations. His impulse was to seize this iniquitous old woman by the throat and choke the bestial life out of her fat body, but with a supreme effort he schooled himself to remain outwardly normal.

As Tanith approached, and taking his hand smiled into his eyes, he knew that she, as well as Simon, must be saved before nightfall from—yes, the old biblical quotation leapt to his mind—'The Power of the Dog,' that was strong upon them.

10

Tanith Proves Stubborn

After the muttering of the old Countess and her veiled allusions to unspeakable depravities Rex felt that even the air had grown stale and heavy, as though charged with some subtle quality of evil, but on the coming of Tanith the atmosphere seemed to lighten. The morning sunshine was lending a pale golden glow to the street outside and in her hand she held one of the sprays of lilac which he had sent up to her. She lifted it to her face as he returned her smile. 'So!' she said in a low clear voice, her eyes mocking him above the fragrant bloom: 'You insisted then that Madame should let you see me?'

'I'd have sat around this place all day if she hadn't,' Rex confessed frankly, 'because now we've met at last I'm hoping you'll let me see something of you.'

'Perhaps—but not today. I have many things to do and already I am late for the dressmaker.'

Rex thanked his stars that the old woman had unwittingly given him a lever in assuming the Duke to be an Adept of great power, and himself his envoy. 'It's mighty important that I should see you today,' he insisted. 'There are certain things we've got to talk about.'

'Got to!' A quick frown clouded Tanith's face. 'I do not understand!'

'*Ma petite,* it is you 'oo do not understan',' Madame D'Urfé broke in hastily. Then she launched into a torrent of low speech in some foreign language, but Rex caught De Richleau's name and the word Ipsissimus, so he guessed that she was giving Tanith some version of the events which had taken place the night before, based on his own misleading statements, and wondered miserably how long he would be able to keep up the impersonation which had been thrust upon him.

Tanith nodded several times and studied him with a new interest as she nibbled a small piece of the lilac blossom between her teeth. Then she said with charming frankness: 'You must forgive me—I had no idea you were such an important member of the Order.'

'Forget it please,' he begged, 'but if you're free I'd be glad if you could join me for lunch.'

'That puts me in a difficulty because I am supposed to be lunching with the wife of the Roumanian Minister.'

'How about this afternoon then?'

Her eyes showed quick surprise. 'But we shall have to leave here by four o'clock if we are to get down by dusk—and I have my packing to do yet.'

He realised that she was referring to the meeting and covered his blunder swiftly. 'Of course—I'm always forgetting that these twisting English roads don't permit of the fast driving I'm used to back home. How would it be if I run you along to your dress place now and then we took a turn round the Park after?'

'Yes—if you will have lots of patience with me, because I take an almost idiotic interest in my clothes.'

'You're telling me!' he murmured to himself as he admired the slim graceful lines of her figure clad so unostentatiously and yet so suitably for the sunshine of the bright spring day. He picked up his hat and beamed at her. 'Let's go—shall we?'

To his amazement he found himself taking leave of the old Countess just as though she were a nice, normal, elderly lady who was chaperoning some young woman to whom he had been formally introduced at a highly respectable dance. And indeed, as they departed, her dark eyes had precisely the same look which had often scared him in mothers who possessed marriageable daughters. Had he not known that such thoughts were anathema to her creed he would have sworn that she was praying that they would be quick about it, so that she could book a day before the end of the season at St. George's, Hanover Square, and was already listing in her mind the guests who should be asked to the reception.

'Where does the great artist hang out?' he asked as he helped Tanith into the car.

'I have two,' she told him. 'Schiaparelli just across the square, where I shall be for some twenty minutes, and after I have also to visit Artelle in Knightsbridge— Are you sure that you do not mind waiting for me?'

'Why, no! we've a whole heap of time before us.'

'And tonight as well,' she added slowly. 'I am glad that you will be there because I am just a little nervous.'

71

'You needn't be!' he said with a sudden tightening of his mouth, but she seemed satisfied with his assurance and had no inkling of his real meaning.

As she alighted in Upper Grosvenor Street he called gaily after her: 'Twenty minutes mind, and not one fraction over,' then he drove across the road and pulled up at the International Sportsman's Club of which he was a member.

The telephone exchange put him through to the British Museum quickly enough, but the operator there nearly drove him frantic. It seemed that it was not part of the Museum staff's duties to search for visitors in the Reading Room, but after urgent prayers about imaginary dead and dying they at last consented to have the Duke hunted out. The wait that followed seemed interminable but at last De Richleau came to the line.

'I've got the girl,' Rex told him hurriedly, 'but how long I'll be able to keep her I don't know. I've had a long talk, too, with the incredible old woman who smokes cigars—you know the one—Madame D'Urfé. They're staying at Claridges together and both of them are going to the party you spoke of tonight. Where it's to be held I don't know, but they're leaving London by car at four o'clock and hope to make the place by nightfall. I've spun 'em a yarn that you're the high and mighty Hoodoo in the you-know-what—a fat bigger bug than Mocata ever was—so the old lady's all for giving him the go-by and sitting in round about your feet, but neither of them knows where Simon is—I'm certain. In fact they've no idea that he made a getaway last night after we got him to your flat—so what's the drill now?'

'I see—well, in that case you must . . .' but Rex never learnt what De Richleau intended him to do for at that moment they were cut off. When he got through to the Museum again it was to break in on a learned conversation about South American antiques which was being conducted on another line and, realising that he had already exceeded his twenty minutes, he had no option but to hang up the receiver and dash out into the street.

Tanith was just coming down the steps of Schiaparelli's as he turned the car to meet her. 'Where now?' he asked when she had settled herself beside him.

'To Artelle. It is just opposite the barracks in Knightsbridge.

72

I will not be more than five minutes this time, but she has a new idea for me. She is really a very clever woman, so I am anxious to hear what she has thought of.'

It was the longest speech he had so far heard her make, as their conversation the night before had been brief and frequently interrupted by Mocata. Her idiom was perfect, but the way in which she selected her words and the care with which she pronounced them made him ask suddenly. 'You're not English—are you?'

'Yes,' she smiled as they turned into Hyde Park, 'but my mother was Hungarian and I have lived abroad nearly all my life. Is my accent very noticeable?'

'Well—in a way, but it sounds just marvellous to me. Your voice has got that deep caressing note about it which reminds me of—well, if you want the truth, it's like Marlene Dietrich on the talkies.'

She threw back her head and gave a low laugh. 'If I believed that I should be tempted to keep it, and as it is I have been working so hard to get rid of it ever since I have been in England. It is absurd that I should not be able to speak my own language perfectly—yet I have talked English so little, except to foreign governesses when I was a young girl.'

'And how old are you now, or is that a piece of rudeness?'

'How old do you think?'

'From your eyes you might be any age, but I've a feeling that you're not much over twenty-two.'

'If I were to live I should be twenty-four next January.'

'Come now,' he protested, laughing, 'what a way to put it, that's only a matter of nine months and no one could say you don't look healthy.'

'I am,' she assured him gravely, 'but let us not talk of death. Look at the colour of those rhododendrons. They are so lovely.'

'Yes, they've jerked this Park up no end since I first saw it as a boy.' As the traffic opened he turned the car into Knightsbridge and two minutes later Tanith got out at the discreet door of her French dressmaker.

While she was inside Rex considered the position afresh, and endeavoured to concoct some cryptic message purporting to come from the Duke, to the effect that she was not to attend the Sabbat but to remain in his care until it was all over. Yet he felt that she would never believe him. It was quite evident that she meant to be present at this unholy Walpurgis-Nacht gathering, and from what the old woman had said all Satanists regarded it with such importance that even warring factions among them sank their differences—for this one night of the year—in order to attend.

Obviously she could have no conception of what she was letting herself in for, but the very idea of her being mishandled by that ungodly crew made his big biceps tighten with the desire to lash out at someone. He had got to keep her with him some-how, that was clear—but how?

He racked his mind in vain for a plausible story but, to his dismay, she rejoined him almost immediately and he had thought of nothing by the time they had turned into the Park again.

'Well—tell me,' she said softly.

'Tell you what?' he fenced. 'That I think you're very lovely?'

'No, no. It is nice that you should have troubled to make pretty speeches about my accent and Marlene Dietrich, but it is time for you to tell me now of the real reason that brought you to Claridges this morning.'

'Can't you guess?'

'No.'

'I wanted to take you out to lunch.'

'Oh, please! Be serious—you have a message for me?'

'Maybe, but even if I hadn't, I'd have been right on the mat at your hotel just the same.'

She frowned slightly. 'I don't understand. Neither of us is free to give our time to that sort of thing.'

'I've reached a stage where I'm the best judge of that,' he announced, with the idea of trying to recover some of the prestige which seemed to be slipping from him.

'Have you then crowned yourself with the Dispersion of Choronzon already?'

Rex suppressed a groan. Here they were off on the Mumbo Jumbo stuff again. He felt that he would never be able to keep it up, so instead of answering he turned the car with sudden determination out into the Kensington Road and headed to-wards Hammersmith.

'Where are you taking me?' she asked quickly.

'To lunch with De Richleau,' he lied. 'I've got no message

for you but the Duke sent me to fetch you because he wants to talk to you himself.' It was the only story he could think of which just might get over.

'I see—where is he?'

'At Pangbourne.'

'Where is that?'

'Little place down the Thames—just past Reading.'

'But that is miles away!'

'Only about fifty.'

'Surely he could have seen me before he left London.'

He caught her eyes, quick with suspicion, on his face, so he answered boldly: 'I know nothing of that, but he sent me to fetch you—and what the Duke says goes.'

'I don't believe you!' she exclaimed angrily. 'Stop this car at once!—I am going to get out.'

11

The Truth Will Always Out

For a second Rex thought of ignoring her protest and jamming his foot on the accelerator, but the traffic in Kensington High Street was thick, and to try to abduct her in broad daylight would be sheer madness. She could signal a policeman and have him stopped before he'd gone two hundred yards.

Reluctantly he drew in to the side of the road, but he stretched his long arm in front of her and gripped the door of the car so that she could not force it open.

Tanith stared at him with angry eyes: 'You are lying to me —I will not go with you.'

'Wait a moment.' He thrust out his chin pugnaciously while he mustered all his resources to reason with her. If he once let her leave the car the chances were all against his having another opportunity to prevent her reaching the secret rendezvous where those horrible Walpurgis ceremonies would take place in the coming night. His determination to prevent her participating in those barbaric rites, of which he was certain she could not know the real nature, quickened his brain to an unusual cunning: 'You know what happened to Simon Aron?' he said.

'Yes, you kidnapped him from his own home last night.'

'That's so—but do you know why?'

'Madame D'Urfé said that it was because the Duke is also seeking for the Talisman of Set. You needed him for your own invocations.'

'Exactly.' Rex paused for a moment to wonder what the Talisman could be. This was the second time he had heard it mentioned. Then he went on slowly: 'It's him being born under certain stars makes his presence essential. We'd hunt for years before we found anyone else who's suitable to do the business and born in the same hour of the same day and year. Well, we need you too.'

'But my number is not eight!'

'That doesn't matter—you're under the Moon, aren't you?' He risked the shot on what he remembered of De Richleau's words about her name.

'Yes,' she admitted. 'But what has that to do with it?'

'A whole heap—believe you me. But naturally you'd know nothing of that. Even Mocata doesn't realise the importance of the Moon in this thing and that's why he's failed to make much headway up to date.'

'Mocata would be furious if I left his Circle—you see I am his favourite medium—so attuned to his vibrations that he would have the very greatest difficulty in replacing me. Perhaps —perhaps he would punish me in some terrible manner.' Tanith's face had gone white and her eyes were staring slightly at the thought of some nameless evil which might befall her.

'Don't worry. De Richleau will protect you—and he's an Ipsissimus remember. If you don't come right along, now he wants to see you, maybe he'll do something to you that'll be far worse.' As Rex lied and threatened he hated himself for it, but the girl had just got to be saved from herself and this form of blackmail was the only line that offered.

'How am I to know? How am I to know?' she repeated quickly. 'You may be lying. Think what might happen to me if Mocata proved the stronger.'

'You had the proof last night. We got Simon Aron away from under his very nose—didn't we?'

'Yes, but will you be able to keep him?'

'Sure,' Rex declared firmly, but he felt sick with misery as he remembered that by Mocata's power Simon had been taken from them under the hour. And where was Simon now? The day was passing, their hope of Tanith being able to put them on his track had proved a failure. How would they find him in time to save him too from the abominations of the coming night?

'Oh, what shall I do?' Tanith gave a little nervous sob. 'It is the first time I have heard of any feud in our Order. I thought that if I only followed the Path I should acquire power and now this hideously dangerous decision is thrust on me.'

Rex saw that she was weakening so he pressed the self-starter. 'You're coming with me and you're not going to be frightened of anything. Get that now—I mean it.'

She nodded. 'All right. I will trust you then,' and the car slid into motion.

For a few moments they sat in silence, then as the car entered Hammersmith Broadway he turned and smiled at her. 'Now let's cut out all talk about this business till we see the Duke and just be normal—shall we?'

'If you wish—tell me about yourself?'

He smothered a sigh of relief at her acquiescence. At least he would be free for an hour or so from the agonising necessity of skating on thin ice of grim parables which had no meaning for him. With all his natural gaiety restored he launched into an account of his life at home in the States, his frequent journeys abroad, and his love of speed in cars and boats and planes and bob-sleighs.

As they sped through Brentford and on to Slough he got her to talk a little about herself. Her English father had died when she was still a baby and the Hungarian mother had brought her up. All her childhood had been spent in an old manor house, dignified by the name of Castle, in a remote village on the southern slopes of the Carpathians, shut in so completely from the world by steep mountains on every side that even the War had passed it by almost unnoticed. After the peace and the disintegration of the Austrian-Hungarian Empire their lands had become part of the new state of Jugo-Slavia, but her life had gone on much the same for, although the War had cost them a portion of their fortune, the bulk of it had been left safe by her father in English Trustee securities. Her mother had died three years before and it was then, having no personal ties and ample money, that she had decided to travel.

'Isn't it just marvellous that I should have seen you such different places about the world,' he laughed.

'The first time that you speak of in Budapest I do not remember,' she replied, 'but I recall the day outside Buenos Aires well. You were in a long red car and I was riding a roan mare. As you drew into the side of the track to let us pass I wondered why I knew your face, and then I remembered quite clearly that our cars had been locked side by side in a traffic jam, months before, in New York.'

'Seems as if we were just fated to meet sometime—doesn't it?'

'We both know that there is no such thing as Chance,' she said slowly. 'I believe you have a wax image of me somewhere and have worked upon it to bring today about.'

The day before he would have instantly assumed her to be joking, despite her apparent seriousness, but now, he realised with a little shock, he no longer considered it beyond the bounds of possibility that actual results might be procured by doing certain curious things to a little waxen doll, so greatly had his recent experiences altered his outlook. He hesitated, unable to confess his ignorance of such practices, and unwilling to admit that he had not done his best to bring about a meeting, but he was saved from the necessity of a reply by Tanith suddenly exclaiming:

'I had forgotten!—luncheon—I shall never be back in time.'

'Easy, put through a call and say you've suddenly been called out of Town,' he told her, and a few miles farther on he pulled up at Skindles Hotel in Maidenhead.

While Tanith was telephoning he stood contemplating the river. Although it was early in the year a period of drought had already checked the spate of the current sufficiently to make boating pleasureable, and he noted that in the gardens of the Hungaria River Club, on the opposite bank, they were setting out their gay paraphernalia preparatory to opening for the Season. Immediately Tanith rejoined him they set off again.

The straggling suburbs of Greater London had already been left behind them before Slough and now, after Maidenhead, the scattered clusters of red-roofed dwellings on the new building estates, which have spread so far afield, also disappeared, giving place to the real country. On certain portions of the road, the fresh green of the beech trees formed a spring canopy overhead and between their trunks, dappled with sunlight, patches of bluebells gave glory to the silent woods; at others they ran between meadows where lazy cattle nibbled the new grass, or fields where the young corn, strong with life, stretched its vivid green shoots upwards to the sun.

The sight and smell of the countryside, unmarred by man or carefully tended in his interests, windswept and clean, gave Rex fresh confidence. He banished his anxiety about Simon for the moment and, thrusting from his mind all thoughts of this gruesome business into which he had been drawn, began to talk all the gay nonsense to Tanith which he would have aired to any other girl whom he had induced to steal a day out of London in which to see the country preparing its May Day garb.

Before they reached Reading he had her laughing, and by the time they entered the little riverside village of Pangbourne, her pale face was flushed with colour and her eyes dancing with new light.

They crossed to the Whitchurch side where the Duke's house stood, some way back from the river, its lawns sloping gently to the water's edge.

Max received them, and while a maid took Tanith upstairs to wash, Rex had a chance to whisper quick instructions to him.

When she entered the low, old-fashioned lounge with its wide windows looking out over the tulip beds to the trees on the further bank she found Rex whistling gaily. He was shooting varying proportions of liquor out of different bottles into a cocktail shaker. Max stood beside him holding a bowl of ice.

'Where is the Duke?' she asked, with a new soberness in her voice.

He had been waiting for the question, and keeping his face averted answered cheerfully: 'He's not made it yet—what time are you expecting him, Max?'

'I should have told you before, sir. His Excellency telephoned that I was to present his excuses to the lady, and ask you, sir, to act as host in his stead. He has been unavoidably detained, but hopes to be able to join you for tea.'

'Well, now, if that isn't real bad luck!' Rex exclaimed feelingly. 'Never mind, we'll go right in to lunch the moment it's ready.' He tasted the concoction which he had been beating up with a large spoon and added: 'My! that's good!'

'Yes, sir—in about five minutes, sir,' Max bowed gravely and withdrew.

Rex knew that there was trouble coming but he presented a glass of the frothing liquid with a steady hand. 'Never give a girl a large cocktail,' he cried gaily, 'but plenty of 'em. Make 'em strong and drink 'em quick—come on now! It takes a fourth to make an appetite— Here's to crime!'

But Tanith set down the glass untasted. All the merriment had died out of her eyes and her voice was full of a fresh anxiety as she said urgently: 'I can't stay here till tea-time—don't you realise that I must leave London by four o'clock.'

It was on the tip of his tongue to say, 'Where is this place you're going to?' but he caught himself in time and substituted: 'Why not go from here direct?' Then he prayed silently that the secret meeting place might not be on the other side of London.

Her face lightened for a moment. 'Of course, I forgot that you were going yourself, and the journey must be so much shorter from here. If you could take me it seems stupid to go all the way back to London—but what of Madame D'Urfé—she expects me to motor down with her—and I must have my clothes.'

'Why not call her on the phone. Ask her to have your stuff packed up and say we'll meet her there. You've got to see the Duke, and whatever happens he'll turn up here because he and I are going down together.'

She nodded. 'If I am to place myself under his protection it is vital that I should see him before the meeting, for Mocata has eyes in the ether and will know that I am here by now.'

'Come on then!' He took her hand and pulled her to her feet. 'We'll get through to Claridges right away.'

Tanith allowed him to lead her out into the hall and when he had got the number he left her at the telephone. Then he returned to the lounge, poured himself another cocktail and began to do a gay little dance to celebrate his victory. He felt that he had got her now, safe for the day, until the Duke turned up. Then trust De Richleau to get something out of her which

80

would enable them to get on Simon's track after all.

At his sixth pirouette he stopped suddenly. Tanith was standing in the doorway, her face ashen, her big eyes blazing with a mixture of anger and fear.

'You have lied to me,' she stammered out, 'Mocata is with the Countess at this moment—he got Simon Aron away from you last night. You and your precious Duke are impostors—charlatans— You haven't even the power to protect yourselves, and for this Mocata may tie me to the Wheel of Ptah—oh, I must get back!' Before he could stop her she had turned and fled out of the house.

12

The Grim Prophecy

In one spring Rex was across the room, another and he had reached the garden. Against those long legs of his Tanith had no chance. Before she had covered twenty yards he caught her arm and jerked her round to face him.

'Let me go!' she panted. 'Haven't you endangered me enough with your lies and interference.'

He smiled down into her frightened face but made no motion to release her. 'I'm awfully sorry I had to tell you all those tarradiddles to get you to this place—but now you're here you're going to stay—understand?'

'It is you who don't understand,' she flashed. 'You and your friend, the Duke, are like a couple of children playing with a dynamite bomb. You haven't a chance against Mocata. He will loose a power on you that will simply blot you out.'

'I wouldn't be too certain of that. Maybe I know nothing of this occult business myself and if anyone had suggested to me that there were practising Satanists wandering around London this time last week, I'd have said they had bats in the belfry. But the Duke's different—and, believe you me, he's a holy terror when he once gets his teeth into a thing. Best save your pity for Mocata—he'll need it before De Richleau's through with him.'

'Is he—is he really an Ipsissimus then?' she hesitated.

'Lord knows—I don't. That's just a word I picked out of some jargon he was talking last night that I thought might impress you.' Rex grinned broadly. All the lying and trickery which he had been forced to practise during the morning had taxed him to the utmost, but now that he was able to face the situation openly he felt at the top of his form again.

'I daren't stay then—I daren't!' She tried to wrench herself free. 'Don't you see that if he is only some sort of dabbler he will never be able to protect me.'

'Don't fret your sweet self. No one shall lay a finger on you as long as I'm around.'

'But, you great fool, you don't understand,' she waved miserably. 'The Power of Darkness cannot be turned aside by bruisers or iron bars. If I don't appear at the meeting tonight, the moment I fall asleep Mocata will set the Ab-humans on to me. In the morning I may be dead or possessed—a raving lunatic.'

Rex did not laugh. He knew that she was genuinely terrified of an appalling possibility. Instead he turned her towards the house and said gently: 'Now please don't worry so. De Richleau does understand just how dangerous monkeying with this business is. He spent half the night trying to convince me of it, and like a fool I wouldn't believe him until I saw a thing I don't care to talk about, but I'm dead certain he'd never allow you to run any risk like that.'

'Then let me go back to London!'

'No. He asked me to get you here so as he could have a word with you—and I've done it. We'll have a quiet little lunch together now and talk this thing over when the Duke turns up. He'll either guarantee to protect you or let you go.'

'He can't protect me I tell you—and in any case I *wish* to attend this meeting tonight.'

'You wish to!' he echoed with a shake of the head. 'Well, that gets me beat, but you can't even guess what you'd be letting yourself in for. Anyhow I don't mean to let you—so now you know.'

'You mean to keep me here against my will?'

'Yes!'

'What is to stop me screaming for help?'

'Nix, but since the Duke's not here the servants know I'm

in charge, so they won't bat an eyelid if you start to yell the house down—and there's no one else about.'

Tanith glanced swiftly down the drive. Except at the white gates tall banks of rhododendrons, heavy with bloom, obscured the lane. No rumble of passing traffic broke the stillness that brooded upon the well-kept garden. The house lay silent in the early summer sunshine. The inhabitants of the village were busy over the midday meal.

She was caught and knew it. Only her wits could get her out of this, and her fear of Mocata was so great that she was determined to use any chance that offered to free herself from this nice, meddling fool.

'You'll not try to prevent me leaving if De Richleau says I may when he arrives?' she asked.

'No. I'll abide by his decision,' he agreed.

'Then for the time being I will do as you wish.'

'Fine—come on.' He led her back to the house and rang for Max, who appeared immediately from the doorway of the dining-room.

'We've decided to lunch on the river,' Rex told him. 'Make up a basket and have it put in the electric canoe.' He had made the prompt decision directly he sensed that Tanith meant to escape if she could. Once she was alone in a boat with him he felt that, unless she was prepared to jump out and swim for it, he could hold her without any risk of a scene just as long as he wanted to.

'Very good, sir—I'll see to it at once.' Max disappeared into the domain of which he was lord and master, while Rex shepherded Tanith back to the neglected cocktails.

He refreshed the shaker while she sat on the sofa eyeing him curiously, but he persuaded her to have one, and when he pressed her she had another. Then Max appeared to announce that his orders had been carried out.

'Let's go—shall we?' Rex held open the french-windows and together they crossed the sunlit lawn, gay with its beds of tulips, polyanthus, wallflowers and forget-me-nots. At the river's edge, upon a neat, white painted landing-stage, a boat-man held the long electric canoe ready for them.

Tanith settled herself on the cushions and Rex took the small perpendicular wheel. In a few moments they were chugging out into midstream and up the river towards Goring, but he preferred not to give her the opportunity of appealing to the lock-keeper, so he turned the boat and headed it towards a small backwater below the weir.

Having tied up beneath some willows, he began passing packages and parcels out of the stern. 'Come on,' he admonished her. 'It's the girl's job to see to the commissariat. Just forget yourself a moment and see what they've given us to eat.'

She smiled a little ruefully. 'If I really thought you realised what you were doing I should look on you as the bravest man I've ever known.'

He turned suddenly, still kneeling at the end of the boat. 'Go on—say it again. I love the sound of your voice.'

'You fool!' She coloured, laughing as she unwrapped the napkins. 'There's some cheese here—and ham and tongue—and brown bread—and salad—and a lobster. We shall never be able to eat all this and—oh, look,' she held out a small wicker basket, '*fraises des bois*.'

'Marvellous. I haven't tasted a wood strawberry since I last lunched at Fontainbleau. Anyhow, it's said the British Army fights on its stomach, so I'm electing myself an honorary member of it for the day. Fling me that corkscrew—will you, and I'll deal with this bottle of Moselle.'

Soon they were seated face to face propped against the cushions, a little sticky about the mouth, but enjoying themselves just as any nice normal couple would in such circumstances; but when the meal was finished he felt that, much as he would have liked to laze away the afternoon, he ought, now the cards were upon the table, to learn what he could of this grim business without waiting for the coming of the Duke. He unwrapped another packet which he had found in the stern of the boat, and passing it over asked half humorously:

'Tell me, does a witch ever finish up her lunch with chocolates? I'd be interested to know on scientific grounds.'

'Oh, why did you bring me back—I have been enjoying myself so much,' her face was drawn and miserable as she buried it in her hands.

'I'm sorry!' He put down the chocolates and bent towards her. 'But we're both in this thing, so we've got to talk of it, haven't we, and though you don't look the part, you're just as much a witch as any old woman who ever soured the neighbour's cream—else you'd never have seen me in that crystal

84

this morning as I sat in the lounge of your hotel.'

'Of course I am if you care to use such a stupid old-fashioned term. She drew her hands away and tossed back her fair hair as she stared at him defiantly. 'That was only child's play—just to keep my hand in—a discipline to make me fit to wield a higher power.'

'For good?' he questioned laconically.

'It is necessary to pass through many stages before having to choose whether one will take the Right or Left Hand Path.'

'So I gather. But how about this unholy business in which you've a wish to take part tonight?'

'If I submit to the ordeal I shall pass the Abyss.' The low, caressing voice lifted to a higher note, and the wise eyes suddenly took on a fanatic gleam.

'You can't have a notion what they mean to do to you or you'd never even dream of it,' he insisted.

'I have, but you know nothing of these things so naturally you consider me utterly shameless or completely mad. You are used to nice English and American girls who haven't a thought in their heads except to get you to marry them—if you have any money—which apparently you have, but that sort of thing does not interest me. I have worked and studied to gain power —real power over other people's lives and destinies—and I know now that the only way to acquire it is by complete surrender of self. I don't expect you to understand my motives but that is why I mean to go tonight.'

He studied her curiously for a moment, still convinced that she could not be fully aware of the abominations that would take place at the Sabbat. Then he broke out: 'How long is it since you became involved in this sort of thing?'

'I was psychic even as a child,' she told him slowly. 'My mother encouraged me to use my gifts. Then when she died I joined a society in Budapest. I loved her. I wanted to keep in touch with her still.'

'What proof have you got it was her?' he demanded with a sudden renewal of scepticism as he recalled the many newspaper exposures of spiritualistic séances.

'I had very little then, but since, I have been convinced of it beyond all doubt.'

'And is she—your own mother, still—yes, your guide—I suppose you'd call it?'

Tanith shook her head. 'No, she has gone on, and it was not for me to seek to detain her, but others have followed, and every day my knowledge of the worlds which lie beyond this grows greater.'

'But it's extraordinary that a young girl like you should devote yourself to this sort of thing. You ought to be dancing, dining, playing golf, going places—you're so lovely you could take your pick among the men.'

She shrugged a little disdainfully. 'Such a life is dull—ordinary—after a year I tired of it, and few women can climb mountains or shoot big game, but the conquest of the unknown offers the greatest adventure of all.'

Again her voice altered suddenly, and the inscrutable eyes which gave her a strange, serious beauty, so fitting for a lady of the Italian Renaissance, gleamed as before.

'Religions and moralities are man-made, fleeting and local; a scandalous lapse from virtue in London may be a matter for the highest praise in Hong Kong, and the present Archbishop of Paris would be shocked beyond measure if it was suggested that he had anything in common, beyond his religious office, with a Medieval Cardinal. One thing and one thing only remains constant and unchanging, the secret doctrine of the way to power. That is a thing to work for, and if need be cast aside all inherent scruples for—as I shall tonight.'

'Aren't you—just a bit afraid?' He stared at her solemnly.

'No, provided I follow the path which is set, no harm can come to me.'

'But it is an evil path,' he insisted, marvelling at the change which had come over her. It almost seemed as if it were a different woman speaking or one who repeated a recitation, learned in a foreign language, with all the appropriate expression yet not understanding its true meaning, as she replied with a cynical little smile.

'Unfortunately the followers of the Right Hand Path obsess themselves only with the well-being of the Universe as a whole, whereas those of the Left exercise their power upon living humans. To bend people to your will, to cause them to fall or rise, to place unaccountable obstacles in their path at every turn or smooth their way to a glorious success—that is more than riches, more than fame—the supreme pinnacle to which any man or woman can rise, and I wish to reach it before I die.'

'Maybe—maybe.' Rex shook his head with a worried frown, 'But you're young and beautiful—just breaking in on all the fun of life—why not think it over for a year or two? It's horrible to hear you talk as though you were a disillusioned old woman.'

Her mouth tightened still further. 'In a way I am—and for me, waiting is impossible because, although in your ignorance I do not expect you to believe it, as surely as the sun will set tonight I shall be dead before the year is out.'

13

The Defeat of Rex Van Ryn

For a moment they sat in silence. The river flowed gently on; the sun still dappled the lower branches of the willows and flecked the water with points of light.

Gradually the fire died out of Tanith's eyes and she sank back against the cushions of the canoe as Rex stared at her incredulously. It seemed utterly impossible that there could be any real foundation for her grim prophecy, yet her voice had held such fatal certainty.

'It isn't true!' Rex seized her hand and gripped it as though, by his own vitality, he would imbue her with continued life. 'You're good for fifty years to come. That's only some criminal nonsense this devil Mocata's got you to swallow.'

'Oh, you dear fool!' She took his other hand and pressed it while, for a moment, it seemed as if tears were starting to her eyes. 'If things were different I think I might like you enormously, but I knew the number of my days long before I ever met Mocata, and there is nothing which can be done to lengthen them by a single hour.'

'Show me your hand,' he said suddenly. It was the only thing even remotely connected with the occult of which Rex had any knowledge. The year before he had ricked an ankle, while after Grizzly in the Rockies, and had had to lie up for a week at a tiny inn where the library consisted of less than a dozen battered volumes. A book on Palmistry, which he had discovered among them, had proved a real windfall and the study of it had whiled away many hours of his enforced idleness.

As Tanith held out her hand he saw at once that it was of the unusual psychic type. Very long, narrow and fragile, the wrist small, the fingers smooth and tapering, ending in long, almond-shaped nails. The length of the first, second and third fingers exceeded that of the palm by nearly an inch, giving the whole a beautiful but useless appearance. The top phalange of the thumb, he noted, was slim and pointed, another sign of lack of desire to grapple with material things.

'You see?' she turned it over showing him the palm. 'The Arabs say that "the fate of every man is bound about his brow," and mine is written here, for all who can, to read.'

Rex's knowledge of the subject was too limited for him to do much but read character and general tendencies by the various shapes of hands, but even he was startled by the unusual markings on the narrow palm.

On the cushion of the hand the Mount of the Moon stood out firm and strong, seeming to spread over and dominate the rest, a clear sign of an exceedingly strong imagination, refinement and love of beauty; but it was tinged with that rare symbol, the Line of Intuition, giving, in connection with such a hand, great psychic powers and a leaning towards mysticism of a highly dangerous kind. A small star below the second finger, upon the Mount of Saturn, caused him additional uneasiness and he looked in vain for squares which might indicate preservation at a critical period. Yet worst of all the Line of Life, more clearly marked than he would have expected, stopped short with a horrifying suddenness at only a little over a third of the way from its commencement, where it was tied to the Line of Head.

He stared at it in silence, not knowing what to say to such sinister portents, but she smiled lightly as she withdrew her hand. 'Don't worry please, but there is no appeal from the verdict of the Stars and you will understand now why marriage —children—a lovely home—all things connected with the future just mean nothing to me.'

'So that's the reason you let yourself get mixed up in this horrible business?'

'Yes. Since I am to die so soon no ordinary emotion can stir me any more. I look as though I were already a great way from it, and what happens to my physical body matters to me not at all. Ten months ago I began seriously to cultivate my psychic sense under real instruction, and the voyages which I can make now into the immensity of the void are the only things left to me which still have power to thrill.'

'But, why in heaven's name involve yourself with Black Magic when you might practise White?'

'Have I not told you? The adepts of the Right Hand Path concern themselves only with the Great Work; the blending of the Microcosm with the Macrocosm; a vague philosophic entity in which one can witness no tangible results. Whereas, those of the Left practise their Art upon human beings and can actually watch the working of their spells.'

'I can't get over your wanting to attend this Satanic festival tonight all the same.'

'It should be an extraordinary experience.'

'Any normal person would be terrified at what might happen.'

'Well, if you like, I will admit that I am just a little frightened but that is only because it is my first participation. By surrendering myself I shall only suffer or enjoy, as most other women do, under slightly different circumstances at some period of their life.'

'Slightly different!' he exclaimed, noting again the sudden change of eyes and voice, as though she were *possessed* by some sinister dual personality which appeared every time she spoke of these horrible mysteries, and blotted out the frank, charming individuality which was natural to her. 'This thing seems worlds apart to me from picking a man you like and taking a sporting chance about the rest.'

'No, in ancient Egypt every woman surrendered herself at the temple before she married, in order that she might acquire virtue, and sacred prostitution is still practised in many parts of the world—for that is what this amounts to. Regarded from the personal point of view, of course, it is loathsome. If I thought of it that way I should never be able to go through with it at all, but I have trained myself not to, and only think of it now as a ritual which *has* to be gone through in order to acquire fresh powers.'

'It's mightly difficult for any ordinary person to see it that way—though I suppose the human brain can shut out certain aspects of a thing.' Rex paused, frowning: 'Still I was really speaking of the hideous danger you will incur from placing yourself in the hands of—well, the Devil if you like.'

She smiled. 'The Devil is only a bogey invented by the Early Church to scare fools.'

'Let's say the Power of Darkness then.'

'You mean by receiving re-Baptism?'

'By attending this Sabbat at all. I imagined from your strange name you had received re-Baptism already.'

'No, Tanith is the name by which I was Christened. It was my mother's choice.'

Rex sat forward suddenly. 'Then you haven't—er—given yourself over completely yet?'

'No, but I shall tonight, for if De Richleau has a tenth of the knowledge which you say he has he will realise the appalling danger to which I should be exposed if he detained me here, so he will let me go immediately he arrives—and remember, you have promised not to interfere with my freedom once he has seen me.'

'But listen,' he caught her hands again. 'It was bad enough that you should have been going to take a part in this abominable business as a graduate—it's a thousand times worse that you should do it while there's still time to back out.'

'Mocata would not allow me to now, even if I had the inclination, but you are so nice it really distresses me that you should worry so. The Satanic Baptism is only an old-fashioned and rather barbarous ritual, but it will give me real status among adepts, and no possible harm can come to me as long as I do not deviate from the Path which must be followed by all members of the Order.'

'You're wrong—wrong—wrong,' Rex insisted boldly. 'De Richleau was explaining the real horror of this thing to me last night. This promise of strange powers is only a filthy trap. At your first Christening your Godparents revoked the Devil and all his Works. Once you willingly rescind that protection, as you'll have to do, something awful will take possession of you and force you into doing its will, an Earthbound Spirit or an Elemental I think he called it.'

She shrugged. 'There are ways of dealing with Elementals.'

'Aw, hell. Why can't I make you understand!' He wrung

his hands together desperately. 'It's easy to see they haven't called on you to do any real devilry yet. They've just led you on by a few demonstrations and encouraging your crystal gazing, but they will—once you're a full member—and then you'll be more scared than ever to refuse, or find it's just impossible under the influence of this thing that will get hold of you.'

'I'm sorry, but I don't believe you. It is I who will make use of them—not they of me, and quite obviously you don't know what you are talking about.'

'The Duke does,' he insisted, 'and he says that you can still get free as long as you haven't been actually re-baptised, but after that all holy protection is taken from you. Why else d'you think we took a chance of breaking up that party last night —if not to try and save Simon from the self-same thing.'

A queer light came into Tanith's eyes. 'Yet Mocata willed him to return so he will receive his nom-du-Diable after all to-night.'

'Don't you be too certain. I've a hunch we'll save him yet.' Rex spoke with a confidence he was very far from feeling.

'And how do you propose to set about it?' she asked with a quick intuition that by some means she might utilise this factor to facilitate her own escape.

'Ah! that's just the rub,' he admitted. 'You see we thought maybe you'd know his whereabouts and I'll be frank about it. That's the reason I went round to Claridges this morning, to see if I couldn't get you down here some way so as De Richleau could question you although I should have called on you anyway for a very different reason. Still you didn't even know Mocata had taken Simon off us till you spoke to the old woman on the wire, so it's pretty obvious you don't know where he is. I believe you could give us a line on Mocata though—if you choose to.'

'I was under the impression that it was at his house that the party where we met was given.'

'No, that was Simon's place, though I gather Mocata's been living there with him for some little time. He must have a hideout of his own somewhere though and that's what we want to get at.'

'I know nothing of his ordinary life, and if I did, I do not think I should be inclined to tell you of it, but why are you so interested in this Mr. Aron? That was a lie you told me

91

about your needing him because you are also searching for the Talisman of Set.'

'He's my very greatest friend, and more than that he risked his life to come out to Soviet Russia and look for me, when I was gaoled for poking my nose into the "Forbidden Territory," a few years back. The Duke came too, and he looks on Simon almost as a son.'

'That does not give you any right to interfere if, like myself, he elects to devote himself to the occult.'

'Maybe, as long as he confines himself to the harmless side, but De Richleau says the game that you and he are playing is the most hideously dangerous that's ever been known to mankind, and after what I saw last night I certainly believe him.'

'Simon Aron did not strike me as a fool. He must be aware of the risks which he is running and prepared to face them for the attainment of his desires.'

'I doubt it—I doubt if you do either. Anyhow, for the moment, we're regarding him as a person who's not quite all there, and nothing you can name is going to stop the Duke and me from saving him from himself if we get half a chance.'

Tanith felt that now was the time to show the bait in the trap which she had been preparing. So she leant forward and said, slowly: 'If you really are so mad as to wish for a chance to pit yourselves against Mocata, I think I could give it to you.'

'Could you?' Rex jerked himself upright and the water gurgled a little at the sides of the canoe.

'Yes, I don't know if he has a house of his own anywhere, but I do know where he will be this evening—and your friend Simon will be with him.'

'You mean the Sabbat eh? And you'll give me the name of the place where it's being held?'

'Oh, no.' The sunlight gleamed golden on her hair as she shook her head. 'But I'll let you take me to it, if you agree to let me go free once we are there.'

'Nothing doing,' he said bluntly.

'I see,' she smiled, 'you are afraid of Mocata after all. Well, that doesn't surprise me because he has ample means of protecting himself against anything you could attempt against him. That is why, of course, I feel that, providing the place is not given away beforehand, he would prefer me to let you know

92

it than detain me here—I'm quite honest you see, but evidently you are not so confident of yourself or interested in your friend as I thought.'

Rex was thinking quickly. Nothing but an actual order from the Duke, based on his assurance that Mocata might punish Tanith in some terrible manner if she failed to appear, would have induced him to let her go to the Sabbat, but on the other hand this was a real chance to reach Simon, in fact, the only one that offered. 'Do you require that I should actually hand you over to Mocata when we get there?' he asked at length.

'No. If you take me to the place that will be sufficient, but there must be no question of gagging me or tying me up.'

In an agony of indecision he pondered the problem again. Dare he risk taking Tanith within the actual sphere of Mocata's influence? Yet he would have the Duke with him, so surely between them they would be able to restrain her from taking any part in the ceremony, and it was impossible to throw away such a chance of saving Simon.

'I'm not giving any promise to let you join the party,' Rex said firmly.

'Well, I intend to do so.'

'That remains to be seen—but I'll accept your offer on those conditions.'

She nodded, confident now that once they reached their destination Mocata would exercise his powers to relieve her of restraint.

'The place must be about seventy miles from here,' she told him, 'and I should like to be there by sundown, so we ought to leave here by six.'

'Wouldn't it be possible to start later?' A worried frown clouded Rex's face. 'The truth is, that message Max gave us before lunch was phony—just a part of my plan for keeping you here. I never did count on De Richleau arriving much before the time you say we ought to start—and I'd just hate to leave without him.'

Tanith smiled to herself. This was an unexpected piece of luck. She had only met the Duke for a moment the night before, but his lean, cultured face and shrewd, grey eyes had impressed her. She felt that he would prove a far more difficult opponent that this nice, bronzed young giant, and if she could get away without having to face him after all, it would be a real relief, so she made a wry face and proceeded to elaborate her story.

'I'm sorry, but there are certain preparations which have to be made before the gathering. They begin at sunset, so I must be at—well, the place to which we are going by a quarter past eight. If I arrive later I shall not be eligible to participate—so I will not go at all.'

'In that case I guess I'm in your hands. Anyhow, now we've settled things, let's get back to the house.' Rex untied the canoe and, setting the motor in motion, steered back to the landing stage.

His first thought was to inform De Richleau of the bargain that he had made, but after pleading once more with the officials at the British Museum to have the Duke sought for, he learned that he was no longer there, and when he got through to the Curzon Street flat the servants could tell him nothing of De Richleau's whereabouts, so it was impossible to expedite his arrival.

For a time Rex strolled up and down the lawn with Tanith, then round the lovely garden, while he talked again of the places that they had both visited abroad and tried to recapture something of the gaiety which had marked their drive down from London in the morning.

Max brought them tea out onto the terrace, and afterwards they played the electric gramophone, but even that failed to relieve Rex of a steadily deepening anxiety that the Duke might not arrive in time.

The shadows of the lilacs and laburnums began to lengthen on the grass. Tanith went upstairs to tidy herself, and when she came down asked if he could find her a road map. He produced a set and for a time she studied two of them in silence, then she refolded them and said quietly: 'I know so little of the English country but I am certain now that I can find it. We must be leaving soon.'

It was already six o'clock, and he had put off shaking a cocktail until the last moment in order to delay their departure as long as possible. Now, he rang for ice as he said casually: 'Don't fuss, I'll get you there by a quarter after eight.'

'I'll give you five miniutes—no more.'

'Well, listen now. Say De Richleau fails to make it. Won't you give me a break? Let me know the name of the place so

94

as I can leave word for him to follow?'

She considered for a moment. 'I will give you the name of a village five miles from it where he can meet you on one condition.'

'Let's hear it.'

'That neither of you seek to restrain me in any way once we reach our destination.'

'No. I'll not agree to that.'

'Then I certainly will not give you any information which will enable your friend to appear on the scene and help you.'

'I'll get him there some way—don't you worry.'

'That leaves me a free hand to prevent you if I can—doesn't it?'

As he swallowed his cocktail she glanced at the clock. 'It's ten past now, so unless you prefer not to go we must start at once.'

Consoling himself with the thought that De Richleau could have got no more out of her even if he had questioned her himself, Rex led her out and settled her in the Rolls then, before starting up the engine, he listened intently for a moment, hoping that even yet he might catch the low, steady purr of the big Hispano which would herald the Duke's eleventh hour arrival, but the evening silence brooded unbroken over the trees and lane. Reluctantly he set the car in motion and as they ran down the gravel sweep, Tanith said quietly, 'Please drive to Newbury.'

'But that's no more than twenty miles from here!'

'Oh, I will give you further directions when we reach it,' she smiled, and for a little time they drove in silence through the quiet byways until they entered the main Bath Road at Theale.

At Newbury, she gave fresh instructions. 'To Hungerford now,' and the fast, low touring Rolls sped out of the town eating up another ten miles of the highway to the west.

'Where next?' he asked, scanning the houses of the market town for its most prosperous-looking inn and mentally registering *The Bear*. It was just seven o'clock—another few miles and they would be about half-way to the secret rendezvous. He did not dare to stop in the town in case she gave him the slip and hired another car or went on by train, but when they were well out in the country again he meant to telephone the Duke, who must have arrived at Pangbourne by this time, and urge him to follow as far as Hungerford at once—then sit tight at *The Bear* until he received further information.

Tanith was studying the map. 'There are two ways from here,' she said, 'but I think it would be best to keep to the main road as far as Marlborough.'

A few miles out of Hungerford the country became less populous with only a solitary farmhouse here and there, peaceful and placid in the evening light. Then these, too, were left behind and they entered a long stretch of darkening woodlands, the northern fringe of Savernake Forest.

Both were silent, thinking of the night to come which was now so close upon them and the struggle of wills that must soon take place. Rex brought the car down to a gentle cruising speed and watched the road-sides intently. At a deserted hairpin bend, where a byway doubled back to the south-east, he found just what he wanted, a telephone call-box.

Turning the car off the main road he pulled up, and noted with quick appreciation that they had entered one of the most beautiful avenues he had even seen. As far as the eye could see it cut clean through the forest, the great branches meeting overhead in the sombre gloom of the falling night, it looked like the nave of some titanic cathedral deserted by mankind; but he had no leisure to admire it to the full, and stepping out, called to Tanith over his shoulder: 'Won't be a minute—just want to put through a call.'

She smiled, but the queer look that he had seen earlier in the day came into her eyes again. 'So you mean to trick me and let De Richleau know the direction we have taken?'

'I wouldn't call it that,' he protested. 'In order to get in touch with Simon I bargained to take you to this place you're so keen to get to, but I reserved the right to stop you taking any part yourself, and I need the Duke to help me.'

'And I agreed, because it was the only way in which I could get away from Pangbourne, but I reserved the right to do all in my power to attend the meeting. However,' she shrugged lightly, 'do as you will.'

'Thanks.' Rex entered the box, spoke to the operator, and having inserted the necessary coins, secured his number. Next minute he was speaking to De Richleau. 'Hello! Rex here. I've got the girl and she's agreed— Oh, Hell!'

He dropped the receiver and leapt out of the box. While

his back was turned Tanith had moved into the driver's seat. The engine purred, the Rolls slid forward. He clutched frantically at the rear mudguard but his fingers slipped and he fell sprawling in the road. When he scrambled to his feet the long blue car was almost hidden by a trail of dust as it roared down the avenue, and while he was still cursing his stupidity, it disappeared into the shadows of the forest.

14

The Duke de Richleau Takes the Field

At 7.20. Rex was through again to the Duke, gabbling out the idiotic way in which he had allowed Tanith to fool him and leave him stranded in Savernake Forest.

At 7.22. De Richleau had heard all he had to tell and was ordering him to return to Hungerford as best he could, there to await instructions at *The Bear*.

At 7.25. Tanith was out of the Forest and on a good road again, some five miles south-east of Marlborough, slowing down to consult her map.

At 7.26. The Duke was through to Scotland Yard.

At 7.28. Rex was loping along at a steady trot through the gathering darkness, praying that a car would appear from which he could ask a lift.

At 7.30. De Richleau was speaking to the Assistant Commissioner at the Metropolitan Police, a personal friend of his. 'It's not the car that matters,' he said, 'but the documents which are in it. Their immediate recovery is of vital importance to me and I should consider it a great personal favour if any reports which come in may be sent at once to the Police Station at Newbury.'

At 7.32. Tanith was speeding south towards Tidworth, having decided that to go round Salisbury Plain via Amesbury would save her time on account of the better roads.

At 7.38. Scotland Yard was issuing the following *communiqué* by wireless: 'All stations. Stolen. A blue touring Rolls, 1934 model. Number OA 1217. Owner, Duke de Richleau. Last seen in Savernake Forest going south-east at 19 hours 15, but reported making for Marlborough. Driven by woman. Age twenty-three—attractive appearance—tall, slim, fair hair, pale face, large hazel eyes, wearing light green summer costume and small hat. Particulars required by Special Department. Urgent. Reports to Newbury.'

At 7.42. De Richleau received a telephone call at Pangbourne. 'Speakin' fer Mister Clutterbuck,' said the voice, 'bin tryin' ter get yer this lars' arf hour, sir. The green Daimler passed through Camberley goin' south just arter seven o'clock.'

At 7.44. Tanith was running past the military camp at Tidworth still going south.

At 7.45. Rex was buying a second-hand bicycle for cash at three times its value from a belated farm-labourer.

At 7.48. The Duke received another call. 'I have a special from Mr. Clutterbuck,' said a new voice. 'The Yellow Sports Sunbeam passed Devizes going south at 7.42.'

At 7.49. Tanith reached the Andover-Amesbury road and turned west along it.

At 7.54. De Richleau climbed into his Hispano. 'My night glasses—thank you,' he said as he took a heavy pair of binoculars from Max. 'Any messages which come in for me up to 8.25 are to be relayed to the police at Newbury, after that to Mr. Van Ryn at the *Bear Inn,* Hungerford, up till 8.40, and from then on to the police at Newbury again.'

At 7.55. Tanith was approaching a small cross-roads on the outskirts of Amesbury. A Police-Sergeant who had left the station ten minutes earlier spotted the number of her car, and stepping out into the road called on her to halt. She swerved violently, missing him by inches, but managed to swing the car into the by-road leading north.

At 7.56. Rex was pedalling furiously along the road to Hungerford with all the strength of his muscular legs.

At 7.58. Tanith, livid with rage that Rex should have put the police on to her as though she were a common car thief, had spotted another policeman near the bridge in Bulford village. Not daring to risk his holding her up in the narrow street, she switched up another side-road leading north-east.

At 7.59. The Amesbury Police-Sergeant dropped off a lorry beside the constable on duty at the main cross-roads of the town and warned him to watch out for a Blue Rolls, number

OA 1217, recklessly driven by a young woman who was wanted by the Yard.

At 8.1. Tanith had slowed down and was wondering desperately if she dared risk another attempt to pass through Amesbury. Deciding against it she ran on, winding in and out through the narrow lanes, to the north-eastward.

At 8.2. Rex had abandoned his bicycle outside the old Almshouses at Froxfield and was begging a lift from the owner of a rickety Ford who was starting into Hungerford.

At 8.3. The Amesbury Police-Sergeant was reporting to Newbury the appearance of the 'wanted' Rolls.

At 8.4. Tanith pulled up, hopelessly lost in a tangle of twisting lanes.

At 8.6. De Richleau swung the Hispano on to the main Bath Road. His cigar tip glowed red in the twilight as he sank his chin into the collar of his coat and settled down to draw every ounce out of the great powerful car.

At 8.8. Tanith had discovered her whereabouts on the map and found that she had been heading back towards the Andover Road.

At 8.9. The Amesbury Police-Sergeant was warning the authorities at Andover to keep a look-out for the stolen car in case it headed back in that direction.

At 8.10. Tanith had turned up a rough track leading north through some woods in the hope that it would enable her to get past the Military Camp at Tidworth without going through it.

At 8.12. Rex was hurrying into *The Bear* Inn at Hungerford.

At 8.14. Tanith was stuck again, the track having come to an abrupt end at a group of farm buildings.

At 8.17. The Duke was hurtling along the straight, about five miles east of Newbury.

At 8.19. Tanith was back at the entrance of the track and turning into a lane that led due east.

At 8.20. The Amesbury Police-Sergeant left the station again. He had completed his work of warning Salisbury, Devizes, Warminster and Winchester to watch for the stolen Rolls.

At 8.21, Tanith came out on the main Salisbury-Marlborough road and, realising that there was nothing for it but to chance being held up at Tidworth, turned north.

At 8.22. Rex had sunk his second tankard of good Berkshire

ale and took up his position in the doorway of *The Bear* to watch for the Duke.

At 8.23. Tanith, possessed now, it seemed, by some inhuman glee, chortled with laughter as a Military Policeman leapt from the road to let her flash past the entrance of Tidworth Camp.

At 8.24. De Richleau entered Newbury Police Station and learned that the Blue Rolls had been sighted in Amesbury half an hour earlier.

At 8.25. Tanith had pulled up, a mile north of Tidworth, and was studying her map again. She decided that her only hope of reaching the secret rendezvous now lay in taking the by-roads across the northern end of Salisbury Plain.

At 8.26. The Duke was reading two messages which had been handed to him by the Newbury Police. One said: 'Green Daimler passed through Basingstoke going west at 7.25. Max per Clutterbuck,' and the other, 'Green Daimler passed through Andover going west at 8.0. Max per Clutterbuck.' He nodded, quickly summing up the position to himself. 'Green is heading west through Amesbury by now, and Blue was seen making in the same direction, while Yellow took the other route and is coming south from Devizes—most satisfactory so far.' He then turned to the Station Sergeant: 'I should be most grateful if you would have any further messages which may come for me relayed to Amesbury. Thank you—Good night.'

At 8.27. Tanith had reached a cross-road two miles north of Tidworth and turning west took a dreary wind-swept road which crosses one of the most desolate parts of the Plain. Dusk had come and with it an overwhelming feeling that whatever happened she must be present at the meeting. The fact that she was about seventeen miles farther from her destination than she had been at Amesbury did not depress her, for she had misled Rex as to the vital necessity of her being there by sunset, and the actual Sabbat did not begin until midnight.

At 8.32. Rex was taking a message over the telephone of *The Bear* at Hungerford.

At 8.35. Tanith was passing the Aerodrome at Upavon, and forced to slow down owing to the curving nature of the road ahead.

At 8.37. De Richleau's Hispano roared into Hungerford, and Rex, who had resumed his position in the doorway of *The Bear*, ran out to meet it. 'Any messages?' the Duke asked as he scrambled in.

'Yep—Max called me. A bird named Clutterbuck says a Yellow Sunbeam passed through Westbury heading south at five minutes past eight.'

'Good,' nodded the Duke, who already had the car in motion again.

At 8.38. Tanith was free of the twisting patch of road by Upavon and out on the straight across the naked Plain once more. If only she could keep clear of the police, she felt that she would be able to reach the meeting-place in another forty-five minutes. A wild, unnatural exaltation drove her on as the Blue Rolls ate up the miles towards the west.

At 8.39. Rex was asking: 'What is all this about a Yellow Sunbeam anyway? It was a Blue Rolls I got stung for.' And the Duke replied, with his grey eyes twinkling: 'Don't worry about the Rolls. The police saw your young friend with it in Amesbury a little after eight. They will catch her for us you may be certain.'

At 8.40. The police at Newbury were relaying a message from Max for the Duke to their colleagues at Amesbury.

At 8.41. De Richleau was saying: 'Don't be a fool, Rex. I only said that I could not call in the police unless these people committed *some definite breach of the law*. Car stealing is a crime, so I have been able to utilise them in this one instance —that's all.'

At 8.44. Two traffic policemen on a motor-cycle combination, which had set out from Devizes a quarter of an hour before, spotted the back number-plate of Blue Rolls number OA 1217 as it switched to the left at a fork road where they were stationed, but Tanith had caught sight of them, and her headlights streaked away, cutting a lane through the darkness to the south-westward.

At 8.45. The Hispano was rocking from side to side as it flew round the bends of the twisting road south-west of Hungerford. The Duke had heard Rex's account of the way Tanith had tricked him but refused to enlighten him about the Yellow Sunbeam. 'No, no,' he said impatiently. 'I want to hear every single thing you learned from the girl—I'll tell you my end later.'

At 8.46. The traffic policemen had their machine going all

101

out and were in full cry after the recklessly driven Rolls.

At 8.47. The Police at Newbury were relaying a second message from Max for the Duke to their colleagues at Amesbury.

At 8.48. Tanith saw the lights of Easterton village looming up in the distance across the treeless grassland as she hurtled south-westward in the Rolls.

At 8.49. The traffic policeman in the side-car said: 'Steady, Bill—we'll get her in a minute.'

At 8.50. The Hispano had passed the cross-roads nine miles south-west of Hungerford and come out on to the straight. De Richleau had now heard everything of importance which Rex had to tell and replied abruptly to his renewed questioning: 'For God's sake don't pester me now. It's no easy matter to keep this thing on the road when we're doing eighty most of the time.'

At 8.51. Tanith clutched desperately at the wheel of the Rolls as with screaming tyres it shot round the corner of the village street. The police siren in her ears shrilled insistently for her to halt. She took another bend practically on two wheels, glimpsed the darkness of the open country again for a second then, with a rending, splintering crash, the off-side mudguards tore down a length of wooden palings. The car swerved violently, dashed up a steep bank then down again, rocking and plunging, until it came to rest, with a sickening thud, against the back of a big barn.

At 9.8. The Duke, with Rex beside him, entered Amesbury Police Station and the two messages which had been 'phoned through from Newbury were handed to him. The first read: 'Green Daimler passed through Amesbury going west at 8.15,' and the second, 'Yellow Sunbeam halted Chilbury 8.22.' Both were signed 'Max per Clutterbuck.'

As De Richleau slipped them into his pocket an Inspector came out of an inner room. 'We've got your car, sir,' he said cheerfully. 'Heard the news only this minute. Two officers spotted the young woman at the roads south of Devizes and gave chase. She made a mucker of that bad bend in Easterton village. Ran it through a garden and up a steep bank.'

'Is she hurt?' asked Rex anxiously.

'No, sir—can't be. Not enough to prevent her hopping out and running for it. I reckon it was that bank that saved her and the car too—for I gather it's not damaged anything to speak of.'

'Has she been caught?' inquired the Duke.

'Not yet, sir, but I expect she will be before morning.'

As De Richleau nodded his thanks, and spread out a map to find the village of Chilbury, the desk telephone shrilled. The constable who answered it scribbled rapidly on a pad and then passed the paper over to him. 'Here's another message for you, sir.'

Rex glanced over the Duke's shoulder and read, 'Green Daimler halted Chilbury 8.30. Other cars parked in vicinity and more arriving. Will await you cross-roads half a mile south of village. Clutterbuck.'

De Richleau looked up and gave a low chuckle. 'Got them!' he exclaimed. 'Now we can talk.'

At 9.14. They were back in the car.

15

The Road to the Sabbat

The big Hispano left the last houses of Amesbury behind and took the long, curving road across the Plain to the west. De Richleau, driving now at a moderate pace, was at last able to satisfy Rex's curiosity.

'It is quite simple, my dear fellow. Immediately I learned from you that Madame D'Urfé was leaving Claridges for the Sabbat at four o'clock, I realised that in her we had a second line of inquiry. Having promised to meet you at Pangbourne, I couldn't very well follow her myself, so I got in touch with an ex-superintendent of Scotland Yard named Clutterbuck, who runs a Private Inquiry Agency.'

'But I thought you said we must handle this business on our own,' Rex protested.

'That is so, and Clutterbuck has no idea of the devilry that we are up against. I only called him in for the purpose of tracing cars and watching people, which is his normal business. After I had explained what I wanted to him he arranged for half a dozen of his assistants to be in readiness with motorcycles. Then I took him round to Claridges in order to point the old woman out to him. As luck would have it, I spotted the Albino that we saw at the party last night come out at half past three and drive off in the Yellow Sports Sunbeam, so that gave us a third line, and Clutterbuck sent one of his men after him. The Countess left in the Green Daimler a good bit after four, and that's why I was delayed in getting down to Pangbourne. Clutterbuck trailed her in his own car, and directly we knew that she was making for the west, sent the rest of his squad ahead in order to pick her up again if by chance he lost her. That is how the reports of the movements of the two cars came through to me.'

'How about Mocata? He was at Claridges when Tanith 'phoned the old woman, round about half past one!'

'Unfortunately, he must have left by the time I came on the scene, but it doesn't matter, because he is certain to be with the rest.'

Rex grinned. 'It was a pretty neat piece of staff work.'

The few miles across the Plain were soon eaten up, and the Duke had scarcely finished giving Rex particulars of his campaign when they reached the lonely wind-swept cross-roads half a mile south of Chilbury. A car was drawn up at the side of the road and near it a group of half a dozen men with motorcycles stood talking in low voices. As the Hispano was brought to a standstill, a tall, thin man left the group and came over to De Richleau.

'The persons you are wanting are in the big house on the far side of the village, sir,' he said. 'You can't miss it because the place is surrounded by trees, and they are the only ones hereabouts.'

'Thank you,' De Richleau nodded. 'Have you any idea how many people have arrived for this party?'

'I should think a hundred or so at a rough guess. There are quite fifty cars parked in the grounds at the back of the house, and some of them had two or three occupants. Will you require my assistance any further?'

'Not now. I am very pleased with the way in which you have handled this little affair, and should I need your help later on, I will get in touch with you again.'

Rex nudged the Duke just as he was about to dismiss Clutterbuck. 'If there's a hundred of them, we won't stand an earthly on our own. Why not keep these people? Eight or nine of us might be able to put up a pretty good show!'

'Impossible,' De Richleau replied briefly, while the detective eyed the two of them with guarded interest, wondering what business they were engaged upon but satisfied in his own mind that, since Rex had suggested retaining him, he had not lent himself to anything illegal. 'If there's nothing else I can do then, sir,' he said, touching his hat, 'I and my men will be getting back to London.'

'Thank you,' De Richleau acknowledged the salute. 'Good night.' As the detective turned away, he let out the clutch of the Hispano.

With the engine just ticking over, they slipped through the silent village. Most of the cottages were already in darkness. The only bright light came from the tap-room of the tiny village inn, while the dull glow from curtained windows in one or two of the upper rooms of the houses showed that those inhabitants of the little hamlet who were not already in bed would very shortly be there.

To the south of the road, on the far side of the village, they came upon a thick belt of ancient trees extending for nearly a quarter of a mile and, although no house was visible behind the high stone wall that shut them in, they knew from Clutterbuck's description that this must be the secret rendezvous.

A chalky lane followed the curve of the wall where it left the main road and, having driven a hundred yards along it, they turned the car so that it might be in immediate readiness to take the road again, and parked it on a grassy slope that edged the lane.

As the Duke alighted, he pulled out a small suitcase. 'These are the results of my morning's research at the British Museum,' he said, opening it up.

Rex leaned forward curiously to survey the strange assortment of things the case contained: a bunch of white flowers, a bundle of long grass, two large ivory crucifixes, several small phials, a bottle—apparently of water—and a number of other items; but he stepped quickly back as a strong, pungent, unpleasant odour struck his nostrils.

De Richleau gave a grim chuckle. 'You don't like the smell of the Asafottida grass and the Garlic flowers, eh? But they are highly potent against evil my friend, and if we can only secure Simon they will prove a fine protection for him. Here, take this crucifix.'

'What'll I do with it?' Rex asked, admiring for a moment the beautiful carving on the sacred symbol.

'Hold it in your hand from the moment we go over this wall, and before your face if we come upon any of these devilish people.'

While De Richleau was speaking, he had taken a little plush box from the suitcase, and out of it a rosary from which dangled a small, gold cross. Reaching up, he hung it about Rex's neck, explaining as he did so: 'Should you drop the big one, or if it is knocked from your hand by some accident, this will serve as a reserve defence. In addition, I want you to set another above a horse-shoe in your aura.'

'How d'you mean?' Rex frowned, obviously puzzled.

'Just imagine if you can that you are actually wearing a horse-shoe surmounted by a crucifix on your forehead. Think of it as glowing there in the darkness an inch or so above your eyes. That is an even better protection than any ordinary material symbol, but it is difficult to concentrate sufficiently to keep it there without long practice, so we must wear the sign as well.' The Duke placed a similar rosary round his own neck and took two small phials from the open case. 'Mercury and Salt,' he added. 'Place one in each of your breast pockets!'

Rex did as he was bid. 'But why are we wearing crucifixes when you put a swastika on Simon before?' he asked.

'I was wrong. That is the symbol of Light in the East, where I learned what little I know of the Esoteric Doctrine. There, it would have proved an adequate barrier, but here, where Christian thoughts have been centred on the Cross for many centuries, the crucifix has far more potent vibrations.'

He took up the bottle and went on: 'This is holy water from Lourdes, and with it I shall seal the nine openings of your body that no evil may enter it at any one of them. Then you must do the same for me.'

With swift gestures, the Duke made the sign of the cross in holy water upon Rex's eyes, nostrils, lips, etc., and then Rex performed a similar service for him.

De Richleau picked up the other crucifix and shut the case. 'Now we can start,' he said. 'I only wish that we had a fragment of the Host apiece. That is the most powerful defence of all, and with it we might walk unafraid into hell itself. But it can only be obtained by a layman after a special dispensation, and I had no time to plead my case for that today.'

The night was fine and clear, but only a faint starlight lit the surrounding country, and they felt rather than saw the rolling slopes of the Plain which hemmed in the village and the house, where they were set in a sheltered dip. The whole length of the high stone wall was fringed, as far as they could see, by the belt of trees, and through their thick, early-summer foliage no glimpse of light penetrated to show the exact position of the house.

Since no sound broke the stillness—although a hundred people were reported to be gathered there—they judged the place to be somewhere in the depths of the wood at a good distance from the wall; yet despite that, as they walked quickly side by side down the chalky lane, they spoke only in whispers, lest they disturb the strange stillness that brooded over that night-darkened valley.

At length they found the thing that they were seeking, a place where the old wall had crumbled and broken at the top. A pile of masonry had fallen into the lane, making a natural step a couple of feet in height, and from it they found no difficulty in hoisting themselves up into the small breach from which it had tumbled.

As they slipped down the other side, they paused for a moment, peering through the great tree-trunks, but here on the inside of the wall beneath the wide-spreading branches of century-old oaks and chestnuts they were in pitch darkness, and could see nothing ahead other than the vague outline of the trees.

'In manus tuas, domine,' murmured the Duke, crossing himself; then holding their crucifixes before them they moved forward stealthily, their feet crackling the dry twigs with a faint snapping as they advanced.

After a few moments the darkness lightened and they came out on the edge of a wide lawn. To their left, two hundred yards away, they saw the dim, shadowy bulk of a rambling old house, and through a shrubbery which separated them from it, faint chinks of light coming from the ground floor windows. Now, too, they could hear an indistinct murmur, which betrayed the presence of many people.

Keeping well within the shadow of the trees, they moved cautiously along until they had passed the shrubbery and could get a clear view of the low, old-fashioned mansion. Only the ground-floor windows showed lights and these were practically obscured by heavy curtains. The upper stories were dark and lifeless.

Still in silence, and instinctively agreeing upon their movements, the two friends advanced again and began to make a circle of the house. On the far side they found the cars parked just as Clutterbuck had described, upon a gravel sweep, and counted up to fifty-seven of them.

'By Jove,' Rex breathed, 'This lot would rejoice an automobile salesman's heart.'

The Duke nodded. Not more than half a dozen out of the whole collection were ordinary, moderately-priced machines. The rest bore out De Richleau's statement that the practitioners of the Black Art in modern times were almost exclusively people of great wealth. A big silver Rolls stood nearest to them; beyond it a golden Bugatti. Then a supercharged Mercedes, another Rolls, an Isotta Fraschini whose bonnet alone looked as big as an Austin Seven, and so the line continued with Alfa Romeos, Daimlers, Hispanos and Bentleys, nearly every one distinctive of its kind. At a low estimate there must have been £100,000 worth of motor-cars parked in that small area.

As they paused there for a moment a mutter of voices and a sudden burst of laughter came from a ground-floor window. Rex tip-toed softly forward across the gravel. De Richleau followed and, crouching down with their heads on a level with the low sill, they were able to see through a chink in the curtains into the room.

It was a long, low billiards-room with two tables, and the usual settees ranged along the walls. Both tables were covered with white cloths upon which were piles of plates, glasses, and an abundant supply of cold food. About the room, laughing, smoking and talking, were some thirty chauffeurs who, having delivered their employers at the rendezvous, were being provided with an excellent spread to keep them busy and out of the way.

The Duke touched Rex on the shoulder, and they tiptoed

quietly back to the shelter of the bushes. Then, making a circle of the drive, they passed round the other side of the house, which was dark and deserted, until they came again to the lighted windows at the back which they had first seen.

The curtains of these had been more carefully drawn than those of the billiards-room where the chauffeurs were supping, and it was only after some difficulty that they found a place at one where they were able to observe a small portion of the room. From what little they could see, the place seemed to be a large reception-room, with parquet floor, painted walls and Italian furniture.

The head of a man, who was seated with his back to the window, added to their difficulty in seeing into the room but the glimpse they could get was sufficient to show that all the occupants of it were masked and their clothes hidden under black dominoes, giving them all a strangely funereal appearance.

As the man by the window turned his head De Richleau, who was occupying their vantage point at the time, observed that his hair was grey and curly and that he had lost the top portion of his left ear, which ended in a jagged piece of flesh. The Duke felt that there was something strangely familiar in that mutilated ear, but he could not for the life of him recall exactly where he had seen it. Not at Simon's party, he was certain but, although he watched the man intently, no memory came to aid his recognition.

The others appeared to be about equal numbers of both sexes as far as the Duke could judge from the glimpses he got of them as they passed and repassed the narrow orbit of his line of vision. The masks and dominoes made it particularly difficult for him to pick out any of the Satanists whom he had seen at the previous party but, after a little, he noticed a man with a dark-skinned, fleshy neck and thin, black hair whom he felt certain was the Babu, and a little later a tall, lank, fair-haired figure who was undoubtedly the Albino.

After a time Rex took his place at their observation post. A short, fat man was standing now in the narrow line of sight. A black mask separated his pink, bald head from the powerful fleshy chin—it could only be Mocata. As he watched, another domino came up, the beaky nose, the bird-like head, the narrow, stooping shoulders of which must surely belong to Simon Aron.

'He's here,' whispered Rex.

'Who—Simon?'

'Yes. But how we're going to get at him in this crush is more than I can figure out.'

'That has been worrying me a lot,' De Richleau whispered back. 'You see, I have had no time to plan any attempt at rescue. My whole day has been taken up with working at the Museum and then organising the discovery of this rendezvous. I had to leave the rest to chance, trusting that an opportunity might arise where we could find Simon on his own if they had locked him up, or at least with only a few people, when there would be some hope of our getting him away. All we can do for the moment is to bide our time. Are there any signs of them starting their infernal ritual?'

'None that I can see. It's only a "conversation piece" in progress at the moment.'

De Richleau glanced at his watch. 'Just on eleven,' he murmured, 'and they won't get going until midnight, so we have ample time before we need try anything desperate. Something may happen to give us a better chance before that.'

For another ten minutes they watched the strange assembly. There was no laughter but, even from outside the window, the watchers could sense a tenseness in the atmosphere and a strange suppressed excitement. De Richleau managed to identify the Eurasian, the Chinaman and old Madame D'Urfé with her parrot beak. Then it seemed to him that the room was gradually emptying. The man with the mutilated ear, whose head had obscured their view, stood up and moved away and the low purr of a motor-car engine came to them from the far side of the house.

'It looks as if they're leaving,' muttered the Duke; 'perhaps the Sabbat is not to be held here after all. In any case, this may be the chance we're looking for. Come on.'

Stepping as lightly as possible to avoid the crunching of the gravel, they stole back to the shrubbery and round the house to the place where the cars were parked. As they arrived a big car full of people was already running down the drive. Another was in the process of being loaded up with a number of hampers and folding tables. Then that also set off with two men on the front seat.

Rex and De Richleau, crouching in the bushes, spent the best

110

part of half an hour watching the departure of the assembly.

Every moment they hoped to see Simon. If they could only identify him among those dark shapes that moved between the cars they meant to dash in and attempt to carry him off. If would be a desperate business but there was no time left in which to make elaborate plans; under cover of darkness and the ensuing confusion there was just a chance that they might get away with it.

No chauffeurs were taken and a little less than half the number of cars utilised. Where the guests had presumably arrived in ones, twos, and threes, they now departed crowded five and six apiece in the largest of the cars.

When only a dozen or so of the Satanists were left the Duke jogged Rex's arm. 'We've missed him I'm afraid. We had better make for our own car now or we may lose track of them,' and, filled with growing concern at the difficulties which stood between them and Simon's rescue, they turned and set off at a quick pace through the trees to the broken place in the wall.

Scrambling over, they ran at a trot down the lane. Once in the car, De Richleau drove it back on to the main road and then pulled up as far as possible in the shadow of the overhanging trees. A big Delage came out of the park gates a hundred yards farther along the road and turning east sped away through the village.

'Wonder if that's the last,' Rex said softly.

'I hope not,' De Richleau replied. 'They have been going off at about two-minute intervals, so as not to crowd the road and make too much of a procession of it. If it is the last, they would be certain to see our lights and become suspicious. With any luck the people in the Delage will take us for the following car if we can slip in now, and the next to follow will believe our rear light to be that of the Delage.' He released his brake, and the Hispano slid forward.

On the far side of the village they picked up the rear light of the Delage moving at an easy pace and followed to the cross-roads where they had met Clutterbuck an hour and a half earlier. Here the car turned north along a by-road, and they followed for a few miles upward on to the higher level of the desolate rolling grassland, unbroken by house or farmstead, and treeless except for, here and there, a coppice set upon a gently sloping hillside.

Rex was watching out of the back window and had assured himself that another car was following in their rear, for upon that open road motor headlights were easily visible for miles.

They passed through the village of Chitterne St. Mary, then round the steep curve to the entrance of its twin parish, Chitterne All Saints. At the latter the car which they were following switched into a track runinng steeply uphill to the northeast, then swiftly down again into a long valley bottom and up the other side on to a higher crest. They came to a crossroads where four tracks met in another valley and turned east to run on for another mile, bumping and skidding on the little-used, pathlike way. After winding a little, the car ahead suddenly left the track altogether and ran on to the smooth short turf.

After following the Delage for a mile or more across the grass, De Richleau saw it pull up on the slope of the downs where the score or so of cars which had brought the Satanists to this rendezvous were parked in a ragged line. He swiftly dimmed his lights, and ran slowly forward, giving the occupants of the Delage time to leave their car before he pulled up the Hispano as far from it as he dared without arousing suspicion in the others. The car following, which seemed to be the last in the procession, passed quite close to them and halted ten yards ahead, also disgorging its passengers. Rex and the Duke waited for a moment, still seated in the darkness of the Hispano, then after a muttered conference, Rex got out to go forward and investigate.

He returned after about ten minutes to say that the Satanists had gone over the crest of the hill into the dip beyond, carrying their hampers and their gear with them.

'We had better drive on then,' said the Duke, 'and park our car with theirs. It's likely to be noticed if the moon gets up.'

'There isn't a moon,' Rex told him. 'We're in the dark quarter. But it would be best to have it handy all the same.'

They drove on until they reached the other cars, all of whose lights had been put out, then, getting out, set off at a stealthy trot in the direction the Satanists had taken.

Within a few moments, they arrived at the brow of the hill and saw that spread below them lay a natural amphitheatre. At the bottom, glistening faintly, lay a small tarn or lake, and De Richleau nodded understandingly.

'This is the place where the devilry will actually be done without a doubt. No Sabbat can be held except in a place which is near open water.' Then the two friends lay down in the grass to watch for Simon among the dark group of figures who were moving about the water's edge.

Some were busy unpacking the hampers, and erecting the small folding-tables which they had brought. The light was just sufficient for Rex to see that they were spreading upon them a lavish supper. As he watched, he saw a group of about a dozen move over to the left towards a pile of ancient stones which, in the uncertain light, seemed to form a rugged, natural throne.

De Richleau's eyes were also riveted upon the spot and, to his straining gaze, it seemed that there was a sudden stirring of movement in the shadows there. The whole body of masked, black-clad figures left the lake and joined those near the stones, who seemed to be their leaders. After a moment the watchers could discern a tall, dark form materialising on the throne and, as they gazed with tense expectancy, a faint shimmer of pale violet light began to radiate from it.

Even at that distance, this solitary illumination of the dark hollow was sufficient for the two friends to realise that the thing which had appeared out of the darkness, seated upon those age-old rocks, was the same evil entity that De Richleau had once taken for Mocata's black servant, and which had manifested itself to Rex with such ghastly clarity in Simon's silent house. The Sabbat was about to commence.

16

The Sabbat

Straining their eyes and ears for every sound and movement from the assembly in the dark shadows below, Rex and the Duke lay side by side on the rim of the saucer-shaped depression in the downland.

As far as they could judge, they were somewhere about half-way between the two hamlets of Imber and Tilshead, with Chitterne All Saints in their rear and the village of Easterton, where Tanith had crashed, about five miles to the north. The country round about was desolate and remote. Once in a while some belated Wiltshire yokel might cross the plain by night upon a special errand created by emergency; but even if such a one had chanced to pass that way on this Walpurgis-Nacht, the hidden meeting-place—guarded by its surrounding hills—was far from the nearest track, and at that midnight hour no living soul seemed to be stirring within miles of the spot which the Satanists had chosen for the worship of their Infernal Master.

In the faint starlight they could see that the tables were now heaped with an abundance of food and wine, and that the whole crowd had moved over towards the throne round which they formed a wide circle, so that the nearest came some little way up the slope and were no more than fifty yards from where the Duke and Rex lay crouched in the grass.

'How long does it last?' Rex asked, beneath his breath, a little nervously.

'Until cock-crow, which I suppose would be at about four o'clock at this time of the year. It is a very ancient belief that the crowing of a cock has power to break spells, so these ceremonies, in which the power to cast spells is given, never last longer. Keep a sharp look out for Simon.'

'I am, but what will they be doing all that time?'

First, they will make their homage to the Devil. Then they will gorge themselves on the food that they have brought and get drunk on the wine; the idea being that everything must be done contrary to the Christian ritual. They will feast to excess as opposed to the fasting which religious people undergo before their services. Look! There are the leaders before the altar now.'

Rex followed the Duke's glance, and saw that half a dozen black figures were placing tall candles—eleven of them in a circle and the twelfth inside it—at the foot of the throne.

As they were lighted the twelve candles burned steadily in the windless night with a strong blue flame, illuminating a circle of fifty feet radius including the tables where the feast was spread. Outside this ring the valley seemed darker than before, filled with pitch-black shadows so that the figures in the area of light stood out clearly as though upon a bright circular stage.

'Those things they have lighted are the special black candles made of pitch and sulphur,' muttered the Duke. 'You will be able to smell them in a minute. But look at the priests: didn't I tell you that there is little difference between this modern Satanism and Voodoo? We might almost be witnessing some heathen ceremony in an African jungle!'

While the crowd had been busy at the tables, their leaders had donned fantastic costumes. One had a huge cat mask over his head and a furry cloak, the tail of which dangled behind him on the ground; another wore the headdress of a repellent toad; the face of a third, still masked, gleamed bluish for a moment in the candle-light from between the distended jaws of a wolf, and Mocata, whom they could still recognise by his squat obesity, now had webbed wings sprouting from his shoulders which gave him the appearance of a giant bat.

Rex shivered. 'It's that infernal cold again rising up the hill,' he said half-apologetically. 'Say—look at the thing on the throne. It's changing shape.'

Until the candles had been lit, the pale violet halo which emanated from the figure had been enough to show that it was human and the face undoubtedly black. But, as they watched, it changed to a greyish colour, and something was happening to the formation of the head.

'It is the Goat of Mendes, Rex!' whispered the Duke. 'My God! this is horrible!' And even as he spoke, the manifestation took on a clearer shape; the hands, held forward almost in an attitude of prayer but turned downward, became transformed into two great cloven hoofs. Above rose the monstrous bearded head of a gigantic goat, appearing to be at least three times the size of any other which they had ever seen. The two slit-eyes, slanting inwards and down, gave out a red baleful light. Long pointed ears cocked upwards from the sides of the shaggy head, and from the bald, horrible unnatural bony skull, which was caught by the light of the candles, four enormous curved horns spread out—sideways and up.

Before the apparition the priests, grotesque and terrifying beneath their beast-head masks and furry mantles, were now swinging lighted censers, and after a little a breath of the noisome incense was wafted up the slope.

Rex choked into his hand as the fumes caught his throat, then whispered: 'What is that filth they're burning?'

'Thorn, apple leaves, rue, henbane, dried nightshade, myrtle and other herbs,' De Richleau answered. 'Some are harmless apart from their stench, but others drug the brain and excite the senses to an animal fury of lust and eroticism as you will see soon enough. If only we could catch sight of Simon,' he added desperately.

'Look, there he is!' Rex exclaimed. 'Just to the left of the toad-headed brute.'

The goat rose, towering above the puny figures of its unhallowed priests, and turned its back on them; upon which one stooped slightly to give the osculam-infame as his mark of homage. The others followed suit, then the whole circle of Satanists drew in towards the throne and, in solemn silence, followed their example, each bending to salute his master in an obscene parody of the holy kiss which is given to the Bishop's ring.

Simon was among the last, and as he approached the throne, Rex grabbed De Richleau's arm. 'It's now or never,' he grunted. 'We've got to make some effort. We can't let this thing go through.'

'Hush,' De Richleau whispered back. 'This is not the baptism. That will not be until after they have feasted—just before the orgy. Our chance *must* come.'

As the two lay there in the rough grass, each knew that the time was close at hand when they must act if they meant to attempt Simon's rescue. Yet, despite the fact that neither of them lacked courage, both realised with crushing despondency how slender their chances of success would be if they ran down the slope and charged that multitude immersed in their ghoulish rites. There were at least a hundred people in that black-robed crowd and it seemed an utter impossibility to overcome such odds.

Rex leaned over towards the Duke and voiced his thoughts aloud, 'We're right up against it this time unless you can produce a brainwave. We'd be captured in ten seconds if we tried getting Simon away from this bunch of maniacs.'

'I know,' De Richleau agreed miserably. 'I did not bargain for them all being shut up together in one room in that house or coming on to this place in a solid crowd. If only they would split up a little we might isolate Simon with just two or three of them, down the rest, and get him away before the main party knew what was happening; but as things are I am worried out of my wits. If we charge in, and they catch us, I have not a single doubt but that we should never be allowed to come up out of this hollow alive. We know too much, and they would kill us for a certainty. In fact, they would probably welcome the chance on a night like this to perform a little human sacrifice in front of that ghastly thing on the stones there.'

'Surely they wouldn't go in for murder even if they do practise this filthy parody of religion?' whispered Rex incredulously.

De Richleau shook his head. 'The Bloody Sacrifice is the oldest magical rite in the world. The slaying of Osiris and Adonis, the mutilation of Attis and the cults of Mexico and Peru, were all connected with it. Even in the Old Testament you read that the sacrifice which was most acceptable to God the Father was one of blood, and St. Paul tells us that "Without the shedding of blood there is no remission".'

'That was just ancient heathen cruelty.'

'Not altogether. The blood is the Life. When it is shed, energy—animal or human as the case may be—is released into the atmosphere. If it is shed within a specially prepared circle, that energy can be caught and stored or redirected in precisely the same way as electric energy is caught and utilised by our modern scientists.'

'But they wouldn't dare to sacrifice a human being?'

'It all depends upon the form of evil they wish to bring upon the world. If it is war they will seek to propitiate Mars with a virgin ram; if they desire the spread of unbridled lust—a goat, and so on. But the human sacrifice is more potent for all purposes than any other, and these wretched people are hardly human at the moment. Their brains are diseased and their mentality is that of the hags and warlocks of the Dark Ages.'

'Oh, Hell!' Rex groaned, 'we've simply got to get Simon out of this some way.'

The Goat turned round again after receiving the last kiss, holding between its hoofs a wooden cross about four feet in length. With a sudden violent motion it dashed the crucifix against the stone, breaking it into two pieces. Then the cat-headed man, who seemed to be acting the part of Chief Priest, picked them up. He threw the broken end of the shaft towards a waiting group, who pounced upon it and smashed it into matchwood with silent ferocity, while he planted the crucifix end upside down in the ground before the Goat. This apparently concluded the first portion of the ceremony.

The Satanists now hurried over to the tables where the banquet was spread out. No knives, forks, spoons or glasses were in evidence. But this strange party, governed apparently by a desire to throw themselves back into a state of bestiality, grabbed handfuls of food out of the silver dishes and, seizing the bottles, tilted them to drink from the necks, gurgling and spitting as they did so and spilling the wine down their dominoes. Not one of them spoke a word, and the whole macabre scene was carried out in a terrible unnatural silence, as though it were a picture by Goya come to life.

'Let's creep down nearer,' whispered the Duke. 'While they are gorging themselves an opportunity may come for us to get hold of Simon. If he moves a few paces away from them for a moment, don't try to argue with him, but knock him out.'

At a stealthy crawl, the two friends moved down the hillside to within twenty yards of the little lake, at the side of which the tables were set. The throne still occupied by the monstrous goat was only a further fifteen yards away from them, and by the light of the twelve black candles burning with an unnaturally steady flame even in that protected hollow among the hills, they could see the clustered figures sufficiently well to recognise those whom they knew among them despite their masks and dominoes.

Simon, like the rest, was gnawing at a chunk of food as though he had suddenly turned into an animal, and, as they watched, he snatched a bottle of wine from a masked woman standing nearby, spilling a good portion of its contents over her and himself; then he gulped down the rest.

For a few moments Rex felt again that he *must* be suffering from a nightmare. It seemed utterly beyond understanding that any cultured man like Simon, or other civilised people such as these must normally be, could behave with such appalling bestiality. But it was no nightmare. In that strange, horrid silence, the Satanists continued for more than half an hour to fight and tumble like a pack of wolfish dogs until the tables had been overthrown and the ground about the lakeside was filthy with the remaining scraps of food, gnawed bones and empty bottles.

At last Simon, apparently three parts drunk, lurched away from the crash and flung himself down on the grass a little apart from the rest, burying his head between his hands.

'Now!' whispered the Duke. 'We've got to get him.'

With Rex beside him, he half rose to his feet, but a tall figure had broken from the mass and reached Simon before they could move. It was the man with the mutilated ear, and in another second a group of two women and three more men had followed him. De Richleau gritted his teeth to suppress an oath and placed a restraining hand on Rex's shoulder.

'It's no good,' he muttered savagely. 'We must wait a bit. Another chance may come.' And they sank down again into the shadows.

The group about the tables was now reeling drunk, and the whole party in a body surged back towards the Goat upon its throne. Rex and De Richleau had been watching Simon so intently they had failed to notice until then that Mocata and the half dozen other masters of the Left Hand Path had erected a special table before the Goat, and were feeding from it. Yet they appeared strangely sober compared with the majority of the crowd who had fed beside the lake.

'So the Devil feeds, too,' Rex murmured.

'Yes,' agreed the Duke, 'or at least the heads of his priest-hood, and a gruesome meal it is if I know anything about it. A little cannibalism, my friend. It may be a stillborn baby or perhaps some unfortunate child that they have stolen and murdered, but I would stake anything that it is human flesh they are eating.'

As he spoke, a big cauldron was brought forward and placed before the throne. Then Mocata and the others with him each took a portion of the food which they had been eating from the table and cast it into the great iron pot. One of them threw in a round ball which met the iron with a dull thud.

Rex shuddered as he realised that the Duke was right. The round object was a human skull.

'They're going to boil up the remains with various other things,' murmured the Duke, 'and then each of them will be given a little flask of that awful brew at the conclusion of the ceremony, together with a pile of ashes from the wood fire they are lighting under the cauldron now. They will be able to use them for their infamous purposes throughout the year until the next Great Sabbat takes place.'

'Oh, Hell!' Rex protested. 'I can't believe that they can work any harm with that human mess, however horrid it may be. It's just not reasonable.'

'Yet you believe that the Blessed Sacrament has power for good,' De Richleau whispered. 'This is the antithesis of the Body of Our Lord, and I assure you, Rex, that, while countless wonderful miracles have been performed by the aid of the Host, terrible things can be accomplished by this blasphemous decoction.'

Rex had no deep religious feeling, but he was shocked and horrified to the depths of his being by this frightful parody of the things he had been taught to hold sacred in his childhood.

'Dear God,' muttered the Duke, 'they are about to commit the most appalling sacrilege. Don't look, Rex—don't look.' He buried his face in his hands and began to pray, but Rex continued to watch despite himself, his gaze held by some terrible fascination.

A great silver chalice was being passed from hand to hand, and very soon he realised the purpose to which it was being put, but could not guess the intention until it was handed back to the cat-headed man. One of the other officiating priests at the infamy produced some round white discs which Rex recognised at once as Communion Wafers—evidently stolen from some church.

In numbed horror he watched the Devil's acolytes break these into pieces and throw them into the brimming chalice, then stir the mixture with the broken crucifix and hand the resulting compound to the Goat, who, clasping it between its great cloven hoofs, suddenly tipped it up so that the whole contents was spilled upon the ground.

Suddenly, at last, the horrid silence was rent, for the whole mob surged forward shouting and screaming as though they had gone insane, to dance and stamp the fragments of the Holy Wafers into the sodden earth.

'Phew!' Rex choked out, wiping the perspiration from his forehead. 'This is a ghastly business. I can't stand much more of it. They're mad, stark crazy, every mother's son of them.'

'Yes, temporarily.'The Duke looked up again.'Some of them

120

are probably epileptics, and nearly all must be abnormal. This revolting spectacle represents a release of all their pent-up emotions and suppressed complexes, engendered by brooding over imagined injustice, lust for power, bitter hatred of rivals in love or some other type of success and good fortune. That is the only explanation for this terrible exhibition of human depravity which we are witnessing.'

'Thank God, Tanith's not here. She couldn't have stood it. She'd have gone mad, I know, or tried to run away. And then they'd probably have murdered her. But what *are* we going to do about Simon?'

De Richleau groaned. 'God only knows. If I thought there were the least hope, we'd charge into this rabble and try to drag him out of it, but the second they saw us they would tear us limb from limb.'

The fire under the cauldron was burning brightly, and as the crowd moved apart Rex saw that a dozen women had now stripped themselves of their dominoes and stood stark naked in the candle-light. They formed a circle round the cauldron, and holding hands, with their backs turned to the inside of the ring, began a wild dance around it anti-clockwise towards the Devil's left.

In a few moments the whole company had stripped off their dominoes and joined in the dance, tumbling and clawing at one another before the throne, with the exception of half a dozen who sat a little on one side, each with a musical instrument, forming a small band. But the music which they made was like no other that Rex had ever heard before, and he prayed that he might never hear the like again. Instead of melody, it was a harsh, discordant jumble of notes and broken chords which beat into the head with a horrible nerve-racking intensity and set the teeth continually on edge.

To this agonising cacophony of sound the dancers, still masked, quite naked and utterly silent but for the swift movement of their feet, continued their wild, untimed gyrations, so that rather than the changing pattern of an ordered ballet the scene was one of a trampling mass of bestial animal figures.

Drunk with an inverted spiritual exaltation and excess of alcohol—wild-eyed and apparently hardly conscious of each other—the hair of the women streaming disordered as they pranced, and the panting breath of the men coming in laboured

121

gasps—they rolled and lurched, spun and gyrated, toppled, fell, picked themselves up again, and leaped with renewed frenzy in one revolting carnival of mad disorder. Then, with a final wailing screech from the violin, the band ceased and the whole party flung themselves panting and exhausted upon the ground, while the huge Goat rattled and clacked its monstrous cloven hoofs together and gave a weird laughing neigh in a mockery of applause.

De Richleau sat up quickly. 'God help us, Rex, but we've got to do something now. When these swine have recovered their wind the next act of this horror will be the baptism of the Neophytes and after that the foulest orgy, with every perversion which the human mind is capable of conceiving. We daren't wait any longer. Once Simon is baptised, we shall have lost our last chance of saving him from permanent and literal Hell in this life and the next.'

'I suppose it's just possible we'll pull it off now they've worked themselves into this state?' Rex hazarded doubtfully.

'Yes, they're looking pretty done at the moment,' the Duke agreed, striving to bolster up his waning courage for the desperate attempt.

'Shall we—shall we chance it?' Rex hesitated. He too was filled with a horrible fear as to the fate which might overtake them once they left the friendly shadows to dash into that ring of evil blue light. In an effort to steady his frayed nerves, he gave a travesty of a laugh, and added: 'The odds aren't quite so heavy against us now they've lost their trousers. No one fights his best like that.'

'It's not the pack that I'm so frightened of, but that ghastly thing sitting on the rocks.' De Richleau's voice was hoarse and desperate. 'The protections I have utilised may not prove strong enough to save us from the evil which is radiating from it.'

'If we have faith,' gasped Rex, 'won't that be enough?'

De Richleau shivered. The numbing cold which lapped up out of the hollow in icy waves seemed to sap all his strength and courage.

'It would,' he muttered. 'It would if we were both in a state of grace.'

At that pronouncement Rex's heart sank. He had no terrible secret crime with which to charge himself, but although circumstances had appeared to justify it at the time, both he

122

and the Duke had taken human life, and who, faced with the actual doorway of the other world, can say that they are utterly without sin?

Desperately now he fought to regain his normal courage. In the dell the Satanists had recovered their wind and were forming in the great semi-circle again about the throne. The chance to rescue Simon was passing with the fleeting seconds, while his friends stood crouched and tongue-tied, their minds bemused by the reek of the noxious incense which floated up from the hollow, their bodies chained by an awful, overwhelming fear.

Three figures now moved out into the open space before the Goat. Upon the left the beast-like, cat-headed high priest of Evil; upon the right Mocata, his gruesome bat's wings fluttering a little from his hunched-up shoulders; between them, naked, trembling, almost apparently in a state of collapse, they supported Simon.

'It's now or never!' Rex choked out.

'No—I can't do it,' moaned the Duke, burying his face in his hands and sinking to the ground. 'I'm afraid, Rex. God forgive me, I'm afraid.'

17

Evil Triumphant

As the blue Rolls, number OA 1217, came to rest with a sickening thud against the back of the big barn outside Easterton Village, Tanith was flung forward against the windscreen. Fortunately the Duke's cars were equipped with splinter-proof glass and so the windows remained intact, but for the moment she was half-stunned by the blow on her head and painfully 'winded' by the wheel, which caught her in the stomach.

For a few sickening seconds she remained dazed and gasping for breath. Then she realised that she had escaped serious injury, and that the police would be on her at any moment. Her head whirling, her breath stabbing painfully, she threw open the door of the Rolls and staggered out on to the grass.

In a last desperate effort to evade capture, she lurched at an unsteady run across the coarse tussocks and just as the torches of the police appeared over the same hillock, which had slowed down the wild career of the car, she flung herself down in a ditch, sheltered by a low hedge, some thirty yards from the scene of the accident.

She paused there only long enough to regain her breath, and then began to crawl away along the runnel until it ended on the open plain. Taking a stealthy look over the hedge, she saw her pursuers were still busy examining the car, so she took a chance and ran for it, trusting in the darkness of the night to hide her from them.

After she had covered a mile she flopped exhausted to the ground, drawing short gulping breaths into her straining lungs —her heart thudding like a hammer. When she had recovered a little, she looked back to find that the village and the searching officers were now hidden from her by a sloping crest of down-land. It seemed that she had escaped—at least for the time being—and she began to wonder what she had better do.

From what she remembered of the map, the house at Chilbury where the Satanists were gathering preparatory to holding the Great Sabbat was at least a dozen miles away. It would be impossible for her to cover that distance on foot even if she were certain of the direction in which it lay, and the fact that she was wanted by the police debarred her from trying to seek a lift in a passing car if she were able to find the main road again. In spite of her desperate attempt to reach the rendezvous in the stolen Rolls, and the frantic excitement of her escape from the police, she found to her surprise that a sudden reaction had set in, and she no longer felt that terrible driving urge to be present at the Sabbat.

Her anger against Rex had subsided. She had tricked him over the car, and he had retaliated by putting the police on her track. She realised now that he could only have done it on account of his overwhelming anxiety to prevent her from joining Mocata, and smiled to herself in the darkness as she thought again of his anxious, worried face as he had tried so hard that afternoon on the river to dissuade her from what she had only considered, till then, to be a logical step in her progress towards gaining supernatural powers.

She began to wonder seriously for the first time if he was

not right, and that during these last months which she had spent with Madame D'Urfé her brain had become clouded almost to the point of mania by this obsession to the exclusion of all natural and reasonable thoughts. She recalled those queer companions who were travelling the same path as herself, most of them far further advanced upon it, of whom she had seen so much in recent times. The man with the hare-lip, the one-armed Eurasian, the Albino and the Babu. They were not normal any one of them and, while living outwardly the ordinary life of monied people, dwelt secretly in a strange sinister world of their own, flattering themselves and each other upon their superiority to normal men and women on account of the strange powers that they possessed, yet egotistical and hard-hearted to the last degree.

This day spent with the buoyant, virile Rex among the fresh green of the countryside and the shimmering sunlight of the river's bank, had altered Tanith's view of them entirely; and now, in a great revulsion of feeling, she could only wonder that her longing for power and forgetfulness of her foreordained death had blinded her to their cruel way of life for so long.

She stood up and, smoothing down her crumpled green linen frock, did her best to tidy herself. But she had lost her bag in the car smash, so not only was she moneyless but had no comb with which to do her hair. However, feeling that now Rex had succeeded in preventing her reaching the meeting-place he would be certain to call off the police, she set out at a brisk pace away from Easterton towards where she believed the main Salisbury-Devizes road to lie; hoping to find a temporary shelter for the night and then make her way back to London in the morning.

Before she had gone two hundred yards, her way was blocked by a tall, barbed-wire fence shutting in some military enclosure, so she turned left along it. Two hundred yards farther on the fence ended, but she was again brought up by another fence and above it the steep embankment of a railway line. She hesitated then, not wishing to turn back in the direction of Easterton, and was wondering what it would be best to do, when a dark, hunched figure seemed to form out of the shadows beside her. She started back, but recovered herself at once on realising that it was only a bent old woman,

'You've lost your way, dearie?' croaked the old crone.

'Yes,' Tanith admitted. 'Can you show me how I get on to the Devizes road?'

'Come with me, my pretty. I am going that way myself,' said the old woman in a husky voice, which seemed to Tanith in some strange way vaguely familiar.

'Thank you.' She turned and walked along the bridle-path that followed the embankment to the west, searching her mind as to where she could have heard that husky voice before.

'Give me your hand, dearie. The way is rough for my old feet,' croaked the ancient crone; and Tanith willingly offered her arm. Then, as the old woman rested a claw upon it, a sudden memory of long ago flooded her mind.

It was of the days when, as a little girl living in the foothills of the Carpathians, she had made a friend of an old gypsy-woman who used to come to the village for the fair and local Saints' Days, with her band of Ziganes. It was from her that Tanith had first learned her strange powers of clairvoyance and second sight. Many a time she had scrambled down from the rocky mount upon which her home was set to the gypsy encampment outside the village to gaze with marvelling eyes at old Mizka who knew so many wonderful things, and could tell of the past and of the future by gazing into a glass of water or consulting her grimy pack of Tarot cards.

Tanith could still see those pasteboards which had such fascinating pictures upon them. The twenty-two cards of the Major Arcana, said by some to be copies of the original *Book of Thoth,* which contained all wisdom and was given to mankind by the ancient ibis-headed Egyptian god. For thousands of years such packs had been treasured and reproduced from one end of the world to the other and were treasured still, from the boudoirs of modern Paris to the tea-houses of Shanghai, wherever people came secretly in the quiet hours to learn, from those who could read them, the secrets of the future.

As she walked on half unconscious of her strange companion, Tanith recalled them in their right and fateful order. The *Juggler* with his table—meaning mental rectitude; the *High Priestess* like a female Pope—wisdom; the *Empress*—night and darkness; the *Emperor*—support and protection; the *Pope*—reunion and society; the *Lovers*—marriage; the *Chariot*—triumph and despotism; *Justice,* a winged figure with sword and scales—

126

the law; the *Hermit* with his lantern—a pointer towards good; the *Wheel of Fortune* carrying a cat and a demon round with it—success and wealth; *Strength,* a woman wrenching open the jaws of a lion—power and sovereignty; the *Hanged Man* lashed by his right ankle to a beam and dangling upside down while holding two money bags—warning to be prudent; *Death* with his scythe—ruin and destruction; *Temperance,* a woman pouring liquid from one vase to another—moderation; the *Devil,* batwinged, goatfaced, with a human head protruding from his belly—force and blindness; the *Lightning-struck Tower* with people falling from it—want, poverty and imprisonment; the *Star*—disinterestedness; the *Moon*—speech and lunacy; the *Sun*—light and science; the *Judgement*—typifying will; the *World,* a naked woman with goat and ram below—travel and possessions; then last but not least the card that has no number, the *Fool,* foretelling dementia, rapture and extravagance.

Old Mizka had been a willing teacher, and Tanith, the child, an eager pupil, for she had spent a lonely girlhood in that castle on the hill separated by miles of jagged valleys difficult to traverse from other children of her own postion, and debarred by custom from adopting the children of the villagers as her playmates. Long before her time she had learned all the secrets of life from the old gipsy, who talked for hours in her husky voice of lovers and marriage and lovers again, and potions to bring sleep to suspicious husbands and philtres which could warm the heart of the coldest man towards a woman who desired his caresses.

'Mizka,' Tanith whispered suddenly. 'It is you—isn't it?'

'Yes, dearie. Yes—old Mizka has come a long way tonight to set her pretty one upon the road.'

'But how did you ever come to England?'

'No matter, dearie. Don't trouble your golden head about that. Old Mizka started you upon the road, and she has been sent to guide your feet tonight.'

Tanith hung back for a second in sudden alarm, but the claw upon her arm urged her forward again with gentle strength as she protested.

'But I don't want to go! Not . . . not to the . . .'

The old crone chuckled. 'What foolishness is this? It is the road that you have taken all your life, ever since Mizka told you of it as a little girl. Tonight is the night that old Mizka has seen for so many years in her dreams—the night when you shall know all things, and be granted powers which come to few. How fortunate you are to have this opportunity when you are yet so young.'

At the old woman's silken words, a new feeling crept into Tanith's heart. She had been dwelling upon Rex's face as she crossed the plain, and all the health-giving freshness of his gay clean modernity, but now she was drawn back into another world; the one of which she had thought so long, in which a very few chosen people could perform the seemingly impossible —bend others to their will—cause them to fall or rise—place unaccountable obstacles in their path at every turn, or smooth their way to a glorious success. That was more than riches, more than fame; the supreme pinnacle to which any man or woman could rise, and all her longing to reach those heights before she died came back to her. Rex was a pleasant, stupid child; De Richleau a meddlesome fool, who did not understand the danger of the things with which he was trying to interfere. Mocata was a Prince in power and knowledge. She should be unutterably grateful that he had considered her worthy of the honour which she was about to receive.

'It is not far, dearie. Not so far as you have thought. The great Festival does not take place in the house at Chilbury. That was only a meeting place, and the Sabbat is to be held upon these downs only a few miles from here. Come with me, and you shall receive the knowledge and the power that you seek.'

A curtain of forgetfulness seemed to be falling over Tanith's mind—a feeling of intoxication—mental and physical, flooded through her. She felt her eyes closing . . . closing . . . as she muttered: 'Yes. Knowledge and Power. Hurry, Mizka! Hurry, or we shall be too late.'

All her previous hesitations had now been blotted out, and although they were walking over coarse grass, it seemed to her that they trod a smooth and even way. Her mind was obsessed again with the sole thought of reaching the Sabbat in time.

'That is my own beautiful one talking now,' crooned the old beldame in a honeyed voice. 'But have no fear, the night is young, and we shall reach the meeting-place of the Covens before the hour when our Master will appear.'

Tanith was holding herself stiffly as she walked. Her golden head thrown back, her eyes dilated to an enormous size—the muscles at the sides of her mouth twitched incessantly as the old woman's smooth babble flowed on.

They crossed the road, although Tanith was hardly conscious of it as, with Mizka beside her, she stepped out, a new strength surging through her despite her long and tiring day. Then as she mounted an earthy bank a dark and furry presence brushed against her legs, and looking down she saw the golden eyes of a great black cat.

For a moment she was startled, but the old woman chuckled in the darkness. 'It is only Nebiros,' she muttered. 'You have played with him often as a child, dearie, and he is so pleased to see you now.'

The cat mewed with pleasure as Tanith stooped for a moment to stroke its furry back. Then they hastened on again.

For hours it seemed they tramped over the grassy tussocks, up gently-sloping hills and down again into lonesome valleys unbroken by trees or cottages or farmsteads, ever on to the secret place where the Satanists would be gathering now, until old Mizka, walking at Tanith's left, suddenly pulled up—clutching at her arm with her bony hand.

'Shut your eyes, dearie,' she hissed in a sharp whisper. 'Shut your eyes. There is something here that it is not good for you to see. I will guide you.'

Tanith did as she was bid mechanically, and although she could no longer see the rough ground over which they were passing, she did not stumble but continued to step forward evenly at a good pace. Yet she had a feeling that she was no longer alone with the old woman, but that a third person was now walking with them at her right hand. Then, a low voice, bell-like and clear, sounded in her ears.

'Tanith, my darling. Look at me, I implore you.'

At the shock of hearing that well-loved voice, the curtain lifted for a moment and Tanith opened her eyes again. To her right, she saw the figure of her mother dressed in white as she had last seen her before she had set out to some great party where she had died of a sudden heart attack. Round her neck hung a rope of pearls, and her head was adorned with a half-hoop of diamond stars. The figure shone by some strange unnatural light in the surrounding darkness, seeming as pure and translucent as carved crystal.

'My dear one,' the voice went on, 'my folly of encouraging your gift of second sight has led you into terrible peril. I beg you by all that is good and holy to draw back while there is yet time.'

Despite the urging hand which clawed upon her arm, Tanith stumbled for the first time in the long grass and, wrenching her arm away, stood still. In a flash of insight which seared through her drugged brain, she knew then that old Mizka was not a living being, but a Dark Angel sent to lead her to the Sabbat, and that her mother had come at this moment from the world beyond as an Angel of Light to draw her back again into the safety and protection of holy things.

Mizka was babbling and crowing upon her left, urging her onward with a terrible force and intensity. The words 'power' —'crowning your life'—'mastery of all' came again and again in her rapid speech, and Tanith moved a few steps forward. But her mother's voice, imploring again, came clearly in her ears.

'Tanith, my darling, I am only allowed to appear to you because of your great danger, and for the briefest space. I am called back already, but I beg you in the name of the love that we had for each other, not to go. There is a better influence in your life. Trust in it while there is still time, otherwise you will be dragged down into the pit and we shall never meet again.' Suddenly the voice changed, becoming cold and commanding. 'Back, Mizka—back whence you came. I order you by the names of Isis, mother of Horus, Kwan-Yin, mother of Hau-Ki, and Mary, mother of Our Lord.'

The voice ceased on a thin wall as though, all unwillingly, the spirit had been drawn back while its abjuration to the demon was only half completed. With a wild cry and arms outstretched, Tanith dashed forward to the place where that nebulous moon-white being had floated, but where the apparition of her mother had been a second before, only a little breeze ruffled the long grasses. A feeling of immense fatigue bowed her shoulders as she turned towards old Mizka and the cat. But they too had vanished.

She sank upon her knees and began to pray, feverishly at first and then less strongly, until her tongue tripped upon the words and at last she fell silent. Almost unconsciously she rose to her feet and found herself, the night wind playing gently in her hair, standing upon a hilltop gazing down into a shallow valley.

A new and terrible fear gripped at her heart, for she saw below her, by the strange unearthly light of a ring of blue candles, the Satanists gathering for their unholy ceremony, and knew that evil powers had led her feet by devious paths to the place of the Great Sabbat that she might participate after all.

She stood for a moment, the blood draining from her face, quick tremors of horror and apprehension running down her body. She wanted to turn and flee into the dark, protective shadows of the night, but she could not tear her eyes away from that terrible figure seated upon the rocky throne, before which the Satanists were making their obscene obeisance. Some terrible uncanny power kept her feet rooted to the spot, and although her mother's warning still rang in her ears, she could not drag her gaze away from that blasphemous mockery of God proceeding in a horrid silence a hundred yards down the slope from where she stood.

Time ceased to exist for Tanith then. An unearthly chill seemed to creep up out of the valley, swirling and eddying about her legs as a cold current suddenly strikes a bather in a warm patch of sea. The chill crept upward to the level of her breasts, numbing her limbs and dulling her faculties until she could have cried out with the pain. She watched the gruesome banquet with loathing and repulsion, but as she saw those ghoul-like figures tilting the bottles to their mouths she was suddenly beset by an appalling desire to drink.

Although her limbs were cold, her mouth seemed parched; her throat swollen and burning. She was seized with an unutterable longing to rush forward, down the slope, and grab one of those bottles with which to slake her all-consuming thirst. Yet she remained rooted, held back by her higher consciousness; the vision of her mother no longer before her physical eyes, but clear in her mentality just as she had seen it, tall, slender and white-clad, with a sparkling hoop of star-like diamonds glistening above the hair drawn back from the high, broad forehead.

At the defamation of the Host, she was seized by a shuddering rigor in all her limbs. She tried to shut her eyes but they remained fixed and staring while silent tears welled from them

131

and gushed down her cheeks. She endeavoured to cross herself, but her hand, numb with that awful cold, refused to do the bidding of her brain and remained hanging limp and frozen at her side. She endeavoured to pray, but her swollen tongue refused its office, and her mind seemed to have gone utterly blank so that she could not recall even the opening words of the Paternoster or Ave Maria. She knew with a sudden appalling clarity that having even been the witness of this blasphemous sacrilege was enough to damn her for all eternity, and that her own wish to attend this devilish saturnalia had been engendered only by a stark madness caught like some terrible contagious disease from her association with these other unnatural beings who were the victims of a ghastly lunacy.

In vain she attempted to cast herself upon her knees, to struggle back from this horror, but she seemed to be caught in an invisible vice and could not lift her glance for one single second from that small lighted circle which stood out so clearly in the surrounding darkness of the mysterious valley.

She saw the Satanists strip off their dominoes and shuddered afresh—almost retching—as she watched them tumbling upon each other in the disgusting nudity of their ritual dance. Old Madame D'Urfé, huge-buttocked and swollen, prancing by some satanic power with all the vigour of a young girl who had only just reached maturity; the Babu, dark-skinned, fleshy, hideous; the American woman, scraggy, lean-flanked and haglike with empty, hanging breasts; the Eurasian, waving the severed stump of his arm in the air as he gavotted beside the unwieldy figure of the Irish bard, whose paunch stood out like the grotesque belly of a Chinese god.

'They are mad, mad, mad,' she found herself saying over and over again, as she rocked to and fro where she stood, weeping bitterly, beating her hands together and her teeth chattering in the icy wind.

The dance ceased on a high wail of those discordant instruments and then the whole of that ghastly ghoul-like crew sank down together in a tangled heap before the Satanic throne. Tanith wondered for a second what was about to happen next, even as she made a fresh effort to drag herself away. Then Simon was led out from among the rest and she knew all too soon that the time of baptism was at hand. As she realised it,

132

a new menace came upon her. Without her own volition, her feet began to move.

In a panic of fear she found herself setting one before the other and advancing slowly down the hill. She tried to scream, but her voice would not come. She tried to throw herself backward, but her body was held rigid, and an irresistible suction dragged at each of her feet in turn, lifting it a few inches from the ground and pulling it forward, so that, despite her uttermost effort of will to resist the evil force, she was being drawn slowly but surely to receive her own baptism.

The weird unearthly music had ceased. An utter silence filled the valley. She was no more than ten yards from the nearest of those debased creatures who hovered gibbering about the throne. Suddenly she whimpered with fright for although she was still hidden by the darkness, the great horned head of the Goat turned and its fiery eyes became fixed upon her.

She knew then that there was no escape. The warnings from Rex and her mother had come too late. Those powers which she had sought to suborne now held her in their grip and she must submit to this loathsome ritual despite the shrinking of her body and her soul, with all the added horror of full knowledge that it meant final and utter condemnation to the bottomless pit.

18

The Power of Light

At the sight of De Richleau's breakdown Rex almost gave in too. The cold sweat of terror had broken out on his own forehead, yet he was still fighting down his fear and, after a moment, the collapse of that indomitable leader to whom he had looked so often and with such certain faith in the worst emergencies brought him a new feeling of responsibility. His generous nature was great enough to realise that the Duke's courage had only proved less than his own on this occasion because of his greater understanding of the peril they were called upon to face. Now, it was as though the elder man had

133

been wounded and put out of action, so Rex felt that it was up to him to take command.

'We can't let this thing be,' he said with sudden firmness, stooping to place an arm round De Richleau's shaking shoulders. 'You stay here. I'm going down to face the music.'

'No—no, Rex.' The Duke grabbed at his coat. 'They'll murder you without a second thought.'

'Will they? We'll see!' Rex gave a grating laugh. 'Well, if they do you'll have something you can fix on them that the police *will* understand. It'll be some consolation to think you'll see to it that these devils swing for my murder if they do me in.'

'Wait! I won't let you go alone,' the Duke stumbled to his feet. 'Don't you realise that death is the least thing I fear. One look from the eyes of the Goat could send you mad—then where is the case to put before the police? Half the people in our asylums may be suffering from a physical lesion of the brain but the others are unaccountably insane. The real reason is demoniac possession brought about by looking upon terrible things that they were never meant to see.'

'I'll risk it.' Rex was desperate now. He held up the crucifix. 'This is going to protect me, because I've got faith that it will.'

'All right then—but even madness isn't the worst that can happen to us. This life is nothing—I'm thinking of the next. Oh, God, if only dawn would come or we had some form of Light that we could bring to bear on these worshippers of Darkness.'

Rex took a pace forward. 'If we'd known what we were going to be up against we'd have brought a searchlight on a truck. That would have given this bunch something to think about if light has the power you say. But it's no good worrying about that now. We've got to hurry.'

'No—wait!' the Duke exclaimed with sudden excitement. 'I've got it. This way—quick!' He turned and set off up the hill at a swift crouching run.

Rex followed, and when they reached the brow easily overtook him. 'What's the idea,' he cried, using his normal voice for the first time for hours.

'The car!' De Richleau panted, as he pelted over the rough grass to the place where they had left the Hispano. 'To attack

134

them is a ghastly risk in any case, but this will give us a sporting chance.'

Rex reached it first and flung open the door. The Duke tumbled in and got the engine going. It purred on a low note as they bumped forward in the darkness to the brow of the hill.

'Out on the running-board, Rex,' snapped De Richleau as he thrust out the clutch. He seemed in those few moments to have recovered all his old steel-like indomitable purpose. 'It's a madman's chance because it's ten to one we'll get stuck going up the hill on the other side, but we must risk that. When I use the engine again, snap on the lights. As we go past, throw your crucifix straight at the thing on the throne. Then try and grab Simon by the neck.'

'Fine!' Rex laughed suddenly, all his tension gone now that he was at last going into action. 'Go to it!'

The car slid forward, silently gathering momentum as it rushed down the steep slope. Next second they were almost upon the nearest of the Satanists. The Duke let in the clutch and Rex switched on the powerful headlights of the Hispano.

With the suddenness of a thunderclap a shattering roar burst upon the silence of the valley—as though some monster plane was diving full upon that loathsome company from the cloudy sky. At the same instant, the whole scene was lit in all its ghastliness by a blinding glare which swept towards them at terrifying speed. The great car bounded forward, the dazzling beams threw into sharp relief the naked forms gathered in the hollow. De Richleau jammed his foot down on the accelerator and, calling with all his will upon the higher powers for their protection, charged straight for the Goat of Mendes upon his Satanic throne.

At the first flash of those blinding lights which struck full upon them, the Satanists rushed screaming for cover. It was as though two giant eyes of some nightmare monster leapt at them from the surrounding darkness and the effect was as that of a fire-hose turned suddenly upon an angry threatening mob.

Their maniacal exaltation died away. The false exhilaration of the alcohol, the pungent herbal incense and the drug-laden ointments which they had smeared upon their bodies, drained from them. They woke as from an intoxicated nightmare to the realisation of their nakedness and helplessness.

For a moment some of them thought that the end had come and that the Power of Darkness had cashed in their bond, claiming them for its own upon this last Walpurgis-Nacht. Others, less deeply imbued with the mysteries of the Evil cult, forgot the terrible entity whose powers they had come to beg in return for their homage and, reverting to their normal thoughts, saw themselves caught and ruined in some ghastly scandal, believing those blinding shafts of light from the great Hispano to herald the coming of the police.

As the grotesque nude figures scattered with shrieks of terror the car bounded from ridge to ridge heading straight for the monstrous Goat. When the lights fell upon it Rex feared for an instant that the malefic rays which streamed from its baleful eyes would overcome the headlights of the car. The lamps flickered and dimmed, but as the Duke clung to the wheel he was concentrating with all the power of his mind upon visualising the horseshoe surmounted by a cross in silver light just above the centre of his forehead, setting the symbol in his aura and, at the same time, repeating the lines of the Ninety-first Psalm which is immensely powerful against all evil manifestations.

'"Whoso dwelleth under the defence of the most High: shall abide under the shadow of the Almighty.

I will say unto the Lord, Thou are my hope, and my stronghold: my God, in Him will I trust.

For He shall deliver thee from the snare of the hunter: and from the noisome pestilence."'

From the time Rex switched on the headlights, it was only a matter of seconds before the big car hurtled forward like a living thing right on to the ground where the Sabbat was being held.

Rex, clinging to the coachwork, and also visualising that symbol which De Richleau had impressed so strongly upon him, leaned from the step of the car and, with all his force, threw the ivory crucifix straight in the terrible face of the monstrous beast.

The Duke swerved the car to avoid the throne and Simon who, alone of all the Satanists, remained standing but apparently utterly unconscious of what was happening.

The blue flames of the black candles set upon the hellish altar went out as though quenched by some invisible hand. The lights of the car regained their full brilliance, and once again they heard the terrible screaming neigh which seemed to echo over the desolate Plain for miles around as the crucifix, shining white in the glow of the headlights, passed through the face of the Goat.

A horrible stench of burning flesh mingled with the choking odour from the sulphur candles, filled the air like some poisonous gas, but there was no time to think or analyse sensations. After that piercing screech, the brute upon the rocks disappeared. At the same instant Rex grabbed Simon by the neck and hauled him bodily on to the step of the car as it charged the farther slope of the hollow.

Jolting and bouncing it breasted the rise, hesitating for the fraction of a second upon the brink as though some awful power was striving to draw it backwards. But the Duke threw the gear lever into low, and they lurched forward again on to level ground.

Rex, meanwhile, had flung open the door at the back and dragged Simon inside where he collapsed on the floor in a senseless heap. Instinctively, although De Richleau had warned him not to do so, he glanced out of the back window down into the valley where they had witnessed such terrible things, but it lay dark, silent, and seemingly deserted.

The car was travelling now at a better pace, although De Richleau did not dare to use the full power of his engine for fear that they should strike a sudden dip or turn over in some hidden gully.

For a mile they raced north-eastward while, without ceasing, the Duke muttered to himself those protective lines:

' "He shall defend thee under his wings, and thou shalt be safe under his feathers: his faithfulness and truth shall be thy shield and buckler.

Thou shalt not be afraid for any terror by night: nor for the arrow that flieth by day;

For the pestilence that walketh in darkness: nor for the sickness that destroyeth in the noon-day." '

Then to his joy, they struck a track at right-angles, and he turned along it to the north-westward, slipping into top gear. The car bounded forward and seemed to fly as though in truth all the devils of Hell were unleashed behind it in pursuit. Swerving, jolting, and bounding across the grassy ruts, they covered five miles in twice as many minutes until they came upon the Lavington-Westbury road.

Even then De Richleau would not slow down but, turning in the direction of London, roared on, swerving from bend to bend with utter disregard for danger in his fear of the greater danger that lay behind.

They flashed through Earlstoke, Market Lavington and then Easterton, where, unseen by them, the Blue Rolls lay just off the road in a ditch where Tanith had crashed it a few hours before; then Bushall, Upavon, Ludgershall and so to Andover, having practically completed a circuit of the Plain. Here at last, at the entrance of the town, the Duke brought the car to a halt and turned in his seat to look at Rex.

'How is he?' he asked.

'About all-in I reckon. He is as cold as blazes, and he hasn't fluttered an eyelid since I hauled him into the car. My God! what a ghastly business.'

'Grim, wasn't it!' De Richleau for once was looking more than his age. His grey face was lined and heavy pouches seemed to have developed beneath his piercing eyes. His shoulders were hunched as he leaned for a moment apparently exhausted over the wheel. Then he pulled himself together with a jerk and thrusting his hand in his pocket, took out a flask which he passed to Rex.

'Give him some of this—as much as you can get him to swallow. It may help to pull him round.'

Rex turned to where Simon lay hunched up beneath the car rugs on the back seat beside him and forcing open his mouth poured a good portion of the old brandy into it.

Simon choked suddenly, gasped, and jerked up his head. His eyes flickered open and he stared at Rex, but there was no recognition in them. Then his lids closed again and his head fell backwards on the seat.

'Well, he's alive, thank God,' murmured Rex. 'While you've been driving like a maniac I've been scared that we had lost poor Simon for good and all. But now we'd best get him back

138

to London or to the nearest doctor just as soon as we can.'

'I daren't.' De Richleau's eyes were full of a desperate anxiety. 'That devilish mob will have recovered themselves and are probably back at the house near Chilbury by now. They will be plotting something against us you may be certain.'

'You mean that as Mocata knows your flat he will concentrate on it to get Simon back—just as he did before?'

'Worse. I doubt if they'd ever let us reach it.'

'Oh, shucks!' Rex frowned impatiently, 'How're they going to stop us?'

'They can control all the meaner things—bats, snakes, rats, foxes, owls—as well as cats and certain breeds of dog like the Wolfhound and Alsatian. If one of those dashed beneath the wheels of the car when we were going at any speed it might turn over. Besides, within certain limits, they can control the elements, so they could ensure a dense local fog surrounding us the whole way, and every mile of it we'd be facing the risk of another car that hadn't seen our lights smashing into us head on at full speed. If they combine the whole of their strength for ill it's a certainty they'll be able to bring about some terrible accident before we can cover the seventy miles to London. Remember too, this is still Walpurgis-Nacht and every force of evil that is abroad will be leagued against us. For every moment until dawn we three remain in the direst peril.'

19

The Ancient Sanctuary

'Well, we can't stay here,' Rex protested.

'I know, and we've got to find some sanctuary where we can keep Simon safe until morning.'

'How about a church?'

'Yes, if we could find one that is open. But they will all be locked up at this hour.'

'Couldn't we get some local parson out of bed?'

'If I knew one anywhere near here I'd chance it, but how can we possibly expect a stranger to believe the story that we should have to tell? He would think us madmen, or probably that it was a plot to rob his church. But wait a moment! By Jove, I've got it! We'll take him to the oldest cathedral in Britain and one that is open to the skies.' With a sudden chuckle of relief, De Richleau set the car in motion again and began to reverse it.

'Surely you're not going back?' Rex asked anxiously.

'Only three miles to the fork-roads at Weyhill, then down to Amesbury.'

'Well, don't you call that going back?'

'Perhaps, but I mean to take him to Stonehenge. If we can reach it, we shall be in safety, even though it is no more than a dozen miles from Chilbury.'

Once more the car rocketed along the road across those grassy, barren slopes, cleaving the silent darkness of the night with its great arced headlights.

Twenty minutes later they passed again through the twisting streets of Amesbury, now silent and shuttered while its inhabitants slept, not even dreaming of the terrible battle which was being fought out that night between the Power of Light and the Power of Darkness, so near to them in actuality and yet so remote to the teeming life of everyday modern England.

A mile outside the town, they ran up the slope to the wire fence which rings in the Neolithic monument, Stonehenge. The Duke drove the car into the deserted car park beside the road and there they left it. Rex carried Simon, wrapped in De Richleau's great-coat and the car rug, while the Duke followed him through the wire with the suitcase containing his protective impedimenta.

As they staggered over the grass, the vast monoliths of the ancient place of worship stood out against the skyline—the timeless symbols of a forgotten cult that ruled Britain, before the Romans came to bring more decorative and more human gods.

They passed the outer circle of great stone uprights upon some of which the lintels forming them into a ring of arches still remain. Then De Richleau led the way between the mighty chunks of fallen masonry to where, beside the two great trilithons, the sandstone altar slab lies half buried beneath the remnants of the central arch.

At a gesture from the Duke, Rex laid Simon, still unconscious, upon it. Then he looked up doubtfully. 'I suppose you know what you're doing, but I've always heard that the Druids, who built this place, were a pretty grim lot. Didn't they sacrifice virgins on this stone and practise all sorts of pagan rites? I should have thought this place would be more sacred to the Power of Evil than the Power of Good.'

'Don't worry, Rex,' De Richleau smiled in the darkness. 'It is true that the Druids performed sacrifices, but they were sun-worshippers. At the summer solstice, the sun rises over the hill-top there, shedding its first beam of light directly through the arch on to this altar stone. This place is one of the most hallowed spots in all Europe because countless thousands of long-dead men and women have worshipped here—calling upon the Power of Light to protect them from the evil things that go in darkness—and the vibrations of their souls are about us now making a sure buttress and protection until the coming of the dawn.'

With gentle hands, they set about a more careful examination of Simon. His body was still terribly cold but they found that, except for where Rex had clawed at his neck, he had suffered no physical injury.

'What do you figure to do now?' Rex asked as the Duke opened his suitcase.

'Exorcise him in due form, in order to try and drive out any evil spirit by which he may be possessed.'

'Like the Roman Catholic priests used to do in the Middle Ages.'

'As they still do,' De Richleau answered soberly.

'What—in these days?'

'Yes. Don't you remember the case of Helene Poirier who died only in 1914. She suffered from such terrible demoniacal possession that many of the most learned priests in France, including Monsiegneur Dupanloup, Bishop of Orleans, and Monsieur Mallet, Superior of the Grand Seminary, had to be called in before, with God's grace, she could be freed from the evil spirit which controlled her.'

'I didn't think the Church admitted the existence of such things as witchcraft and black magic.'

'Then you are very ignorant, my friend. I do not know the official views of others, but the Roman Church, whose authority comes unbroken over nineteen centuries from the

141

time when Our Lord made St. Peter his viceregent on earth, has ever admitted the existence of the evil power. Why else should they have issued so many ordinances against it, or at the present time so unhesitatingly condemn all spiritualistic practices which they regard as the modern counterparts of necromancy, by which Hell's emissaries seek to lure weak, foolish and trusting people into their net?'

'I can't agree to that,' Rex demurred. 'I know a number of Spiritualists, men and women of the utmost rectitude.'

'Perhaps.' De Richleau was arranging Simon's limp body. 'They are entitled to their opinion and he who thinks rightly lives rightly. No doubt their high principles act as a protective barrier between them and the more dangerous entities of the spirit world. However, for the weak-minded and mentally frail such practices hold the gravest peril. Look at that Bavarian family of eleven people, all of whom went out of their minds after a Spiritualistic séance in 1921. The case was fully reported by the Press at the time and I could give you a dozen similar examples, all attributable to Diabolic possession, of course. In fact, according to the Roman Church, there is no phenomenon of modern Spiritism which cannot be paralleled in the records of old witch trials.'

'According to them, maybe, but Simon's not a Catholic.'

'No matter, there is nothing to prevent a member of the Roman Church asking Divine aid for any man whatever his race or creed. Fortunately I was baptised a Catholic and, although I may not be a good one, I believe that with the grace of God, power will be granted to me this night to help our poor friend.

'Kneel down now and pray silently, for all prayers are good if the heart is earnest and perhaps those of the Church of England more efficacious than others since we are now in the English countryside. It is for that reason I recite certain psalms from the book of Common Prayer. But be ready to hold him if he leaps up for, if he is possessed, the Demon within him will fight like a maniac.'

De Richleau took up the holy water and sprinkled a few drops on Simon's forehead. They remained there a moment and then trickled slowly down his drawn, furrowed face. But he remained corpse-like and still.

'May the Lord be praised,' murmured the Duke.

'What is it?' breatned Rex.

'He is not actually possessed. If he were the holy water would have scalded him like boiling oil, and at its touch the Demon would have screamed like a hell cat.'

'What now then?'

'He still reeks of evil so I must employ the banishing ritual to purge the atmosphere about him and do all things possible to protect him from Mocata's influence. Then we will see if this coma shows any signs of lifting.'

The Duke produced a crutch of Rowan wood then proceeded to certain curious and complicated rites; consisting largely in stroking Simon's limbs with a brushing motion towards the feet; the repetition of many Latin formulas with long intervals in which, led by the Duke, the two men knelt to pray beside their friend.

Simon was anointed with holy water and with holy oil. The gesture of Horus was made to the north, to the south, to the east and to the west. The palms of his hands were sprinkled and the soles of his feet. Asafœtida grass was tied round his wrists and his ankles. An orb with the cross upon it was placed in his right hand, and a phial of quicksilver between his lips. A chain of garlic flowers was hung about his neck, and the sacred oil placed in a cross upon his forehead. Each action upon him was preceded by prayer, concentration of thought, and invocation to the archangels, the high beings of Light, and to his own higher consciousness.

At last, after an hour, all had been accomplished in accordance with the ancient lore and De Richleau examined Simon again. He was warmer now and the ugly lines of distress and terror had faded from his face. He seemed to have passed out of his dead faint into a natural sleep and was breathing regularly.

'I think that with God's help we have saved him,' declared the Duke. 'He looks almost normal now, but we had best wait until he wakes of his own accord; I can do no more, so we will rest for a little.'

Rex passed his hand across his eyes as De Richleau sank down beside him. 'I'll say I need it. Would it be . . . er . . . sacrilegious or anything if I had a smoke?'

'Of course not.' De Richleau drew out his cigars. 'Have a

Hoyo. It is thoughts, not formalities, which make an atmosphere of good or evil.'

For a little while the two friends sat silent, the points of their cigars glowing faintly in the darkness until a pale greyness in the eastern sky made clearer the ghostly outlines of the great oblong stones towering at varying angles to twenty feet about their heads.

'What a strange place this is,' Rex murmured. 'How old do you suppose it to be?'

'About four thousand years.'

'As old as that, eh?'

'Yes, but that is young compared with the Pyramids and, beside them, for architecture and scientific alignment, this thing is a primitive toy.'

'Those ancient Britons must have been a whole heap cleverer than we give them credit for all the same, to get these great blocks of stone set up. It would tax all the resources of our modern engineers, I reckon. Some of them must weigh a hundred tons apiece.'

De Richleau nodded. 'Only the piety of many thousand willing hands, hauling on skin ropes, and manipulating vast levers, could have accomplished it, but what is even more remarkable is that the foreign stones were transported from a quarry nearly two hundred miles from here.'

'What do you mean by "foreign stones"?'

'The stones which form the inner ring and the inner horseshoe are called so because they were brought from a great distance—a place in Pembrokeshire, I think.'

'Horseshoe,' Rex repeated with a puzzled look. 'I thought all the stones were placed in rings.'

'It is hardly discernible in the ruins now, but originally this great temple consisted of an outer ring formed of big arches, then a concentric circle of smaller uprights. Inside that, five great separate trilithons of arches, two of which you can see still standing, set in the form of a horseshoe and then another horseshoe of the smaller stones.'

'The Druids used the horseshoe, too, then?'

'Certainly. As I have told you, it is a most potent symbol indissolubly connected with the Power of Light. Hence my use of it in connection with the swastika and the cross.'

They fell silent again for some time, then Simon stirred beside them and they both stood up. He slowly turned over and looked about him with dull eyes until he recognised his friends, and asked in a stifled voice where he was.

Without answering, De Richleau drew him down between Rex and himself on to his knees, and proceeded to give thanks for his restoration. 'Repeat after me,' he said, 'the words of the fifty-first Psalm.

' "*Have mercy upon me, O God, after thy great goodness: according to the multitude of thy mercies do away mine offences.*

Wash me thoroughly from my wickedness: and cleanse me from my sin.

For I acknowledge my faults and my sin is ever before me." '

To the end of the beautiful penitent appeal the Duke read in a solemn voice from the Prayer Book by the aid of a little torch while the others repeated verse by verse after him. Then all three stood up and began at last to talk in their normal voices.

De Richleau explained what had taken place, and Simon sat upon the altar-stone weeping like a child as now, with a clear brain, he began at last to understand the terrible peril from which his friends had rescued him.

He remembered the party which had been given at his house and that the Duke had hypnotised him in Curzon Street. After that—nothing, until he found himself present in the Sabbat which had been held that night, and even then he could only see vague pictures of it, as though he had not participated in it himself, but watched the whole of the ghastly proceedings from a distance; horrified to the last degree to see a figure that seemed to be himself taking part in those abominable ceremonies, yet mentally chained and powerless to intervene or stop that body, so curiously like his own, participating in that godless scene of debauchery.

Dawn was now breaking in the eastern sky, as De Richleau placed his arm affectionately round Simon's shoulders. 'Don't take it to heart so, my friend,' he said kindly. 'For the moment at least you have been spared, and praise be to God you are still sane, which is more than I dared to hope for when we got you here.'

Simon nodded. 'I know—I've been lucky,' he said soberly. 'But am I really free—for good? I'm afraid Mocata will try and get me back somehow.'

'Now we're together again you needn't worry,' Rex grinned. 'If the three of us can't fight this horror and win out we're not the men I always thought we were.'

'Yes,' Simon agreed, a little doubtfully. 'But the trouble is that I was born at a time when certain stars were in conjunction, so in a way I'm the key to a ritual which Mocata's set his heart on performing.'

'The invocation to Saturn coupled with Mars,' the Duke put in.

'I'm scared he'll exercise every incantation in the book to drag me back to him despite myself.'

'Isn't that danger over? Surely it should have been done two nights ago, but we managed to prevent it then.'

'Ner,' Simon used his favourite negative with a little wriggle of his bird-like head. 'That would have been the most suitable time of all, but the ritual can be performed with a reasonable prospect of success any night while the two planets remain in the same house of the Zodiac.'

'Then the longer we can keep you out of Mocata's clutches, the less chance he stands of pulling it off as the two planets get farther apart,' Rex commented.

De Richleau sighed. His face looked grey and haggard in the early morning light. 'In that case,' he said slowly, 'Mocata will exert his whole strength when twilight comes again, and we shall have to fight with our backs to the wall throughout this coming night.'

20

The Four Horsemen

Now that the sun was up Rex's resilient spirit reasserted itself. 'Time enough to worry about tonight when we are through to-day,' he declared cheerfully. 'What we need most just now is a good hot breakfast.'

The Duke smiled. 'I thoroughly agree, and in any case we can't stay here much longer. While we feed we'll discuss the safest place to which we can take Simon.'

'We can't take him anywhere at the moment,' Rex grinned. 'Not as he is—with only the car rug and your great-coat to cover his birthday suit.'

Simon tittered into his hand. It was the gesture which both his friends knew so well, and which it delighted them to see again. 'I must look pretty comic as I am,' he chuckled. 'And it's chilly too. One of you had better try and raise me a suit of clothes.'

'You take the car, Rex,' said the Duke, 'and drive into Amesbury. Knock up the first clothes dealer you can find and buy him an outfit. Have you enough money?'

'Plenty. I was going down to Derby yesterday for the first Spring Race Meeting if this business hadn't cropped up overnight. So I'd drawn fifty the day before.'

'Good,' the Duke nodded. 'We shan't move from here until you return.' Then, as Rex strode away across the grass to the Hispano, which was now visible where they had left it in the car-park, he turned to Simon:

'Tell me,' he said, 'while Rex is gone. How did you ever get drawn into this terrible business?'

Simon smiled. 'Well,' he said hesitantly, 'it may seem a queer thing to say, but you are partly responsible yourself.'

'I!' exclaimed the Duke. 'What the deuce do you mean?'

'I'm not blaming you, of course, in the least, but do you remember that long chat we had when we were both down at Cardinals Folly for Christmas? It started by your telling us about the old Alchemists and how they used to make gold out of base metals.'

De Richleau nodded. 'Yes, and you threw doubt upon my statement that the feat had actually been performed. I cited the case of the scientist Helvetius, I remember, who was bitterly opposed to the pretentions of the Alchemists, but who, when he was visited by one at the Hague in December, 1666, managed to secrete a little of the reddish powder which the man showed him under his finger-nail, and afterwards succeeded in transmuting a small amount of lead into gold with it. But you would not believe me, although I assured you, that no less a person than Sponoza verified the experiment at the time.'

'That's right,' said Simon. 'Well, I was sceptical but interested, so I took the trouble to check up as far as possible

147

on all you'd said. It was Spinoza's testimony that impressed me because he was so very sane and unbiased.'

'So was Helvetius himself for that matter.'

'I know. Anyhow, I dug up the fact that Povelius, the chief tester of the Dutch Mint, assayed the metal seven times with all the leading goldsmiths at the Hague and they unanimously pronounced it to be pure gold. Of course there was a possibility that Helvetius deceived them by submitting a piece of gold obtained through the ordinary channels, but it hardly seemed likely that he practised deliberate fraud, because he had no motive. He had always declared his disbelief in alchemy and he couldn't make any more because he hadn't got the powder —so there was no question of his trying to float a bogus company on the experiment. He couldn't even claim any scientific kudos from it either because he frankly admitted that he had stolen the powder from the stranger who showed it to him. After that I went into the experiment of Berigord de Pisa and Van Helmont.'

'And what did you think of those?' asked the Duke, his lined face showing quick interest in the early morning light.

'They shook my unbelief a lot. Van Helmont was the greatest chemist of his time, and like Helvetius, he'd always said the idea of transmitting base metals into gold was sheer nonsense until a stranger gave him a little of that mysterious powder with which he, too, performed the experiment successfully; and he again had no personal axe to grind.'

'There are plenty of other cases as well,' remarked the Duke. 'Raymond Lully made gold for King Edward III of England, and George Ripley gave £100,000 of alchemical gold to the Knights of Rhodes. The Emperor Augustus of Saxony left 17,000,000 Rix dollars and Pope John XXII of Avignon 25,000,000 florins, sums which were positively gigantic for those days. Both were poor men with slender revenues which could not have accounted in a hundred years for such fortunes. But both were alchemists, and transmutation is the only possible explanation of the almost fabulous treasure which was actually found in their coffers after their deaths.'

Simon nodded. 'I know. And if one rejects the sworn evidence of men like Spinoza and Van Helmont, why should one believe the people who say they can measure the distance to the stars, or the scientists of the last century who produced electrical phenomena?'

'The difference is that the mass mind will not accept scientific truths unless they can be demonstrated freely and harnessed to the public good. Everyone accepts the miracle that sulphur can be converted into fire because they see it happen twenty times a day and we all carry a box of matches in our pockets, but if it had been kept as a jealously guarded secret by a small number of initiates, the public would still regard it as impossible. And that, you see, is precisely the position of the alchemist.

'He stands apart from the world and is indifferent to it. To succeed in the Great Work he must be absolutely pure, and to such men gold is dross. In most cases he makes only sufficient to supply his modest needs and refuses to pass on his secret to the profane; but that does not necessarily mean that he is a fraud and a liar. The theory that all matter is composed of atoms, molecules and electrons in varying states is generally accepted now. Milk can be made as hard as concrete by the new scientific process, glass into women's dresses, wood and human flesh decay into a very similar dust, iron turns to rust, and crystals are known to grow although they are a type of stone. Even diamonds can be made synthetically.'

'Of course,' Simon agreed, with his old eagerness, so absorbed now in the discussion as to be apparently oblivious of his surroundings. 'And as far as metals are concerned, they are all composed of sulphur and mercury and can be condensed or materialised by means of a salt. Only the varying proportions of those three Principals account for the difference between them. Metals are the fruits of mineral nature, and the baser ones are still unripe because the sulphur and mercury had no time to combine in the right proportions before they solidified. This powder, or the Philosophers' Stone as they call it, is a ferment that forces on the original process of Nature and ripens the base metals into gold.'

'That is so. But do you mean to tell me that you have been experimenting yourself?'

'Ner,' Simon shook his narrow head. 'I soon found out that to do so would mean a lifetime of æstheticism and then perhaps failure after all. It is hardly in my line to become a "Puffer." Besides it's obvious that transmutation in its higher sense is the supreme mystery of turning Matter into Light. Metals are

149

like men, the baser corresponding to the once born, and both gradually become purified—metals by geological upheavals—men by successive reincarnations, and the part played by the secret agent which hurries lead to gold is the counterpart of esoteric initiation which lifts the spirit towards light.'

'Was that your aim then?'

'To some extent. You know how one thing leads to another. I discovered that the whole business is bound up with the Quabalah so, being a Jew, I began to study the esoteric doctrine of my own people.'

De Richleau nodded. 'And very interesting you found it, I don't doubt.'

'Yes, it took a bit of getting into, but after I'd tackled a certain amount of the profane literature to get a grounding, I read the *Sepher Ha Zoher,* the *Sepher Jetyirah* and some of the *Midraschim.* Then I began to see a little daylight.'

'In fact you began to believe, like most people who have really read considerably and had a wide experience of life, that our western scientists have only been advancing in one direction and that we have even lost the knowledge of many things with which the wise men of ancient times were well acquainted.'

'That's so,' Simon smiled again. 'I've always been a complete sceptic. But once I began to burrow beneath the surface I found such a mass of evidence that I could no longer doubt the existence of strange hidden forces which can be chained and untilised if one only knows the way.'

'Yes. And plenty of people still interest themselves in these questions and use the Quabalah to promote their own well-being and the general good. But where does Mocata come into all this?'

Simon shuddered slightly at the name and drew the car rug more closely about his shoulders. 'I met him in Paris,' he said, 'at the house of a French banker with whom I've sometimes done business.'

'Castelnau!' exclaimed the Duke. 'The man with the jagged ear. I knew last night that I had seen that ear somewhere before, but for the life of me I couldn't recall where.'

Simon nodded quickly. 'That's right—Castelnau. Well, I met Mocata at his place, and I don't quite know how it started, but the conversation drifted round to the Quabalah and, as I had been soaking myself in it at the time, I was naturally interested. He said he had a lot of books upon it and suggested that I might like to visit the house where he was staying and have a look through them. Of course I did. Then he told me that he was conducting an experiment in Magic the following night, and asked if I would care to be present.'

'I see. That's how the trouble started.'

'Yes. The experiment was quite a harmless affair. He made certain ritual conjurations with the four elements, Fire, Air, Water and Earth, then told me to look into a mirror with him. It was an old Venetian piece, a bit spotted at the back but otherwise quite ordinary you know. As I watched, it clouded over with a sort of mist, then when it cleared again I could no longer see my reflection in it, but a sheet of newspaper instead. It was the financial page of *Le Temps* giving all the quotations of the Paris Bourse, which sounds pretty prosaic I suppose, but the queer part is that this issue was dated three days ahead.'

De Richleau stroked his lean face with his slender fingers. 'I saw a similar demonstration in Cairo once,' he commented gravely. 'But on that occasion it was the name of the new Commander-in-Chief, who had only been appointed by the War Office in London that afternoon, which appeared in the mirror. You took a note of some of the Bourse quotations I suppose?'

'Um. The list wasn't visible for more than ten seconds then the mirror clouded over again and went back to its normal state, but that was quite long enough for me to memorise the stocks I was interested in, and when I checked up afterwards they were right to a fraction.'

'What happened then?'

'Mocata offered to instruct me in the attainment of the knowledge and conversation of my Holy Guardian Angel as the first step on the road to obtaining similar powers myself.'

'My poor Simon!' The Duke made an unhappy grimace. 'You are not the first to be trapped by a Brother of the Left Hand Path who is recruiting for the Devil by such a promise. If you had known more of Magic you would have realised that it is proper to pass through the six stages of Probationer, Neophyte, Zelator, Practicus, Philosophus and Dominus Liminis before, as an Adeptus Inferior after many years of study and experience, you would be qualified to take the risk of attempting to pass the Abyss. Besides, there are no precise rules for

151

attaining the knowledge and conversation of one's Holy Guardian Angel. It is a thing which each man must work out for himself and no other can help one to it. Mocata invoked your Evil Angel, of course, to act a blasphemous impersonation while your Holy Guardian wept impotent tears to see the terrible danger into which you were being drawn.'

'I suppose so, although, of course, I couldn't know that at the time. Anyhow, I had to go back to London a few days later, and I was so impressed by that time that I asked Mocata to let me know directly he arrived, because he spoke of coming over. He turned up a fortnight later and rang me up at once to urge me to unload a lot of stock that he knew I was carrying. I had faith in it myself but in view of what I'd seen in his mirror I took his tip and saved myself quite a packet, because the market broke almost immediately after.'

'Was that when you asked him to go and live with you?' inquired the Duke.

'Yes. I suggested that he should stay with me while he was in London because he had no suitable place in which to practise his evocations at his hotel. He moved over to St. John's Wood then and after that we used to sit up together in the observatory pretty well every night. That's why I saw so little of you during that time. But the results were extraordinary—utterly amazing.'

'He gave you more information which governed your financial transactions, I suppose.'

'Yes, but more than that. He foretold the whole of the Stravinsky scandal. I'm not a poor man as you know, but if I hadn't been forewarned about that, it would have darn nearly broken me. As it was, I cleared every single share in the dud companies before the storm broke and got out with an immense profit.'

'By that time you had begun to dabble in Black Magic I imagine?'

Simon's dark eyes flickered away from the Duke's for a moment, then he nodded. 'Just a bit. He asked me to recite the Lord's Prayer backwards one night, and I was a bit unhappy about it but . . . well, I did. He said that since I wasn't a Christian anyhow no harm could come to me from it.'

'It is horribly potent all the same,' the Duke commented.

'Perhaps,' agreed Simon miserably. 'But Mocata is so

152

devilish glib and according to him there is no such thing as Black Magic anyhow. The harnessing of supernatural powers to one's will is just Magic—neither black nor white, and that's all there is to it.'

'Tell me about this man.'

'Oh, he's about fifty, I suppose, bald-headed, with curious light blue eyes and a paunch that would rival Dom Gorenflot's.'

'I know,' agreed the Duke impatiently. 'I've seen him. But I meant his personality, not his appearance.'

'Of course, I forgot,' Simon apologised. 'You know for weeks now I hardly know what I've been doing. It's almost as though I had been dreaming the whole time. But about Mocata: he possesses extraordinary force of character, and he can be the most charming person when he likes. He's clever of course—amazingly so, and seems to have read pretty well every book that one can think of. It's extraordinary, too, what a fascination he can exercise over women. I know half a dozen who are simply "bats" about him.'

'What can you tell me of his history?'

'Not much, I'm afraid. His Christian name is Damien and he is a Frenchman by nationality, but his mother was Irish. He was educated for the Church. In fact, he actually took Orders, but finding the life of a priest did not suit him, he chucked it up.'

De Richleau nodded. 'I thought as much. Only an ordained priest can practise the Black Mass, and since he is so powerful an adept of the Left Hand Path, it was pretty certain that he was a renegade priest of the Roman Church. But what more can you tell me? Every scrap of information which you have may help us in our fight, because you must remember, Simon, that you have only achieved a very temporary security. The battle will begin again when he exercises his dominance over you to call you back.'

Simon shifted his position on the stones and then replied thoughtfully. 'He does the most lovely needlework, petit point and that sort of thing you know, and he's terribly fastidious about keeping his plump little hands scrupulously clean. As a companion he is delightful to be with except that he will smother himself in expensive perfumes and is as greedy as a schoolboy about sweets. He had huge boxes of fondants,

153

crystallised fruits, and marzipan sent over from Paris twice a week when he was at St. John's Wood.

'Ordinarily he was perfectly normal and his manners were charming, but now and again he used to get irritable fits. They came on about once a month and after he had been boiling up for twenty-four hours, he use to clear out for a couple of days and nights. I don't know where he used to go to at those times, but I ran into him one morning early, when he had just returned from one of these bouts, and he was in a shocking state: filthy dirty, a two days' growth of beard on his chin, his clothes all torn and absolutely stinking of drink. It looked to me as if he hadn't been to bed at all the whole time but had been wallowing in every sort of debauchery down in the slums of the East End.

'He is quite an exceptional hypnotist, of course, and keeps himself in touch with what is going on in Paris, Berlin, New York and a dozen other places by throwing various women, who used to come and visit him regularly, into a trance. One of them was a girl called Tanith, a perfectly lovely creature. You may have seen her at the party, and he says she is by far the best medium he's ever had. He can use her almost like a telephone and plug in right away to whatever he wants to know about. Whereas with the others there are very often hitches and delays.'

'You let him hypnotise you, too, of course?'

'Yes, in order to get these financial results.'

'I thought as much,' De Richleau nodded. 'And after you had allowed him to do it willingly for some little time he was able to block out your own mentality entirely and govern your every thought. That's why you've failed to realise what's been going on. It is just as though he'd been keeping you drugged the whole time.'

'Um,' Simon agreed miserably. 'It makes me positively sick to think of it, but I suppose he has been gradually preparing me for this Ritual to Saturn which he meant to perform two nights ago and . . .' He broke off suddenly as Rex appeared between two of the great monoliths.

Grinning from ear to ear, Rex displayed his purchases for their inspection. A pair of grey flannel shorts, a khaki shirt, black and white check worsted stockings, a gaudy tie of revolting magenta hue, a pair of waders, a cricket cap quartered in alternate triangular sections of orange and mauve, and a short, dark blue bicyclist's cape.

'Only things I could get,' he volunteered cheerfully. 'The people who run the local Co-op don't live on the premises, so I had to knock up a sports outfitter.'

De Richleau sat back and roared with laughter while Simon fingered the queer assortment of garments doubtfully. 'You're joking Rex,' he protested with a sheepish grin. 'I can't return to London in this get-up.'

'We're not going to London,' the Duke announced. 'But to Cardinals Folly.'

'What—to Marie Lou's?' Rex looked at him sharply. 'How did you come to get that idea ...'

'Something that Simon said just after you left us.'

Simon shook his head jerkily. 'I don't like it—not a little bit. I'd never forgive myself if I brought danger into their home.'

'You will do as you're told my friend,' De Richleau's voice brooked no further argument. 'Richard and Marie Lou are the most mentally healthy couple that I know. The atmosphere of their sane and happy household will be the very best protection we could find for you and all of us are certain of a warm welcome. No harm will come to them if we exercise reasonable precautions, and the help of their right-thinking minds will give us the extra strength we need. Besides, they are about the only people to whom we can explain the whole situation without being taken for madmen. Now hurry up and array yourself like the champion of next year's Olympic games.'

With a shrug of his narrow shoulders Simon disappeared behind the stones while Rex added: 'That's right. I ordered ham and eggs to be got ready at the local inn and I'm mighty anxious to start in on them.'

'Eggs and fruit,' cut in the Duke, 'but no ham for any of us. It is essential that we should avoid meat for the moment. If we are to retain our astral strength our physical bodies must undergo a semi-fast at least.'

Rex groaned. 'Why, oh, why dear Simon, did you ever go hunting Talisman and let your friends in for this? When I went to Russia after the Shulimoff jewels and you came to get me out of trouble, at least it didn't prevent your feeding decently when you had the chance.'

'That reminds me,' De Richleau threw over his shoulder in the direction where Simon was struggling into his queer garments. 'What is this Talisman? Rex mentioned it last night.'

'It's the reason why Mocata is certain to make every effort to get possession of me again,' Simon's voice came back. 'It is buried somewhere, and adepts of the Left Hand Path have been seeking it for centuries. It conveys almost limitless powers upon its possessor and Mocata has discovered that its where-abouts will be revealed if he can practise the ritual to Saturn in conjunction with Mars with someone who was born in a certain year at the hour of the conjunction. There can't be many such, but for my sins I happen to be one, and even if he can find others they might not be suitable for various reasons.'

'Yes, I realise that. But what is the Talisman?'

'I don't really know. Except for conducting my business on the lines suggested by Mocata, I don't think my brain has been functioning at all in the last two months. But it's called the Talisman of Set.'

'What!' The Duke sprang to his feet as Simon appeared grotesquely attired in his incongruous new clothes, his long knees protruding beneath the shorts, the absurd cricket cap set at a rakish angle on his head, and the cycling cloak flapping about his shoulders.

Rex dissolved into tears of laughter, but the Duke's grim face quickly sobered his mirth.

'The Talisman of Set,' De Richleau repeated almost in a whisper.

'Yes, it has something to do with four horsemen I think—but what on earth's the matter?' Simon's big mouth fell open in dismay at the sight of the Duke's horror-stricken eyes.

'It has indeed! The Four Horsemen of the Apocalypse,' De Richleau grated out. 'War, Plague, Famine and Death. We all know what happened the last time those four terrible entities were unleashed to cloud the brains of statesmen and rulers.'

'You're referring to the Great War I take it.' Rex said soberly.

'Of course, and every adept knows that it started because one of the most terrible Satanists who ever lived found one of the secret gateways through which to release the four horse-men.'

'I thought the Germans got a bit above themselves,' Rex

hazarded, 'although it seems that lots of other folks were pretty well as much to blame.'

'You fool!' De Richleau suddenly swung upon him. 'Germany did not make the War. It came out of Russia. It was Russia who instigated the murder at Sarajevo, Russia who backed Serbia to resist Austria's demands, Russia who mobilised first and Russia who invaded Germany. The monk Rasputin was the Evil genius behind it all. He was the greatest Black Magician that the world has known for centuries. It was he who found one of the gateways through which to let forth the four horsemen that they might wallow in blood and destruction—and I know the Talisman of Set to be another. Europe is ripe now for any trouble and if they are loosened again, it will be final Armageddon. This is no longer a personal matter of protecting Simon. We've got to kill Mocata before he can secure the Talisman and prevent his plunging the world into another war.'

21

Cardinals Folly

Richard Eaton read the telegram a second time:

> *'Eat no lunch this vitally important Simon ill Rex and I bringing him down to you this afternoon Marie Lou must stop eating too kiss Fleur love all.—De Richleau.'*

He passed one hand over the smooth brown hair which grew from his broad forehead in an attractive widow's peak, and handed the wire to his wife with a puzzled smile.

'This is from the Duke. Do you think he has gone crazy—or what?'

'*What,* darling,' said Marie Lou promptly. 'Definitely *what.* If he stood on his handsome head in Piccadilly and the whole world told me he was crazy I should still maintain that dear old Greyeyes was quite sane.'

'But really,' Richard protested. 'No lunch—and you told

me that the shrimps from Morecambe Bay came in this morning. I was looking forward...'

'My sweet!' Marie Lou gave a delicious gurgle of laughter as she flung one arm round his neck and drew him down on to the sofa beside her. 'What a glutton you are. You simply live for your tummy.'

He nuzzled his head against her thick chestnut curls. 'I don't. I eat only in order to maintain sufficient strength to deal with you.'

'Liar,' she pushed him away suddenly. 'There must be some reason for this extraordinary wire, and poor Simon ill too! What can it mean?'

'God knows! Anyhow it seems that virtuous and upright wife orders preparations of rooms for guests while miserable worm husband goes down into dark, dirty cellar to select liquid sustenance for same.' Richard paused for a moment. A wicked little smile hovered round his lips as he looked at Marie Lou curled up on the sofa with her slim legs tucked under her like a very lovely Persian kitten, then he added thoughtfully: 'I think tonight perhaps we might give them a little of the Chateau Lafite '99.'

'Don't you dare,' she cried, springing to her feet. 'You know that it's my favourite.'

'Got you—got you,' chanted Richard merrily. 'Who's a glutton now?'

'You beast,' she pouted deliciously, and for the thousandth time since he had brought her out of Russia her husband felt himself go a little giddy as his eyes rested on the perfection of her heart-shaped face, the delicately flushed cheeks and the heavy-lidded blue eyes. With a sudden movement, he jerked her to him and swinging her off her feet, picked her up in his arms.

'Richard—put me down—stop.' Her slightly husky voice rose to a higher note in a breathless gasp of protest.

'Not until you kiss me.'

'All right.'

He let her slide down to her feet, and although he was not a tall man, she was so diminutive that she had to stand on tiptoe to reach her arms round his neck.

'There,' she declared, a trifle breathlessly, after he had crushed her soft lips under his. 'Now go and play with your

158

bottles, but spare the Lafite, beloved. That's our own special wine, and you mustn't even give it to our dearest friends—unless it's for Simon and he's really ill.'

'I won't,' he promised. 'But whatever I give them, we shall all be tight if we're not to be allowed to eat anything. I wish to goodness I knew what De Richleau is driving at.'

'Something it is worth our while to take notice of, you may be certain. Greyeyes never does anything without a purpose. He's a wily old fox if ever there was one in this world.'

'Yes—wily's the word,' Richard agreed. 'But it's nearly lunch-time now, and I'm hungry. Surely we're not going to take serious notice of this absurd telegram?'

'Richard!' Marie Lou had curled herself up on the sofa again. But now she sat forward suddenly, almost closing her big eyes with their long curved lashes. 'I do think we ought to do as he says, but I was looking round the strawberry house this morning.'

'Oh were you!' He suppressed a smile. 'And picking a few just to see how they were getting on, I don't mind betting.'

'Three,' she answered gravely. 'And they are ripening beautifully. Now if we took a little cream and a little sugar, it wouldn't be cheating really to go and have another look at them instead of having lunch—would it?'

'No,' said Richard with equal gravity. 'But we have an ancient custom in England when a girl takes a man to pick the first strawberries.'

'But, darling, you have so many ancient customs and they nearly always end in kissing.'

'Do you dislike them on that account?'

'No.' She smiled, extending a small, strong hand by which he pulled her to her feet. 'I think that is one of the reasons why I enjoy so much having become an Englishwoman.'

They left Marie Lou's comfortable little sitting-room and, pausing for a moment for her to pull on a pair of gum-boots which came almost up to her knees while Richard gave orders cancelling their luncheon, went out into the garden through the great octagonal library.

The house was a rambling old mansion, parts of which dated back to the thirteenth century, and the library, being one of the oldest portions of it, was sunk into the ground so that they had to go up half a dozen steps from its french windows

159

on to the long terrace which ran the whole length of the southern side of the house.

A grey stone balustrade patched with moss and lichens separated the terrace from the garden, and from the former two sets of steps led down to a broad, velvety lawn. An ancient cedar graced the greensward towards the east end of the mansion where the kitchen quarters lay, hiding the roofs of the glass-houses and the walled garden with its espaliered peach and nectarine trees.

At the bottom of the lawn tall yew hedges shut in the outer circle of the maze, beyond which lay the rose garden and the swimming-pool. To the right, just visible from the library windows, a gravel walk separated the lawn from a gently sloping bank, called the Botticelli Garden. It was so named because in spring it had all the beauty of the Italian master's paintings. Dwarf trees of apple, plum, and cherry, standing no more than six feet high and separated by ten yards or more from each other, stood covered with white and pink blossom while, rising from the grass up the shelving bank, clumps of polyanthus, pheasant's-eye narcissus, forget-me-nots and daffodils were planted one to the square yard.

This spring garden was in full bloom now and the effect of the bright colours against the delicate green of the young grass was almost incredibly lovely. To walk up and down that two hundred yard stretch of green starred by its many-hued clumps of flowers with Richard beside her was, Marie Lou thought —sometimes with a little feeling of anxiety that her present happiness was too great to last—as near to Heaven as she would ever get. Yet she spent even more time in the long walk that lay beyond it, for that was her own, in which the head gardener was never allowed to interfere. It consisted of two glorious herbaceous borders rising to steep hedges on either side, and ending at an old sun-dial beyond which lay the pond garden, modelled from that at Hampton Court, sinking in rectangular stages to a pool where, later in the year, blue lotus flowers and white water-lilies floated serenely in the sunshine.

As they came out on to the terrace, there were shrieks of 'Mummy—Mummy,' and a diminutive copy of Marie Lou, dressed in a Russian peasant costume with wide puffed sleeves of lawn and a slashed vest of colourful embroidery threaded with gold, came hurtling across the grass. Her mother and father went down the steps of the terrace to meet her, and as she arrived like a small whirlwind Richard swung her up shoulder high in his arms.

'What is it Fleur d'amour?' he asked, with simulated concern, calling her by the nick-name that he had invented for her. 'Have you crashed the scooter again or is it that Nanny's been a wicked girl today?'

'No—no,' the child cried, her blue eyes, seeming enormous in that tiny face, opened wide with concern. 'Jim's hurted hisself.'

'Has he?' Richard put her down. 'Poor Jim. We must see about this.'

'He's hurted bad,' Fleur went on, tugging impulsively at her mother's skirt. 'He's cutted hisself on his magic sword.'

'Dear me,' Marie Lou ran her fingers through Fleur's dark curls. She knew that by 'magic sword' Fleur meant the gardener's scythe, for Richard always insisted that the lawn at Cardinals Folly was too old and too fine to be ruined by a mowing machine, and maintained the ancient practice of having it scythe-cut. 'Where is he now, my sweet?'

'Nanny binded him up and I helped a lot. Then he went wound to the kitchen.'

'And you weren't frightened of the blood?' Richard asked with interest.

Fleur shook her curly head. 'No. Fleur's not to be frightened of anyfink, Mummy says. Why would I be frightened of the blug?'

'Silly people are sometimes,' her father replied. 'But not people who know things like Mummy and you and I.'

At that moment Fleur's nurse joined them. She had heard the last part of the conversation. 'It's nothing serious, madam,' she assured Marie Lou. 'Jim was sharpening his scythe and the hone slipped, but he only cut his finger.'

'But fink if he can't work,' Fleur interjected in a high treble.

'Why?' asked her father gravely.

'He's poor,' announced the child after a solemn interval for deep thought. 'He-has-to-work-to-keep-his-children. So if he can't work, he'll be in a muddle—won't he?'

Richard and Marie Lou exchanged a smiling glance as Simon's expression for any sort of trouble came so glibly to the child's lips.

'Yes, that's a serious matter,' her father agreed gravely, 'What are we going to do about it?'

'We mus' all give him somefink,' Fleur announced breathlessly.

'Well, say I give him half-a-crown,' Richard suggested. 'How much do you think you can afford?'

'I'll give half-a-cwown too.' Fleur was nothing if not generous.

'But have you got it, Batuskha?' inquired her mother.

Fleur thought for a bit, and then said doubtfully: 'P'r'aps I haven't. So I'll give him a ha'-penny instead.'

'That's splendid, darling, and I'll contribute a shilling,' Marie Lou declared. 'That makes three shillings and sixpence halfpenny altogether, doesn't it?'

'But Nanny must give somefink,' declared Fleur suddenly turning on her nurse, who smiling said that she thought she could manage fourpence.

'There,' laughed Richard. 'Three and tenpence halfpenny! He'll be a rich man for life, won't he? Now you had better toddle in to lunch.'

This domestic crisis having been satisfactorily settled, Richard and Marie Lou strolled along beneath the balustraded terrace, past the low branches of the old cedar, and so to the hot-houses. Their butler, Malin, had just arrived with sugar and fresh cream, and for half an hour they made a merry meal of the early strawberries.

They had hardly finished when, to their surprise, since it was barely two o'clock, Malin returned to announce the arrival of their guests. So they hurried back to the house.

'There they are,' cried Marie Lou as the three friends came out from the tall windows of the drawing-room on to the terrace. 'But, darling, look at Simon—they *have* gone mad.'

Well might the Eatons think so from Simon's grotesque appearance in shorts, cycling cape and the absurd mauve and orange cricketing cap. Hurried greetings were soon exchanged and the whole party went back into the drawing-room.

'Greyeyes, darling,' Marie Lou exclaimed as she stood on tiptoe again to kiss De Richleau's lean cheek. 'We had your telegram and we are dying to know what it's all about. Have our servants conspired to poison us or what?'

'*What*,' smiled De Richleau. 'Definitely *what*, Princess. We have a very strange story to tell you, and I was most anxious you should avoid eating any meat for today at all events.'

Richard moved towards the bell. 'Well, we're not debarred from a glass of your favourite sherry, I trust.'

The Duke held up a restraining hand. 'I'm afraid we are. None of us must touch alcohol under any circumstances at present.'

'Good God!' Richard exclaimed. 'You don't mean that—you can't. You *have* gone crazy!'

'I do,' the Duke assured him with a smile. 'Quite seriously.'

'We're in a muddle—a nasty muddle,' Simon added with a twisted grin.

'So it appears,' Richard laughed, a trifle uneasily. He was quite staggered by the strange appearance of his friends, the tense electric atmosphere which they had brought into the house with them, and the unnatural way in which they stood about—speaking only in short jerky sentences.

He glanced at Rex, usually so full of gaiety, standing huge, gloomy and silent near the door, then he turned suddenly back to the Duke and demanded: 'What *is* Simon doing in that absurd get-up? If it was the right season for it I should imagine that he was competing for the fool's prize at the Three Arts' Ball.'

'I can quite understand your amazement,' the Duke replied quietly, 'but the truth is that Simon has been very seriously bewitched.'

'It is obvious that something's happened to him,' agreed Richard curtly. 'But don't you think it would be better to stop fooling and tell us just what all this nonsense *is* about?'

'I mean it,' the Duke insisted. 'He was sufficiently ill advised to start dabbling in Black Magic a few months ago, and it's only by the mercy of Providence that Rex and I were enabled to step in at a critical juncture with some hope of arresting the evil effects.'

Richard's brown eyes held the Duke's grey ones steadily. 'Look here,' he said, 'I am far too fond of you ever to be rude intentionally, but hasn't this joke gone far enough? To talk about magic in the twentieth century is absurd.'

'All right. Call it natural science then.' De Richleau leaned a little wearily against the mantelpiece. 'Magic is only a name for the sciences of causing change to occur in conformity with will,'

163

'Or by setting natural laws in action quite inadvertently,' added Marie Lou, to everyone's surprise.

'Certainly,' the Duke agreed after a moment, 'and Richard has practised that type of magic himself.'

'What on earth are you talking about?' Richard exclaimed.

De Richleau shrugged. 'Didn't you tell me that you got a Diviner down from London when you were so terribly short of water here last summer, and that when you took his hazel twig from him you found out quite by accident that you could locate an underground spring in the garden without his help?'

'Yes,' Richard hesitated. 'That's true, and as a matter of fact, I've been successful in finding places where people could sink wells on several estates in the neighbourhood since. But surely that has something to do with electricity? It's not magic.'

'If you were to say vibrations, you would be nearer the mark,' De Richleau replied seriously. 'It is an attunement of certain little-understood vibrations between the water under the ground and something in yourself which makes the forked hazel twig suddenly begin to jump and revolve in your hands when you walk over a hidden spring. That is undoubtedly a demonstration of the lesser kind of magic.'

'The miracle of Moses striking the rock in the desert from which the waters gushed forth is only another example of the same thing,' Simon cut in.

Marie Lou was watching the Duke's face with grave interest. 'Everyone knows there is such a thing as magic,' she declared, 'and witchcraft. During those years that I lived in a little village on the borders of the Siberian Forest I saw many strange things, and the peasants went in fear and trembling of one old woman who lived in a cottage all alone outside the village. But what do you mean by lesser magic?'

'There are two kinds,' De Richleau informed her. 'The lesser is performing certain operations which you believe will bring about a certain result without knowing why it should be so. If you chalk a line on the floor and take an ordinary hen, hold its beak down for a little time on to the line and then release it, the hen will remain there motionless with its head bent down to the floor. The assumption is that, being such a stupid creature, it believes that it has been tied down to the line and it is therefore useless to endeavour to escape. But nobody knows for certain. All we do know is that it happens. That is a fair example of an operation in minor magic. The great majority of the lesser witches and wizards in the part had no conception as to *why* their spells worked, but had learned from their predecessors that if they performed a given operation a certain result was almost sure to follow it.'

Rex looked up suddenly and spoke for the first time. 'I'd say they were pretty expert at playing on the belief of the credulous by peddling a sort of inverted Christian Science, faith healing, Coueism and all that as well.'

'Of course,' De Richleau smiled faintly. 'But they were far too clever to tell a customer straight out that if he concentrated sufficiently on his objective he would probably achieve it— even if they realised that themselves. Instead, they followed the old formulas which compelled him to develop his will power. If a man is in love with a girl and is told that he will get her if he rises from his bed at seven minutes past two every night for a month, gathers half a dozen flowers from a new-made grave in the local churchyard and places them in a spot where the girl will walk over them the following day, he does not get much chance to slacken in his desire and we all know that persistence can often work wonders.'

'Perhaps,' Richard agreed with mild cynicism. 'But would you have us believe that Simon is seeking the favour of a lady by wandering about in this lunatic get-up?'

'No, there is also the greater magic which is only practised by learned students of the Art who go through long courses of preparation and initiation, after which they understand not only that certain apparently inexplicable results are brought about by a given series of actions, but the actual reason why this should be so. Such people are powerful and dangerous in the extreme, and it is into the hands of one of these that our poor friend has fallen.'

Richard nodded, realising at last that the Duke was perfectly serious in his statement. 'This seems a most extraordinary affair,' he commented. 'I think you'd better start from the beginning and give us the whole story.'

'All right. Let's sit down. If you doubt any of the statements that I am about to make, Rex will guarantee the facts and vouch for my sanity.'

'I certainly will,' Rex agreed with a sombre smile.

De Richleau then told the Eatons all that had taken place

in the last forty-eight hours, and asked quite solemnly if they were prepared to receive Simon, Rex and himself under their roof in spite of the fact that it might involve some risk to themselves.

'Of course,' Marie Lou said at once. 'We would not dream of your going away. You must stay just as long as you like and until you are quite certain that Simon is absolutely out of danger.'

Richard, sceptical still, but devoted to his friends whatever their apparent folly, nodded his agreement as he slipped an arm through his wife's. 'Certainly you must stay. And,' he added generously without the shadow of a smile, 'tell us exactly how we can help you best.'

'It's awfully decent of you,' Simon hazarded with a ghostly flicker of his old wide-mouthed grin. 'But I'll never forgive myself if any harm comes to you from it.'

'Don't let's have that all over again,' Rex begged. 'We argued it long enough in the car on the way here, and De Richleau's assured you time and again that no harm will come to Richard and Marie Lou providing we take reasonable precautions.'

'That is so,' the Duke nodded. 'And your help will be invaluable. You see, Simon's resistance is practically nill owing to his having been under Mocata's influence for so long, and Rex and I are at a pretty low ebb after last night. We need every atom of vitality which we can get to protect him, and your coming fresh into the battle should turn the scale in our favour. What we should have done if you had thrown us out I can't think, because I know of no one else who wouldn't have considered us all to be raving lunatics.'

Richard laughed. 'My dear fellow, how can you even suggest such a thing? You would still be welcome here if you'd committed murder.'

'I may have to before long,' De Richleau commented soberly. 'The risk to myself is a bagatelle compared to the horrors which may overwhelm the world if Mocata succeeds in getting possession of the Talisman—but I won't involve you in that of course.'

'This Sabbat you saw . . .' Richard hazarded after a moment. 'Don't think I'm doubting your account of it, but isn't it just possible that your eyes deceived you in the darkness? I mean about the Satanic part. Everyone knows that Sabbats took place all over England in the sixteenth and seventeenth centuries. But it is generally accepted now that they were only an excuse for a bit of a blind and a sexual orgy. Country people had no motor bikes and buses to take them in to local cinemas then, and the Church frowned on all but the mildest forms of amusement, so the bad hats of the community used to sneak off to some quiet spot every now and again to give their repressed complexes an airing. Are you sure that it was not a revival of that sort of thing staged by a group of wealthy decadents?'

'Not on your life,' Rex declared with a sudden shiver. 'I've never been scared all that bad before and, believe you me, it was the real business.'

'What do you wish us to do, Greyeyes dear?' Marie Lou asked the Duke.

He hoisted himself slowly out of the chair into which he had sunk. 'I must drive to Oxford. An old Catholic priest whom I know lives there and I am going to try and persuade him to entrust me with a portion of the Blessed Host. If he will, that is the most perfect of all protections which we could have to keep with us through the night. In the meantime, I want the rest of you to look after Simon.' He smiled affectionately in Simon's direction. 'You must forgive me treating you like a child for the moment, my dear boy, but I don't want the others to let you out of their sight until I return.'

'That's all right,' Simon agreed cheerfully. 'But are you certain that I'm not—er—carrying harmful things about with me still?'

'Absolutely. The purification ceremonies which I practised on you last night have banished all traces of the evil. Our business now is to keep you free of it and get on Mocata's trail as quickly as we can.'

'Then I think I'll rest for a bit.' Simon glanced at Richard as he followed the Duke towards the door. 'The nap we had at the hotel in Amesbury after breakfast wasn't long enough to put me right—and afterwards perhaps you could lend me a decent suit of clothes?'

'Of course,' Richard smiled, 'Let's see Greyeyes off, then I'll make you comfortable upstairs.'

The whole party filed into the hall and, crowding about the low nail-studded oaken door, watched De Richleau, who promised to be back before dark, drive off. Then Richard, taking Simon by the arm, led him up the broad Jacobean stairway, while Marie Lou turned to Rex.

'What do you really think of all this?' she asked gravely, the usual merriment of her deep blue eyes clouded by a foreboding of coming trouble.

He stared down at her upturned heart-shaped face from his great height and answered soberly. 'We've struck a gateway of Hell all right, my dear, and I'm just worried out of my wits. De Richleau didn't give you the whole story. There's a girl in this that I'm—well—that I'm crazy about.'

'Rex!' Marie Lou laid her small strong hand on his arm. 'How awful for you. Come into my room and tell me everything.'

He followed her to her sitting-room and for half an hour poured into her sympathetic ears the strange tale of his three glimpses of Tanith at different times abroad, and then his unexpected meeting with her at Simon's party. Afterwards he related with more detail than the Duke had done their terrible experiences on Salisbury Plain and was just beginning his anxious speculation as to what could have happened to Tanith when Malin, the butler, softly opened the door.

'Someone is asking for you on the telephone, Mr. Van Ryn, sir.'

'For me!' Rex stood up and, excusing himself to Marie Lou, hurried out, wondering who in the world it could be since no one knew his whereabouts. He was soon enlightened. A lilting voice, which had a strong resemblance to that of Marlene Dietrich, came over the wire as he placed the receiver to his ear.

'Is that you, Rex? Oh, I am so glad I have found you. I must see you at once—quickly—without a moment's delay.'

'Tanith!' he exclaimed. 'How did you tumble to it that I was here?'

'Oh, never mind that! I will tell you when I see you. But hurry, please.'

'Where are you then?'

'At the village inn, no more than a mile from you. Do come at once. It is very urgent.'

For a second Rex hesitated, but only for a second. Simon would be safe enough in the care of Richard and Marie Lou, and Tanith's voice had all the urgency and agitation of extreme fear. Anxiety for her had been gnawing at his heart ever since he had heard of her crash the previous evening. He knew that he loved her now—loved her desperately.

'All right,' he answered, his voice shaking a little. 'I'll be right over.'

Running back across the hall, he explained breathlessly to Marie Lou what had happened.

'You must go of course,' she said evenly. 'But you'll be back before nightfall won't you, Rex?'

'Sure.' All his animation seemed suddenly to have returned to him as, with a quick grin, he hurried out, snatched up his hat and, leaving the house, set off at a long easy loping trot by the short cut across the meadows to the village.

Unnoticed by him, a short figure entered the drive just as he disappeared beyond the boundary of the garden. A few moments later the newcomer was in conversation with Malin. The butler knew that his master was upstairs sitting with his friend Mr. Aron while the latter rested, and had given orders that he was not to be disturbed, so leaving the visitor in the hall he crossed to Marie Lou's sitting-room.

'There is a gentleman to see you, madam,' he announced quietly. 'A Mr. Mocata.'

22

The Satanist

For a moment Marie Lou hesitated, her eyes round with surprise, staring at the butler. In the last hour she had heard so much about this strange and terrifying visitor, but it had not occurred to her for one instant that she might be called upon to face him in the flesh so soon.

Her first impulse was to send upstairs for Richard, but like many people who possess extremely small bodies, her brain was exceptionally quick. Rex and the Duke were both absent, and, if she sent for Richard, Simon would be left alone—the one thing that De Richleau had been so insistent should not be allowed to happen. True, she and Richard would have the principal enemy under observation themselves, but he had allies. It flashed upon her that this girl Tanith was one perhaps and had purposely decoyed Rex away to the inn. Mocata might have others already waiting to lure Simon out of the house while they were busy talking to him. Almost instantly her mind was made up. Richard must not leave Simon, so she would have to interview Mocata on her own.

'Show him in,' she told the butler evenly. 'But if I ring you are to come at once—immediately, you understand?'

'Certainly, madam.' Malin softly withdrew, while Marie Lou seated herself in an armchair with her back to the light and within easy reach of the bell-push.

Mocata was shown in, and she studied him curiously. He was dressed in a suit of grey tweeds and wore a black stock tie. His head, large, bald and shiny, reminded her of an enormous egg, and the several folds of his heavy chin protruded above his stiff collar.

'I do hope you'll forgive me, Mrs. Eaton,' he began in a voice that was musical and charming, 'for calling on you without any invitation. But you may perhaps have heard my name.'

She nodded slightly, carefully ignoring the hand which he half extended as she motioned him to the armchair on the opposite side of the fireplace. Marie Lou knew nothing of Esoteric Doctrines, but quite enough from the peasants' superstitions which had been rife in the little village where she had lived, an outcast of the Russian Revolution, to be aware that she must not touch this man, not offer him any form of refreshment while he was in her house.

The afternoon sunshine played full upon Mocata's pink, fleshy countenance as he went on. 'I thought perhaps that would be the case. Whether the facts have been rightly represented to you, I don't know, but Simon Aron is a very dear friend of mine, and during his recent illness I have been taking care of him.'

'I see,' she answered guardedly. 'Well, it was hardly put to me in that way, but what is the purpose of your visit?'

'I understand that Simon is with you now?'

'Yes,' she replied briefly, feeling that it was senseless to deny it, 'and his visit to us will continue for some little time.'

He smiled then, and with a little shock Marie Lou suddenly

170

caught herself thinking that he was really quite an attractive person. His strange light-coloured eyes showed a strong intelligence and, to her surprise, a glint of the most friendly humour, which almost suggested that he was about to conspire with her in some amusing undertaking. His lisping voice, too, was strangely pleasant and restful to listen to as he spoke again in perfect English periods, only a curious intonation of the vowel sounds indicating his French extraction.

'The country air would no doubt be excellent for him, and I am certain that nothing could be more charming for him than your hospitality. Unfortunately there are certain matters, of which you naturally know nothing, but which make it quite imperative that I should take him back to London tonight.'

'I am afraid that is quite impossible.'

'I see,' Mocata looked thoughtfully for a moment at his large elastic-sided boots. 'I feared that you might take this attitude to begin with, because I imagine our friend De Richleau has been filling the heads of your husband and yourself with the most preposterous nonsense. I don't propose to go into that now or his reason for it, but I do ask you to believe me, Mrs. Eaton, when I say that Simon will be in very considerable danger if you do not allow me to take him back into my care.'

'No danger will come to him as long as he is in my house,' said Marie Lou firmly.

'Ah, my dear young lady,' he sighed a little wistfully. 'I can hardly expect anyone like yourself to understand precisely what will happen to our poor Simon if he remains here, but his mental state has been unsatisfactory for some little time, and I alone can cure him of his lamentable condition. Chocolates!' he added suddenly and irrelevantly as his eyes rested upon a large box on a nearby table. 'You'll think me terribly rude, but may I? I simply adore chocolates.'

'I'm so sorry,' Marie Lou replied without the flicker of an eyelash, 'but that box is empty. Do go on with what you were saying about Simon.'

Mocata withdrew his hand, feeling himself unable to challenge her statement by opening the box to see, and Marie Lou found it difficult to repress a smile as he made a comically rueful face like some greedy schoolboy who has been disappointed of a slice of cake.

'Really!' he exclaimed. 'What a pity. May I put it in the

171

waste-paper basket for you then? To leave it about is such a terrible temptation for people like myself.' Before she could stop him he had reached out again and picked up the box, realising immediately by its weight that she had lied to him.

'No, please,' she put out her hand and almost snatched the box from his pudgy fingers. 'I gave it to my little girl to put her marbles in—we mustn't throw it away.' The box gave a faint rustle as she laid it down beside her, so she added swiftly: 'She puts each one in the little paper cups that the chocolates are packed in and arranges them in rows. She would be terribly distressed if they were upset.'

Mocata was not deceived by that ingenious fiction. He guessed at once her true reason for denying him the chocolates and was quick to realise that in this lovely young woman, who stood no taller than a well-grown child, he was up against a far cleverer antagonist than he had at first supposed. However, he was amply satisfied with the progress he had made so far, sensing that her first antagonism had already given way to a guarded interest. He must talk to her a little, his eyes and voice would do the rest. For a moment they stared at each other in silence. Then he opened his attack in a new direction.

'Mrs. Eaton, it is quite obvious to me that you distrust me and, after what your friends have told you, I am not surprised. But your intelligence emboldens me to think that I am likely to serve my purpose better by putting my cards on the table than by beating about the bush.'

'It will make no difference what you do,' said Marie Lou quietly.

He ignored the remark and went on in his low, slightly lisping voice. 'I do not propose to discuss with you the rights or wrongs of practising the Magic Art. I will confine myself to saying that I am a practitioner of some experience and Simon, who has interested himself in these things for the past few months, shows great promise of one day achieving considerable powers. Monsieur De Richleau has probably led you to suppose that I am a most evil person. But in fairness to myself I must protest that such a view of me is quite untrue. In magic, there is neither good nor evil. It is only the science of causing change to occur by means of will. The rather sinister reputation attaching to it is easily accounted for by the fact that it had to be practised in secret for many centuries owing to the ban

172

placed upon it by the Church. Anything which is done in secret naturally begets a reputation for mystery and, since it dare not face the light of day, the reverse of good. Few people understand anything of these mysteries, and I can hardly assume that you have more than vague impressions gathered from casual reading; but at least I imagine you will have heard that genuine adepts in the secret Art have the power to call certain entities, which are not understood or admitted by the profane, into actual being.

'Now these are perfectly harmless as long as they are under the control of the practitioner, just as a qualified electrician stands no risk in adjusting a powerful electric battery from which a child, who played foolishly with it, might receive a serious shock or even death. This analogy applies to the work Simon and I are engaged upon. We have called a certain entity into being just as workers in another sphere might have constructed an electrical machine. It needs both of us to operate this thing with skill and safety, but if I am to be left to handle it alone, the forces which we have engendered will undoubtedly escape and do the very gravest harm both to Simon and myself. Have I made the position clear?'

'Yes,' murmured Marie Lou. During that long explanatory speech he had been regarding her with a steady stare, and as she listened to his quiet, cultured voice expressing what seemed such obvious truths, she felt her whole reaction to his personality changing. It suddenly seemed to her absurd that this nice, charming gentleman in the neat grey suit could be dangerous to anyone. His face seemed to have lost its puffy appearance even while he was speaking, and now her eyes beheld it as only hairless, pink and clean like that of some elderly divine.

'I am so glad,' he went on in his even, silky tone. 'I felt quite sure that if you allowed me a few moments I could clear up this misunderstanding which has only arisen through the over-eagerness of your old friend the Duke, and that charming young American, to protect Simon from some purely imaginary danger. If I had only had the opportunity to explain to them personally I am quite convinced that I should have been able to save them a great deal of worry, but I only met them for a few moments one evening at Simon's house. It is a charming little place that, and he very kindly permits me to share it with him while I am in England. If you are in London during the next few weeks, I do hope that you will come and see us there. We both know without asking that Simon would be delighted, and it would give me the very greatest pleasure to show you my collection of perfumes, which I always take with me when I travel.

'As a matter of fact, I am rather an expert in the art of blending perfumes, and quite a number of my women friends have allowed me to make a special scent for them. It is a delicate art, and interesting, because each woman should have her own perfume made to conform to her aura and personality. You have an outstanding individuality, Mrs. Eaton, and it would be a very great pleasure if you would allow me some time to see if I could not compound something really distinctive in that way for you.'

'It sounds most interesting,' Marie Lou's voice was low and Mocata's eyes still held hers. Really, she felt, despite his bulk, he was a most attractive person, and she had been quite stupid to be a little frightened of him when he first entered the room. The May sunshine came in gently-moving shafts through the foliage of a tree outside the window, so that the dappled light played upon his face, and it was that, she thought, which gave her the illusion that his unblinking eyes were larger than when she had first looked into them.

'When will the Duke be back?' he asked softly. 'Unfortunately, my visit today must be a brief one, but I should so much have liked to talk this matter over quietly with him before I go.'

'I don't know,' Marie Lou found herself answering. 'But I'm afraid he won't be back before six.'

'And our American friend—the young giant,' he prompted her.

'I've no idea. He has gone down to the village.'

'I see. What a pity, but of course your husband is here entertaining Simon, is he not?'

'Yes, they are upstairs together.'

'Well, presently I should like to explain to your husband, just as I have to you, how very important it is that I should take Simon back with me tonight, but I wonder first if I might beg a glass of water. Walking from the village has given me quite a thirst.'

'Of course,' Marie Lou rose to her feet automatically and

pressed the bell. 'Wouldn't you prefer a cup of tea or a glass of wine and some biscuits?' she added, completely now under the strange influence that radiated from him.

'You are most kind, but just a glass of water and a biscuit if I may.'

Malin already stood in the doorway and Marie Lou gave orders for these slender refreshments. Then she sat down again, and Mocata's talk flowed on easily and glibly, while her ears became more and more attuned to that faint musical lisping intonation.

The butler appeared with water and biscuits on a tray and set them down beside Mocata, but for the moment he took no notice of it. Instead he looked again at Marie Lou, and said: 'I do hope you'll forgive me asking, but have you recently been ill? You are looking as though you were terribly run down and very, very tired.'

'No,' said Marie Lou slowly. 'I haven't been ill.' But at that moment her limbs seemed to relax where she was sitting and her heavy eyelids weighed upon her eyes. For some unaccountable reason, she felt an intense longing to shut them altogether and fall asleep.

Mocata watched her with a faint smile curving his full mouth. He had her under his dominance now and knew it. Another moment and she would be asleep. It would be easy to carry her into the next room and leave her there, ring for the servant, ask him to find his master and when Richard arrived, say that she had gone out into the garden to find him. Then another of those quiet little talks which he knew so well how to handle, even when people were openly antagonistic to him to begin with, and the master of the house would also pass into a quiet, untroubled sleep. Then he would simply call Simon by his will and they would leave the house together.

Marie Lou's eyes flickered and shut. With a shake of her head she jerked them open again. 'I'm so sorry,' she said sleepily. 'But I am tired, most awfully tired. What was it that you were talking about?'

Mocata's eyes seemed enormous to her now, as they held her own with a solemn, dreamy look. 'We shall not talk any more,' he said. 'You will sleep, and at four o'clock on the afternoon of 7th May, you will call on me at Simon's house in St. John's Wood.'

175

Marie Lou's heavy lashes fell on her rounded cheeks again, but next second her eyes were wide open, for the door was flung back and Fleur came scampering into the room.

'Darling, what is it?' Marie Lou struggled wide awake and Mocata snapped his plump fingers with a little angry, disappointed gesture. The sudden entrance of the child had broken the current of delicate vibrations.

'Mummy—mummy,' Fleur panted. 'Daddy-sent-me-to-find-you. We'se playing hosses in the garden, an' Uncle Simon says he's a dwagon, an' not a hoss at all. Daddy says you're to come and tell him diffwent.'

'So this is your little daughter? What a lovely child,' Mocata said amiably, stretching out a hand to Fleur. 'Come here, my . . .'

But Marie Lou cut short his sentence as full realisation of the danger to which she had exposed herself flooded her mind. 'Don't you touch her!' she cried, snatching up the child with blazing eyes. 'Don't you dare!'

'Really, Mrs. Eaton,' he raised his eyebrows in mild protest. 'Surely you cannot think that I meant to hurt the child? I thought too, that we were beginning to understand each other so well.'

'You beast,' Marie Lou cried angrily as she jabbed her finger on the bell. 'You tried to hypnotise me.'

'What nonsense,' he smiled good-humouredly. 'You were a little tired, but I fear I bored you rather with a long dissertation upon things which can hardly interest a woman so young and charming as yourself. It was most stupid of me, and I hardly wonder that you nearly fell asleep.'

As Malin arrived on the scene she thrust Fleur into the astonished butler's arms and gasped: 'Fetch Mr. Eaton—he's in the garden— quickly—at once.'

The butler hurried off with Fleur and Mocata turned on her. His eyes had gone cold and steely. 'It is vital that I should at least see Simon before I leave this house.'

'You shan't,' she stormed. 'You had better go before my husband comes. D'you hear?' Then she found herself looking at him again, and quickly jerked her head away so that she should not see his eyes, yet she caught his gesture as he stooped to pick up the glass of water from the table.

Furious now at the way she had been tricked into ordering it for him, and determining that he should not drink, she sprang forward and, before he could stop her, dashed the little table to the ground. The plate caught the carafe as it fell and smashed it into a dozen pieces, the biscuits scattered and the water spread in a shallow, widening lake upon the carpet. Mocata swung round with an angry snarl. This small, sensuous, catlike creature had cheated him at the last, and the placid, kindly expression of his face changed to one of hideous demoniacal fury. His eyes, muddled now with all the foulness of his true nature, stripped and flayed her, threatening a thousand unspeakable abominations in their unwinking stare as she faced him across the fallen table.

Suddenly, with a fresh access of terror, Marie Lou cowered back, bringing up her hands to shield her face from those revolting eyeballs. Then a quick voice in the doorway exclaimed: 'Hello! What is all this?'

'Richard,' she gasped. 'Richard, it's Mocata! I saw him because I thought you'd better stay with Simon, but he tried to hypnotise me. Have him thrown out. Oh, have him thrown out.'

The muscles in Richard's lean face tightened as he caught the look of terror in his wife's eyes and thrusting her aside he took a quick step towards Mocata. 'If you weren't twice my age and in my house, I'd smash your face in,' he said savagely. 'And that won't stop me either unless you get out thundering quick.'

With almost incredible swiftness Mocata had his anger under control. His face was benign and smiling once more, as he shrugged, showing no trace of panic. 'I'm afraid your wife is a little upset,' he said mildly. 'It is this spring weather, and while we were talking together, she nearly fell asleep. Having heard all sorts of extraordinary things about me from your friends, she scared herself into thinking that I tried to hypnotise her. I apologise profoundly for having caused her one moment's distress.'

'I don't believe one word of that,' replied Richard. 'Now kindly leave the house.'

Mocata shrugged again. 'You are being very unreasonable, Mr. Eaton. I called this afternoon in order to take Simon Aron back to London.'

'Well, you're not going to.'

'Please,' Mocata held up his protesting hand. 'Hear me for one moment. The whole situation has been most gravely misrepresented to you, as I explained to your wife, and if she hadn't suddenly started to imagine things we should be discussing it quite amicably now. In fact, I even asked her to send for you, as she will tell you herself.'

'It was a trick,' cried Marie Lou angrily. 'Don't look at his eyes, Richard, and for God's sake turn him out!'

'You hear,' Richard's voice held a threatening note and his face was white. 'You had better go—before I lose my temper.'

'It's a pity that you are so pig-headed, my young friend,' Mocata snapped icily. 'By retaining Simon here, you are bringing extreme peril both on him and on yourself. But since you refuse to be reasonable and let me take him with me, let me at least have five minutes' conversation with him alone.'

'Not five seconds,' Richard stood aside from the door and motioned through it for Mocata to pass into the hall.

'All right! If that is your final word!' Mocata drew himself up. He seemed to grow in size and strength even as he stood there. A terrible force and energy suddenly began to shake his obese body. They felt it radiating from him as his words came low and clear like the whispering splash of death-cold drops falling from icicles upon a frozen lake.

'Then I will send the Messenger to your house tonight and he shall take Simon from you alive—or dead!'

'Get out,' gritted Richard between his teeth. 'Damn you—get out!'

Without another word Mocata left them. Marie Lou crossed herself, and with Richard's arm about her shoulder they followed him to the door.

He did not turn or once look back, but plodded heavily, a very ordinary figure now, down the long, sunlit drive.

Richard suddenly felt Marie Lou's small body tremble against him, and with a little cry of fright she buried her head on his shoulder. 'Oh, darling,' she wailed. 'I'm frightened of that man—frightened. Did you see?'

'See what, my sweet?' he asked, a little puzzled.

'Why!' sobbed Marie Lou. 'He is walking in the sunshine—but he has no shadow!'

23

The Pride of Peacocks

The inn which served the village near Cardinals Folly was almost as old as the house. At one period it had been a hostelry of some importance, but the changing system of highways in the eighteenth century had left it denuded of the coaching traffic and doomed from then on to cater only for the modest wants of the small local population. It had been added to and altered many times; for one long period falling almost wholly into disrepair, since its revenue was insufficient for its upkeep, and so it had remained until a few years earlier upon the retirement of Mr. Jeremiah Wilkes, the ex-valet of a wealthy peer who lived not far distant.

Only the fact that Mr. Wilkes suffered from chronic sciatica, which rendered it impossible for him to travel any more with his old master, had made his retirement necessary, and through those long years of packing just the right garments that his lordship might need for Cowes, Scotland or the French Riviera and exercising his incomparable facility for obtaining the most comfortable seats upon trains which were already full, he had always had it in the back of his mind that he would like to be the proprietor of a gentlemanly 'house.'

When the question of his retirement had been discussed, and Jeremiah had named the ambition of his old age, his master had most generously suggested the purchase and restoration of the old inn, but voiced his doubts of Jeremiah's ability to run it at a profit; stating that capital was very necessary to the success of any business, and adding in his innocence that he did not feel Jeremiah could have saved a sufficient sum despite the long period in his employment.

In this, of course, his lordship was entirely wrong. Jeremiah's wage might have been a modest one but, while protecting his master from many generations of minor thieves, he had gathered in the time-honoured perquisites which were his due and, since he had stoutly resisted the efforts of his fellow servants to interest him in 'the horses,' he owned investments in property which would have considerably amazed his master.

Mr. Wilkes, therefore, had modestly stated that he thought he might manage providing that his lordship would be good enough to send him such friends or their retainers as could not be accommodated at the Court when shooting parties and such like were in progress. This having been arranged satisfactorily, Mr. Wilkes underwent the metamorphosis from a gentleman's gentleman to host of 'The Pride of Peacocks.'

Very soon the old inn began to thrive again; quietly, of course, since it was no road-house for noisy motorists. But it became well known among a certain select few who enjoyed a peaceful weekend in lovely scenery, and Mr. Wilkes' admirable attention to these, together with his wife's considerable knowledge of the culinary art, never caused them to question their Monday morning bill.

Jeremiah had further added to the attraction of the place by stocking a cellar with variety and taste from his lordship's London wine merchant on terms extremely advantageous to himself, and moreover to the added well-being of the neighbourhood. The hideous and childish tyranny of licensing hours never affected him in the least for the simple reason that all his customers were personal friends, including, of course, the magistrates upon the local bench, and had some officious policeman from the town ever questioned the fact that gentlemen were to be found there quite frequently in the middle of the afternoon taking a little modest refreshment, they would have quailed under the astonished and supercilious glance of the good Mr. Wilkes, together with the freezing statement that this was no monetary transaction, but the gentlemen concerned were doing him the honour to give him their opinion upon his latest purchase in the way of port.

In short, it will be gathered that this ancient hostelry could provide all the comfort which any reasonable person might demand, and was something a little out of the ordinary for a village inn. Rex, of course, knew the place well from his previous visits to Cardinals Folly and, a little out of breath from the pace at which he had come, hurried into the low, comfortably furnished lounge, the old oak beams of which almost came down to his head.

Tanith was there alone. Immediately she saw him she jumped up from her chair and ran to meet him, gripping both his hands in hers with a strength surprising for her slender fingers.

180

She was pale and weary. Her green linen dress was stained and mired from her terrible journey on the previous night, although obviously she had done her best to tidy herself. Her eyes were shadowed from strain and lack of sleep, seeming unnaturally large, and she trembled slightly as she clutched at him.

'Oh, thank God you've come!' she cried.

'But how did you know I was at Cardinals Folly?' he asked her quickly.

'My dear,' she sank down in the chair again, drawing her hand wearily across her eyes. 'I am terribly sorry about last night. I think I was mad when I stole your car and tried to get to the Sabbat. I crashed of course, but I expect you will have heard about that—and then I did the last five miles on foot.'

'Good God! Do you mean to say you got there after all?'

She nodded and told him of that nightmare walk from Easterton to the Satanic Festival. As she came to the part in her story where, against her will, she had been drawn down into the valley, her eyes once more expressed the hideous terror which she had felt.

'I could not help myself,' she said. 'I tried to resist with all my mind but my feet simply moved against my will. Then, for a moment, I thought that the heavens had opened and an angry God had suddenly decided to strike those blasphemous people dead. There was a noise like thunder and two giant eyes like those of some nightmare monster seemed to leap out of the darkness right at me. I screamed, I think, and jumped aside. I remember falling and springing up again. The power that had held my feet seemed to have been suddenly released and I fled up the hill in absolute panic. When I got to the top I tripped over something and then I must have fainted.'

Rex smiled. 'That was us in the car,' he said. 'But how did you know where to find me?'

'It was not very difficult,' she told him. 'When I came to, I was lying on the grass and there wasn't a sound to show that there was a living soul within miles of me. I started off at a run without the faintest idea where I was going—my only thought being to get away from that terrible valley. Then when I was absolutely exhausted I fell again, and I must have been so done in that I slept for a little in a ditch.

'When I woke up, it was morning and I found that I was quite near a main road. I limped along it not knowing what I should come to and then I saw houses and a straggling street and, after a little, I discovered that I had walked into Devizes.

'I went into the centre of the town and was about to go into an hotel when I realised that I had no money; but I had a brooch, so I found a jeweller's and sold it to them—or rather, they agreed to advance me twenty pounds, because I didn't want to part with it and it must be worth at least a hundred. An awfully nice old man there agreed to keep it as security until I could send him the money on from London. Then I did go to the hotel, took a room and tried to think things over.

'Such an extraordinary lot seemed to have happened since you took me off in your car from Claridges yesterday that at first I could not get things straight at all, but one thing stood out absolutely clearly. Whether it was you or the vision of my mother, I don't know, but my whole outlook had changed completely. How I could ever have allowed myself to listen to Madame D'Urfé and do the things I've done I just can't think. But I know now that I've been in the most awful danger, and that I must try and get free of Mocata somehow. Anyone would think me mad, and possibly I am, to come to you like this when I hardly know you, but the whole thing has been absolutely outside all ordinary experiences. I am terribly alone, Rex, and you are the only person in the world that I can turn to.'

She sank back in her chair almost exhausted with the effort of endeavouring to impress him with her feelings, but he leant forward and, taking one of her hands in his great leg-of-mutton fist, squeezed it gently.

'There, there, my sweet.' Speaking from his heart he used the endearment quite naturally and unconsciously. 'You did the right thing every time. Don't you worry any more. Nobody is going to hurt a hair of your head now you've got here safely. But how in the world did you do it?'

Her eyes opened again and she smiled faintly. 'My only hope was to throw myself on your protection, so I had to find you somehow and that part wasn't difficult. All systems of divination are merely so many methods of obscuring the outer vision, in order that the inner may become clear. Tea-leaves, crystals, melting wax, lees of wine, cards, water, entrails, birds, sieve-turning, sand and all the rest.

'I wanted sleep terribly when I got to that hotel bedroom, but I knew that I mustn't allow myself to, so I took some

182

paper from the lounge, and borrowed a pencil. Then I threw myself into a trance with the paper before me and the pencil in my hand. When I looked at it again I had quite enough information scribbled down to enable me to follow you here.'

Rex accepted this amazing explanation quite calmly. Had he been told such a thing a few days before he would have considered it fantastic, but now it never even occurred to him that it was in any way extraordinary that a woman desiring to know his whereabouts should throw herself into a trance and employ automatic writing.

She glanced at the old grandfather clock which stood ticking away in a corner of the low-raftered room. Half an hour had sped by already and he was feeling guilty now at having left Simon. He would never be able to forgive himself if, in his absence, any harm befell his friend. Now that he knew Tanith was safe he must get back to Cardinals Folly, so he announced abruptly: 'I'm mighty sorry, but I've got Simon to look after so I can't stay here much longer.'

'Oh, Rex,' her eyes held his imploringly. 'You must not unless you take me with you. If you leave me alone, Mocata will be certain to get me.'

For a moment Rex hesitated miserably, wrestling with the quandary that faced him. If Tanith was telling the truth, he couldn't possibly leave her to be drawn back by that terrible power of evil. But was she? So far she had been Mocata's puppet. How much truth was there in this pretended change of heart? Had Mocata planted her there in order to lure him deliberately away from Simon's side?

It occurred to him that he might take her back with him to Cardinals Folly, for if she was speaking the truth she was in the same case as Simon. They could keep the two of them together and concentrate their forces against the black magician. But he dismissed the idea almost as soon as it entered his mind. To do so would be playing Mocata's game with a vengeance. If Tanith were acting consciously or unconsciously under his influence, God alone knew what powers she might possess to aid her master once they accepted her as a friend in their midst. If he took her there it would be like introducing one of the enemy into a beleaguered fortress.

'What are you afraid might happen if I leave you?' he asked suddenly.

'You can't—you mustn't,' her eyes pleaded with him. 'Not only for my own sake, but your friends' as well. Mocata has a hundred means of knowing where Simon is and where I am too. He may arrive here at any moment. It's no good pretending Rex. I know beyond any question that I cannot resist him and he'll work through me, however much my will is set against it. He's told me a dozen times that he has never met a woman who is such a successful medium for him as myself. So you can be certain that he is on his way here now.'

'What d'you think he'll do when he turns up?'

'He will throw me into a trance and call Simon to him. Then if Simon fails to come Mocata may curse him through me.'

Rex shrugged. 'Don't worry. De Richleau's a wily old bird. He'll turn the curse aside some way.'

'But you don't seem to understand,' she sobbed. 'If a curse is sent out it must lodge somewhere, and if it fails to reach its objective because there is an equally strong influence working against it, the vibrations recoil and impinge upon the sender.'

'Steady now.' He took her hands and tried to soothe her. 'If that is so I guess we couldn't find a better way to tickle up Mocata.'

'No—no!! He never does things himself—at least I have never known him to—just in case he fails, because then he would have to pay the penalty. Instead, he uses other people —hypnotises them and makes them throw out the thought or the wish. That is what he will do to me. If he succeeds, you will no longer be able to protect Simon, and if he fails, it is I who will pay the price. That is why you've just got to stay with me and prevent him using me as his instrument.'

'Holy smoke! Then we're in a proper jam!' Rex's brain was working swiftly. If she were telling the truth, she was in real danger. If not, at least Simon still had Richard and Marie Lou to take care of him until the Duke's return.

All his chivalry and his love for her which seemed to have blossomed overnight welled up and told him that he must chance her honesty and remain there to protect her. 'All right, I'll stay,' he said after a moment.

'Oh, thank God!' she sighed. 'Thank God!'

'But tell me,' he went on, 'just why is it you're such a king-pin medium to this man? What about old Madame D'Urfé and the rest? Can't he do his stuff through them?'

Tanith looked at him through tear-dimmed eyes and shook her head. 'Not in the same way. You see there is rather an unusual link between us. My number is twenty and so is his.'

Rex frowned. 'What exactly do you mean by that?' he asked in a puzzled voice.

'I mean our astrological number,' she replied quietly. 'Give me a piece of paper, and I will show you.'

Rex handed her a few sheets from a nearby table and a pencil from his waistcoat pocket, then she quickly drew out a list of the numerical values to the letters of the alphabet: —

A=1	K=2	S=3
B=2	L=3	T=4
C=3	M=4	U=6
D=4	N=5	V=6
E=5	O=7	W=6
F=5	P=8	X=5
G=3	Q=1	Y=1
H=5	R=2	Z=7
I or J=1		

'There!' she went on. 'By substituting numbers for letters in anyone's name and adding them up you get their occult number which indicates the planet that influences them most in all spiritual affairs. It must be the name by which they are most generally known—even if it is a pet name. Now look!'

M=4	T=4
O=7	A=1
C=3	N=5
A=1	I=1
T=4	T=4
A=1	H=5
──	──
20 2+0=2	20 2+0=2

'You see how closely our vibrations are attuned. Two is the value of the Moon, to which both he and I are subject, and any names having a total numerical value which reduce by progresssive additions to two, such as eleven or twenty-nine or thirty-eight or forty-seven, would give us some affinity, but that

185

they actually add up to the same *compound* number shows that we are attuned to a very remarkable degree. That is why I have proved such an exceptionally good medium for him to work through.'

'But you are utterly different from him,' Rex protested.

'Of course,' she nodded gravely. 'One's birth date gives the *material* number, which is generally that of another planet and modifies the influence of the *spiritual* number considerably. As it happens mine is May 2nd—again a two you see, so I am an almost pure type. Moon people are intensely imaginative, artistic, romantic, gentle by nature and not very strong physically. They are rather over-sensitive and lacking in self-confidence, unsettled too, and liable to be continually changing their plans, but most of them, of course, have some balancing factor. Mocata gets all his imaginative and psychic qualities from the Moon, but his birthday is April 24th which adds up to six, and six being the number of Venus, he is very strongly influenced by that planet. Venus people are extremely magnetic. They attract others easily and are usually loved and worshipped by those under them, but very often they are obstinate and unyielding. It is that in his nature which balances the weakness of the Moon and makes him so determined in carrying out his plans.'

'What do I come under?' Rex asked with sudden curiosity. 'My names are so short that I'm generally known by all three.'

Again Tanith took the paper and quickly worked out the equivalent of his name.

$$
\begin{aligned}
R &= 2 \\
E &= 5 \\
X &= 5 \\
\hline
&= 12 \\
V &= 6 \\
A &= 1 \\
N &= 5 \\
\hline
&= 12 \\
R &= 2 \\
Y &= 1 \\
N &= 5 \\
\hline
&= 8
\end{aligned}
$$

32 and 3+2=5

She looked at him sharply. 'Yes, I am not surprised. Five is a fortunate and magic number which comes under Mercury. Such people are versatile and mercurial, quick in thought and decisions, impulsive in action and detest plodding work. They make friends easily with every type and have a wonderful elasticity of character which can recover at once from any setback. Even though I do not know you well, I am certain that all this is true of you. I expect you are a born speculator as well and every type of risk attracts you.'

'That certainly is so,' Rex grinned as she went on thoughtfully: 'But I should have thought that there was a good bit of the Sun about you because you have such strong individuality and you are so definite in your views.'

'I was born on the 19th of August if that gives you a line.'

She smiled. 'Yes, 19 is 1+9 which equals ten and 1+0 equals 1, the number of the Sun. So I was right, and it is that part of you which I think attracts me so much. Sun and Moon people always get on well together.'

'I don't know anything about that,' Rex said softly. 'But I'm dead sure I could never see too much of you.'

She lifted her eyes from his quickly as though almost in fright and to break the pause that followed he asked: 'What number is Simon associated with?'

'He was born under Saturn as we know only too well, and his occult number is certain to be the Saturnian eight,' Tanith replied promptly, scribbling the name and numbers on the paper.

$$
\begin{array}{l}
S=3 \\
I=1 \\
M=4 \\
O=7 \\
N=5 \\
\overline{}=20 \\
A=1 \\
R=2 \\
O=7 \\
N=5 \\
\overline{}=15 \\
\end{array}
$$

35 and 3+5=8

'By Jove! That's queer,' Rex murmured as he saw the name worked out quite simple to the number she had predicted.

'He is a typical number eight person too,' she went on. 'They have deep, intense natures and are often lonely at heart because they are frequently misunderstood. Sometimes they play a most important part on life's stage and nearly always a fatalistic one. They are almost fanatically loyal to persons they are fond of or causes they take up, and carry things through regardless of making enemies. It is not a fortunate number to be born under as a rule, and such people usually become great successes or great failures.'

Rex drew the paper towards him, and taking the pencil from her began to work out for himself the numerical symbols of De Richleau, Richard Eaton and Marie Lou.

$$R=2$$
$$I=1$$

$$D=4 \qquad C=3$$
$$E=5 \qquad H=5$$
$$\overline{}=9 \qquad A=1 \qquad M=4$$
$$R=2 \qquad A=1$$
$$R=2 \qquad D=4 \qquad R=2$$
$$I=1 \qquad \overline{}=18 \qquad I=1$$
$$C=3 \qquad E=5$$
$$H=5 \qquad \overline{}=13$$
$$L=3 \qquad E=5$$
$$E=5 \qquad A=1$$
$$A=1 \qquad T=4 \qquad L=3$$
$$U=6 \qquad O=7 \qquad O=7$$
$$\overline{}=26 \qquad N=5 \qquad U=6$$
$$\overline{}=22 \qquad \overline{}=16$$

$$35=8 \qquad\qquad 40=4 \qquad\qquad 29=11=2$$

'This is amazing,' Tanith exclaimed when he had finished. 'The Duke not only comes under the eight like Simon, but their compound number—thirty-five—is the same as well. He should have immence influence with Simon through that affinity, just as Mocata has over me, and the nine in his name gives him the additional qualities of the born leader, independence, success, courage and determination. If anyone in the world can save your friend, that extraordinary combination of

188

strength and sympathy will enable De Richleau to do so.'

'But d'you see that the names Richleau and Ryn boil down to eight as well, linking us both with Simon. That's strange, isn't it?'

'Not altogether. Any numerologist who knew of your devotion to each other would expect to find some such affinity in your numbers. You will see, too, that your other friend, Richard Eaton, is a four person, which accounts for his sympathy towards you. The eight is formed by two halves or circles and, four being the half of eight, persons with those numbers will always incline towards each other. Then his wife, like myself, is a two which is again linked to all four of you because it is divisible into eight.'

Rex nodded. 'It's the strangest mystery I've met up with in the whale of a while. There isn't a single odd number in the whole series, but tell me, would this combination of eights be a good thing d'you reckon—or no?'

'It is very, very potent,' she said slowly. '888 is the number given to Our Lord by students of Occultism in his aspect as the Redeemer. Add them together and you get twenty-four. $2+4=6$ which is the number of Venus, the representative of Love. That is the complete opposite of 666 which Revelations give as the number of the Beast. The three sixes add to eighteen, and $1+8=9$, the symbol of Mars—De Richleau's secondary quality which makes him a great leader and fighter, but in its pure state represents Destruction, Force and War.'

At the mention of War, Rex's whole mind was jerked from the quiet, comfortable, old-fashioned inn parlour to a mental picture of De Richleau as he had stood only a few hours before with the light of dawn breaking over Stonehenge. He saw again the Duke's grey face and unnaturally bright eyes as he spoke of the Talisman of Set; that terrible gateway out of Hell through which, if Mocata found it, those dread four horsemen would come riding, invisible but all-powerful, to poison the thoughts of peace-loving people and manipulate unscrupulous statesmen, influencing them to plunge Europe into fresh calamity.

Not only had they to fight Mocata for Simon's safety and Tanith's as well but, murder though it might be to people lacking in understanding, they had to kill him even if they were forced to sacrifice themselves.

189

With sudden clarity Rex saw that Tanith's appeal for protection offered a golden opportunity to carry the war into the enemy's camp. She was so certain that Mocata would appear to claim her, and De Richleau had stated positively that while daylight lasted the Satanist was no more powerful than any other thug.

'Why,' Rex thought, with a quick tightening of his great muscles, 'should he not seize Mocata by force when he arrived; then send for the Duke to decide what they should do with him.'

Only one difficulty seemed to stand in the way. He could hardly attack a visitor and hold him prisoner in 'The Pride of Peacocks.' Mr. Wilkes might object to that. But apparently Mocata could find Tanith with equal ease wherever she was, so she must be got out of the inn to some place where the business could be done without interference.

For a moment the thought of Cardinals Folly entered his mind again, but if he once took Tanith there, they could hardly turn her out later on, and she might become a highly dangerous focus in the coming night; besides, Mocata might not care to risk a visit to the house in daylight with the odds so heavily against him, and that would ruin the whole plan. Then he remembered the woods at the bottom of the garden behind the inn. If he took Tanith there and Mocata did turn up he would have a perfectly free hand in dealing with him. He glanced across at Tanith and suggested casually: 'What about a little stroll?'

She shook her fair head, and lay back with half-closed eyes in the arm-chair. 'I would love to, but I am so terribly tired. I had no proper sleep you know last night.'

He nodded. 'We didn't get much either. We were sitting around Stonehenge the best part of the time till dawn. After that we went into Amesbury where the Duke took a room. The people there must have thought us a queer party—one room for three people and beds being specially shifted into it at half-past seven in the morning, but he was insistent that we shouldn't leave Simon for a second. So we had about four hours' shut-eye on those three beds, all tied together by our wrists and ankles; but it's a glorious afternoon and the woods round here are just lovely now it's May.'

'If you like.' She rose sleepily. 'I dare not go to sleep in any

190

case. You mustn't let me until to-morrow morning. After midnight it will be May 2nd, the mystic two again you see, and my birthday. So during the dark hours tonight I shall be passing into my fatal day. It may be good or evil, but in such circumstances it is almost certain to bring some crisis in my life, and I'm afraid, Rex, terribly afraid.'

He drew her arm protectively through his and led her out through the back door into the pleasant garden which boasted two large, gay archery targets, a pastime that Jeremiah Wilkes had seen fit to institute for the amusement of the local gentry, deriving considerable profit therefrom when they bet each other numerous rounds of drinks upon their prowess with the six-foot bow.

A deep border of dark wallflowers sent out their heady scent at the farther end of the lawn and beyond them the garden opened on to a natural wooded glade. A small stream marked the boundary of Mr. Wilkes' domain and when they reached it, Rex passed his arm round Tanith's body, lifted her before she could protest, and with one spring of his long legs cleared the brook. She did not struggle from his grasp, but looked up at him curiously as she lay placid in his arms.

'You must be very strong,' she said. 'Most men can lift a woman, but it can't be easy to jump a five-foot brook with one.'

'I'm strong enough,' he smiled into her face, not attempting to put her down. 'Strong enough for both of us. You needn't worry.' Then, still carrying her in his arms, he walked on into the depths of the wood until the fresh, green beech trees hid them from the windows of the inn.

'You will get awfully tired,' she said lazily.

'Not me,' he declared, shaking his head. 'You may be tall, but you're only a featherweight. I could carry you a mile if I wanted, and it wouldn't hurt me any.'

'You needn't,' she smiled up at him. 'You can put me down now and we'll sit under the trees. It's lovely here. You were quite right—much nicer than the inn.'

He laid her down very gently on a sloping bank, but instead of rising, knelt above her with one arm still about her shoulders and looked down into her eyes. 'You love me,' he said suddenly. 'Don't you?'

'Yes,' she confessed with troubled shadows brooding in her

golden eyes. 'I do. But you mustn't love me, Rex. You know what I told you yesterday. I'm going to die. I'm going to die soon—before the year is out.'

'You're not,' he said, almost fiercely. 'We'll break this devil Mocata—De Richleau will, I'm certain.'

'But, my dear, it's nothing to do with him,' she protested sadly. 'It's just Fate, and you haven't known me long, so it's not too late yet for you to keep a hold on yourself. You mustn't love me, because if you do, it will make you terribly unhappy when I die.'

'You're not going to die,' he repeated, and then he laughed suddenly, boyishly, all his mercurial nature rising to dispel such gloomy thoughts. 'If we both die tomorrow,' he said suddenly, 'we've still got today, and I love you, Tanith. That's all there is to it.'

Her arms crept up about his neck and with sudden strength she kissed him on his mouth.

He grabbed her then, his lips seeking hers again and again, while he muttered little phrases of endearment, pouring out all the agony of anxiety that he had felt for her during the past night and the long run from Amesbury in the morning. She clung to him, laughing a little hysterically although she was not far from tears. This strange new happiness was overwhelming to her, flooding her whole being now with a desperate desire to live; to put behind her those nightmare dreams from which she had woken shuddering in the past months at visions of herself torn and bleeding, the victim of some horrible railway accident, or trapped upon the top storey of a blazing building with no alternative but to leap into the street below. For a moment it almost seemed to her that no real foundation existed for the dread which had haunted her since childhood. She was young, healthy and full of life. Why should she not enjoy to the full all the normal pleasures of life with this strong, merry-eyed man who had come so suddenly into her existence.

Again and again he assured her that all those thoughts of fatality being certain to overtake her were absurd. He told her that once she was out of Europe she would see things differently; the menace of the old superstition-ridden countries would drop away and that, in his lovely old home in the southern states, they would be able to laugh at Fate together.

Tanith did not really believe him. Her habit of mind had

grown so strongly upon her; but she could not bring herself to argue against his happy auguries, or spoil those moments of glorious delight as they both confessed their passion for each other.

As he held her in his arms a marvellous languor began to steal through all her limbs. 'Rex,' she said softly. 'I'm utterly done in with this on top of all the rest. I haven't slept for nearly thirty-six hours. I ought not to now, but I'll never be able to stay awake tonight unless I do. No harm can come to me while you're with me, can it?'

'No,' he said huskily. 'Neither man nor devil shall harm you while I'm around. You poor sweet, you must be just about at the end of your tether. Go to sleep now—just as you are.'

With a little sigh she turned over, nestling her fair head into the crook of his arm, where he sat with his back propped up against a tree-trunk. In another moment she was sound asleep.

The afternoon drew into evening. Rex's arms and legs were cold and stiff, but he would not move for fear of waking her. A new anxiety began to trouble him. Mocata had not appeared, and what would they think had become of him at Cardinals Folly? Marie Lou knew he had gone to the inn, and they would probably have rung up by now. But, like a fool, he had neglected to leave any message for them.

The shadows fell, but still there was no sign of Mocata, and the imps of doubt once more began to fill Rex's mind with horrible speculations as to the truth of Tanith's story. Had she consciously or unconsciously lured him from Simon's side on purpose? Simon would be safe enough with Richard and Marie Lou, and De Richleau had promised to rejoin them before dusk—but perhaps Mocata was plotting some evil to prevent the Duke's return. If that were so—Rex shivered slightly at the thought—Richard knew nothing of those mysterious protective barriers with which it would be so necessary to surround Simon in the coming night—and he, who at least knew what had been done the night before—would be absent. By his desertion of his post poor Simon might fall an easy prey to the malefic influence of the Satanist.

He thought more than once of rousing Tanith, but she looked so peaceful, so happy, so lovely there, breathing gently and resting in his strong arms with all her limbs relaxed that he could not bring himself to do it. The shadows lengthened, night drew on, and at last darkness fell with Tanith still sleeping. The night of the ordeal had come and they were alone in the forest.

24

The Scepticism of Richard Eaton

At a quarter to six, De Richleau arrived back at Cardinals Folly and Richard, meeting him in the hall, told him of Mocata's visit.

'I am not altogether surprised,' the Duke admitted sombrely. 'He must be pretty desperate to come here in daylight on the chance of seeing Simon, but of course, he is working against time—now. Did he threaten to return?'

'Yes.' Richard launched into full particulars of the Satanist's attempt on Marie Lou and the conversation that had followed. As he talked he studied De Richleau's face, struck by his anxious harassed expression. Never before had he thought of the Duke as old, but now for the first time it was brought home to him that De Richleau must be nearly double his own age. And this evening he showed it. He seemed somehow to have shrunk in stature, but perhaps that was because he was standing with bent shoulders as though some invisible load was borne upon them. Richard was so impressed by that tired, lined face that he found himself ending quite seriously: 'Do you really think he can work some devilry tonight?'

De Richleau nodded. 'I am certain of it, and I'm worried Richard. My luck was out today. Father Brandon, whom I went to see, was unfortunately away. He has a great knowledge of this terrible "other world" that we are up against, and knowing me well, would have helped us, but the young priest I saw in his place would not entrust me with the Host, nor could I persuade him to come with it himself, and that is the only certain protection against the sort of thing Mocata may send against us.'

'We'll manage somehow,' Richard smiled, trying to cheer him.

'Yes, we've *got* to.' A note of the old determination came

194

into De Richleau's voice. 'Since the Church cannot help us we must rely upon my knowledge of Esoteric formulas. Fortunately, I have the most important aids with me already, but I should be glad if you would send down to the village blacksmith for five horseshoes. Tell whoever you send, that they must be brand new—that is essential.'

At this apparently childish request for horseshoes all Richard's scepticism welled up with renewed force, but he concealed it with his usual tact and agreed readily enough. Then, the mention of the village having reminded him of Rex, he told the Duke how their friend had been called away to the inn.

De Richleau's face fell suddenly. 'I thought Rex had more sense!' he exclaimed bitterly. 'We must telephone at once.'

Richard got on to Mr. Wilkes, but the landlord could give them little information. A lady had arrived at about three, and the American gentleman had joined her shortly after. Then they had gone out into the garden and he had seen nothing of them since.

De Richleau shrugged angrily. 'The young fool! I should have thought that he would have seen enough of this horror by now to realise the danger of going off with that young woman. It's a hundred to one that she is Mocata's puppet if nothing else. I only pray to God that he turns up again before nightfall. Where is Simon now?'

'With Marie Lou. They are upstairs in the nursery I think—watching Fleur bathed and put to bed.'

'Good. Let us go up then. Fleur can help us very greatly in protecting him tonight.'

'Fleur!' exclaimed Richard in amazement.

The Duke nodded. 'The prayers of a virgin woman are amazingly powerful in such instances, and the younger she is the stronger her vibrations. You see, a little child like Fleur who is old enough to pray, but absolutely unsoiled in any way, is the nearest that any human being can get to absolute purity. You will remember the words of Our Lord: "Except ye become as little children ye shall not enter into the Kingdom of Heaven." You have no objection I take it?'

'None,' agreed Richard quickly. 'Saying a prayer for Simon cannot possibly harm the child in any way. We'll go up through the library.'

Seven sides of the great octagonal room were covered ceiling

195

high with books and the eighth consisted of wide french windows through which half-a-dozen stone steps, leading up to the terrace, could be seen and beyond, a portion of the garden.

Richard led the way to one of the book-lined walls and pressed the gilded cardinal's hat upon a morocco binding. A low doorway, masked by dummy bookbacks, swung open disclosing a narrow spiral stairway hewn out of the solid wall. They ascended the stone steps and a moment later entered Fleur's nursery on the floor above, through a sliding panel in the wall.

When they arrived the nursery was empty, but in the bathroom beyond they found Simon, with Nanny's apron tied about his waist, quite solemnly bathing Fleur while Marie Lou sat on the edge of the bath and chortled with laughter.

It was an operation which Simon performed on every visit that he had made to Cardinals Folly so Fleur was used to the business and regarded it as a definite treat; but this tubbing of his friend's child was a privilege which De Richleau had never claimed, and as he entered Fleur suddenly exhibited signs of maidenly modesty surprising in one so young.

'Oh, Mummy,' she exclaimed. 'He mussent see me, muss he, 'cause he's a man.' On which the whole party gave way to a fit of laughter.

'Sen' him away!' yelled the excited Fleur, standing up and clutching an enormous bath sponge to her chest.

De Richleau's firm mouth twitched with his old humour, as he apologised most gravely and backed into the nursery beside Richard. A few minutes later the others joined them, and the Duke held a hurried conversation in whispers with Marie Lou.

'Of course,' she said. 'If it will help, do just what you think, I will get rid of Nanny for a few minutes.'

Walking over, he smiled down at Fleur. 'Does Mummy watch you say your prayers every night?' he asked gently.

'Oh, yes,' she lisped. 'And you shall all hear me now.'

He smiled again. 'Have you ever heard her say hers?'

Fleur thought hard for a moment. 'No,' she shook her dark head and the big blue eyes looked up at him seriously. 'Mummy says her prayers to Daddy when I'se asleep.'

He nodded quietly. 'Well, we're all going to say them together tonight.'

'Ooo,' cooed Fleur. 'Lovely. It'll be just as though we'se playing a new game, won't it?'

'Not a game, dearest,' interjected Marie Lou quietly. 'Because prayers are serious, and we mean them.'

'Yes, we mean them very much tonight, but we could all kneel down in a circle couldn't we and put Uncle Simon in the middle?'

'Jus' like kiss-in-the-ring,' added Fleur.

'That's right,' the Duke agreed, 'or Postman's Knock. And you shall be the postman. But this is very serious, and instead of touching him on the shoulder, you must hold his hand very tight.'

They all knelt down then and Fleur extended her pudgy palm to Simon, but the Duke gently laid his hand on her shoulder. 'No,' he whispered. 'Your left hand, my angel, in Uncle Simon's right. You shall say your prayers first, just as you always do, and then I shall say one for all of us afterwards.'

The first few lines of the Our Father came tumbling out from the child's lips in a little breathless spate as they knelt with bowed heads and closed eyes. Then there was a short hesitation, a prompting whisper from Marie Lou, and an equally breathless ending. After that, the little personal supplication for Mummy and Daddy and Uncle Simon and Uncle Rex and Uncle Greyeyes and dear Nanny were hurried through with considerably more gusto.

'Now,' whispered De Richleau. 'I want you to repeat everything I say word for word after me,' and in a low, clear voice he offered up an entreaty that the Father of All would forgive His servants their sins and strengthen them to resist temptation, keeping at bay by His limitless power all evil things that walked in darkness, and bringing them safely by His especial mercy to see again the glory of the morning light.

When all was done and Fleur, tucked up and kissed, left between Mr. Edward Bear and Golliwog, the others filed downstairs to Marie Lou's cosy sitting-room.

De Richleau was worried about Rex, but a further 'phone call to the inn failed to elicit any later information. He had not returned, and they sat round silently, a little subdued. Richard, vaguely miserable because it was sherry time and the Duke had once again firmly prohibited the drinking of any alcohol,

197

asked at length: 'Well, what do you wish us to do now?'

'We should have a light supper fairly early,' De Richleau announced. 'And after, I should like you to make it quite clear to Malin that none of the servants are to come into this wing of the house until tomorrow morning. Say, if you like, that I am going to conduct some all-night experiments with a new wireless or television apparatus, but in no circumstances must we be disturbed or any doors opened and shut.'

'Hadn't we . . . er . . . better disconnect the telephone as well?' Simon hazarded. 'In case it rings after we've settled down.'

'Yes, with Richard's permission I will attend to that myself.'

'Do, if you like, and I'll see to the servants,' Richard agreed placidly. 'But what do you call a light supper?'

'Just enough to keep up our strength. A little fish if you have it. If not eggs will do, with vegetables or a salad and some fruit, but no meat or game and, of course, no wine.'

Richard grunted. 'That sounds a jolly dinner I must say. I suppose you wouldn't like to shave my head as well, or get us all to don hair shirts if we could find them. I'm hungry as a hunter, and owing to your telegram, we had no lunch.'

The Duke smiled tolerantly. 'I am sorry, Richard, but this thing is deadly serious. I am afraid you haven't realised quite how serious yet. If you had seen what Rex and I did last night, I'm certain that you wouldn't breathe a word of protest about these small discomforts, and realise at once that I am acting for the best.'

'No,' Richard confessed. 'Quite frankly, I find it very difficult to believe that we haven't all gone bug-house with this talk of witches and wizards and magic and what-not at the present day.'

'Yet you saw Mocata yourself this afternoon.'

'I saw an unpleasant pasty-faced intruder I agree, but to credit him with all the powers that you suggest is rather more than I can stomach at the moment.'

'Oh, Richard!' Marie Lou broke in. 'Greyeyes is right. That man is horrible. And to say that people do not believe in witches at the present day is absurd. Everybody knows that there are witches just as there have always been.'

'Eh!' Richard looked at his lovely wife in quick surprise,

198

'Have you caught this nonsense from the others already? I've never heard you air this belief before.'

'Of course not,' she said a little sharply. 'It is unlucky to talk of such things, but one knows about them all the same. Of witches in Siberia I could tell you much—things that I have seen with my own eyes.'

'Tell us, Marie Lou,' urged the Duke. He felt that in their present situation scepticism might prove highly dangerous. If Richard did not believe in the powers that threatened them, he might relax in following out the instructions for their protection and commit some casual carelessness, bringing, possibly, a terrible danger upon them all. He knew how very highly Richard esteemed his wife's sound common sense. It was far better to let her convince him than to press arguments on Richard himself.

'There was a witch in Romanovsk,' Marie Lou proceeded. 'An old woman who lived alone in a house just outside the village. No one, not even the Red Guards, with all their bluster about having liquidated God and the Devil, would pass her cottage alone at night. In Russia there are many such and one in nearly every village. You would call her a wise woman as well perhaps, for she could cure people of many sicknesses and I have seen her stop the flow of blood from a bad wound almost instantly. The village girls used to go to her to have their fortunes told and, when they could afford it, to buy charms of philtres to make the young men they liked fall in love with them. Often, too, they would go back again afterwards when they became pregnant and buy the drugs which would secure their release from that unhappy situation. But she was greatly feared, for everyone knew that she could also put a blight on crops and send a murrain on the cattle of those who displeased her. It was even whispered that she could cause men and women to sicken and die if any enemy paid her a high enough price to make it worth her while.'

'If that is so I wonder they didn't lynch her,' said Richard quietly.

'They did in the end. They would not have dared to do that themselves. But a farmer whom she had inflicted with a plague of lice appealed to the local commissar and he went with twenty men to her house one day. All the villagers and I among them—for I was only a little girl then and naturally curious—went with them in a frightened crowd hanging well behind. They brought the old woman out and examined her, and having proved she was a witch, the commissar had her shot against the cottage wall.'

'How did they prove it?' Richard asked sceptically.

'Why—because she had the marks of course.'

'What marks?'

'When they stripped her they found that she had a teat under her left arm, and that is a certain sign.'

De Richleau nodded. 'To feed her familiar with, of course. Was it a cat?'

Marie Lou shook her head. 'No. In this case, it was a great big fat toad that she used to keep in a little cage.'

'Oh, come!' Richard protested. 'This is fantastic. They slaughtered the poor old woman because she had some malformation and kept an unusual pet.'

'No, no,' Marie Lou assured him. 'They found the Devil's mark on her thigh and they swam her in the village pond. It was very horrible, but it was all quite conclusive.'

'The Devil's mark!' interjected Simon suddenly. 'I've never heard of that,' and the Duke answered promptly:

'It is believed that the Devil or his representative touches these people at their baptism during some Satanic orgy and that spot is for ever afterwards free from pain. In the old witch trials, they used to hunt for it by sticking pins into the suspected person because the place does not differ in appearance from any other portion of the body.'

Marie Lou nodded her curly head. 'That's right. They bandaged this old woman's eyes so that she could not see what part of her they were sticking the pin into and then they began to prick her gently in first one place and then another. Of course she cried out each time the pin went in, but after about twenty cries, the head man of the village pushed the pin into her left thigh and she didn't make a sound. He took it out then and stuck it in again, but still she did not cry out at all so he pushed it in right up to the head, and she didn't know he'd even touched her. So you see, everyone was quite satisfied then that she was a witch.'

'Well, *you* may have been,' Richard said slowly. 'It seems a horribly barbarous affair in any case. I dare say the old woman deserved all she got, but it's pretty queer evidence to shoot anyone on.'

'Er . . . Richard . . .' Simon leaned forward suddenly. 'Do you believe in curses?'

'What—the old bell and book business! Not much. Why?'

'Because the actual working of a curse is evidence of the supernatural.'

'They're mostly old wives' tales of coincidences I think.'

'How about the Mackintosh of Moy?'

'Oh, Scotland is riddled with that sort of thing. But what is supposed to have happened to the Mackintosh?'

'Well, this was in seventeen something,' Simon replied slowly. 'They story goes that he was present at a witch burning or jilted one—I forget exactly. Anyhow she put a curse on him and it went like this:

"Mackintosh, Mackintosh, Mackintosh of Moy
  If you ever have a son *he shall never have a boy*."'

Richard smiled. 'And what happened then?'

'Well, whether the story's true or not I can't say, but it's a fact that the Chieftainship of the Clan has gone all over the shop ever since. Look it up in the records of the Clans if you doubt me.'

'My dear chap, you'll have to produce something far more concrete than that to convince me.'

'All right,' Marie Lou gazed at him steadily out of her large blue eyes. 'You know very little about such things, Richard, but in Russia people are much closer to nature and everyone there still accepts the supernatural and diabolic possession as part of ordinary life. Only about a year before you brought me to England they caught a were-wolf in a village less than fifty miles from where I lived.

He moved over to the sofa and, taking her hand, patted it gently. 'Surely, darling, you don't really ask me to believe that a man can actually turn into a beast—leave his bed in the middle of the night to go out hunting—then return and go to his work in the morning as a normal man again?'

'Certainly,' Marie Lou nodded solemnly. 'Wolves, as you know, nearly always hunt in packs, but that part of the country had been troubled for months by a lone wolf which seemed possessed of far more than normal cunning. It killed sheep and dogs and two young children. Then it killed an old woman. She was found with her throat bitten out, but she had been ravished too, so that's how they knew that it must be a were-wolf. At last it attacked a woodman and he wounded it in the shoulder with his axe. Next day a wretched half-imbecile creature, a sort of village idiot, died suddenly, and when the women went to prepare his body for burial they found that he had died from loss of blood and that there was a great wound in his right shoulder just where the woodman had struck the wolf. After that there were no other cases of slaughtered sheep or people being done to death. So it was quite clear that he was the were-wolf.'

Richard looked thoughtful for a moment. 'Of course,' he remarked, 'the man may have done all that without actually changing his shape at all. If anyone is bitten by a mad dog and gets hydrophobia, they bark, howl, gnash their teeth and behave just as though they were dogs and certainly believe at the time that they are. Lycanthropy, of which this poor devil seems to have been the victim, may be some rare disease of the same kind.'

Marie Lou shrugged lightly and stood up. 'Well, if you won't believe me—there it is. I don't know enough to argue with you, only what I believe myself, so I shall go and order supper.'

As the door closed behind her the Duke said quietly: 'That may be a possible explanation, Richard, but there is an enormous mass of evidence in the jurisprudence of every country to suggest that actual shape shifting does occur at times. The form varies of course. In Greece it is often of the were-boar that one hears. In Africa of the were-hyena and were-leopard. China has the were-fox; India the were-tiger; and Egypt the were-jackal. But even as near home as Surrey I could introduce you to a friend of mine, a doctor who practices among the country people, who will vouch for it that the older cottagers are still unshakable in their beliefs that certain people are were-hares, and have power to change their shape at particular phases of the moon.'

'If you really believe these fantastic stories,' Richard smiled a little grimly, 'perhaps you can give me some reasonable explanation as to what makes such things possible.'

'By all means.' De Richleau hoisted himself out of his chair and began to pace softly up and down the fine, silk Persian prayer rug before the fireplace while he expounded again the Esoteric doctrine just as he had to Rex two nights before.

Simon and Richard listened in silence until the Duke spoke of the eternal fight which, hidden from human eyes, has been waged from time immemorial between the Powers of Light and the Powers of Darkness. Then the latter, his serious interest really aroused for the first time, exclaimed:

'Surely you are proclaiming the Manichaean heresy? The Manichees believed in the Two Principals, Light and Darkness, and the Three Moments, Past, Present and Future. They taught that in the *Past* Light and Darkness had been separate; then that Darkness invaded Light and became mingled with it, creating the *Present* and this world in which evil is mixed with good. They preached the practice of æstheticism as the means of freeing the light imprisoned in human clay so that in some distant *Future* Light and Darkness might be completely separated again.'

The Duke's lean face lit with a quick smile. 'Exactly, my friend! The Manichees had a credo to that effect.

> "Day by day diminishes
> The number of Soul below
> As they are *distilled and mount above*."

The basis of the belief is far, far older of course, pre-Egyptian at the least, but where before it was a jealously guarded mystery the Persian Mani proclaimed it to the world.'

'It became a serious rival to Christianity at one time, didn't it?'

'Um,' Simon took up the argument. 'And it survived despite the most terrible persecution by the Christians. Mani was crucified in the third century after Christ and, by their own creed, his followers were not allowed to enlist converts. Yet somehow it spread in secret. The Albigenses followed it in Southern France in the twelfth century until they were stamped out. Then in the thirteenth, a thousand years after Mani's death, it swept Bohemia. A form of it was still practised there by certain sects as late as the 1840's and even today many thinking people scattered all over the world believe that it holds the core of the only true religion.'

'Yes, I can understand that,' Richard agreed, 'Brahminism, Budism, Taoism, all the great philosophers which have passed

203

beyond the ordinary limited religions with a personal God are connected up with the Prana, Light, and the Universal Life Stream, but that is a very different matter to asking me to believe in were-wolves and witches.'

'They only came into the discussion because they illustrate certain manifestations of supernatural *Evil*,' De Richleau protested; 'just as the appearance of wounds similar to those of Christ upon the Cross in the flesh of exceptionally pious people may be taken as evidence for the existence of supernatural *Good*. Emminent surgeons have testified again and again that stigmata are not due to trickery. It is a changing of the material body by the holy saints in their endeavour to approximate to its highest form, that of Our Lord, so, I contend, base natures, with the assistance of the Power of Darkness, may at times succeed in altering their form to that of were-beasts. Whether they change their shape entirely it is impossible to say because at death they always revert to human form, but the belief is world-wide and the evidence so abundant that it cannot lightly be put aside. In any case what you call madness is actually a very definite form of diabolic possession which seizes upon these people and causes them to act with the same savagery as the animal they believe themselves for the time to be. Of its existence, no one who has read the immense literature upon it, can possibly doubt.'

'Perhaps,' Richard admitted grudgingly. 'But apart from Marie Lou's story, all the evidence is centuries old and mixed up with every sort of superstition and fairy story. In the depths of the Siberian forests or the Indian jungle the belief in such things may perhaps stimulate some poor benighted wretch to act the part now and again and so perpetuate the legend. But you cannot cite me a case in which a number of people have sworn to such happenings in a really civilised country in modern times!'

'Can't I?' De Richleau laughed grimly. 'What about the affair at Uttenheim near Strasbourg. The farms in the neighbourhood had been troubled by a lone wolf for weeks. The Garde-Champetre was sent out to get it. He tracked it down. It attacked him and he fired—killing it dead. Then he found himself bending over the body of a local youth. That unfortunate rural policeman was tried for murder, but he swore by all that was holy that it was a wolf at which he had shot, and the entire population of the village came forward to give evidence on his behalf—that the dead man had boasted time and again of his power to change his shape.'

'Is that a fifteenth or sixteenth century story?' murmured Richard.

'Neither. It occurred in November, 1925.'

25

The Talisman of Set

For a while longer De Richleau strode up and down, patiently answering Richard's questions and ramming home his arguments for a belief in the power of the supernatural to affect mankind until, when Marie Lou rejoined them, Richard's brown eyes no longer held the half-mocking humour which had twinkled in them an hour before.

The Duke's explanation had been so clear and lucid, his earnestness so compelling that the younger man was at least forced to suspend judgment, and even found himself toying with the idea that Simon might really be threatened by some very dangerous and potent force which it would need all their courage to resist during the dark hours that lay ahead.

It was eight o'clock now. Twilight had fallen and the trees at the bottom of the garden were already merged in shadow. Yet with the coming of darkness they were not filled with any fresh access of fear. It seemed that their long talk had elucidated the position and even strengthened the bond between them. Like men who are about to go into physical battle, they were alert and expectant but a little subdued, and realised that their strongest hope lay in putting their absolute trust in each other.

At Marie Lou's suggestion they went into the dining-room and sat down to a cold supper which had already been laid out. Having eaten so lightly during the day, their natural inclination was to make a heavy meal but, without any further caution from De Richleau, they all appreciated now that the situation was sufficiently serious to make restraint imperative.

Even Richard denied himself a second helping of his favourite Morecambe Bay shrimps which had arrived that morning.

When they had finished the Duke leant over him. 'I think the library would be the best place to conduct my experiments, and I shall require the largest jug you have full of fresh water, some glasses and it would be best to leave the fruit.'

'By all means,' Richard agreed, glancing towards his butler. 'See to that please, Malin—will you.' He then went on to give clear and definite instructions that they were not to be disturbed on any pretext until the morning, and concluded with an order that the table should be cleared right away.

With a bland, unruffled countenance the man signified his understanding and motioned to his footman to begin clearing the table. So bland in fact was the expression that it would have been difficult for them to visualise him half an hour later in the privacy of the housekeeper's room declaring with a knowing wink:

'In my opinion it's spooks they're after—the old chap's got no television set. And behaving like a lot of heathens with not a drop of drink to their dinner. Think of that with young Simon there who's so mighty particular about his hock. But spiritualists always is that way. I only hope it doesn't get 'em bad or what's going to happen to the wine bill I'd like to know?'

When Richard had very pointedly wished his henchman 'good night,' they moved into the library and De Richleau, who knew the room well, surveyed it with fresh interest.

Comfortable sofas and large arm-chairs stood about the uneven polished oak of the floor. A pair of globes occupied two angles of the book-lined walls, and a great oval mahogany writing-table of Chippendale design stood before the wide french window. Owing to its sunken position in the old wing of the house the lighting of the room was dim even on a summer's day. Yet its atmosphere was by no means gloomy. A log fire upon a twelve-inch pile of ashes was kept burning in the wide fireplace all through the year, and at night, when the curtains were drawn and the room lit with the soft radiance of the concealed ceiling lights, which Richard had installed, it was a friendly, restful place well suited for quiet work or idle conversation.

'We must strip the room—furniture, curtains, everything!'

said the Duke. 'And I shall need brooms and a mop to polish the floor.'

The three men then began moving the furniture out into the hall while Marie Lou fetched a selection of implements from the house-maid's closet.

For a quarter of an hour they worked in silence until nothing remained in the big library except the serried rows of gilt-tooled books.

'My apologies for even doubting the efficiency of your staff!' the Duke smiled at Marie Lou. 'But I would like the room gone over thoroughly, particularly the floor, since evil emanations can fasten on the least trace of dust to assist their materialisation. Would you see to it, Princess, while I telephone the inn again to find out if Rex has returned.'

'Of course, Greyeyes, dear,' said Marie Lou and, with Richard's and Simon's help, she set about dusting, sweeping and polishing until when De Richleau rejoined them, the boards were so scrupulously clean that they could have eaten from them.

'No news of Rex, worse luck,' he announced with a frown. 'And I've had to disconnect the telephone now in case a call makes Malin think it necessary to disregard his instructions. We had better go upstairs and change next.'

'What into?' Richard inquired.

'Pyjamas. I hope you have a good supply. You see none of us tonight must wear any garment which has been even slightly soiled. Human impurities are bound to linger in one's clothes even if they have only been worn for a few hours, and it is just upon such things that elementals fasten most readily.'

'Shan't we be awfully cold?' hazarded Simon with an unhappy look.

'I'll fit you out with shooting stockings and an overcoat,' Richard volunteered.

'Stockings if you like, providing that they are fresh from the wash—but no overcoats, dressing-gowns or shoes,' said the Duke. 'However, there is no reason why we should not wear a couple of suits apiece of Richard's underclothes, beneath the pyjamas, to keep us warm. The essential point is that everything must be absolutely clean.'

The whole party then migrated upstairs, the men congregating in Richard's dressing-room where they ransacked his wardrobe for suitable attire. Marie Lou joined them a little later looking divinely pretty in peach silk pyjamas and silk stockings into the tops of which, above the knees, the bottoms of her pyjamas were neatly tucked.

'Now for a raid on the linen cupboard,' said De Richleau. 'Cushions, being soiled already, are useless to us, but I am dreading that hard floor so we will take down as many sheets as we can carry, clean bath towels and blankets too. Then we shall have some sort of couch to sit on.'

In the library once more, they set down their bundles and De Richleau produced his suitcase, taking from it a piece of chalk, a length of string, and a footrule. Marking a spot in the centre of the room, he asked Marie Lou to hold the end of the string to it, measuring off exactly seven feet and then, using her as a pivot, he drew a large circle in chalk upon the floor.

Next, the string was lengthened and an outer circle drawn. Then the most difficult part of the operation began. A five-rayed star had to be made with its points touching the outer circle and its valleys resting upon the inner. But, as the Duke explained, while such a defence can be highly potent if it is constructed with geometrical accuracy, should the angles vary to any marked degree or the distance of the apexes from the central point differ more than a fraction, the pentacle would prove not only useless but even dangerous.

For half an hour they measured and checked with string and rule and marking chalk; but Richard proved useful here, for all his life he had been an expert with maps and plans and was even something of amateur architect. At last the broad chalk lines were drawn to the Duke's satisfaction, forming the magical five pointed star, in which it was his intention that they should remain while darkness lasted.

He then chalked in, with careful spacing round the rim of the inner circle, the powerful exorcism: —

In nomina Pa ✠ tris et Fi ✠ lii et Spiritus ✠ Sancti! ✠ El ✠ Elohym ✠ Sother ✠ Emmanuel ✠ Sabaoth ✠ Agia ✠ Tetragammaton ✠ Agyos ✠ Otheos ✠ Ischiros ✠—and, after reference to an old book which he had brought with him, drew certain curious and ancient symbols in the valleys and the mounts of the microcosmic star.

Simon, whose recent experience had taught him something of pentacles, recognised ten of them as Cabbalistic signs taken

208

from the Sephirotic Tree; *Kether, Binah, Ceburah, Hod, Malchut* and the rest. But others, like the Eye of Horus, were of Egyptian origin, and others again in some ancient Aryan script which he did not understand.

When the skeleton of this astral fortress was completed, the clean bedding was laid out inside it for them to rest upon and De Richleau produced further impedimenta from his case.

With lengths of asafœtida grass and blue wax he sealed the windows, the door leading to the hall, and that concealed in the bookshelves which led to the nursery above, each at both sides and at the tops and at the bottoms, making the sign of the Cross in holy water over every seal as he completed it.

Then he ordered the others inside the pentacle, examined the switches by the door to assure himself that every light in the room was on, made up the fire with a great pile of logs so that it would last well through the night and there be no question of their having to leave the circle to replenish it and, joining them where they had squatted down on the thick mat of blankets, produced five little silver cups, which he proceeded to fill two-thirds full with Holy water. These he placed, one in each valley of the pentacle.

Then, taking five long white tapering candles, such as are offered by devotees to the Saints in Catholic Churches, he lit them from an old-fashioned tinder-box and set them upright, one at each apex of the five-pointed star. In their rear he placed the five brand new horseshoes which Richard had secured from the village with their horns pointing outward, and beyond each vase of holy water he set a dried mandrake, four females and one male, the male being in the valley to the north.

These complicated formulas for the erection of outward barriers being at last finished, the Duke turned his attention to the individual protection of his friends and himself. Four long wreaths of garlic flowers were strung together and each of the party placed one about his neck. Rosaries, with little golden crucifixes attached, were distributed, medals of Saint Benedict holding the Cross in his right hand and the Holy Rule in his left, and phials of salt and mercury; lengths of the asafœtida grass were again tied round Simon's wrists and ankles, and he was placed in their midst facing towards the north. The Duke then performed the final rites of sealing the nine openings of each of their bodies.

All this performance had entirely failed to impress Richard. In fact, it tended to revive his earlier scepticism. It was his private belief that a blackmailing gang were playing tricks upon Simon and the Duke so, before coming downstairs, he had tucked a loaded automatic comfortably away beneath his pyjama jacket. In deference to De Richleau's obvious concern that nothing soiled should be brought within the circle he had first, half-ashamedly, cleansed the weapon in a bath of spirit but, if Mr. Mocata was so ill-advised as to break into his house that night with the intention of staging any funny business, he meant to use it. After a little pause he looked cheerfully round at the others. 'Well—here we are! What happens now?'

'We have ample room here,' replied De Richleau. 'So there is no reason why we should not lie down with our feet towards the rim of the circle and try to get some sleep, but there are certain instructions I would like to give you before we settle down.'

'I never felt less like sleep in my life,' remarked Simon.

'Nor I,' agreed Richard. 'It's early yet and if only Marie Lou weren't here I'd tell you some bawdy stories to keep you gay.'

'Don't mind me, darling,' cooed Marie Lou. 'I'm human— even if you are right about my having an angelic face.'

'No!' He shook his head quickly. 'Somehow they fail to amuse me when you're about. That's why I never tell you any. It needs men on their own sitting round a bottle of something to get the best out of a bawdy jest. My God! I wish we'd got a bottle of brandy with us now!'

'Mean pig,' she murmured amiably, snuggling up against him. 'If Greyeyes and Simon didn't know you so well they would think you nothing but an awful little drunk from the way you talk, whereas you're a nice person really.'

'Am I? Well, anyway it's fine that you should think so.' He fondled her short curly hair with his long fingers. 'My present lust for liquor is only because I've been done out of my fair ration today. But what shall we talk about? Greyeyes—this Talisman that all the bother centres on—tell us about it before you give us your final orders for the night.'

'You know the legend of Isis and Osiris?' the Duke asked.

'Yes—vaguely,' Richard replied. 'They were the King and Queen of Heaven who came to earth in human form and taught the Egyptians all they knew weren't they? The old business of a fairhaired god arriving among a dusky people and importing all sorts of new ideas about agriculture and architecture and justice—in fact—what we call civilisation.'

De Richleau nodded. 'That is so. But I mean the story of how Osiris came to die?'

'He was murdered wasn't he?' volunteered Simon. 'But I've forgotten how.'

'Well, this is the account which has been handed down to us through many thousands of years. Osiris was, apparently, as Richard says, a fair-haired, light-skinned man, alien to the Egyptian race, who became their King and, ruling them with great intelligence, brought them many blessings. But he had a brother named Set—and here again you get the two principals of Good and Evil, Light and Darkness—for Set was a dark man. The legend is, of course, apocryphal up to a point but, eliminating the overlay of myth with which the priests later embroidered it, the whole story had such a genuine ring of human tragedy that it is very difficult to doubt that these two men and the woman Isis actually lived, as the progenitors of a Royal dynasty, in the Nile valley long before the Pyramids were built.

'It always amazes me, whenever I re-read the story in the Greek Classics, how Set, particularly, stands out as a definite and living figure after all these countless generations. The characters in our seventeenth century plays even are quite unreal to us now—with a very few exceptions; but Set remains, timeless and unchanging, the charming but unscrupulous rogue who might have entertained you with lavish hospitality and brilliant conversation yesterday—yet would do you down without the least compunction if he met you in the street tomorrow.

'He was tall and slim and dark and handsome; a fine athlete and a great hunter, but a cultured, amusing person too, and a boon companion who knew how to carry his wine at table. The type whose lapses men are always ready to condone on account of their delightful personality, and whose wickedness women persuade themselves is only waywardness—while they succumb almost at a glance to that dark, male virility.

'Set was younger than Osiris and jealous of his authority.

211

Then he fell in love with Isis, his brother's wife. The old story of the human triangle you see, or rather the original, for all others in the whole literature of the world which deal with the same subject are plagiarisms. Set conspired, therefore, to slay the King and seize his wife and power for himself.

'To assassinate Osiris openly would have been a difficult matter because he was always surrounded by the older nobles, who loved him and knew that he kept the peace while the land flourished and grew prosperous. Set knew that they would defend the King's person with their lives, and he was faced with another problem too. Osiris was a god, and even if he could lure him to a place where the deed could be done in secret, he dared not spill one drop of the divine blood.

'He planned then a superlatively clever murder. You all know that the Egyptians considered this present life to be only an interlude and that almost from the age at which they could think at all their thoughts were largely focused on the life to come. Many of them spent their entire fortune upon preparing some magnificent place of burial for themselves, and at every banquet, when the slaves served the dessert, the head wine butler carried round a miniature coffin with a skeleton inside to remind the guests that death was waiting round the corner for them all.

'With diabolical cunning, Set utilised the national preoccupation with death and ceremonial burial to ensnare his brother. First, by a clever piece of trickery he secured Osiris' exact measurements. Then he had made the most beautiful sarcophagus that had ever been seen. It was a great heavy chest of fine cedar wood with the figures of the forty-two assessors of the dead, who form the jury of the gods, painted in lapis blue, and the minutest hieroglyphics in black and red; line upon line of them reciting the most effective protections against black magic, and every requisite line of ritual from the great Book of the Dead.

'As soon as this wonderful coffin was completed, Set prepared a great banquet to which he invited Osiris and seventy-two of the younger nobles, all of whom he had corrupted and drawn one by one into his conspiracy.

'Then on the night of the feast he had the beautiful sarcophagus placed in a small anteroom through which every guest had to pass on his arrival.

212

'You can imagine how envious they were when they saw it, and how each commented on the workmanship and the artistry of the designs—Osiris no less than the others.

'They dined, drank heavily of wine, watched the Egyptian dancing girls, saw Ethiopian contortionists, and listened to the best stringed music of the day. Then as a final hospitality to his guests, the Prince Set rose from his couch and proclaimed:

' "You have all seen the sarcophagus which stands in the little anteroom, and it is my wish that one of you should receive it as a gift. He whom it fits may take it with my blessing."

'Picture to yourselves the nobles as they scrambled up from their couches, thrusting the dancing girls aside, and elbowing their way out into the anteroom, each hoping that the princely gift might fall to him.

'One after another they got inside and lay down, but not one of them fitted it exactly. Then Set led Osiris into the anteroom and, waving his hand towards the handsome chest said with a little laugh: "Why don't you try it brother. It is worthy of a King. Even of the Lord of the Two Lands, the Upper and the Lower Nile."

'With a smile Osiris lowered himself into the masterpiece. And behold, it fitted his tall, broad-shouldered body to a hair's breadth. No sooner was he inside than the principal conspirators, who were in the secret, rushed forward with the weighty lid. In frantic haste they nailed it down and poured molten lead upon it, so that Osiris may have survived an hour in agony but died at last of suffocation.

'Set thus succeeded in his treacherous design of killing his brother without spilling one drop of his blood. He and his turbulent followers then hastened to their chariots, rode forth, and seized the Kingdom. But Isis was warned in time and managed to escape.

'The coffer had been left with Osiris in it and, the Egyptian religion being so strongly bound up with the worship of the dead, it was vital to Set's newly established authority that the body should be disposed of at the earliest possible moment. Otherwise, if the priests got hold of it, they would bury it in state and erect a mighty shrine to the dead King's memory which would form a rallying point for all the best elements in the Kingdom where they would league themselves against the murderer.

'Next morning, therefore, immediately he got home, Set had the chest cast into the Nile. But Isis recovered it, and after certain magical ceremonies, succeeded in impregnating herself by means of her husband's dead body. Then she fled to the papyrus marshes of the Delta, taking Osiris' body with her in the chest since there was no time to give it proper burial.

'When Set learned what had happened, he swore that he would hunt Isis down and kill her, and that he would find Osiris' body and destroy it for ever.

'Again now, in the story, we get one of those strange glimpses of happenings many thousands of years ago which we can see more clearly than the things of yesterday.

'In a few phrases it is recounted how Set searched for months in vain, and then one night, the pregnant ex-Queen Isis, now a destitute refugee alone and unattended, is seated beneath a cluster of palm trees in the desert. Her husband's body, roughly embalmed, is in the wooden chest beside her and she is conscious of the movements of the child she bears. Suddenly her sorrowful meditations are disturbed by a distant rumble breaking the stillness of the night. The noise increases to a drumming thunder as a party of horsemen come galloping across the sand. Isis runs for cover to a nearby papyrus swamp and crouches waist high in the water watching from amidst the reeds. The dusky riders come thundering past. She sees that it is Set and his dissolute nobles hunting by the brilliant light of the Egyptian moon. One of them recognises the chest. With cries of triumph they fling themselves from their saddles, break it to pieces and drag out the body of Osiris. Hidden there, fearful and trembling, Isis watches Set's dark, proud profile as he orders the body to be torn into fourteen pieces and the parts distributed throughout the length and breadth of the Kingdom so that they might never be brought together again.

'Years later, Horus, the son of Isis, the Great God, the Hawk of Light, who restored its blessings to mankind and lifted again the veil of darkness that Set's treachery had brought to dim the world, became master of the Kingdom. Then Isis roamed the country seeking for the dismembered portions of her husband. She did not attempt to assemble them again, but wherever she found one she erected a great temple to his

214

memory. In all, she succeeded in finding thirteen pieces of the body, but the fourteenth she never found. That Set had carefully embalmed and kept himself. It was for this reason that, although Horus defeated Set three times in battle he was never able to slay him. The portion that Set retained was the most potent of all charms—the phallus of the dead god, his brother.

'In the secret histories of esoterism it is stated that it has since been heard of many times. For long periods through the ages it has been completely lost. But whenever it is found it brings calamity upon the world, and that is the thing which we have to prevent Mocata securing at all costs today—the Talisman of Set.'

When De Richleau had ceased speaking, they sat silent for a while until Marie Lou said softly: 'I am feeling rather tired now, Greyeyes, dear, and I think I'd like to rest, even if it is impossible to sleep with all these lights.'

'All right. Then I'll say what I have to Princess. But please, all of you'—the Duke paused to look at each of them in turn —'listen carefully, because this is vitally serious.

'What may happen I have no idea. Perhaps nothing at all and the worst we'll have to face is an uncomfortable night. But Mocata threatened to get Simon away from us by hook or by crook, and I feel certain that he meant it. I cannot tell you what form his attack is likely to take, but I am sure he will literally do his damnedest to break us up and get Simon out of our care tonight.

'He may send the most terrible powers against us, but there is one thing above all others that I want you to remember. As long as we stay inside this pentacle we shall be safe, but if any of us sets one foot outside it we risk eternal damnation.

'We may be called upon to witness the sort of horrors which it is difficult for you to conceive. I mean visions such as you have read of in Gustave Flaubert's *Temptation of Saint Anthony,* or seen in pictures by the old Flemish masters such as Brueghel. But they cannot do us the least harm as long as we remain where we are.

'Again, we may see nothing, but the attack may develop in a far more subtle form. That is to say, inside ourselves. Any, or all of us, may find our reason being undermined by insidious argument so that we may start telling each other that there is nothing in the world to be frightened of and that we are utter fools to spend a miserable night sitting here when we might all be comfortably in bed upstairs. If that happens, it is a lie. Even if I appear to change my mind and tell you that I have thought of new arrangements which would be safer, you must not believe me because it will not be my true self speaking. It may be that an awful thirst will come upon us. That is why I have had this big jug of water brought in. We may be assailed by hunger, but to meet that we have the fruit. It is possible that we may be afflicted with earache or some other bodily pain which, ordinarily, would make us want to go upstairs to seek relief. If that happens we've just got to stick it till the morning.

'Poor old Simon is likely to be afflicted worst because the campaign will centre on an attempt to make him break out of the circle. But we've got to stop him—by force, if need be. There are two main defences which we can bring into play if any manifestations do take place, as I fear they may.

'One is the Blue vibration. Shut your eyes and try to think of yourselves as standing in an oval of blue light. The oval is your aura, and the colour blue exceedingly potent in all things pertaining to the spirit; the other is prayer. Do not endeavour to make up complicated prayers or your words may become muddled and you will find yourself saying something that you do not mean. Confine yourselves to saying over and over again: "Oh, Lord, protect me! Oh, Lord, protect me!" and not only say it but think it with all the power of your will, visualising, if you can, Our Lord upon the Cross with blue light streaming from His body towards yourselves; but if you think you see Him outside this pentacle beckoning you to safety while some terrible thing threatens you from the other side, *still you must remain within.*'

As De Richleau finished there was a murmur of assent. Then Richard, with an arm about Marie Lou's shoulders said quietly: 'I understand, and we'll do everything you say.'

'Thank you. Now, Simon,' the Duke went on. 'I want you to say clearly and distinctly seven times, *"Om meni padme aum."* That is the invocation to *manathaer*—your higher self.'

Simon did as he was bid, then they knelt together and each offered a silent prayer that the Power of Light might guard and protect them from all uncleanness, and that each might be granted strength to aid the others should they be faced with any peril.

They lay down then and tried to rest despite the burning candles and the soft glow of the electric light. Sleep was utterly impossible to them in such circumstances. Yet no one there had more to say upon any point that mattered and, after a little time, no one felt that they could break the stillness by endeavouring to make ordinary conversation.

The steady ticking of a clock came faintly from somewhere in the depths of the house. Occasionally a log fell with a loud plop and hissed for a moment in the fire grate. Then the little noises of the night were hushed, and an immense silence, brooding and mysterious, seemed to have fallen upon them. In some strange way it did not seem as though the quite octagonal room was any longer a portion of the house or that outside the window lay the friendly, well-cared-for garden that they knew so well. Watchful, listening, intent, they lay silent, waiting to see what the night would bring.

26

Rex Learns of the Undead

Tanith slept peacefully, curled up in Rex's arms, her golden head pillowed upon his chest. For a little time anxious thoughts occupied his mind. He reproached himself for having left Simon, and the gnawing worm of doubt raised its head again to whisper that Tanith had planned to lure him away from protecting his friend, but he dismissed such thoughts almost immediately. Simon would be safe enough in the care of Richard and Marie Lou. Tanith was alone and needed him, and he soon convinced himself that in remaining there he was breaking a lance against the enemy as well, by preventing Mocata securing her again to assist him, all unwillingly, in his hostilities.

The shadows lengthened and the patches of sunlight dimmed, yet still Tanith slept on—the sleep of utter exhaustion—brought about by the terrible nervous crisis through which she had passed from hour to hour during the previous day, the past night, and that morning, in her attempt to seek safety with him.

With infinite precaution not to disturb her he looked at his watch and found that the time was nearly eight o'clock. De Richleau should be back by now and after all it was unlikely that Mocata could prevent his return before sundown. De Richleau might have lost his nerve for a few moments the night before, but he had retrieved it brilliantly in that headlong dash at the wheel of the Hispano down into the hellish valley where the Satanists practised their grim rites. Now that they had secured Simon safe and sound once more, Rex had an utter faith that De Richleau would fight to the last ditch, with all the skill and cunning of his subtle brain, and that stubborn, tenacious courage that Rex knew so well, before he would surrender their friend to the evil powers again.

It was dark now; even the afterglow had faded, leaving the trees as vague, dark sentinels in that silent wood. The undergrowth was massed in bulky shadows and the colour had faded from the grasses and wild-flowers on the green, mossy bank where he lay with Tanith breathing so evenly in his embrace.

His back and arms were aching from his strained position but he sat on while the moments fled, sleepy himself now, yet determined not to give way to the temptation, even to doze, lest silent evil should steal upon them where they lay.

Another hour crept by and then Tanith stirred slightly. Another moment, and she had raised her head, shaking the tumbled golden hair back from her face and blinking up at him a little out of sleepy eyes.

'Rex, where are we?' she murmured indistinctly. 'What has happened? I've had an awful dream.'

He smiled down at her and kissed her full on the lips.

'Together,' he said. 'That's all that matters, isn't it? But if you must know, we're in the wood behind the road-house.'

'Of course,' she gave a little gasp, and hurriedly began to tidy herself. 'But we can't stay here all night.'

The thought of taking her back to Cardinals Folly occurred to him again, but in these timeless hours he had witnessed so many things he would have thought impossible a few days before that he dismissed the idea at once. Tanith, he felt convinced, was not lying to him. She was genuinely repentant and terrified of Mocata. But who could say what strange powers that sinister man might not be able to exercise over her at a distance. He dared not risk it. However, she was certainly right in saying that they could not stay where they were all night.

'We'd best go back to the road-house,' he suggested. 'They will be able to knock us up a meal, and after, it'll be time enough to figure out what we mean to do.'

'Yes,' she sighed a little. 'I am hungry now—terribly hungry. Do let us go back and see if they can find us something to eat.'

Her arm through his, their fingers laced together, they walked back the quarter of a mile to the little stream which separated the wood from the inn garden. He lifted her over it again and when they reached the lounge of the 'Pride of Peacocks' they found that it was already half-past nine.

Knowing that his friends would be anxious about him, Rex tried to telephone immediately he got in, but the village exchange told him that the line to Cardinals Folly was out of order. Then he sent the trim maid for Mr. Wilkes, and when that worthy arrived on the scene, inquired if it was too late for them to have a hot meal.

'Not at all, sir,' Mr. Wilkes bent, quiet-voiced, deferential, priestlike, benign. 'My wife will be very happy to cook you a little dinner. What would you care for now? Fish is a little difficult in these parts, except when I know that I have guests staying and can order in advance, and game, of course, is unfortunately out of season. But a nice young duckling perhaps, or a chicken? My wife, if I may say so, does a very good Chicken Maryland, sir, of which our American visitors have been kind enough to express their approval from time to time.'

'Chicken Maryland,' exclaimed Rex. 'That sounds grand to me. How about you, honey?'

Tanith nodded. 'Lovely, if only it is not going to take too long.'

'Some twenty minutes, madam. Not more. Mrs. Wilkes will see to it right away, and in the meantime, I've just had in a very nice piece of smoked salmon, which comes to me from a London house. I could recommend that if you would like to start your dinner fairly soon.'

Rex nodded, and the aged Wilkes went on amiably: 'And now sir—to drink? Red wine, if I might make so bold would be best with the grill, perhaps. I have a little of the Clos de Vougeot 1920 left, which Mr. Richard Eaton was good enough to compliment me on when he dined here last, and his Lordship, my late master, always used to say that he found a glass

219

of Justerini's Amontillado before a meal lent an edge to the appetite.'

For a second Rex wavered. He recalled De Richleau's prohibition against alcohol, but he had been far from satisfied by the brief rest which he had snatched that morning and was feeling all the strain now of the events which had taken place in the last forty-eight hours. Tanith, too, was looking pale and drawn, despite her sleep. A bottle of good burgundy was the very thing they needed to give them fresh strength and courage. He could have sunk half a dozen cocktails with the greatest ease and pleasure, but by denying himself those spirits, he felt that he was at least carrying out the kernel of the Duke's instructions. Good wine could surely harm no one—so he acquiesced.

A quarter of an hour later, he was seated opposite to Tanith at a little corner table in the dining-room, munching fresh, warm toast and the smoked salmon with hungry relish, while the neat little maid ministered to their wants, and the pontifical Mr. Wilkes hovered eagle-eyed in the background. The chicken was admirably cooked, and the wine lent an additional flavour by the fact that his palate was unusually clean and fresh from having denied himself those cocktails before the meal.

When the chicken was served, Mr. Wilkes murmured something about a sweet and Rex, gazing entranced into Tanith's big eyes, nodded vaguely. Which sign of assent resulted, a little later, in the production of a flaming omelette au kirsch. Then Wilkes came forward once more, with a suggestion that the dinner should be rounded off by allowing him to decant a bottle of his Cockburn's '08. But here, Rex was firm. The burgundy had served its purpose, stimulated his brain and put fresh life into his body. To drink a vintage port after it would have been pleasant he knew, but certain to destroy the good effect and cause him to feel sleepy. So he resisted Mr. Wilkes' blandishments.

After the meal Rex tried to get on to Cardinals Folly again but the line was still reported out of order, so he scribbled a note to Richard, saying that he was safe and well and would ring them in the morning, then asked Wilkes to have it sent up to the house by hand.

When the landlord had left them, they moved back into the lounge and discussed how they should pass the night. Tanith was as insistent as ever that under no circumstances should

Rex leave her to herself, even if she asked him later on to do so. She felt that her only hope of safety lay in remaining with him beside her until the morning, so it was decided that they spend the night together in the empty lounge.

Tanith had already booked a room and so, to make all things orderly in the mind of the good Mr. Wilkes, Rex booked another, but told the landlord that, as Tanith suffered from insomnia, they would probably remain in the lounge until very late, and so he was not to bother about them when he locked up. As a gesture he also borrowed from Wilkes a pack of cards, saying that they meant to pass an hour or two playing nap.

The fire was made up and they settled down comfortably under the shelter of the big mantel in the inglenook with a little table before them upon which they spread out the cards for appearance sake. But no sooner had the maid withdrawn than they had their arms about each other once more and blissfully oblivious of their surroundings, began that delightful first exchange of confidences about their previous lives, which is such a blissful hour for all lovers.

Rex would have been in the seventh heaven but for the thought of this terrible business in which Tanith had got herself involved and the threat of Mocata's power hanging like a sword of Damocles above her head.

Again and again, from a variety of subjects and experiences ranging the world over, and from their childhood to the present day, they found themselves continually and inexplicably caught back to that macabre subject which both were seeking to avoid. In the end, both surrendered to it and allowed the thoughts which were uppermost in their minds to enter their conversation freely.

'I'm still hopelessly at sea about this business,' Rex confessed, 'It's all so alien, so bizarre, so utterly fantastic. I know I wasn't dreaming last night or the night before. I know that if Simon hadn't got himself into trouble I wouldn't be holding your loveliness in my arms right now. Yet, every time I think of it, I feel that I must have been imagining things, and that it just simply can't be true.'

'It is, my dear,' she pressed his hand gently. 'That is just the horror of it. If it were any ordinary tangible peril, it wouldn't be quite so terrifying. It wouldn't be quite so bad even if we were living in the middle ages. Then at least, I could seek

221

sanctuary in some convent where the nuns would understand and the priests who were learned in such matters, exert themselves to protect me. But in these days of modern scepticism there is no one I can turn to; police and clergymen and doctors would all think me insane. I only have you and after last night I'm frightened, Rex, frightened.' A sudden flush mounted to her cheeks again.

'I know, I know,' Rex soothed her gently. 'But you must try all you know not to be. I've a feeling that you're scaring yourself more than is really necessary. I'll agree that Mocata might hypnotise you if he got you on your own again, and maybe use you in some way to get poor Simon back into his net, but what could he actually do to you beyond that? He's not going to take a chance on murdering anybody, so that the police could take a hand, even if he had sufficient motive to want to try.'

'I am afraid you don't understand, dearest,' she murmured gently. 'A Satanist who is as far along the Path as Mocata does not need a motive to do murder, unless you can call malicious pleasure in the deed a motive in itself, and my having left him in the lurch at such a critical time is quite sufficient to anger him into bringing about my death.'

'I tell you, sweet, he'll never risk doing murder. In this country it is far too dangerous a game.'

'But his murders are not like ordinary murders. He can kill from a distance if he likes.'

'What—by sticking pins in a little wax figure with your name scratched on it, or letting it melt away before the fire until you pine and die?'

'That is one way, but he is more likely to use the blood of white mice.'

'How in the world do you mean?'

'I don't know very much about it except what I have picked up from Madame D'Urfé and a few other people. They say that when a very advanced adept wishes to kill someone, he feeds a white mouse on some of the holy wafers that they compel people to steal from churches for them. The sacrilegious aspect of the thing is very important, you see. Then they perform the Catholic ceremony of baptism over the mouse, christening it with the same name as that of their intended victim. That creates an affinity between the mouse and the person far stronger than carving their name on any image.'

'Then they kill the mouse, eh?'

'No, I don't think so. They draw off some of its blood, impregnate that with their malefic will, vaporise it, and call up an elemental to feed upon its essence. Then they perform a mystic transfusion in their victim's veins causing the elemental to poison them. But, Rex——'

'Yes, my sweet.'

'It is not that I am afraid to die. In any case, as I have told you, there is no hope of my living out the year, but that has not troubled me for a long time now. It is what may come after that terrifies me so.'

'Surely he can't harm anybody once they're dead,' Rex protested.

'But he can,' Tanith burst out with a little cry of distress and fear. 'If he kills me *that* way, he can make me dead to the world, but I shall live on as an *undead,* and that would be horrible.'

Rex passed his hand wearily across his eyes. 'Don't speak in riddles, treasure. What is this thing you're frightened of? Just tell me now in ordinary, plain English.'

'All right. I suppose you have heard of a vampire.'

'Why, yes. I've read of them in fiction. They're supposed to come out of their graves every night and drink the blood of human beings, aren't they? Until they're found out, then their graves are opened up for a priest to cut off their head and drive stakes through their hearts. Is that what you call an undead?'

Tanith nodded slowly. 'Yes, that is an undead—a foul, revolting thing, a living corpse that creeps through the night like a great white slug, and a body bloated from drinking people's blood. But have you never read of them in other books beside nightmare fiction?'

'No, I wouldn't exactly say I have as far as I can remember. The Duke would know all about them for a certainty —and Richard Eaton too, I expect—because they're both great readers. But I'm just an ordinary chap who's content to take his reading from the popular novelists who can turn out a good, interesting story. Do you mean to tell me seriously that such creatures have ever existed outside the thriller writer's imagination?'

'I do. In the Carpathians, where I come from, the whole countryside is riddled with vampire stories from real life. You hear of them in Poland and Hungary and Roumania, too. All through Middle Europe and right down into the Balkan countries there have been endless cases of such revolting Satanic manifestations. Anyone there will tell you that time and again, when graves have been opened on suspicion, the corpses of vampires have been found, months after burial, without the slightest sign of decay, their flesh pink and flushed, their eyes wide-open, bright and staring. The only difference to their previous appearance is the way in which their canine teeth have grown long and pointed. Often, even, they have been found with fresh blood trickling out of the sides of their mouths.'

'Say, that sounds pretty grim,' Rex exclaimed with a little shudder. ' I reckon De Richleau would explain that by saying that the person was possessed before he died and that after, although the actual soul passed on, the evil spirit continued to make a doss-house of its borrowed body. But I can't think that anything so awful would ever happen to you.'

'It might, my dear. That is what scares me so. And if Mocata did get hold of me again he would not need to perform those ghastly rites with impregnated blood. He could just throw me into the hypnotic state and, after he had made me do all he wished, allow some terrible thing to take possession of me at once. The elemental would still remain in my body when he killed me, and I should become one of those loathsome creatures—the undead, if that happened, this very night.'

'Stop! I can't bear to think of it,' Rex drew her quickly to him again. 'But he shan't get hold of you. We'll fight him till all's blue, and I'm going to marry you to-morrow so that I can be with you constantly. We'll apply for a special licence first thing in the morning.'

She nodded, and a new light of hope came into her eyes. 'If you wish it, Rex,' she whispered, 'and I do believe that by your love and strength, you can save me. But you mustn't leave me for a single second tonight, and we mustn't sleep a wink. Listen!'

She paused a moment as the bell in the village steeple chimed the twelve strokes of midnight, which came to them clearly

224

in the stillness of the quiet room. 'It is the second of May now —my fatal day.'

He smiled indulgently. 'Sure, I won't leave you, and we won't sleep either. One of us might drop off if we were all alone, but together we'll prod each other into keeping awake. Though I just can't think that'll be necessary, with all the million things I've got to tell you about your sweet self.'

She stood up then, raising her arms to smooth back her hair, and making a graceful, slender silhouette against the flickering flames of the heaped-up fire.

'No. The night will slip away before we know it,' she agreed more cheerfully. 'Because I've got a thousand things to tell you too. I must just slip upstairs to powder my nose now, and when I come back, we'll settle down in earnest to make a night of it together.'

A quick frown crossed his face. 'I thought you said I wasn't to let you leave me even for a second. I don't like your going upstairs alone at all.'

'But, my dear!' Tanith gave a little laugh. 'I can hardly take you with me, and I shan't be more than a few moments.'

Rex nodded, reassured as he saw her standing there, smiling down at him in the firelight so happy and normal in every way. He felt certain that he would know at once if Mocata was trying to exert his power on her from a distance, by that strange far-away look which had come into her eyes and the fanatical note that had raised the pitch of her voice each time she had spoken of the imperative necessity of her reaching the meeting-place for the Sabbat on the previous day. There was not the faintest suggestion of that other will, imposed upon her own, in her face or voice now, and obviously it would have been childish to attempt to prevent her carrying out so sensible a suggestion before settling down. The best part of six hours must elapse before daylight began to filter greyly through the old-fashioned bow window at the far end of the room.

'All right,' he laughed. 'I'll give you five minutes by that clock—but no more, remember, and if you're not down then, I'll come up and get you.'

'Dear lover!' she stooped suddenly and kissed him, then slipped out of the room closing the door softly behind her.

Rex lay back, spreading his great limbs now in the comfortable corner of the inglenook, and stretching out his long legs to the glow of the log fire. He wasn't sleepy, which amazed him when he thought how little sleep he had had since he woke in his state-room on the giant Cunarder the morning of the day that he dined with De Richleau. That seemed ages ago now, weeks, months, years. So many things had happened, so many new and staggering thoughts come to seethe and ferment in his brain, yet Simon's party had been held only a bare two nights before.

His hand moved lazily to his hip pocket to get a cigarette, but half way to it he abandoned the attempt as too much trouble, wriggling down instead more comfortably about the cushions.

He wasn't sleepy—not a bit. His brain had never been more active and his thoughts turned for a moment to his friends at Cardinals Folly. They, too, would be wide awake, braced, no doubt, under De Richleau's determined leadership, to face an attack from the powers of evil. De Richleau must be feeling pretty sleepy he thought. Neither of them had had more than three hours that morning after their exhausting night. They hadn't got to bed much before dawn the night before either, and the Duke had been up, according to Max, at seven in order to be at the British Museum directly it opened. Say six hours in sixty. That wasn't much, but De Richleau was an old campaigner and he would stick it all right, Rex had no doubt.

He glanced at the clock, thinking it almost time that Tanith should rejoin him, but saw that the slow-moving hand had only advanced two minutes. 'Amazing how time drags when one is watching it,' he thought, and his mind wandered on to the reflection that he had been mighty wise not to drink anything but that one glass of sherry and the burgundy for dinner. He would probably have been horribly drowsy by now if he had been fool enough to fall for the cocktails or the port. But he wasn't sleepy—not a bit.

His mind began to form little mental pictures of some of those strange episodes which he had lived through in the last two days—old Madame D'Urfé smoking her cigar and then Tanith; Max arranging the cushions in De Richleau's electric canoe at Pangbourne, and then Tanith again. That plausible old humbug Wilkes serving the Clos de Vougeot with meticulous care—a mighty fine thing he made out of this pub no doubt —and then Tanith once more, sitting opposite him at table,

226

with the soft glow of the shaded electric lamp lighting her oval face and throwing strange shadows in the silken web of her golden hair.

He glanced at the clock again—another minute had crawled by, and then he pictured Tanith as he had seen her only a few moments before, bending to kiss him, her face warm and flushed by the firelight, and those strange, deep, age-old eyes of hers smiling tenderly into his beneath their heavy half-lowered lids. It must be this strange wonderful love for her, he thought, which kept him so alive and alert, for ordinarily his healthy body demanded its fair share of sleep and he would have been nodding his head off by this time. He could still see those glorious golden eyes of hers smiling into his. The face above them was indistinct and vague, but they remained clear and shining in the shadows on the far side of the fireplace. The eyes were changing now a little—losing their colour and fading from gold to grey and then to a palish blue. Yet their brightness seemed to increase and they grew bigger as he held them with his mental gaze.

He thought for a second of glancing at the clock again. It seemed that Tanith had left him ages ago now, but judging by the time it had taken for that long hand to crawl through three minutes' space he felt that it could hardly yet have covered the other two. Besides, he did not want to lose the focus of those strange, bright eyes which he could see so plainly when he half closed his own.

Rex wasn't sleepy—not a bit. But time is an illusion, and Rex never afterwards knew how long he sat awake there in the semi-darkness. Perhaps during the first portion of his watch some strange power deluded his vision and the clock had in reality moved on while he only thought that the minutes dragged so heavily. In any case, those eyes that watched him from the shadows were his last conscious thought, and next moment Rex was sound asleep.

27

Within the Pentacle

While Rex slumbered evenly and peacefully before the dying fire in the lounge of the 'Pride of Peacocks,' Richard, Marie Lou, the Duke and Simon waited in the pentacle, on the floor of the library at Cardinals Folly, for the dreary hours of night to drag their way to morning.

They lay with their heads towards the centre of the circle and their feet towards the rim, forming a human cross, but although they did not speak for a long time after they had settled down, none of them managed to drop off to sleep.

The layer of clean sheets and blankets beneath them was pleasant enough to rest on for a while, but the hard, unyielding floorboards under it soon began to cause them discomfort. The bright flames of the burning candles and the steady glow of the electric light showed pink through their closed eyelids, making repose difficult, and they were all keyed up to varying degrees of anxious expectancy.

Marie Lou was restless and miserable. Nothing but her fondness for Simon, and the Duke's plea that the presence of Richard and herself would help enormously in his protection, would have induced her to play any part in such proceedings. Her firm belief in the supernatural filled her with grim forebodings, and she tried in vain to shut out her fears by sleep. Every little noise that broke the brooding stillness, the creaking of a beam as the old house eased itself upon its foundations, or the whisper of the breeze as it rustled the leaves of the trees in the garden, caused her to start wide awake again, her muscles taut with alarm and apprehension.

Richard did not attempt to sleep. He lay revolving a number of problems in his mind. Fleur d'amour's birthday was in a couple of weeks' time. The child was easy, but a present for Marie Lou was a different question. It must be something that she wanted and yet a surprise. A difficult matter when she already had everything with which his fine fortune could endow her, and jewellery was not only banal but absurd. The sale of the lesser stones among the Shulimoff treasure, which they had brought out of Russia, had realised enough to provide her with a handsome independent income and her retention of the finer gems alone equipped her magnificently in that direction. He toyed with the idea of buying her a two-year-old. He was not a racing man but she was fond of horses and it would be fun for her to see her own run at the lesser meetings.

After a while he turned restlessly on to his tummy, and began to ponder this wretched muddle into which Simon had got himself. The more he thought about it the less he could subscribe to the Duke's obvious beliefs. That so-called Black Magic was still practised in most of the Continental capitals and many of the great cities in America, he knew. He had even met a man, a few years before, who had told him that he had attended a celebration of the Black Mass at a house in the Earls Court district of London, yet he could not credit that it had been anything more than a flimsy excuse for a crowd of intellectual decadents to get disgustingly drunk and participate in a wholesale sexual orgy. Simon was not that sort, or a fool either, so it was certainly queer that he should have got himself mixed up with such beastliness.

Richard turned over again, yawned, glanced at his friend whom, he decided, he had never seen look more normal, and wondered if, out of courtesy to the Duke, he could possibly continue to play his part in this tedious farce until morning.

The banishing rituals which De Richleau had performed upon Simon the previous night at Stonehenge had certainly proved successful, and he had had a good sleep that afternoon. His brain was now quick and clear as it had been in the old days and, although Mocata's threats were principally directed against himself, he was by far the most cheerful of the party. Despite his recent experiences, his natural humour bubbling up very nearly caused him to laugh at the thought of them all lying on that hard floor because he had made an idiot of himself, and Richard's obvious disgust at the discomforts imposed by the Duke caused him much amusement. Nevertheless, he recognised that his desire to laugh was mainly due to nervous tension, and accepted with full understanding the necessity for these extreme precautions. To think, for only a second, of how narrow his escape had been was enough to sober instantly any tendency to mirth and send a quick shudder through his limbs. He was only anxious now, having dragged his friends into this horrible affair, to cause them as little further trouble as possible by following the Duke's leadership without question. With resolute determination he kept his thoughts away from any of his dealings with Mocata and set himself to endure his comfortless couch with philosophic patience.

To outward appearances De Richleau slept. He lay perfectly still on his back breathing evenly and almost imperceptibly, but he had always been able to do with very little sleep. Actually he was recruiting his forces in a manner that was not possible to the others. That gentle rhythmic breathing, perfectly but unconsciously timed from long practice, was the way of the Raja Yoga which he had learnt when young, and all the time he visualised himself, the others, the whole room as blue—blue—blue, the colour vibration which gives love and sympathy and spiritual attainment. Yet he was conscious of every tiny movement made by the others; the gentle sighing of the breeze outside, and the occasional plop of burning logs as they fell into the embers. For over two hours he barely moved a muscle but all his senses remained watchful and alert.

The night seemed never-ending. Outside the wind dropped and a steady rain began to fall, dripping with monotonous regularity from the eaves on to the terrace. Richard became more and more sore from the hard floor. He was tired now and bored by this apparently senseless vigil. He thought that it must be about half past one, and daylight would not come to release them from their voluntary prison before half past five or six. That meant another four hours of this acute and momentarily increasing discomfort. As he tossed and turned it grew upon him with ever-increasing force how stupid and futile this whole affair seemed to be. De Richleau was so obviously the victim of a gang of clever tricksters, and his wide reading on obscure subjects had caused his imagination to run away with him. To pander to such folly any longer simply was not good enough. With these thoughts now dominating his mind Richard suddenly sat up.

'Look here,' he said. 'I'm sick of this. A joke's a joke, but we've had no lunch and precious little dinner, and I haven't had a drink all day. Some of you have got far too lively an imagination, and we are making utter fools of ourselves. We had better go upstairs. If you're really frightened of anything happening to Simon we could easily shift four beds into one room and all sleep within a hand's reach of each other. Nobody will be able to get at him then. But frankly, at the moment, I think we're behaving like a lot of lunatics.'

De Richleau rose with a jerk and gave him a sharp look from beneath his grey slanting devil's eyebrows. 'Something's beginning to happen,' he told himself swiftly. 'They're working upon Richard, because he's the most sceptical amongst us, to try and make him break up the pentacle.' Aloud he said quietly: 'So you're still unconvinced that Simon is in real danger, Richard?'

'Yes, I am.' Richard's voice held an angry aggressive note quite foreign to his normal manner. 'I regard this Black Magic business as stupid nonsense. If you could cite me a single case where so-called magicians have actually done their stuff before sane people it would be different. But they're charlatans—every one of them. Take Cagliostro—he was supposed to make gold but nobody ever saw any of it, and when the Inquisition got hold of him they bunged him in a dungeon in Rome and he died there in abject misery. His Black Magic couldn't even procure him a hunk of bread. Look at Catherine de Medici. She was a witch on the grand scale if ever there was one—built a special tower at Vincennes for Cosimo Ruggeri, an Italian sorcerer. They used to slit up babies and practise all sorts of abominations there together night after night to ensure the death of Henry of Navarre and the birth of children to her own sons. But it didn't do her a ha'porth of good. All four died childless so that at last, despite all her bloody sacrifices, the House of Valois was extinct, and Henry, the hated Bearnais, became King of France after all. Come nearer home if you like. Take that absurd fool Elipas Levi who was supposed to be the Grand High Whatnot in Victorian times. Did you ever read his book, *The Doctrine and Ritual of Magic*? In his introduction he professes that he is going to tell you all about the game and that he's written a really practical book, by the aid of which anybody who likes can raise the devil, and perform all sorts of monkey tricks. He drools on for hundreds of pages about fiery swords and tetragrams and the terrible aqua poffana, but does he tell you anything? Not a blessed thing. Once it comes to a showdown he hedges like the crook he was and tells you that such mysteries are *far too terrible and dangerous to be entrusted to the profane.* Mysterious balderdash my friend. I'm going to have a good strong nightcap and go to bed.'

Marie Lou looked at him in amazement. Never before had she heard Richard denounce any subject with such passion and venom. Ordinarily, he possessed an extremely open mind and, if he doubted any statement, confined himself to a kindly but slightly cynical expression of disbelief. It was extraordinary that he should suddenly forget even his admirable manners and be downright rude to one of his greatest friends.

De Richleau studied his face with quiet understanding and as Richard stood up he stood up too, laying his hand upon the younger man's shoulder. 'Richard,' he said. 'You think I'm a superstitious fool, don't you?'

'No.' Richard shrugged uncomfortably. 'Only that you've been through a pretty difficult time and, quite frankly, that your imagination is a bit overstrained at the moment.'

The Duke smiled. 'All right, perhaps you are correct, but we have been friends for a long time now and this business tonight has not interfered with our friendship in any way, has it?'

'Why, of course not. You know that.'

'Then, if I begged of you to do something for my sake, just because of that friendship, you would do it, wouldn't you?'

'Certainly I would,' Richard's hesitation was hardly perceptible and the Duke cut in quickly, taking him at his word.

'Good! Then we will agree that Black Magic may be nothing but a childish superstition. Yet I happen to be frightened of it, so I ask you, my friend, who is not bothered with such stupid fears, to stay with me tonight—and not move outside this pentacle.'

Richard shrugged again, and then smiled ruefully. . . .

'You've caught me properly now so I must make the best of it; quite obviously if you say that, it is impossible for me to refuse.'

'Thank you,' De Richleau murmured as they both sat down again, and to himself he thought: 'That's the first move in the game to me.' Then as a fresh silence fell upon the party, he began to ruminate upon the strangeness of the fact that elementals and malicious spirits may be very powerful, but their nature is so low and their intelligence so limited that they can

232

nearly always be trapped by the divine spark of reason which is the salvation of mankind. The snare was such an obvious one and yet Richard's true nature had reasserted itself so rapidly that the force, which had moved him to try and break up their circle for its benefit, had been scotched almost before it had had a chance to operate.

They settled down again but in some subtle way the atmosphere had changed. The fire glowed red on its great pile of ashes, the candles burned unflickeringly in the five points of the star, and the electric globes above the cornices still lit every corner of the room with a soft diffused radiance, yet the four friends made no further pretence of trying to sleep. Instead they sat back to back, while the moments passed, creeping with leaden feet towards the dawn.

Marie Lou was perplexed and worried by Richard's outburst, De Richleau tense with a new expectancy, now he felt that psychic forces were actually moving within the room. Stealthy —invisible—but powerful; he knew them to be feeling their way from bay to bay of the pentacle, seeking for any imperfection in the barrier he had erected, just as a strong current swirls and eddies about the jagged fissures of a reef searching for an entrance into a lagoon.

Simon sat crouched, his hands clasped round his knees, staring, apparently with unseeing eyes, at the long lines of books. It seemed that he was listening intently and the Duke watched him with special care, knowing that he was the weak spot of their defence. Presently, his voice a little hoarse, Simon spoke:

'I'm awfully thirsty. I wish we'd got a drink.'

De Richleau smiled, a little grimly. Another of the minor manifestations—the evil was working upon Simon now but only to give another instance of its brutish stupidity. It overlooked the fact that he had provided for such an emergency with that big carafe of water in the centre of the pentacle. The fact that it had caused Simon to forget its presence was of little moment. 'Here you are, my friend,' he said, pouring out a glass. 'This will quench your thirst.'

Simon sipped it and put it aside with a shake of his narrow head. 'Do you use well-water, Richard?' he asked jerkily. 'This stuff tastes beastly to me—brackish and stale.'

'Ah!' thought De Richleau. 'That's the line they are trying, is it? Well, I can defeat them there,' and taking Simon's glass he poured the contents back into the carafe. Then he picked up his bottle of Lourdes water. There was very little in it now for the bulk of it had been used to fill the five cups which stood in the vales of the pentagram—but enough—and he sprinkled a few drops into the water in the carafe.

Richard was speaking—instinctively now in a lowered voice —assuring Simon that they always used Burrows Malvern for drinking purposes, when the Duke filled the glass again and handed it back to Simon. 'Now try that.'

Simon sipped again and nodded quickly. 'Um, that seems quite different. I think it must have been my imagination before,' and he drank off the contents of the glass.

Again for a long period no one spoke. Only the scraping of a mouse behind the wainscot, sounding abnormally loud, jarred upon the stillness. That frantic insistent gnawing frayed Marie Lou's nerves to such a pitch that she wanted to scream, but after a while that, too, ceased and the heavy silence, pregnant with suspense, enveloped them once more. Even the gentle patter on the window-panes was no longer there to remind them of healthy, normal things, for the rain had stopped, and in that soundless room the only movement was the soft flicker of the logs, piled high in the wide fireplace.

It seemed that they had been crouching in that pentacle for nights on end and that their frugal dinner lay days away. Their discomfort had been dulled into a miserable apathy and they were drowsy now after these hours of strained uneventful watching. Richard lay down again to try and snatch a little sleep. The Duke alone remained alert. He knew that this long interval of inactivity on the part of the malefic powers was only a snare designed to give a false sense of security before the renewal of the attack. At length he shifted his position slightly and as he did so he chanced to glance upwards at the ceiling. Suddenly it seemed to him that the lights were not quite so bright as they had been. It might be his imagination, due to the fact that he was anticipating trouble, but somehow he felt certain that the ceiling had been brighter when he had looked at it before. In quick alarm he roused the others.

Simon nodded, realising why De Richleau had touched him on the shoulder and confirming his suspicion. Then with straining eyes, they all watched the cornice, where the concealed

234

lights ran round the wall above the top of the bookshelves.

The action was so slow, that each of them felt their eyes must be deceiving them, and yet an inner conviction told them that it was true. Shadows had appeared where no shadows were before. Slowly but surely the current was failing and the lights dimming as they watched.

There was something strangely terrifying now about that quiet room. It was orderly and peaceful, just as Richard knew it day by day, except for the absence of the furniture. No nebulous ghost-like figure had risen up to confront them, but there, as the minutes passed, they were faced with an un-accountable phenomenon—those bright electric globes hidden from their sight were gradually but unquestionably being dimmed.

The shadows from the bookcases lengthened. The centre of the ceiling became a dusky patch. Gradually, gradually, as with caught breath they watched, the room was being plunged in darkness. Soundless and stealthy, that black shadow upon the ceiling grew in size and the binding of the books became obscure where they had before been bright until, after what seemed an eternity of time, no light remained save only the faintest line just above the rim of the top bookshelf, the five candles burning steadily in the points of the five-starred pentagram, and the dying fire.

Richard shuddered suddenly. 'My God! It's cold,' he exclaimed, drawing Marie Lou towards him. The Duke nodded, silent and watchful. He felt that sinister chill draught beginning to flow upon the back of his neck, and his scalp prickled as he swung round with a sudden jerk to face it.

There was nothing to be seen—only the vague outline of the bookcases rising high and stark towards the ceiling where the dull ribbon of light still glowed. The flames of the candles were bent now at an angle under the increasing strength of the cold invisible air current that pressed steadily upon them.

De Richleau began to intone a prayer. The wind ceased as suddenly as it had begun, but a moment later it began to play upon them again—this time from a different quarter.

The Duke resumed his prayer—the wind checked—and then came with renewed force from another angle. He swung to meet it but it was at his back again.

A faint, low moaning became perceptible as the unholy

blast began to circle round the pentacle. Round and round it swirled with ever-increasing strength and violence, beating up out of the shadows in sudden wild gusts of arctic iciness, and tearing at them with chill, invisible, clutching fingers, so that it seemed as if they were standing in the very vortex of a cyclone. The candles flickered wildly—and went out.

Richard, his scepticism badly shaken, quickly pushed Marie Lou to one side and whipped out his matches. He struck one, and got the nearest candle alight again but, as he turned to the next, that cold damp evil wind came once more, chilling the perspiration that had broken out upon his forehead, snuffing the candle that he had re-lit and the half-burnt match which he still held between his fingers.

He lit another and it spluttered out almost before the wood had caught—another—and another, but they would not burn.

He glimpsed Simon's face for an instant, white, set, ghastly, the eyeballs protruding unnaturally as he knelt staring out into the shadows—then the whole centre of the room was plunged in blackness.

'We must hold hands,' whispered the Duke. 'Quick, it will strengthen our resistance,' and in the murk they fumbled for each other's fingers, all standing up now, until they formed a little ring in the very centre of the pentagram, hand clasped in hand and bodies back to back.

The whirling hurricane ceased as suddenly as it had begun. A unnatural stillness descended on the room again. Then without warning, an uncontrollable fit of trembling took possession of Marie Lou.

'Steady, my sweet,' breathed Richard, gripping her hand more tightly, 'you'll be all right in a minute.' He thought that she was suffering from the effect of that awful cold which had penetrated the thin garments of them all, but she was standing facing the grate and her knees shook under her as she stammered out:

'But look—the fire.'

Simon was behind her but the Duke and Richard, who were on either side, turned their heads and saw the thing that had caused her such excess of terror. The piled-up logs had flared into fresh life as that strange rushing wind had circled round the room, but now the flames had died down and, as their eyes rested upon it, they saw that the red hot embers were turning black. It was as though some monstrous invisible hand was dabbing at it, then almost in a second, every spark of light in that great, glowing fire was quenched.

'Pray,' urged the Duke, 'for God's sake, pray.'

After a little their eyes grew accustomed to this new darkness. The electric globes hidden behind the cornice were not quite dead. They flickered and seemed about to fail entirely every few moments, yet always the power exerted against them seemed just not quite enough, for their area of light would increase again, so that the shadows across the ceiling and below the books were driven back. The four friends waited with pounding hearts as they watched that silent struggle between light and darkness and the swaying of the shadows backwards and forwards, that ringed them in.

For what seemed an immeasurable time they stood in silent apprehension, praying that the last gleam of light would hold out, then, shattering that eerie silence like the sound of guns there came three swift, loud knocks upon the window-pane.

'What's that?' snapped Richard.

'Stay still,' hissed the Duke.

A voice came suddenly from outside in the garden. It was clear and unmistakable. Each one of them recognised it instantly as that of Rex.

'Say, I saw your light burning. Come on and let me in.'

With a little sigh of relief at the breaking of the tension, Richard let go Marie Lou's hand and took a step forward, But the Duke grabbed his shoulder and jerked him back:

'Don't be a fool,' he rasped. 'It's a trap.'

'Come on now. What in heck is keeping you?' the voice demanded. 'It's mighty cold out here, let me in quick.'

Richard alone remained momentarily unconvinced that it was a superhuman agency at work. The others felt a shiver of horror run through their limbs at the perfect imitation of Rex's voice, which they were convinced was a manifestation of some terrible entity endeavouring to trick them into leaving their carefully constructed defence.

'Richard,' the voice came again, angrily now. 'It's Rex I tell you—Rex. Stop all this fooling and get this door undone.' But the four figures in the pentacle now remained tense, silent and unresponsive.

The voice spoke no more and once again there was a long interval of silence.

De Richleau feared that the Adversary was gathering his forces for a direct attack and it was that, above all other things, which filled him with dread. He was reasonably confident that his own intelligence would serve to sense out and avoid any fresh pitfalls which might be set, providing the others would obey his bidding and remain steadfast in their determination not to leave the pentacle, but he had failed in his attempt to secure the holy wafers of the Blessed Sacrament that afternoon, the lights were all but overcome, the sacred candles had been snuffed out. The holy water, horseshoes, garlic and the pentacle itself might only prove a partial defence if the dark entities which were about them made an open and determined assault.

'What's that!' exclaimed Simon, and they swung round to face the new danger. The shadows were massing into deeper blackness in one corner of the room. Something was moving there.

A dim phosphorescent blob began to glow in the darkness; shimmering and spreading into a great hummock, its outline gradually became clearer. It was not a man form nor yet an animal, but heaved there on the floor like some monstrous living sack. It had no eyes or face but from it there radiated a terrible malefic intelligence.

Suddenly there ceased to be anything ghostlike about it. The Thing had a whitish pimply skin, leprous and unclean, like some huge silver slug. Waves of satanic power rippled through its spineless body, causing it to throb and work continually like a great mass of new-made dough. A horrible stench of decay and corruption filled the room; for as it writhed it exuded a slimy poisonous moisture which trickled in little rivulets across the polished floor. It was solid, terribly real, a living thing. They could even see long, single, golden hairs, separated from each other by ulcerous patches of skin, quivering and waving as they rose on end from its flabby body—and suddenly it began to laugh at them, a low, horrid, chuckling laugh.

Marie Lou reeled against Richard, pressing the back of her hand against her mouth and biting into it to prevent a scream.

His eyes were staring, a cold perspiration broke out upon his face.

De Richleau knew that it was a Saiitii manifestation of the

most powerful and dangerous kind. His nails bit into the palms of his hands as he watched that shapeless mass, silver white and putrescent, heave and ferment.

Suddenly it moved, with the rapidity of a cat, yet they heard the squelching sound as it leapt along the floor, leaving a wet slimy trail in its wake, that poisoned the air like foul gases given off by animal remains.

They spun round to face it, then it laughed again, mocking them with that quiet, diabolical chuckle that had the power to fill them with such utter dread.

It lay for a moment near the window pulsating with demoniac energy like some enormous livid heart. Then it leapt again back to the place where it had been before.

Shuddering at the thought of that ghastliness springing upon their backs they turned with lightning speed to meet it, but it only lay there wobbling and crepitating with unholy glee.

'Oh, God!' gasped Richard.

The masked door which led up to the nursery was slowly opening. A line of white appeared in the gap from near the floor to about three feet in height. It broadened as the door swung back poiselessly upon its hinges, and Marie Lou gave a terrified cry.

'It's Fleur!'

The men, too, instantly recognised the little body, in the white nightgown, vaguely outlined against the blackness of the shadows, as the face with its dark aureole of curling hair became clear.

The Thing was only two yards from the child. With hideous merriment it chuckled evilly and flopping forward, decreased the distance by a half.

With one swift movement, De Richleau flung his arm about Marie Lou's neck and jerked her backwards, her chin gripped fast in the crook of his elbow. 'It's not Fleur,' he cried desperately. 'Only some awful thing which has taken her shape to deceive you.'

'Of course it's Fleur—she walking in her sleep!' Richard started forward to spring towards the child, but De Richleau grapped his arm with his free hand and wrenched him back.

'It's not,' he insisted in an agonised whisper. 'Richard, I beg you! Have a little faith in me! Look at her face—it's blue! Oh, Lord protect us!'

At that positive suggestion, thrown out with such vital force at a moment of supreme emotional tension, it did appear to them for an instant that the child's face had a corpse-like bluish tinge then, upon the swift plea for Divine aid, the lines of the figure seemed to blur and tremble. The Thing laughed, but this time with thwarted malice, a high-pitched, angry, furious note. Then both the child and that nameless Thing became transparent and faded. The silent heavy darkness, undisturbed by sound or movement, settled all about them once again.

With a gasp of relief the straining Duke released his prisoners. 'Now do you believe me?' he muttered hoarsely, but there was not time for them to reply. The next attack developed almost instantly.

Simon was crouching in the middle of the circle. Marie Lou felt his body trembling against her thigh. She put her hand on his shoulder to steady him and found that he was shaking like an epileptic in a fit.

He began to gibber. Great shudders shook his frame from head to toe and suddenly he burst into heart-rending sobs.

'What is it, Simon,' she bent towards him quickly, but he took no notice of her and crouched there on all fours like a dog until, with a sudden jerk, he pulled himself upright and began to mutter:

'I won't—I won't I say—I won't. D'you hear—— You mustn't make me—no—no—— No!' Then with a reeling, drunken motion he staggered forward in the direction of the window. But Marie Lou was too quick for him and flung both arms about his neck.

'Simon darling—Simon,' she panted. 'You mustn't leave us.'

For a moment he remained still, then, his body twisted violently as though his limbs were animated by some terrible inhuman force, and he flung her from him. The mild good-natured smile had left his face and it seemed, in the faint light which still glowed from the cornice, that he had become an utterly changed personality—his mouth hung open showing the bared teeth in a snarl of ferocious rage—his eyes glinted hot and dangerous with the glare of insanity—a little dribble of saliva ran down his chin.

'Quick, Richard,' cried the Duke. 'They've got him—for God's sake pull him down!'

Richard had seen enough now to destroy his scepticism for

life. He followed De Richleau's lead, grappling frantically with Simon, and all three of them crashed struggling to the floor.

'Oh, God,' sobbed Marie Lou. 'Oh, God, dear God!'

Simon's breath came in great gasps as though his chest would burst. He fought and struggled like a maniac, but Richard, desperate now, kneed him in the stomach and between them they managed to hold him down. Then De Richleau, who, fearing such an attack, had had the forethought to provide himself with cords, succeeded in tying his wrists and ankles.

Richard rose panting from the struggle, smoothed back his dark hair, and said huskily to the Duke. 'I take it all back. I'm sorry if I've been an extra nuisance to you.'

De Richleau patted him on the elbow. He could not smile for his eyes were flickering, even as Richard spoke, from corner to corner of that grim, darkened room, seeking, yet dreading, some new form in which the Adversary might attempt their undoing.

All three linked their arms together and stood, with Simon's body squirming at their feet, jerking their heads from side to side in nervous expectancy. They had not long to wait. Indistinct at first, but certain after a moment, there was a stirring in the blackness near the door. Some new horror was forming out there in the shadows beyond the pointers of the pentacle—just on a level with their heads.

Their grip upon each other tightened as they fought desperately to recruit their courage. Marie Lou stood between the others, her eyes wide and distended, as she watched this fresh manifestation gradually take shape and gain solidity.

Her scalp began to prickle beneath her chestnut curls. The Thing was forming into a long, dark, beast-like face. Two tiny points of light appeared in it just above the level of her eyes. She felt the short hairs at the back of her skull lift of their own volition like the hackles of a dog.

The points of light grew in size and intensity. They were eyes. Round, protuberant and burning with a fiery glow, they bored into hers, watching her with a horrible unwinking stare.

She wanted desperately to break away and run, but her knees sagged beneath her. The head of the Beast merged into powerful shoulders and the blackness below solidified into strong thick legs.

241

'It's a horse!' gasped Richard. 'A riderless horse.'

De Richleau groaned. It was a horse indeed. A great black stallion and it had no rider that was visible to them, but he knew its terrible significance. Mocata, grown desperate by his failures to wrest Simon from their keeping, had abandoned the attempt and, in savage revenge, now sent the Angel of Death himself to claim them.

A saddle of crimson leather was strapped upon the stallion's back, the pressure of invisible feet held the long stirrup leathers rigid to its flanks, and unseen hands held the reins taut a few inches above its withers. The Duke knew well enough that no human who has beheld that dread rider in all his sombre glory has ever lived to tell of it. If that dark Presence broke into the pentacle they would see him all too certainly, but at the price of death.

The sweat streaming down his face, Richard held his ground, staring with fascinated horror at the muzzle of the beast. The fleshy nose wrinkled, the lips drew back, barring two rows of yellowish teeth. It champed its silver bit. Flecks of foam, white and real, dripped from its loose mouth.

It snorted violently and its heated breath came like two clouds of steam from its quivering nostrils warm and damp on his face. He heard De Richleau praying, frantically, unceasingly, and tried to follow suit.

The stallion whinnied, tossed its head and backed into the bookcases drawn by the power of those unseen hands, its mighty hoofs ringing loud on the boards. Then, as though rowelled by knife-edged spurs, it was launched upon them.

Marie Lou screamed and tried to tear herself from De Richleau's grip, but his slim fingers were like a steel vice upon her arm. He remained there, ashen-faced but rigid, fronting the huge beast which seemed about to trample all three of them under foot.

As it plunged forward the only thought which penetrated Richard's brain was to protect Marie Lou. Instead of leaping back, he sprang in front of her with his automatic levelled and pressed the trigger.

The crash of the explosion sounded like a thunder-clap in that confined space. Again—again—again, he fired while blinding flashes lit the room as though with streaks of lighting. For a succession of seconds the whole library was as bright as day and the gilded bookbacks stood out so clearly that De Richleau could even read the titles across the empty space where, so lately, the great horse had been.

The silence that descended on them when Richard ceased fire was so intense that they could hear each other breathing, and for the moment they were plunged in utter darkness.

After that glaring succession of flashes from the shots, the little rivers of light around the cornice seemed to have shrunk to the glimmer of night lights coming beneath heavy curtains. They could no longer even see each other's figures as they crouched together in the ring.

The thought of the servants flashed for a second into Richard's mind. The shooting was bound to have fetched them out of bed. If they came down their presence might put an end to this ghastly business. But the minutes passed. No welcome sound of running feet came to break that horrid stillness that had closed in upon them once more. With damp hands he fingered his automatic and found that the magazine was empty. In his frantic terror he had loosed off every one of the eight shots.

How long they remained there, tense with horror, peering again into those awful shadows, they never knew, yet each became suddenly aware that the steed of the Dark Angel, who had been sent out from the underworld to bring about their destruction, was steadily re-forming.

The red eyes began to glow in the long dark face. The body lengthened. The stallion's hoof-beats rang upon the floor as it stamped with impatience to be unleashed. The very smell of the stable was in the room. That gleaming harness stood out plain and clear. The reins rose sharply from its polished bit to bend uncannily in that invisible grip above its saddle bow. The black beast snorted, reared high in to the air, and then the crouching humans faced that terrifying charge again.

The Duke felt Marie Lou sway against him, clutch at his shoulder, and slip to the floor. The strain had proved too great and she had fainted. He could do nothing for her—the beast was actually upon them.

It baulked, upon the very edge of the pentacle, its fore hoofs slithering upon the polished floor, its back legs crashing under it as though faced with some invisible barrier,

With a neigh of fright and pain it flung up its powerful head

243

as though its face had been brought into contact with a red-hot bar. It backed away champing and whinnying until its steaming hindquarters pressed against the book-lined wall.

Richard stooped to clasp Marie Lou's limp body. In their fear they had all unconsciously retreated from the middle to the edge of the circle. As he knelt his foot caught one of the cups of Holy Water set in the vales of the pentacle. It toppled over. The water spilled and ran to waste upon the floor.

Instantly a roar of savage triumph filled the room, coming from beneath their feet. The ab-human monster from the outer circle—that obscene sack-like Thing—appeared again. Its body vibrated with tremendous rapidity. It screamed at them with positively frantic glee. With incredible speed the stallion was swung by its invisible rider at the gap in the protective barrier. The black beast plunged, scattering the gutted candles and dried mandrake, then reared above them, its great, dark belly on a level with their heads, its enormous hoofs poised in mid-air about to batter out their brains.

For one awful second it hovered there while Richard crouched gazing upward, his arms locked tight round the unconscious Marie Lou, De Richleau stood his ground above them both, the sweat pouring in great rivulets down his lean face.

Almost, it seemed, the end had come. The the Duke used his final resources, and did a thing *which shall never be done except in the direst emergency when the very soul is in peril of destruction*. In a clear sharp voice he pronounced the last two lines of the dread Sussamma Ritual.

A streak of light seemed to curl for a second round the stallion's body, as though it had been struck with unerring aim, caught in the toils of some gigantic whip-lash and hurled back. The Thing disintegrated instantly in sizzling atoms of opalescent light. The horse dissolved into the silent shadows.

Those mysterious and unconquerable powers, the Lord of Light, the Timeless Ones, had answered; compelled by those mystic words to leave their eternal contemplation of Supreme Beatitude for a fraction of earthly time, to intervene for the salvation of those four small flickering flames that burned in the beleaguered humans.

An utter silence descended upon the room. It was so still that De Richleau could hear Richard's heart pounding in his breast. Yet he knew that by that extreme invocation they had been carried out of their bodies on to the fifth Astral plane. His conscious brain told him that it was improbable that they would ever get back. To call upon the very essence of light requires almost superhuman courage, for Prana possesses an energy and force utterly beyond the understanding of the human mind. As it can shatter darkness in a manner beside which a million candle power searchlight becomes a pallid beam, so it can attract all lesser light to itself and carry it to realms undreamed of by infinitesimal man.

For a moment it seemed that they had been ripped right out of the room and were looking down into it. The pentacle had become a flaming star. Their bodies were dark shadows grouped in its centre. The peace and silence of death surged over them in great saturating waves. They were above the house. Cardinals Folly became a black speck in the distance. Then everything faded.

Time ceased, and it seemed that for a thousand thousand years they floated, atoms of radiant matter in an immense immeasurable void—circling for ever in the soundless stratosphere—being shut off from every feeling and sensation, as though travelling with effortless impulse five hundred fathoms deep below the current levels of some uncharted sea.

Then, after a passage of eons in human time they saw the house again, infinitely far beneath them, their bodies lying in the pentacle and that darkened room. In an utter eerie silence the dust of centuries was falling . . . falling. Softly, impalpably, like infinitely tiny particles of swansdown, it seemed to cover them, the room, and all that was in it, with a fine grey powder.

    *   *   *   *   *

De Richleau raised his head. It seemed to him that he had been on a long journey and then slept for many days. He passed his hand across his eyes and saw the familiar bookshelves in the semi-darkened library. The bulbs above the cornice flickered and the light came full on.

Marie Lou had come to and was struggling to her knees while Richard fondled her with trembling hands, and murmured: 'We're safe, darling—safe.'

Simon's eyes were free now from that terrible maniacal

glare. The Duke had no memory of having unloosened his bonds but he knelt beside them looking as normal as he had when they had first entered upon that terrible weaponless battle.

'Yes, we're safe—and Mocata is finished,' De Richleau passed a hand over his eyes as if they were still clouded. 'The Angel of Death was sent against us tonight, but he failed to get us, and he will never return empty-handed to his dark Kingdom. Mocata summoned him so Mocata must pay the penalty.'

'Are—are you sure of that?' Simon's jaw dropped suddenly.

'Certain. The age-old law of retaliation cannot fail to operate. He will be dead before the morning.'

'But—but,' Simon stammered. 'Don't you realise that Mocata never does these things himself. He throws other people into a hypnotic trance and makes them do his devilish business for him. One of the poor wretches who are in his power will have to pay for this night's work.'

Even as he spoke there came the sound of running footsteps along the flagstones of the terrace. A rending crash as a heavy boot landed violently on the woodwork of the french-windows.

They burst open, and framed in them stood no vision but Rex himself. Haggard, dishevelled, hollow-eyed, his face a ghastly mask of panic, fear and fury.

He stood there for a moment staring at them as though they were ghosts. In his arms he held the body of a woman; her fair hair tumbled across his right arm, and her long silk-stockinged legs dangled limply from the other.

Suddenly two great tears welled up into his eyes and trickled slowly down his furrowed cheeks. Then as he laid the body gently on the floor they saw that it was Tanith, and knew, by her strange unnatural stillness, that she was dead.

28

Necromancy

'Oh, Rex!' Marie Lou dropped to her knees beside Tanith, knowing that this must be the girl of whom he had raved to her that afternoon. 'How awful for you!'

'How did this happen?' the Duke demanded. It was imperative that he should know at once every move in the enemy's game, and the urgent note in his voice helped to pull Rex together.

'I hardly know,' he gasped out. 'She got me along because she was scared stiff of that swine Mocata. I couldn't call you up this afternoon and later when I tried your line was blocked, but I had to stay with her. We were going to pass the night together in the parlour, but around midnight she left me and then—oh, God! I fell asleep.'

'How long did you sleep for?' asked Richard quickly.

'Several hours, I reckon. I was about all in after yesterday, but the second I woke I dashed up to her room and she was, dressed as she is now—lying asleep, I figured—in an armchair. I tried to wake her but I couldn't. Then I got real scared—grabbed hold of her—and beat it down those stairs six at a time. You've just no notion how frantic I was to get out of that place and next thing I knew—I saw your light and came bursting in here. She—she's not dead, is she?'

'Oh, Rex, you poor darling,' Marie Lou stammered as she chafed Tanith's cold hands. 'I—I'm afraid——'

'She isn't—she can't be!' he protested wildly. 'That fiend's only thrown her into a trance or something.'

Richard had taken a little mirror from Marie Lou's bag. He held it against Tanith's bloodless lips. No trace of moisture marred its surface. Then he pressed his hand beneath her breast.

'Her heart's stopped beating,' he said after a moment. 'I'm sorry, old chap, but—well, I'm afraid you've got to face it.'

'The old-fashioned tests of death are not conclusive,' Simon whispered to the Duke. 'Scientists say now that even arteries can be cut and fail to bleed, but life still remains in the body.

They've all come round to the belief that we're animated by a sort of atomic energy—call it the soul if you like—and that the body may retain that vital spark without showing the least sign of life. Mightn't it be some form of catalepsy like that?'

'Of course,' De Richleau agreed. 'It has been proved time and again that the senses are only imperfect vessels for collecting impressions. There is something else which can see when the eyes are closed and hear while the body is being painlessly cut to ribbons under an anaesthetic. All the modern experimenters agree that there are many states in which the body is not wholly alive or wholly dead, but I fear there is little hope in this case. You see we know that Mocata used her as his catspaw, so the poor girl has been forced to pay the price of failure. I haven't a single doubt that she is dead.'

Rex caught his last words and swung upon him frantically. 'God! this is frightful. I—I tried to kid myself but I think I knew it the moment I picked her up. Her prophecy's come true then.' He passed his hand over his eyes. 'I can't quite take it in yet—this and all of you seem terribly unreal—but is she *really* dead? She was so mighty scared that if she died some awful thing might remain to animate her body.'

'She is dead as we know death,' said Richard softly. 'So what could remain?'

'I know what he means,' the Duke remarked abruptly. 'He is afraid that an elemental may have taken possession of her corpse. If so drastic measures will be necessary.'

'No!' Rex shook his head violently. 'If you're thinking of cutting off her head and driving a stake through her heart, I won't have it. She's mine, I tell you—mine!'

'Better that than the poor soul should suffer the agony of seeing its body come out of the grave at night to fatten itself on human blood,' De Richleau murmured. 'But there are certain tests, and we can soon find out. Bring her over here.'

Simon and Richard lifted the body and carried it over to the mat of sheets and blankets in the centre of the pentacle, while De Richleau fiddled for a moment among his impedimenta.

'The Undead,' he said slowly, 'have certain inhibitions. They can pass as human, but they cannot eat human food and they cannot cross running water except at sunset and sunrise. Garlic is a most fearsome thing to them, so that they scream if only

248

touched by it, and the Cross, of course, is anathema. We will see if she reacts to them.'

As he spoke he took the wreath of garlic flowers from round his neck and placed it about Tanith's. Then he made the sign of the Cross above her and laid his little gold crucifix upon her lips.

The others stood round, watching the scene with horrified fascination. Tanith lay there, calm and still, her pale face shadowed by the golden hair, her tawny eyes now closed under the heavy, blue-veined lids, the long, curved eyelashes falling upon her cheeks. She had the look of death and yet, as De Richleau set about his grim task, it seemed to them that her eyelids might flicker open at any moment. Yet, when the garlic flowers were draped upon her, she remained there cold and immobile, and when the little crucifix was laid upon her lips she showed no consciousness of it, even by the twitching of the tiniest muscle.

'She's dead, Rex, absolutely dead,' De Richleau stood up again. 'So, my poor boy, at least your worst fears will not be realised. Her soul has left her body but no evil entity has taken possession of it. I am certain of that now.'

A new hush fell upon the room. Tanith looked, if possible, even more beautiful in death that she had in life, so that they marvelled at her loveliness. Rex crouched beside her, utterly stricken by this tragic ending to all the wonderful hopes and plans which had seethed in his mind the previous afternoon after she had told him that she loved him. He had known her by sight for so long, dreamed of her so often, yet having gained her love a merciless fate had deprived him of it after only a few hours of happiness. It was unfair—unfair. Suddenly he buried his face in his hands, his great shoulders shook, and for the first time in his life he gave way to a passion of bitter tears.

The rest stood by him in silent sympathy. There was nothing which they could say or do. Marie Lou attempted to soothe his anguish by stroking his rebellious hair, but he jerked his head away with a quick angry movement. Only a few hours before, in those sunlit woods, Tanith had run her fingers through his curls again and again during the ecstasy of the dawning of their passion for each other, and the thought that she would never do so any more filled him with the almost unbearable grief and misery.

After a while the Duke turned helplessly away and Simon, catching his eye, beckoned him over towards the open window out of earshot from the others. The seemingly endless night still lay upon the garden, and now a light mist had arisen. Wisps of it were creeping down the steps from the terrace and curling into the room. De Richleau shivered and refastened the windows to shut them out.

'What is it?' he asked quickly.

'I—er—suppose there *is* no chance of her being made animate again?' hazarded Simon.

'None. If there had been anything there it would never have been able to bear the garlic and the crucifix without giving some indication of its presence.'

'I wasn't thinking of that. The vital organs aren't injured in any way as far as we know, and *rigor mortis* has not set in yet. I felt her hand just now and the fingers are as flexible as mine.'

De Richleau shrugged. 'That makes no difference. *Rigor mortis* may have been delayed for a variety of reasons but she will be as stiff as a board in a few hours' time just the same. Of course her state does resemble that of a person who has been drowned, in a way, but only superficially; and if you are thinking that we might bring her back to life by artificial respiration I can assure you that there is not a chance. It would only be a terrible unkindness to hold out such false hopes to poor Rex.'

'Ner—you don't see what I'm driving at.' Simon's dark eyes flickered quickly from De Richleau's face to the silent group in the centre of the pentagram and then back again. 'No ordinary doctor could do anything for her, I know that well enough; but since her body is still in the intermediate stage there *are* a few people in this world who could, and I was wondering if you——'

'What!' The Duke started suddenly then went on in a whisper: 'Do you mean that *I* should try and bring her back?'

'Um,' Simon nodded his head jerkily up and down. 'If you know the drill—and you seem to know so much about the great secrets, I thought it just on the cards you might?'

De Richleau looked thoughtful for a moment. 'I know something of the ritual,' he confessed at length, 'but I have never seen it done, and in any case it's a terrible responsibility.'

At that moment there was a faint sighing as the breeze rippled the leaves of the trees out in the garden. Both men heard it and they looked at each other questioningly.

'Her soul can't be very far away yet,' whispered Simon.

'No,' the Duke agreed reluctantly. 'But I don't like it, Simon. The dead are not meant to be called back. They do not come willingly. If I attempt this and succeed it would only be by the force of incredibly powerful conjurations which the soul dare not disobey, and we are not justified in taking such steps. Besides, what good could it do? At best, I should not be able to bring her back for more than a few moments.'

'Of course, I know that; but you still don't seem to get my idea,' Simon went on hurriedly. 'As far as Rex is concerned, poor chap, she's gone for good and all, but I was thinking of Mocata. You were hammering it into us last night for all you were worth that it's up to us to destroy him before he has the chance to secure the Talisman. Surely this is our opportunity. In Tanith's present physical state her spirit can't have gone far from her body. If you could bring it back for a few moments, or even get her to talk, don't you see that she'll be able to tell us how best to try and scotch Mocata. From the astral plane, where she is now, her vision and insight are limitless, so she'll be able to help us in a way that she never could have done before.'

'That's different,' De Richleau's pale face lit up with a tired smile. 'And you're right, Simon. I have been under such a strain for the past few hours that I had forgotten the thing that matters most of all. I would never consent to attempt it for any other purpose, but to prevent suffering and death coming to countless millions of people we are justified in anything. I'll speak to Rex.'

Rex nodded despondently, numb now with misery, when the Duke had explained what he meant to try to do. 'Just as you like,' he said slowly. 'It won't hurt in any way, though— I mean her soul—will it?'

'No,' De Richleau assured him. 'In the ordinary way it might. To recall the soul of a dead person is to risk interfering with their *karma,* but Tanith has virtually been murdered and, although it is not the way of the spirit to seek revenge against people for things which may have happened in this life, it is almost a certainty that she is actually wanting to come back for just long enough to tell us how to defeat Mocata, because of her love for you.'

'All right then,' Rex muttered, 'only let's get over with it as quickly as we can.'

'I'm afraid it will take some time,' De Richleau warned him, 'and even then it may not be successful, but the issues at stake are so vital, you must try and put aside your personal grief for a bit.'

He began to clear the pentacle of all the things which he had used the previous evening to form protective barriers, the holy water, the little cups, the horseshoes, placing them with the garlic and dried mandrake back in the suitcase. He then took from it seven small metal trays, a wooden platter, and a box of powered incense; and pouring a little heap of the dark powder on the platter went up to Rex.

'I'm afraid I've got to trouble you if we're going to see this through.'

'Trouble away,' said Rex grimly, with a flash of his old spirit. 'You know I'm with you in anything which is likely to let me get my hands on that devil's throat.'

'Good.' The Duke took out his pocket knife and held the blade for a moment in the flame of a match. 'You've seen enough of this business now to know that I don't do anything without a purpose, and I want a little of your blood. I will use my own if you like but yours is far more likely to have the desired effect, since you felt so strongly for this poor girl and she, apparently, for you.'

'Go ahead.' Rex pulled up his cuff and bared his forearm, but De Richleau shook his head.

'No. Your finger will do, and it will hardly be more than a pin-prick. I only need a few drops.'

With a swift movement he took Rex's hand and, having made a slight incision in the little finger, squeezed out seven drops of blood on to the incense.

Then he walked over to Tanith and, kneeling down, took seven long golden hairs from her head. Next he proceeded to form the mixture of incense and blood into a paste out of which he made seven cones, in each of which was coiled one of Tanith's long golden hairs.

With Richard's assistance he carefully oriented the body so that her feet were pointing towards the north and drew a

252

fresh chalk circle, just large enough to contain her and the bedding, seven feet in diameter.

'Now if you will turn your backs, please,' he told them all, 'I will proceed with the preparation.'

For a few moments they gazed obediently at the book-lined walls while he did certain curious things, and when he bade them turn again he was placing the seven cones of incense on the seven little metal trays, each engraved with the Seal of Solomon, in various positions round the body.

'We shall remain outside the circle this time,' he explained, 'so that the spirit, if it comes, is contained within it. Should some evil entity endeavour to impersonate her soul it will thus be confined within the circle and unable to get at us.'

He lit the seven cones of incense, completed the barrier round about the body with numerous fresh signs, and then, walking over to the doorway, switched out the lights.

The fire was quite dead now, and the candles had never been re-lit, but after a moment greyness began to filter through the french-windows. The light was just sufficient for them to see each other as ghostly forms moving in the darkness, while the body, lying in the circle, was barely visible, its position being indicated by the seven tiny points of light from the cones of incense burning round it.

Simon laid an unsteady hand on the Duke's arm. 'Is it—is it—quite safe to do this? I mean, mightn't Mocata have another cut at us now we're in the dark and no longer have the protection of the pentacle?'

'No,' De Richleau answered decisively. 'He played his last card tonight when he sent the Dark Angel against us and caused Tanith's death. That stupendous operation will have exhausted his magical powers for the time at least. Come over here, all of you, and sit down on the floor in a circle.'

Leading them over to Tanith's feet he arranged them so that Rex and Marie Lou both had their backs to the body and would be spared the sight of any manifestations which might take place about it. He sat facing it himself, with Richard and Simon either side of him; all five of them clasped hands.

Then he told them that they must preserve complete quiet and under no circumstances break the circle they had formed. He warned them too, that if they felt a sudden cold they were not to be frightened by it as they had been of the

253

horrible wind which had swirled so uncannily in that room a few hours before. It would be caused by the ectoplasm which might be drawn from Tanith's body and, he went on to add, if a voice addressed them they were not to answer. He would do any talking which was necessary and they were to remain absolutely still until he gave orders that the circle should be broken up.

They sat there, hand in hand, in silence, while it seemed that an age was passing. The square frame of the window gradually lightened but so very slowly that it was barely perceptible, and if dawn was breaking at last upon the countryside it was shut out from them by the grey, ghostly fog.

The cones of incense burned slowly, giving a strange, acrid smell, mixed with some queer and sickly eastern perfume. From their position in the circle Richard and Simon could see the faint wreaths of smoke curling up for a few inches above the tiny points of light to disappear above, lost in the darkness. Tanith's body lay still and motionless, a shadowy outline upon the thin mat of makeshift bedding.

De Richleau had closed his eyes and bowed his head upon his chest. Once more he was practising that rhythmic, inaudible Raja Yoga breathing, which has such power to recruit strength or to send it forth, and he was using it now while he concentrated on calling the spirit of Tanith to him.

Richard watched the body with curious expectancy. His experience of the last few hours had been too recent for him to collate his thoughts, and while he had so sturdily rejected the idea of Black Magic the night before he would more or less have accepted the fact of Spiritualism. It was a much more general modern belief, and this business as far as he could see, except in a few minor particulars such as the incense compounded with blood, was very similar to the spiritualistic séances of which he had often heard. The only real difference being that, in this instance, they had a newly dead body to operate on and therefore were far more likely to get results. As time wore on, however, he became doubtful, for if their vigil had lasted many hours this one, now that he was utterly weary, seemed like a succession of nights.

It was Simon who first became aware that something was happening. He was watching the seven cones of incense intently, and it seemed to him that the one which was farthest from him, set at Tanith's head, gave out a greater amount of smoke than the rest. Then he realised that he could see the cone more clearly and the eddying curls of aromatic vapour which it sent up had taken on a bluish hue which the rest had not.

He pressed De Richleau's hand and the Duke raised his head. Richard too had seen it, and as they watched, a faint blue light became definitely perceptible.

It gradually solidified into a ball about two inches in diameter and moved slowly forward from the head until it reached the centre of Tanith's body. There it remained for a while, growing in brightness and intensity until it had became a strong blue light. Then it rose a little and hovered in the air above her, so that by its glow they could clearly see the curves of her figure and her pale, beautiful face, lit by that strange radiance.

Intensely alert now, they sat still and watchful, until the ball of light began to lose colour and diffuse itself over a wider area. The smoke of the incense wreathed up towards it from the seven metal platters, and it seemed to gather this into itself, forming from it the vague outline of a head and shoulders, still cloudy and transparent but, after another few moments, definitely recognisable as an outline of the bust of the figure which lay motionless beneath it.

With pounding hearts they watched for new developments, and now it seemed that the whole process of materialisation was hurried forward in a few seconds. The bust joined itself, by throwing out a shadowy torso, to the hips of the dead body, the face and shoulders solidified until the features were distinct, and the whole became surrounded by an aureole of light.

Upon the strained silence there came the faintest whisper of a voice:

'You called me. I am here.'

'Are you in truth, Tanith?' De Richleau asked softly.

'I am.'

'Do you acknowledge our Lord Jesus Christ?'

'I do.'

A sigh of relief escaped De Richleau, for he knew that no impersonating elemental would ever dare to testify in such a manner, and he proceeded quietly:

'Do you come here of your own free will, or do you wish to depart?'

'I come because you called, but I am glad to come.'

'There is one here whose grief for your passing is very great. He does not seek to draw you back, but he wishes to know if it is your desire to help him in the protection of his friends and the destruction of evil for the well-being of the world.'

'It is my desire.'

'Will you tell us all that you can of the man Mocata which may prove of help?'

'I cannot, for I am circumscribed by the Law, but you may ask me what you will and, because you have summoned me, I am bound by your command to answer.'

'What is he doing now?'

'Plotting fresh evil against you.'

'Where is he now?'

'He is quite near you.'

'Can you not tell me where?'

'I do not know. I cannot see distinctly, for he covers himself with a cloak of darkness, but he is still in your neighbourhood.'

'In the village?'

'Perhaps.'

'Where will he be this time tomorrow?'

'In Paris.'

'What do you see him doing in Paris?'

'I see him talking with a man who has lost a portion of his left ear. It is a tall building. They are both very angry.'

'Will he stay in Paris for long?'

'No. I see him moving at great speed towards the rising sun.'

'Where do you see him next?'

'Under the earth.'

'Do you mean that he is dead—to us?'

'No. He is in a stone-flagged vault beneath a building which is very *very* old. The place radiates evil. The red vibrations are so powerful that I cannot see what he does there. The light which surrounds me now protects me from such sights.'

'What is he planning now?'

'To draw me back.'

'Do you mean that he is endeavouring to restore your soul to your body?'

'Yes. He is already bitterly regretting that in his anger

256

against you he risked the severance of the two. He could force me to be of great service to him on your plane but he cannot do so on this.'

'But is it possible for him to bring you back—permanently?'

'Yes. If he acts at once. While the moon is still in her dark quarter.'

'Is it your wish to return?'

'No, unless I were free of him—but I have no choice. My soul is in pawn until the coming of the new moon. After that I shall pass on unless he has succeeded.'

'How will he set about this thing?'

'There is only one way. The full performance of the Black Mass.'

'You mean with sacrifice of a Christian child?'

'Yes. It is the age-old law, a soul for a soul. That is the only way and the soul of a baptised child will be accepted in exchange for mine. Then if my body remains uninjured I shall be compelled to return to it.'

'What are——'

The Duke's next question was cut short by Rex, who could stand the strain no longer. He did not know that De Richleau was only conversing with Tanith's astral body and thought that he had succeeded in restoring the corpse which lay behind him, at least to temporary life again.

'Tanith,' he cried, breaking the circle and flinging himself round. 'Tanith!'

In a fraction of time the vision disintegrated and disappeared. His eyes blazing with anger, De Richleau sprang to his feet.

'You fool!' he thundered. 'You stupid fool.' In the pale light of dawn which was now at last just filtering through the fog, he glared at Rex. Then, as they stood there, angry recriminations about to burst from their lips, the whole party were arrested in their every movement and remained transfixed.

A shrill, clear cry had cut like a knife into the heavy, incense-laden atmosphere, coming from the room above.

'That's Fleur,' gasped Marie Lou. 'My precious, what is it?'

In an instant, she was dashing across the room to the little door in the bookshelves which led to the staircase up to the nursery. Yet Richard was before her.

In two bounds he had reached the door and was fumbling

for the catch. His trembling fingers found it. He gave a violent jerk. The little metal ring which served to open it came away in his hand.

Precious moments were lost as they clawed at the bookbacks. At last it swung free. Richard pushed Marie Lou through ahead of him and followed, pressing at her heels. The others stumbled up the old stone stairs in frantic haste behind them.

They reached the night nursery. Rex ran to the window. It was wide open. The grey mist blanketed the garden outside. Marie Lou dashed to the cot. The sheets were tumbled. The imprint of a little body lay there fresh and warm—but Fleur was gone.

29

Simon Aron Takes a View

'Here's the way they went,' cried Rex. 'There's a ladder under this window.'

'Then for God's sake get after him,' Richard shouted, racing across the room. 'If that damn door hadn't stuck we'd have caught him red-handed—he can't have got far.'

Rex was already on the terrace below, Simon shinned down the ladder and Richard flung his leg over the sill of the window to follow.

Marie Lou was left alone with De Richleau in the nursery. She stared at him with round, tearless eyes, utterly overcome by this new calamity. The Duke stared back, shaken to the very depths by this appalling thing which he had brought upon his friends. He wanted most desperately to comfort and console her, but realised how hopelessly inadequate anything that he could say would be. The thought of that child having been seized by the Satanist to be offered up in some ghastly sacrifice, was utterly unbearable.

'Princess,' he managed to stammer, 'Princess.' But further words would not come, and for once in his life he found himself powerless to deal with a situation.

Marie Lou just stood there motionless and staring, held

urgent need to comfort De Richleau. Her poor 'Greyeyes' was feeling desperately unhappy, she knew, and held himself entirely responsible for the terrible thing which could not possibly be true. When he mentioned breakfast she said at once: 'I will go down and cook you some eggs or something.'

'No, no, my dear,' De Richleau looked round and then lowered his eyes quickly, his heart wrung at the sight of her dead-white face. 'Please go down to the library and read this letter of Mocata's through again quietly with Richard. Then you can talk it over together and will have made up your minds what you think best by the time the rest of us get back.'

Richard gave in to the Duke's wishes for the moment. They all descended to the ground floor again and, when the other three had gone off to the kitchen quarters, he remained with Marie Lou and read Mocata's letter quickly.

As he finished he looked up at her in miserable indecision. 'My poor sweet. This is ghastly for you.'

'It's just as bad for you,' she said softly. Then, with a little cry, she flung her arms round his neck. 'Oh, Richard, darling, what are we to do?'

'Dearest.' He hugged her to him, soothing her gently as best he could now that the storm had broken. Her small body heaved with desperate sobbing, while great tears ran down her cheeks, falling in large, damp splashes upon his hands and neck.

As he held her, murmuring little phrases of endearment and optimistic comfort, he thought her weeping would never cease. Her body trembled as it was swept with terrible emotion at the loss of her cherished Fleur.

'Marie Lou, my angel,' he whispered softly, 'try and pull yourself together, do, or else you'll have me breaking down as well in a minute. No harm can have happened to her yet, and it isn't likely to until tonight at the earliest. Even then, he'll think twice before he carries out his threat. Only a fool destroys his hostage to spite his enemy. Mocata may be every sort of rogue, but he's a civilised one at least, so he won't maltreat her in any way, you can be sure of that, and if we only play our cards properly, we'll get her back before it comes to any question of his carrying out this appalling threat.'

'But what can we do, Richard? What can we do?' she cried, looking at him wildly from large, tear-dimmed eyes.

'Get after him the second the others come back,' Richard

declared promptly. 'He's human, isn't he? He had to use a ladder to get up to the nursery just like any other thug. If we act at once we'll have him under lock and key by nightfall.'

De Richleau's quiet voice broke in from behind them. 'You have decided, then, to call in the police?'

'Of course.' Richard turned to stare at him. 'This is totally different from last night's affair. It is a case of kidnapping, pure and simple, and I'm going to pull every gun I know to get the police of the whole country after him in the next half hour. If you've reconnected that line, I'll get straight through to Scotland Yard—now.'

'Yes, the telephone is all right. I've been through to the inn and had old Wilkes out of bed. He remembers Rex and Tanith dining there last night, of course, but when I described Mocata to him, he said he hadn't seen anyone who answers to that description there at all, either yesterday or this morning. Have you written that letter for the servants?'

'Not yet. I will.' Richard left the library just as Simon and Rex came in, carrying a collection of plates and dishes on two trays, prominent upon which were a large China teapot and the half of a York ham.

'Please don't phone Scotland Yard just yet,' Marie Lou called after Richard. 'I simply must talk to you again before we burn our boats.'

The Duke gave her a sharp glance from under his grey eyebrows. 'You are not then in favour of calling in the police?'

'I don't know what to do,' she confessed miserably. 'Richard is so sane and practical that I suppose he's right, but you read the letter and I should never forgive myself if our calling in the police forced Mocata's hand. Do you—do you really think that he has the power to find out if we go against his instructions?'

De Richleau nodded. 'I'm afraid so. But Simon can tell you more of his capabilities in that direction than I can.'

Simon and Rex had put down their trays and were reading Mocata's letter together. The former looked up swiftly.

'Um. He can see things when he wants to in that mirror I told you of, and once he gets to London he'll have half-a-dozen mediums that he can throw into a trance to pick us up. It will be child's play for a man of his powers to find out if we leave this room,'

'That's my view,' the Duke agreed. 'And if we once turn to the police, we have either to go to them or else bring them here. Telephoning won't be sufficient. They will want photographs of Fleur and to question every one concerned, so Mocata stands a pretty good chance of seeing us in conference with them, if he keeps us under psychic observation, whichever way we set to work.'

'We should be mad to even think of it,' said Simon jerkily. 'It's pretty useless for me to say I'm sorry, but I brought this whole trouble on you all and there's only one thing to do, that obvious.'

'For us to sit here like a lot of dummies while you go off to give yourself up at twelve o'clock, I suppose?' Richard, who had just rejoined them, cut in acidly.

'I have been expecting that, knowing Simon,' the Duke observed. 'Terrible as the consequences may be for him and although the idea of surrender makes my blood boil I must confess that I think he's right, with certain modifications!'

'Oh, isn't there some other way?' Marie Lou exclaimed desperately, catching at Simon's hand. 'It's too awful that because of our own trouble we should even talk of sacrificing you.'

One of those rare smiles that made him such a lovable person lit Simon's face. 'Ner,' he said softly, 'it's been my muddle from the beginning. I'm terribly grateful to you all for trying to get me out of it, but Mocata's been too much for us, and I must throw my hand in now. It's the only thing to do.'

'It is my damned incompetence which has let us in for this,' grunted the Duke. 'I deserve to take your place, Simon, and I would—you know that—if it were the least use. The devil of it is that it's you he wants, not me.'

Rex had been cutting thin slices from the ham and pouring out the tea. Richard took a welcome cup of his favourite Orange Pekoe from him and said firmly:

'Stop talking nonsense, for God's sake! Neither of you is to blame. After what we've all been through together in the past you did quite rightly to come here. Who should we look to for help in times of trouble if not each other? If I was in a real tight corner I shouldn't hesitate to involve either of you—and I know that Marie Lou feels the same. This blow couldn't possibly have been foreseen by anyone. It was just—

well, call it an accident, and the responsibility for protecting Fleur was ours every bit as much as yours. Now let's get down to what we mean to do.'

'That's decent of you, Richard.' De Richleau tried to smile, knowing what it must have cost his friend to ease their feeling of guilt when he must be so desperately anxious about his child.

'Damned decent,' Simon echoed. 'But all the same I'm going to keep the appointment Mocata's made for me. It's the only hope we've got.'

Richard stuck out his chin. 'You're not, old chap. You placed yourself in my hands by coming to my house, and I won't have it. The business we went through last night scared me as much as anyone, I admit it; but because Greyeyes has proved right about Satanic manifestations, there is no reason for you all to lose your sense of proportion about what the evil powers can do. They have their limitations, just like anything else. Greyeyes admitted last night that they were based on natural laws, and this swine's gone outside them. He's operating now in country that is strange to him. He confesses as much in his letter. You can see he is scared of calling in the police, and that's the very way we're going to get him. You people seem to have lost your nerve.'

'No,' the Duke said sadly. 'I haven't lost my nerve, but look at it if you like on the basis which you suggest, Richard—that this is a perfectly normal kidnapping. Say Fleur were being held to ransom by a group of unscrupulous gangsters, such as operate in the States, the gang being in a position to to know what is going on in your house. They have threatened to kill Fleur if you bring the police into the business. Now, would you be prepared to risk that in such circumstances?'

'No, I should pay up, as most wretched parents seem to, on the off-chance that the gang gave me a square deal and I got the child back unharmed. But this is different. I'll stake my oath that Mocata means to double-cross us anyhow. If it were only Simon that he wanted he might be prepared to let us have Fleur back in exchange. You seem to forget what Tanith told you. He doesn't know that we know his intentions, but she was absolutely definite on three points. One, he means to do his damnedest to bring her back. Two, he will fail unless he makes the attempt in the next few days. Three, *the only*

266

*way that can be done is by performing a full Black Mass,
including the sacrifice of a baptised child.* Kidnappings take
time to plan in a civilised country unless you want the police
on your track. Mocata has succeeded in one where he thinks
there is a fair chance of keeping the police out of it, and no
one in their senses could suggest that he's the sort of man
who would run the risk of doing another just for the joy of
keeping his word with us. It's as clear as daylight that he is
using Fleur as bait to get hold of Simon and then he'll do us
down by killing the child in the end.'

De Richleau slit open a roll and slipped a slice of ham inside
it. 'Well,' he said as he began to trim the ragged edges neatly,
'it is for you and Marie Lou to decide. The prospect of sitting
in this room for hours on end doing nothing is about the grim-
mest I've ever had to face in a pretty crowded lifetime. I
would give most things I really value for a chance to have
another cut at him. The only thing that deters me for one
moment is the risk to Fleur.'

'I know that well enough,' Richard acknowledged, 'but I
am convinced our only chance of seeing her alive again is to
call in the police, and trust to running him to earth before
nightfall.'

'I wouldn't,' Simon shook his head, 'I wouldn't honestly,
Richard. He's certain to find out if we take steps against him.
We shall waste hours here being questioned by the local big-
wigs, and it's a hundred to one against their being able to
corner him in a single day. Fleur is safe for the moment—for
God's sake don't make things worse than they are. I know the
man and he's as heartless as a snake. It's signing Fleur's death
warrant to try and tackle him like this.'

Marie Lou listened to these conflicting arguments in miserable indecision. She was torn violently from side to side by
each in turn. Simon spoke with such absolute conviction that
it seemed certain Richard's suggested intervention would pre-
cipitate her child's death, and yet she felt, too, how right
Richard was in his belief that Mocata was certain to double-
cross them, and having trapped them into surrendering Simon,
retain Fleur for this abominable sacrifice which Tanith had
told them he was so anxious to make. The horns of the
dilemma seemed to join and form a vicious circle which went
round and round in her aching head.

The others fell silent and Richard looked across at her. 'Well, dearest, which is it to be?'

'Oh, I don't know,' she moaned. 'Both sides seem right and yet the risk is so appalling either way.'

He laid his hand gently on her hair. 'It's beastly having to make such a decision, and if we were alone in this I wouldn't dream of asking you. I'd do what I thought best myself unless you were dead against it, but as the others disagree with me so strongly what can I do but ask you to decide?'

Wringing her hands together in agonised distress at this horrible problem with which she was faced, Marie Lou looked desperately from side to side, then her glance fell on Rex. He was sitting hunched up in a dejected attitude on the far side of Tanith's body, his eyes fixed in hopeless misery on the dead girl's face.

'Rex,' she said hoarsely, 'you haven't said what you think yet. Both these alternatives seem equally ghastly to me. What do you advise?'

'Eh?' He looked up quickly 'It's mighty difficult and I was just trying to figure it out. I hate the thought of doing nothing, waiting about when you've got a packet of trouble is just real hell to me, and I'd like to get after this bird with a gun. But Simon's so certain that if we did it would be fatal to Fleur, and I guess the Duke thinks that way to. They both know him, you must remember, and Richard doesn't, which is a point to them, but I've got a hunch that we are barking up the wrong tree, and that this is a case for what Greyeyes calls his masterly policy of inactivity. The old game of giving the enemy enough rope so he'll hang himself in the end.

'Any sort of compromise is all against my nature, but I reckon it's the only policy that offers now. If we stay put here and carry out Mocata's instructions to the letter, we'll at least be satisfied in our minds that we are not bringing any fresh danger on Fleur. But let's go that far and no farther. We all know Simon is willing enough to cash in his checks, but I don't think we ought to let him. Instead, we'll keep him here. That is going to force Mocata to scratch his head a whole heap. He'll not do Fleur in before he's had another cut at getting hold of Simon, so it will be up to him to make the next move in the game, and that may give us a fresh opening. The situation can't be worse than it is at present, and when he shows his hand again, given a spot of luck, we might be able to ring the changes on him yet.'

De Richleau smiled, for the first time in days, it seemed. 'My friend, I salute you,' he said, with real feeling in his voice. 'I am growing old, I think, or I should have thought of that myself. It is by far and away the most sensible thing that any of us have suggested yet.'

With a sigh of relief, Marie Lou moved over and, stooping down, kissed Rex on the cheek. 'Rex, darling, bless you. In our trouble we've been forgetting yours, and it is very wonderful that you should have thought of a real way out for us in the midst of your sorrow. I dreaded having to make that decision just now more than anything that I have had to do in my whole life.'

He smiled rather wanly. 'That's all right, darling. There's nothing so mighty clever about it, but it gives us time, and you must try and comfort yourself with the thought that time and the angels are on our side.'

Even Richard's frantic anxiety to set out immediately in search of his Fleur d'amour was overcome for the time being by Rex's so obviously sensible suggestion. In his agitation he had eaten nothing yet, but now he sat down to cut some sandwiches, and set about persuading Marie Lou that she must eat the first of them in order to keep up her strength. Then he looked over at the Duke.

'I left that note for Malin where he's bound to see it—slipped it under his bedroom door, so we shan't be disturbed here. Is there anything at all that we can do?'

'Nothing, I fear, only possess ourselves with such patience as we can, but we're all at about the end of our tether, so we ought to try and get some sleep. If Mocata makes some fresh move this evening it's on the cards that we shall be up again all night.'

'I'll get some cushions,' Simon volunteered. 'I suppose there's no harm in bringing used articles into this room now?'

'None. You had better collect all the stuff you can and we'll make up some temporary beds on the floor.'

Simon, Richard and Rex left the room and returned a few moments later with piles of cushions and all the rugs that they could find. They placed some fresh logs on the smouldering ashes of the fire and then set about laying out five make-shift resting-places.

When they had finished, Marie Lou allowed Richard to lead her over to one of them and tuck her up, although she protested that, exhausted though she was, she would never be able to sleep. The rest lay down, and then Richard switched out the light.

Full day had come at last, but it was of little use, for the range of vision was limited to about fifteen yards. The mist outside the windows seemed, if anything, denser than before, and it swirled and eddied in curling wreaths above the damp stones of the terrace, muffling the noises of the countryside and shutting out the light.

None of them felt that they would be able to sleep. Rex's gnawing sorrow for Tanith preyed upon his mind. The others, racked with anxiety for Fleur, turned restlessly upon their cushions. Every now and then they heard Marie Lou give way to fits of sobbing as though her heart would break. But the stress of those terrible night hours and the emotions they had passed through since had exhausted them completely. Marie Lou's bursts of sobbing became quieter and then ceased. Richard fell into an uneasy doze. De Richleau and Rex breathed evenly, sunk at last in a heavy sleep.

Hours later Marie Lou was dreaming that she was seated in an ancient library reading a big, old-fashioned book, the cover of which was soft and hairy like a wolf's skin, and that as she read it a circle of iron was bound about her head. Then the scene changed. She was in the pentacle again, and that loathsome sack-like Thing was attacking Fleur. She awoke —started up with a sudden scream of fear.

Her waking was little better than the nightmare when memory flooded back into her mind. Yet that too and the present only seemed other phases of the frightful dream; the comfortable library denuded of its furniture; Tanith's dead body lying in the centre of the floor and the dimness of the room from those horrible fog banks shutting out the sunshine. They could not possibly be anything but figments of the imagination.

The men had roused at once, and crowded round her, shadowy figures in the uncertain light. De Richleau pressed the electric switch. They blinked a little, and looked at each other sleepily, then their eyes turned to the place where Simon had lain.

With one thought their glances shifted to the window and they knew that while they slept their friend had gone out, into that ghostly unnatural night, to keep his grim appointment.

30

Out Into the Fog

It was Rex who noticed the chalk marks on the floor. He stepped over and saw that Simon, lacking pencil and paper, had used these means to leave them a short message. Slowly he deciphered the scribbled words and read them out:

'Please don't fuss or try to come after me. This is my muddle, so am keeping appointment. Do as Mocata has ordered. Am certain that is only chance of saving Fleur.

Love to all.   SIMON.'

'Aw, Hell!' exclaimed Rex as he finished. 'The dear heroic little sap has gone and put paid to my big idea. Mocata has got him *and* Fleur now on top of having killed Tanith. If you ask me we're properly sunk.'

De Richleau groaned. 'It is just like him. We ought to have guessed that he would do this.'

'You're right there,' Richard agreed sadly. 'I've known him longer than any of you, and I did my damnedest to prevent him sacrificing himself for nothing, but it seems to me he's only done the very thing you said he should.'

'That's not quite fair,' the Duke protested mildly. 'I only said I thought it right that he should *with certain modifications*. I had it in my mind that we might follow him at a distance. We should have arrived at the rendezvous before Mocata could have known that we had left this place, and we might have pulled something off. As it was, I thought Rex's idea so much better that I abandoned mine.'

'I'm sorry,' Richard apologised huskily. 'But Simon's my

271

oldest friend you know, and this on top of all the rest . . .'

'Do you—do you think the poor sweet is right, and that his having given himself up will be of any use?' whispered Marie Lou.

Richard shrugged despondently. 'Not the least, dearest. I hate to seem ungracious, and you all know how devoted I am to Simon but in his anxiety to do the right thing he's handed Mocata our only decent card. We can sit here till Doomsday, but there's no chance now of making any fresh move which might give us a new opening. We've wasted the Lord knows how many precious hours, and we're in a worse hole than we were before. I'm going to carry out my original intention and get on to the police.'

'I wouldn't do that,' Rex caught him by the arm. 'It'll only mean our wasting further time in spilling long dispositions to a bunch of cops, and you're all wrong about our not having made anything on the new deal. We've had a sleep which we needed mighty badly, and we've lulled Mocata into a false sense of security. Just because we've remained put here all morning like he said and Simon's come over with the goods, he'll think he's sitting pretty now and maybe let up on his supervision stunt. Let's cut out bothering with the police and get after him ourselves this minute.'

Marie Lou shivered slightly and then nodded. 'Rex is right, you know. Mocata has got what he wants now, so it is very unlikely that he is troubling to keep us under observation any more, but how do you propose to try to find him?'

'We will go straight to Paris,' De Richleau announced, with a display of his old form. 'You remember Tanith told us that by tonight he would be there holding a conversation with a man who had lost the upper portion of his left ear. That is Castelnau, the banker, I am certain, so the thing for us to do is to make for Paris and hunt him out.'

'How do you figure on getting there?' asked the practical Rex.

'By plane, of course. Mocata is obviously travelling that way or he could never get there by tonight. Richard must take us in his four-seater, and if Mocata has to motor all the way to Croydon before he can make a start, we'll be there before him. Is your plane in commission, Richard?'

'Yes, the plane's all right. It's in the hangar at the bottom of the meadow, and when I took her out three days ago she was running perfectly. I don't much like the look of this fog, though, although, of course, it's probably only a ground mist.'

They all glanced out of the window again. The grey murk still hung over the terrace, shutting out the view of the Botticelli garden where, on this early May morning, the polyanthus and forget-me-nots and daffodils, shedding their green cocoons, were bursting into colourful life.

'Let's go,' said Rex, impatiently. 'De Richleau's right. 'You'd best get some clothes on, then we'll beat it for Paris the second you're fit.'

The rest followed him out into the hall and upstairs to the rooms above. The house was silent and seemingly deserted. The servants were obviously taking Richard's orders in their most literal sense and, released for once from their daily tasks, enjoying an unexpected holiday in their own quarters.

Marie Lou looked into the nursery and almost broke down again for a moment as she once more saw the empty cot, but she hurried past it to the nurse's bedroom and found the woman still sleeping soundly.

In Richard's dressing-room the men made hasty preparations. Rex was clad in the easy lounge suit which he had put on in De Richleau's flat, but Richard and the Duke were still in pyjamas. When they were dressed Richard fitted the others out as well as he could with top clothes for their journey. The Duke was easy, being only a little taller than himself, and a big double overcoat was found for Rex, into which he managed to scramble despite the breadth of his enormous shoulders. Marie Lou joined them a few moments later, clad in her breeches and leather flying coat, which she always used whenever she went up with Richard.

Downstairs again, they paused in the library to make another hurried meal. Then the door was locked, and after casting a last unhappy glance at Tanith's body, which remained unaltered in appearance, Rex led the way out on the terrace.

They walked quickly down the gravel path beside the Botticelli border, the sound of their footsteps muffled by the all-pervading mist—through Marie Lou's own garden, with its long herbaceous borders, and past the old sundial—round the quadrangles of tessellated pavement which fell in a succession

273

of little terraces to the pond garden, with its water lilies, and so to the meadow beyond.

When they reached the hangar Richard and Rex ran out the plane and got it in order for the flight. De Richleau stood watching their operations with Marie Lou beside him, both of them fretting a little at the necessary delay, since now that the vital decision had been taken every member of the party was impatient to set out.

They settled themselves in the comfortable four-seater. Rex swung the propeller, well accustomed to the ways of aeroplanes, and the engine purred upon a low steady note. He watched it for a second, and then, as he scrambled aboard, there came the long conventional cry: '*All set.*'

The plane moved slowly forward into the dank mist. The hedges and trees on either side were shut out by banks of fog, but Richard knew the ground so well that he felt confident of judging his distance and direction. He taxied over the even grass of the long field, and turned to rise. The plane lifted, touched ground again gently twice, and they were off.

As they left the earth a new feeling came over Richard. He was passionately fond of flying, and it always filled him with exhilaration, but this was different. It was as though he had suddenly come out into the daylight after having been walking down a long, dark, smoky tunnel for many hours. At long intervals there had been brightly lit recesses in the sides of it where figures stood like tableaux at a waxworks show. The slug-like Thing and Fleur; Rex standing at the window with Tanith in his arms; Simon whispering something to the Duke; Marie Lou's face as she stood with her hand resting on the rail of Fleur's empty cot, and a dozen others. The rest of that strange journey he seemed to have made, consisted of long periods of blankness only punctuated by little cries of fear and scraps of reiterated argument, the purpose of which he could no longer remember. Now—his brain was clear again, and he settled himself with new purpose to handle the plane with all his skill.

In those few moments they had risen clear of the ground mist and were soaring upwards into the blue above. As De Richleau looked down he saw a very curious thing. Not only was the fog that had hemmed them in local, but it seemed to be concentrated entirely upon Cardinals Folly. He could just make out the chimneys of the house rising in its centre, as from a grey sea, and from the buildings it spread out in a circular formation for half a mile or so on every side, hiding the gardens from his view and obscuring the meadows between the house and the village, but beyond, all was clear in the brilliant sunshine of the early summer afternoon.

Rex was beside Richard in the cockpit. Automatically he had taken on the job of navigator, and, like Richard, his brain numbed before with misery, had started to function properly again directly he set to busying himself with the maps and scales.

The Duke, sitting in the body of the machine with Marie Lou, felt that there was nothing he could say to comfort her, but he took her hand in his and held it between his own. From his quick gesture she felt again his intense distress that he should ever have been the means of bringing her this terrible unhappiness, so, to distract his thoughts, she put her mouth right up against his ear and told him of the odd dream she had had; about reading the old book. He gave her a curious glance and began to shout back at her.

She could not catch all he said owing to the noise of the engine, but enough to tell that he was intensely interested. He seemed to think that she had been dreaming of the famous Red Book of Appin, a wonderful treatise on Magic owned by the Stewards of Invernahyle, who were now extinct. The book had been lost and not heard of for more than a hundred years, but her description of it, and the legend that it might only be read with understanding by those who wore a circlet of iron above their brow made him insistent that it must be this which she had seen in her dream. He pressed her to try and remember if she had understood any portion of it.

After some trouble she managed to convey to him that she had read one sentence on a faded vellum page, and that although the lettering was quite different from anything which she had ever seen before, she understood it at the time, but could not recall the meaning now. Then, as talking was so difficult, they fell silent.

At a hundred miles an hour the plane soared above the English counties, but they took little heed of the fields and hedges, woods and hills, which fled so swiftly from beneath them. Somehow they seemed to have stepped out of their old

275

life altogether. Time no longer existed for them, only the will to arrive at their destination in order to be active once again. All their thoughts were concentrated now upon Paris and the man who had lost half his ear. Would he be there? Could they find him if he was? And would they arrive before Mocata?

They passed over the Northern end of the English Channel almost without noticing it; Marie Lou felt a little shock when the plane banked steeply and Richard brought it circling down.

The sun was sinking behind great banks of cloud and, as the plane tilted, she saw that a thick mist lay below them in which glowed dull patches of half-obscured light. Richard and Rex knew them, however, to be fog flares of the Le Bourget landing ground.

A few seconds more and they had seen the last of the sunset. A thin greyness closed about them. One of the flares showed bright, and the plane bounded along the earth until Richard brought it to a standstill.

Almost in a daze they answered the questions of the officers at the airport and passed the Customs, secured a fast-looking taxi and, packed inside it, were heading for the centre of Paris.

As they ran through the streets, with the familiar high-pitched note of the taxi's horn continually sounding and the subtle smell of the *epiceries* in their nostrils—the very scent of Paris—they noticed half-unconsciously that night had fallen once more.

Here and there the electric sky-signs on the tall buildings, advertising Savan Cadum or Byrrh, glowed dully through the murk, and the lights of the cafés illuminated little spaces of the boulevards through which they passed, throwing up the figures that sat sipping their aperitifs at the marble-topped tables and dappling the young green of the stunted trees that lined the pavements.

None of them spoke as the taxi swerved and rushed, seeking every opportunity to nose its way through the traffic. Only Rex leant forward once, soon after they left the aerodrome, and murmured: 'I told him the Ritz. We'll be able to hunt up this bird's address when we get there.'

They ran past the Opera, down the Boulevard de la Madeleine, and turned left into the Place Vendôme. The cab pulled

276

up with a jerk. A liveried porter hurried forward to fling open the door, and they scrambled out.

'Pay him off, with a good tip,' Rex ordered the hotel servant. 'I'll see-yer-later, inside.' Then he led the way into the hotel.

One of the under-managers at the bureau recognised him and came forward with a welcoming smile.

'Monsieur Van Ryn, what a pleasure! You require accomodation for your party? How many rooms do you desire? I hope that you will stay with us some time.'

'Two single rooms and one double, with bathrooms, and we'd best have ⅂ sitting-room on the same floor,' replied Rex curtly. 'How long we'll be staying I can't say. I've got urgent business to attend to this trip. Do you happen to know a banker named Castelnau—elderly man, grey-haired, with a hatchet face, who's had a slice taken out of his left ear?'

'*Mais oui, monsieur.* He lunches here frequently.'

'Good. D'you know where he lives?'

'For the moment, no, but I will ascertain. You permit?' The manager moved briskly away and disappeared into the office. A few moments later he returned with a Paris telephone directory open in his hand.

'This will be it, monsieur, I think. Monsieur Laurent Castelnau, 72, Maison Rambouillet, Parc Monceau. That is a block of flats. Do you wish to telephone his apartment?'

'Sure,' Rex nodded. 'Call him right away, please.' Then, as the Frenchman hurried off, he nodded quietly to the Duke: 'Best leave this to me. I've got a hunch how to fix him.'

'Go ahead,' the Duke acquiesced. He had been keeping well in the background, and now he smiled a little unhappily as he went on in a low voice:

'How I love Paris. The smell and the sight and the sound of it. I have not been back here for fifteen years. The Government have never forgiven me for the part that I played in the Royalist rising which took place in the 90's. I was young then. How long ago it all seems now. But never since have I dared to venture back to France, except a few times, secretly on the most urgent business. I believe the authorities would still put me into some miserable fortress if they discovered me on French soil.'

'Oh, Greyeyes, dear! You ought never to have come.' Marie Lou turned to him impulsively. 'With all these awful things

277

happening I had forgotten. Somehow I always think of you really as an Englishman, not as a French exile who lives in England as the next best thing. It would be terrible if you were arrested and tried as a political offender after all these years.'

He shrugged and smiled again. 'Don't worry, Princess. The authorities have almost forgotten my existence, I expect, and the only risk I run is in knowing so many people who constantly travel through France. If someone recognised me and spoke my name too loud it is just possible that it might strike a chord in some police spy's memory, but beyond that there is very little danger.

They sat down at a little table in the lounge while Rex was telephoning. When he rejoined them he nodded cheerfully.

'We're in luck, and Lord knows we need it. I spoke to Castelnau himself, used the name of my old man's firm—The Chesapeake Banking and Trust Corporation—and spun a yarn that he had sent me over on a special mission to Europe connected with the franc. Told him the whole thing was far too hush-hush for me to make a date to see him at his office tomorrow morning, where his clerks might recognise me as the representative of an American banking house, and that I must see him tonight privately. He hedged a bit until I put it to him that I had power to deal in real big figures, and he fell for that like a sucker. He couldn't see me yet though, because he's busy putting on his party frock for some official banquet, but he figures he'll be back at the apartment round about ten o'clock, so I said I'd be along to state my business then.'

'To fill in time we might go upstairs and have a bath, remarked Richard, feeling his bristly chin. 'Then we'd better go out and dine somewhere, though God knows, I've never felt less like food in my life.'

'All right,' De Richleau agreed, 'only let us go somewhere quiet for dinner. If we go to one of the smart places it will add to the chance of my running into somebody that I know.'

'What about Le Vert Galant?' Richard suggested. 'It's on the right bank down by La Cité, old-fashioned, quiet, but excellent food, and you're unlikely to see the sort of people that we know there in the evening.'

'Is that still running?' De Richleau smiled. 'Then let us go there by all means. It's just the place.' And they moved over towards the lift.

Upstairs they bathed and tidied themselves, but almost automatically, for their uneasy sleep that morning seemed to have done little to recruit their lowered energy. As though still in a bad dream, Marie Lou undressed, and dressed again, while Richard moved about the room, for once apparently unconscious of her presence, silently and mechanically eliminating the traces of the journey. Then he submitted to the ministrations of the hotel barber with one curt order, that the man was to shave him and not to talk.

Rex finished first and wandered into their room, where he sat uncomfortably perched upon a corner of the bed, but he stared at his large feet the whole time that he sat there and did not make any effort whatever at conversation.

De Richleau joined them shortly afterwards, and Marie Lou, rousing for a moment from her abject misery, noted with a little start how spick and span he had become again, after the attentions of the barber and his bath. He had produced one of his long Hoyos, and appeared to be smoking it with quiet enjoyment. Richard and Rex, despite the removal of their incipient beards, still looked woebegone and haggard, as though they had not slept for days, and were almost contemplating suicide, but the Duke still maintained his air of the great gentleman for whose pleasure and satisfaction this whole existence is ordered.

Actually his appearance was no more than a mask with which long habit had accustomed him to disguise his emotions, and at heart he was racked by an anxiety equal to that of any of the others. He was suppressing his impatience to get hold of Castelnau only by a supreme effort; his feet itched to be on the move, and his fingers to be on the throat of the adversary; but as he came into the room he smiled round at them, kissed Marie Lou's hand with his usual gallantry, and presented a huge bunch of white violets to her.

'A few flowers, Princess, for your room.'

Marie Lou took them without a word; the tears brimming in her eyes spoke her thanks that he should have thought of such a thing at such a time, and his perfect naturalness served to steady them all a little as they went down afterwards in the lift. Rex changed some money at the *caisse,* and they went out into the night again.

'Queer—isn't it,' remarked Richard as he looked out of the

taxi window at the fog-bound streets. 'I've always said what fun it is to make a surprise visit for a couple of nights to Paris —in May. It's like stealing in on summer in advance—tea in the open at Armenonville—a drive to Fontainebleau, with the forest at its very best—and all that. 'I never thought I might come to Paris one May like this.'

'I've a feeling there's something wrong about it—or us,' said Rex slowly. 'Those servants in the hotel back there didn't seem any more natural than the weather to me. It was as though I was watching them act in some kind of play.'

De Richleau nodded. 'Yes, I felt the same, and I believe Mocata is responsible. Perhaps he surrounded Cardinals Folly with a strong atmospheric force, and we have brought the vibrations of it with us, or he may be interfering with our auras in some way. I'm only guessing, of course, and can't possibly explain it.'

At the Vert Galant De Richleau ordered dinner without reference to any of them. He was a great gourmet, and knew from past experience the dishes that pleased them best, but as a meal it was one of the most dismal failures which it had ever been his misfortune to witness.

He knew and they knew that his apparent preoccupation with food and wine was nothing but a bluff; an attempt to smother their anxiety and occupy their thoughts until the time to go to Castelnau's apartment should arrive. The cooking was excellent, the service everything that one could desire, and the cellar of Le Vert Galant provided wines to which even De Richleau's critical taste gave full approval, but their hearts were not in the business.

They toyed with the Lobster Cardinal, sent away the Pauillac Lamb untasted, and drank the wines as a beverage to steady their nerves rather than with the consideration and pleasure which they deserved.

The fat *maître d'hôtel* supervised the service of each course himself, and it passed his understanding how these three men and the beautiful little lady could show so little appreciation. With hands clasped upon a large stomach, he stood before the Duke and murmured his distress that the dishes they had ordered should not appear to please them, but the Duke waved him away, even summoning up a little smile to assure him that

280

it was no fault of the restaurant and only their unfortunate lack of appetite.

Throughout the meal De Richleau talked unceasingly. He was a born raconteur, and ordinarily, with his charm and wit, could hold any audience enthralled. Tonight, despite his own anxiety, he made a supreme attempt to lift the burden from the shoulders of his friends by exploiting every venue of memory and conversation, but never in his life had his efforts met with such a cold reception. In vain he attempted to divert their thoughts, laughing a little to himself, as he reached the denouement in each of his stories, and hoping against hope that he might raise a smile in those three anxious faces that faced him across the table.

For Marie Lou the meal was just another phase of that horrible nightmare through which she had been passing since the early hours of the morning. Mechanically she sampled the dishes which were put before her, but each one seemed to taste the same, and after a few mouthfuls she laid down her fork, submitting miserably to the frantic, gnawing thoughts which pervaded her whole being.

Richard said nothing, ate little, and drank heavily. He was in that state when he knew quite well that it was impossible for him to drink too much. Great happiness or great distress has that effect upon certain men, and he was one of them. Every other minute he glanced at the clock on the wall, as it slowly registered the passage of time until they could set forth once more on their attempt to save his daughter.

There was still half an hour to go when the fruit and brandy were placed upon the table, and then at last De Richleau surrendered.

'I've been talking utter nonsense all through dinner,' he confessed gravely; 'only to keep my thoughts off this wretched business, you understand. But now the time has come when we can speak of it again with some advantage. What do you intend to do, Rex, when you see this man?'

Marie Lou lifted her eyes from the untasted grapes which lay upon her plate. 'You've been splendid, Greyeyes, dear. I haven't been listening to you really, but a sentence here and there has been just enough to take my mind off a picture of the worst that may happen, which keeps on haunting me.'

He smiled across at her gratefully. 'I'm glad of that. It's

281

the least that I could try to do. But come now, Rex, let's hear your plan.'

'I've hardly got one,' Rex confessed, shrugging his great shoulders. 'We know he'll see me, and that's as far as I have figured it out. I presume it'll boil down to my jumping on him after a pretty short discussion and threatening to gouge out his eyeballs with my hands unless he's prepared to come clean with everything he knows about Mocata.'

De Richleau shook his head. 'That is roughly the idea, of course, but there are certain to be servants in the flat, and we must arrange it that you have a free field for your party.'

'Can't you take us along with you?' Richard suggested. 'Say that we're privately interested in this deal you're putting up. If only the three of us can get inside that flat God help anybody who tries to stop us forcing him to talk.'

'Sure,' Rex agreed. 'I see no sort of objection to that. We can park Marie Lou at the Ritz again, on our way, before we beat this fellow up.'

'No!' Marie Lou gave a sudden dogged shake of her head. 'I am coming with you. I'm quite capable of taking care of myself, and I will keep out of the way if there is any trouble. You cannot ask me to go back to the hotel and sit there on my own while you are trying to obtain news of Fleur. I should go mad and fling myself out of the window. I've got to come, so please don't argue about it.'

Richard took her hand and caressed it softly. 'Of course you shall, my sweet. It would be better, perhaps, for you not to be with us when we see Castelnau, but there's no reason why you shouldn't wait for us in his hall.'

De Richleau nodded. 'Yes, in the circumstances it is impossible to leave Marie Lou behind, but about these servants —did you bring that gun that you had last night with you?'

'Yes, I brought it through the Customs in my hip pocket, and it's fully loaded.'

'Right. Then if necessary you can use it to intimidate the servants while Rex and I tackle Castelnau. It is a quarter to. Shall we go?'

Rex sent for the bill and paid it, leaving a liberal tip which soothed the dignity of the injured *maître d'hôtel,* then they filed out of the restaurant.

'Maison Rambouillet, Parc Monceau,' De Richleau told

282

the driver sharply as they climbed into the taxi, and not a
word was spoken until the cab drew up before a palatial block
of modern flats, facing on to the little green park where the
children of the rich in Paris take their morning airing.

'Monsieur Castelnau?' the Duke inquired of the concierge.

'This way, monsieur'; the man led them through a spacious
stone faced hall to the lift.

It shot up to the fifth floor and as he opened the gates, the
concierge pointed to a door upon the right.

'Number Seventy-two,' he said quietly. 'I think Monsieur
Castelnau has just come in.'

The gates clanged behind them, and the lift flashed silently
down again to the ground floor. De Richleau gave Rex a
swift glance and, stepping towards the door of Number Seventy-
two, pressed the bell.

31

The Man With the Jagged Ear

The tall, elaborately carved door was opened by a bald,
elderly man-servant in a black alpaca coat. Rex gave his name,
and the servant looked past him with dark, inquiring eyes at
the others.

'These are friends of mine who're seeing Monsieur Castelnau
on the same business,' Rex said abruptly, stepping into the
long, narrow hall. 'Is he in?'

'Yes, monsieur, and he is expecting you. This way, if you
please.'

Marie Lou perched herself on a high couch of Cordova
leather, while the other three followed the back of the alpaca
jacket down the corridor. Another tall, carved door was thrown
open, and they entered a wide, dimly-lit *salon,* furnished in the
old style of French elegance: gilt ormolu, tapestries, bric-à-
brac, and a painted ceiling where cupids disported themselves
among roseate flowers.

Castelnau stood, cold, thin, angular and hatchet-faced, with
his back to a large porcelain stove. He was dressed in the

clothes which he had worn at the banquet. The wide, watered silk ribbon with the garish colours of some foreign order cut across his shirt front and a number of decorations were pinned to the lapel of his evening coat.

'Monsieur Van Ryn.' He barely touched Rex's hand with his cold fingers and went on in his own language. 'It is a pleasure to receive you. I know your house well by reputation, and from time to time in the past my own firm has had some dealings with yours.' Then he glanced at the others sharply. 'These gentlemen are, I assume, associated with you in this business?'

'They are.' Rex introduced them briefly. 'The Duke de Richleau—Mr. Richard Eaton.'

Castelnau's eyebrows lifted a fraction as he studied the Duke's face with new interest. 'Of course,' he murmured. 'Monsieur le Duc must pardon me if I did not recognise him at first. It is many years since we have met, and I was under the impression that he had never found the air of Paris good for him; but perhaps I am indiscreet to make any reference to that old trouble.'

'The business which has brought me is urgent, monsieur,' De Richleau replied suavely. 'Therefore I elected to ignore the ban which a Government of bourgeois and socialists placed upon me.'

'A grave step, monsieur, since the police of France have a notoriously long memory. Particularly at the present time when the Government has cause to regard all politicals who are not of its party with suspicion. However,' the banker bowed slightly, 'that, of course, is your own affair entirely. Be seated, gentlemen. I am at your service.'

None of the three accepted the proffered invitation, and Rex said abruptly: 'The bullion deal I spoke of when I called you on the telephone was only an excuse to secure this interview. The three of us have come here tonight because we know that you are associated with Mocata.'

The Frenchman stared at him in blank surprise and was just about to burst into angry protest when Rex hurried on. 'It'll cut no ice to deny it. We know too much. The night before last we saw you at that joint in Chilbury, and afterwards with the rest of those filthy swine doing the devil's business on Salisbury

Plain. You're a Satanist, and you're going to tell us all you know about your leader.'

Castelnau's dark eyes glittered dangerously in his long, white face. They shifted with a sudden furtive glance towards an open escritoire.

Before he could move, Richard's voice came quiet but steely. 'Stay where you are. I've got you covered, and I'll shoot you like a dog if you flicker an eyelid.'

De Richleau caught the banker's glance, and with his quick, cat-like step had reached the ornate desk. He pulled out a few drawers, and then found the weapon that he felt certain must be there. It was a tiny .2 pistol, but deadly enough. Having assured himself that it was loaded, he pointed it at the Satanist. 'Now,' he said, icily, 'are you prepared to talk, or must I make you?'

Castelnau shrugged, then looked down at his feet. 'You cannot make me,' he replied with a quiet confidence, 'but if you tell me what you wish to know, I may possibly give you the information you require in order to get rid of you.'

'First, what do you know of Mocata's history?'

'Very little, but sufficient to assure you that you are exceedingly ill-advised if, as it appears, you intend to pit yourself against him.'

'To hell with that!' Rex snapped angrily; 'get on with the story.'

'Just as you wish. It is the Canon Damien Mocata to whom you refer, of course. When he was younger he was an officiating priest at some church in Lyons, I believe. He wa; always a difficult person, and his intellectual gifts made a thorn in the sides of his superiors. Then there was some scandal and he left the Church; but long before that he had become an occultist of exceptional powers. I met him some years ago and became interested in his operations. Your apparent disapproval of them does not distress me in the least. I find their theory an exceptionally interesting study, and their practice of the greatest assistance in governing my business transactions. Mocata lives in Paris for a good portion of the year, and I see him from time to time socially in addition to our meetings for esoteric purposes. I think that is all that I can tell you.'

'When did you see him last?' asked the Duke.

'At Chilbury two nights ago, when we gathered again after

the break-up of our meeting. I suppose you were responsible for that?' Castelnau's thin lips broke into a ghost of a smile. 'If so, believe me, you will pay for it.'

'You have not seen him then today—this evening?'

'No, I did not even know that he had returned to Paris.' There was a ring in the banker's voice which made it difficult for his questioners to doubt that he was telling them the truth.

'Where does he live when he is in Paris?' the Duke enquired.

'I do not know. I have visited him at many places. Often he stays with various friends, who are also interested in his practices, but he has no permanent address. The people with whom he was staying last left Paris some months ago for the Argentine, so I have no idea where you are likely to find him now.'

'Where do you meet him when these Satanic gatherings take place?'

'I am sorry but I can't tell you.' The Frenchman's voice was firm.

De Richleau padded softly forward and thrust the little pistol into Castelnau's ribs, just under his heart. 'I am afraid you've got to,' he purred silkily. 'The matter that we are engaged upon is urgent.'

The banker held his ground, and to outward appearances remained unruffled at the threat. 'It is no good,' he said quietly, 'I cannot do it, even if you intend to murder me. Each one of us goes into a self-induced hypnotic trance before proceeding to these meetings, and wakes upon his arrival. In my conscious state I have no idea how I get there; so this apache attitude of yours is completely useless.'

'I see.' De Richleau nodded slowly and withdrew the automatic. 'However, you are going to tell me just the same, because it happens that I am something of a hypnotist. I shall put you under now, and we shall proceed to follow all the stages of your unconscious journey.'

For the first time Castelnau's face showed a trace of fear. 'You can't,' he muttered quickly. 'I won't let you.'

De Richleau shrugged. 'Your opposition will make it slightly more difficult, but I shall do it, nevertheless. However, as it may take some time, we will make fresh arrangements in order to ensure that we are not disturbed. Press the bell, and when your servant comes, give him definite instructions that as we shall be engaged in a long conference, upon no pretext whatsoever are you to be disturbed.'

'And if I refuse?' Castelnau's dark eyes suddenly flashed rebellion.

'Then you will never live to give another order. The affair we are engaged upon is desperate, and whatever the consequences may be, I shall shoot you like the rat you are. Now ring.' De Richleau put the pistol in his pocket but still held the banker covered, and after a moment's hesitation Castelnau pressed the bell.

'You, Richard,' the Duke said in a sharp whisper, 'will leave us when the servant has taken his instructions. Wait for us with Marie Lou in the entrance hall. You have your gun. Prevent anyone leaving the apartment until we have finished. Open the door to anyone who rings yourself, and if Mocata arrives, as he may at any moment, don't argue—shoot. I take all responsibility.'

'I am only waiting for the chance,' said Richard grimly, just as the servant entered.

Castelnau gave his orders in an even voice, with one eye upon the Duke's pocket, then Richard, in his normal voice, remarked casually:

'Well, since the matter is confidential, I had better wait outside with my wife until you are through,' and followed the elderly alpaca-coated man out into the hall.

'Rex,' De Richleau lost not an instant once the door was closed. 'Take that telephone receiver off its stand so that we are not interrupted by any calls. And you,' he turned to the banker, 'sit down in that chair.'

'I won't!' exclaimed Castelnau furiously. 'This is abominable. You invade my apartment like brigands. I give you such information as I can, but what you are about to do will bring me into danger, and I refuse—I refuse, I tell you.'

'I shall neither argue with you nor kill you,' De Richleau answered frigidly. 'You are too valuable to me alive. Rex, knock him out!'

Castelnau swung round and threw up his arms in a gesture of defence, but Rex broke through his guard. The young American's mighty fist caught him on the side of the jaw and he crumpled up, a still heap on his own hearth-rug.

When the banker came to he found himself sitting in a straight chair; his hands were lashed to the back and his ankles to the legs with the curtain cords. His head ached abominably and he saw De Richleau standing opposite to him, smiling relentlessly down into his face.

'Now,' said the Duke, 'look into my eyes. The sooner we get this business over the sooner you will be able to get to bed and nurse your sore head. I am about to place you under, and you are going to tell us what you do when you go to these satanic meetings.'

For answer Castelnau quickly closed his eyes and lowered his head on to his chest, resisting De Richleau's powerful suggestion with all the force of his will.

'This doesn't look to me as though it's going to be any too easy,' Rex muttered dubiously. 'I've always thought that it was impossible to hypnotise people if they were unwilling. You'd better let me put the half-Nelson on him until he becomes more amenable and sees reason.'

'That might make him agree verbally,' De Richleau replied, 'but it won't stop him lying to us afterwards, and it is quite possible to hypnotise people against their will. It is often done to lunatics in asylums. Get behind him now, hold back his head and lift his eyelids with your fingers so that he cannot close them. We've got to find out about this place. It is our only hope of geting on to Mocata.'

Rex did as he was bid. The Duke stood before the chair, his steel-grey eyes fastened without a flicker upon those of the unwilling Satanist.

Time passed, and every now and then De Richleau's voice broke the silence of the quiet, dimly-lit room. 'You are tired now, you will sleep. I command you.' But all his efforts were unavailing. The Satanist sat there rigid and determined not to succumb.

The ormolu clock upon the mantelpiece ticked with a steady, monotonous note, until Rex was filled with the mad desire to throw something at it. The hands crawled round the white enamelled dial; its silvery chime rang out, marking the hours eleven, twelve, one. Still the Frenchman endured De Richleau's steady gaze. He knew that they were expecting Mocata to arrive at his apartment. Mocata was immensely powerful. If only he could hold out until then the whole position might be saved. With a fixed determination not to give in, his eyelids held back by Rex's forefingers, he stared blankly at De Richleau's chin.

Outside, on the sofa of Cordova leather, Richard and Marie Lou sat side by side. It seemed to her again that she must be dreaming. The whole fantastic business of this flight to Paris and their dinner at the Vert Galant had been utterly unreal. It could not be real now that Mocata was somewhere in this city preparing to kill her darling Fleur in some ungodly rite, while she sat there with Richard in that strange, silent apartment and the night hours laboured on.

She thought that she slept a little, but she was not certain. Ever since she had fainted in the pentacle and come to with the sensation that she was above Cardinals Folly, floating in the soundless ether, all her movements had been automatic and her vision of their doings distorted, so that whole sections of time were blotted out from her mind, and only these glimpses of strange places and faces seemed to register.

The black-coated servant appeared once at the far end of the corridor, but seeing them still there, disappeared again.

Almost the whole of that long wait Richard sat with his eyes glued to the front door, his hand clasped ready on the pistol in his pocket, expecting the ring that would announce Mocata's arrival.

He too felt that somehow this person, grown desperate from an unbearable injury and lusting with the desire to kill, regardless of laws and consequences, could not possibly be himself. With every movement that he made he expected to wake and find himself safely in bed at Cardinals Folly, with Marie Lou snuggled down close against him and Fleur peacefully asleep only a few doors away.

Had he wholly believed that Fleur had been taken from him and that he was never to see her again, he could not possibly have endured those dreary hours of enforced idleness while the Duke battled with Castelnau. He would have been forced to interrupt them or at least leave his post to watch their proceedings, for his inactivity would have become unbearable.

In the richly furnished *salon*, Rex and the Duke continued their long-sustained effort without a second's intermission. The clock struck two, and as Rex stood behind the Frenchman's chair, shifting his weight from foot to foot now and then, he seemed at times to drop off into a sort of half-sleep where he stood.

At last, a little after two, he was roused to a fresh attention by a sudden sob breaking from the dry lips of the banker.

'I will not let you, I will not,' he cried hysterically, and then began to struggle violently with the curtain cords that tied him to the chair.

'You will,' De Richleau told him firmly, the pupils of his grey eyes now distended and gleaming with an unnatural light.

Castelnau suddenly ceased to struggle; a cold sweat broke out on his bony forehead, and his head sagged on his neck, but Rex held it firmly and continued to press back his eyelids so that it was impossible for him to escape the Duke's relentless stare.

He began to sob then, like a child who is being beaten, and at last De Richleau knew that he had broken the Frenchman's will. In another ten minutes Rex was able to remove his fingers from the banker's eyelids for he no longer had the power to close them, but sat there gazing at De Richleau with an imbecile glare.

In a low voice the Duke began to question him and, after one last feeble effort at resistance, it all came out. The meeting place was in a cellar below a deserted warehouse on the banks of the Seine at Asnières. They secured full directions as to the way to reach it and how to get into it when they arrived.

As Castelnau answered the last question, De Richleau glanced at the clock. 'Three and a quarter hours,' he said with a sigh of weariness. 'Still, it might well have taken longer in a case like this.'

'What'll we do with him?' Rex motioned towards the Frenchman who, with his head fallen forward on his chest, was now sound asleep.

'Leave him there,' answered the Duke abruptly. 'The servants will find him in the morning, and he's so exhausted that he will sleep until then. But stuff your handkerchief in his mouth just in case he wakes and tries to make any trouble for us. Be quick!'

Castelnau did not even blink an eyelid as Rex gagged him. They left him there and hurried out to the others.

'Come on!' cried the Duke.

'What about Mocata?' Richard asked. 'If we leave here we may miss him.'

'We must chance that.' De Richleau pulled open the door and made for the stairs.

As they dashed down the long flights he flung over his shoulder: 'Tanith may have been wrong. Messages from the astral plane are often unreliable about time. As it does not exist there, they have difficulty in judging it. She may have seen him here a week hence or in the past even. It's so late now that I doubt if he will turn up tonight. Anyhow, we got out of Castelnau the place where he's most likely to be—and God knows what he may be doing if he is there. We've got to hurry!' They fled after him out of the silent building.

Round the corner they managed to pick up a taxi and, at the promise of a big tip, the man got every ounce out of his engine as he whirled the four harassed-looking people away through the murky streets up towards the Boulevard de Clichy. Topping the hill, they descended again towards the Seine, crossed the river and entered Asnières.

In that outlying slum of Paris with its wharves and warehouses, narrow, sordid-looking streets and dimly-lit passages, there was little movement at that hour of the morning. They paid off the taxi outside a closed café which faced upon a dirty-looking square. A market wagon rumbled past with its driver huddled on the seat above the horses, his cape drawn close to protect him from the damp mist rising from the river. The bedraggled figure of a woman was huddled upon the steps of a shop with 'Tabac' in faded blue letters above it, but otherwise there was no sign of life.

Turning up the collars of their coats and shivering afresh from the damp chill of the drifting fog, they followed the Duke's lead along an evil-looking street of tumbledown dwelling houses. Then, between two high walls, along a narrow passage where the rays of a solitary lamp, struggling through grimy glass, were barely sufficient to dispel a small circle of gloom in its own area. When they had passed it the rest was darkness, foul smells, greasy mud squishing from beneath their feet, and wisps of mist curling cold about their faces.

At the end of that long dark alley-way they came out upon a deserted wharf. De Richleau turned to the left and the others followed. To one side of them the steep face of a tall brick building, from which chains and pulleys hung in slack festoons, towered up into the darkness. On the other, a few feet away, the river surged, oily, turgid, yellow and horrible as it hurried to the sea.

As if in a fresh phase of their nightmare, they stumbled forward over planks, hawsers and pieces of old iron, the neglected debris of the riverside, until fifty yards farther on De Richleau halted.

'This is it,' he announced, fumbling with a rusty padlock. 'Castelnau hadn't got a key and so we'll have to break this thing. Hunt around, and see if you can find a piece of iron that we can use as a jemmy. The longer the better. It will give us more purchase.'

They rummaged round in the semi-darkness, broken only by a riverside light some distance away along the wharf and the masthead lanterns of a few long barges anchored out on the swiftly flowing waters.

'This do?' Richard pulled a rusty lever from a winch and, grabbing it from him, the Duke thrust the narrow end into the hoop of the padlock.

'Now then,' he said, as he gripped the cold, moist iron, 'steady pressure isn't any good. It needs a violent jerk, so when I say "go!" we must all throw our weight on the bar together. Ready? Go!'

They heaved downwards. There was a sudden snap. The tongue of the padlock had been wrenched out of the lock. De Richleau removed it from the chain and in another moment they had the tall wooden door open.

Once inside, De Richleau struck a match, and while he shaded it with his hands the others looked about them. From what little they could see, the place appeared to be empty. They moved quickly forward, striking more matches as they went, in the direction where Castelnau had told them they would find a trap-door leading to the cellars.

In a far corner they halted. 'Stand back all of you.' whispered Rex, and while the Duke held up a light he pulled at the second in a row of upright iron girders, apparently built in to strengthen the wall. As Castelnau had said in his trance, it was a secret lever to operate the trap. The girder came forward and a large square of flooring lifted noiselessly on well-oiled hinges.

De Richleau blew out his match and produced the small automatic which he had taken from the banker. 'I will go first,' he said, 'and you, Rex, follow me. Richard, you have the other gun so you had better come last. You can look after Marie Lou and protect our rear. No noise now, because if we're lucky our man is here.'

Feeling about with his foot he ascertained that a flight of stairs led downwards. His shoes made no noise, and it was evident that they were covered with a thick carpet. Swiftly but cautiously he began to descend the flight and the others followed him down into the pitchy darkness.

At the bottom of the stairs they groped their way along a tunnel until the Duke was brought up sharply by a wooden partition at which it seemed to end. He fumbled for the handle, thinking that it was a door. The sides were as smooth and polished as the centre, yet it moved gently under his touch, and after a moment he found it to be a sliding panel. With the faintest click of ball bearings it slid back on its runners.

Straining their eyes they peered into the great apartment upon which it opened. A hundred feet long at least and thirty wide, it stretched out before them. Two lines of thick pillars, acting as supporters to the roof above, and rows of chairs divided in the centre by an aisle which led up to a distant altar, gave it the appearance of a big private chapel. It was lit by one solitary lamp which hung suspended before the altar, and that distant beacon did not penetrate to the shadows in which they stood.

On tiptoe and with their weapons ready they moved forward along the wall. De Richleau peered from side to side as he advanced, his pistol levelled. Rex crept along beside him, the iron winch lever which they had used to smash the padlock gripped tight in his big fist. At any moment they expected their presence to be discovered.

As they crept nearer to the hanging lamp, they saw that the place had been furnished with the utmost luxury and elegance for those unholy meetings. It was, indeed, a superbly equipped temple for the worship of the Devil. Above the altar a great and horrible representation of the Goat of Mendes, worked in the loveliest coloured silks, leered down at them; its eyes were two red stones which had been inset in the tapestry. They flickered with dull malevolence in the dim light of the solitary lamp.

On the side walls were pictures of men, women and beasts practising obscenities only possible of conception in the brain of a mad artist. Below the enormous central figure, which had hideous, distorted, human faces protruding from its elbows, knees and belly, was a great altar of glistening red stone, worked and inlaid with other coloured metals in the Italian fashion. Upon it reposed the ancient 'devil's bibles' containing all liturgies of hell; broken crucifixes and desecrated chalices stolen from churches and profaned here at the meetings of the Satanists.

Luxurious armchairs upholstered in red velvet and gold with eleborate canopies of lace above, such as High Prelates use in cathedrals when assisting at important ceremonies, flanked the altar on either side. Below the steps to the short chancel, on a level with where they stood, were arranged rows and rows of cushioned *prie-dieux* for the accommodation of the worshippers.

No sound or movement disturbed the stillness of the heavy incense laden air and with a sinking of the heart De Richleau knew that they had lost their man. He had gambled blindly upon Tanith's message and she had proved wrong as to time. Mocata might not be in Paris for days to come; perhaps he had divined their journey and, knowing that he would be unmolested while they were abroad, returned to Simon's house where, even now, he might be foully murdering poor little Fleur. It seemed that their last hope had gone.

Then as they stepped from the side aisle they suddenly saw a thing that had been hidden from them by the rows of chair backs—a body, clad in a long white robe with mystic signs embroidered on it in black and red, lay spreadeagled, face downwards on the floor, at the bottom of the chancel steps.

'It's Simon!' breathed the Duke.

'Oh, hell, they've killed him!' Rex ran forward and knelt beside the body of their friend. They turned him over and felt his heart. It was beating slowly but rhythmically. The Duke pulled out of his waistcoat pocket a little bottle, without which he never travelled, and held it beneath Simon's nose. He shuddered suddenly and his eyes opened, staring up at them.

'Simon, darling, Simon. It's us—we're here.' Marie Lou

grasped his limp hands between her own.

He shuddered again and struggled into a sitting position. 'What—what's happened?' he murmured, but his voice was normal.

'You left us, you dear, pig-headed ass!' exclaimed Richard. 'Gave yourself up and ruined our whole plan of campaign. What's happened to *you*? That's what we want to know.'

'Well, I met him.' Simon gave the ghost of a smile. 'And he took me to Paris in his plane. Then to some place down on the riverside.' He gazed round and added quickly: 'But this is it. How did you get here?'

'Never mind that,' De Richleau urged him. 'Have you seen Fleur?'

'Yes. He sent a car for me, and when I reached the plane she was already in it. We had an argument and he swore he'd keep his word unless I went through with this.'

'The ritual to Saturn?' asked De Richleau.

'Um. He said that if I'd do it without making any fuss he'd let me take Fleur out of here immediately afterwards and back to England.'

'He's double-crossed you, as we thought he would,' Rex grunted. 'There's not a soul in this place. He's quit, and taken Fleur with him. Can't you say where he'll be likely to make for?'

'Ner.' Simon shook his head. 'Directly we started on the ritual he put me under. I let him, but of course he would have done that anyway. The last I saw of Fleur she was sound asleep in that armchair and the next thing I knew you were all staring down at me just now.'

'If you completed the ritual, Mocata knows now where the Talisman is,' De Richleau said abruptly.

'Yes,' Simon nodded.

'Then he will have gone to wherever it is—from here.'

'Of course,' Richard cut in. 'That's his main objective. He wouldn't lose a second.'

'Then Simon must know the place to which he's gone.'

'How's that? I don't quite get you.' Rex looked at the Duke with a puzzled frown.

'In his subconscious, I mean. Our only hope now is for me to put Simon under again and make him repeat every word that he said when the ritual was performed. That will give

us the hiding-place of the Talisman and the place to which
I'll stake my life Mocata is heading at the present moment.
Are you game, Simon?'

'Yes, of course. You know that I would do anything to
help.'

'Right.' The Duke took him by the arm and pushed him
gently. 'Sit down in that chair to the right of the altar and
we'll go ahead.'

Simon settled himself and leaned back on the comfortable
cushions, his white robe with its esoteric designs in black and
red settling about his feet like the long skirts of a woman. De
Richleau made a few swift passes. 'Sleep, Simon,' he commanded.

Simon's eyelids trembled and closed. After a moment he
began to breathe deeply and regularly. The Duke went on:
'You are in this temple with Mocata. The ritual to Saturn is
about to begin. Repeat the words that he made you speak
then.'

Dreamily but easily, Simon spoke the words of power which
were utterly meaningless to Richard, Rex and Marie Lou,
who stood, a tensely anxious audience, at the bottom of the
chancel steps.

'On,' commanded De Richleau. 'Jump a quarter of an hour.'
Simon spoke again, more sentences incomprehensible to the
uninitiate.

'On again,' commanded De Richleau. 'Another quarter of an
hour has passed.'

'——was built above the place where the Talisman is
buried,' said Simon. 'It will be found in the earth beneath
the right hand stone of the altar.'

'Go back one minute,' ordered De Richleau, and Simon
spoke once more.

'——Attila's death the Greek secreted it and took it to his
own country. In the city of Yanina, upon his return, he became
possessed of devils and was handed over to the brethren at
the monastery above Metsovo, which stands in the mountains
twenty miles east of the city. They failed to cast out the spirits
which inhabited his body and so imprisoned him in an underground cell and there, before he died, he buried the
Talisman. Seven years later the dungeons were demolished
and the crypt built in their place on the same site, with the

296

great church above it. The Talisman remained undisturbed in its original hiding place. Its power gradually pervaded the whole of the Brotherhood, filling it with lechery and greed, so that it disintegrated and was finally disbanded before the invasion by the Turks. The chapel to the left in the crypt was built above the place where the Talisman is buried.'

'Stop,' ordered the Duke. 'Awake now.'

'By Jove, we've got it!' exclaimed Rex. But as he spoke a slight noise behind them made him swing upon his heel.

Four figures stood there in the shadows. The tallest suddenly stepped forward.

Richard's hand leapt to his gun but the tall man snapped: 'Stand still, *mon vieux*, I have you covered,' and they saw that he held an automatic.

The other two strangers came forward. The fourth was Castelnau.

The leader of the party turned to a little old man, who stood beside him wearing an out-of-date bowler hat that came almost down to his ears, then nodded towards the Duke.

'Is that De Richleau, Verrier? You should be able to recognise him, since he was in your time.'

'*Oui monsieur*,' declared the little old man. 'That is the famous Royalist who caused us so much trouble when I was young. I would know his face again anywhere.'

'*Bon!* All this is very interesting.' The tall, hard-eyed man glanced from the obscene pictures on the walls to the magnificent appurtenances of Satanic worship upon the altar, and went on in a silky tone: 'I have had an idea for some time that a secret society has been practising devil worship in Paris and is responsible for certain disappearances, but I could never lay my hands on them before. Now I have got five of you red-handed.'

He paused for a moment then gave a jerky little bow. '*Madame et Messieurs,* permit me to introduce myself. I am *le Chef de la Sûreté,* Daudet. *Monsieur le Duc,* I arrest you as an enemy of the Government upon the old charge. The rest of you I shall hold with him, as persons suspected of kidnapping and the murder of young children at the practice of infamous rites.'

32

The Gateway of the Pit

For ten seconds the friends stood there staring at the detective. Castelnau's presence gave them the key to this grotesque but highly dangerous situation. Mocata must have left the warehouse at almost the same time they had left the banker's apartment. Perhaps their taxis had even passed within a few feet of each other, racing in opposite directions. Tanith had proved right after all when she had told them that she could see Mocata talking with Castelnau that night in his flat.

Mocata had found the banker there, released and revived him, and then listened to his story; realising at once that, since it was possible for De Richleau to hypnotise Castelnau against his will, it would be easy for him to do the same to Simon, learn the hiding place of the Talisman, and follow him to it.

Now that they had discovered the secret Satanic temple which was his headquarters in Paris, the place would be useless to him and only a source of danger. Unmentionable crimes had been committed there, and it would be far too great a risk for him ever to visit it again. Then the brilliant decision that, since the place had to be abandoned, he could at least use it to destroy his enemies.

The whole thing flashed through De Richleau's brain in those few seconds. Mocata's first idea that, if only he could get the police to the warehouse before they left it, he would have involved them in all the crimes associated with such a place and thrown them off his trail for good. Next, the vital question, how to get the police there in time. Would they act at once if Castelnau were sent to tell them a tale about Satanic orgies or only laugh at him? What practical crime could his enemies be charged with? Then the perfect inspiration. If the authorities were told that De Richleau, the Royalist exile, was a party to the business they would not lose a second, but seize on it as a heaven-sent opportunity to throw discredit upon their political opponents. What a magnificent scandal for the Government Press to handle. 'Secret Royalist Society practises Black Art'—'Satanic Temple raided at Asnières'—

'Notorious exile arrested while performing Blasphemous Rites.'
The Duke could see the scurrilous headlines and hear the news-
boy's cry.

And the trick had worked. They had actually been discovered in that house of hell with Simon in the tell-tale robes,
seated before the altar, while he performed what must certainly
have appeared to the police as some evil ceremony and the
other three had stood there, forming a small congregation.

How could they possibly hope to persuade the tall, suspic-
ious-eyed *Monsier le Chef de la Sûreté* Daudet of their innocence, much less get him to agree to their immediate release?
Yet, as they stood there, Mocata was on his way to the place
where he kept his special plane, if not already aboard it.
Night flying would have no terrors for him who, if he wished,
could invoke the elements to his aid. Fleur would be with
him and he meant to murder her as certainly as they stood
there. His determination to secure the return of Tanith made
the sacrifice of a baptised child imperative, and before another
twenty-four hours had gone he would be in possession of the
Talisman of Set, bringing upon the world God alone knew
what horrors of war, famine, disablement and death.

De Richleau knew that there was only one thing for it—even
if he was shot down there and then—he sprang like a panther
at the *Chef de la Sûreté's* throat.

The detective fired from his hip. Flame stabbed the semi-
darkness of the vault. The crash hit their eardrums like the
explosion of a slab of gelignite. The bullet seared through the
Duke's left arm, but his attack hurled the Police-Chief to the
ground.

Simon and Marie Lou flung themselves simultaneously upon
the old detective Verrier. The thoughts which had passed
through De Richleau's mind in those breathless seconds had
also raced through hers. If they submitted to arrest their last
hope would be gone of saving her beloved Fleur.

Richard had no chance to pull his gun. The third man had
grabbed him round the body but Rex rapped the policeman
on the back of the head with his iron bar. The man grunted
and toppled on the the chancel steps.

Rex leapt over the body straight for Castelnau. Quick as a
flash, the banker turned and ran, his long legs flicking past
each other as he bounded down the empty aisle, but Rex's legs

were even longer. He caught the Satanist at the entrance of the passage and grabbed him by the back of the neck. Castelnau tore himself away and stood panting for a second, half crouching with bared teeth, his back against the wall. Then for the second time that night Rex's leg-of-mutton fist took him on the chin and he slid to the ground like a pole-axed ox.

De Richleau, his wounded arm hanging limp and useless, writhed beneath the *Chef de la Sûreté* who had one hand on his throat and with the other was groping for his fallen gun.

His fingers closed upon it. He jerked it up and fired at Richard, who was dashing to De Richleau's help. The shot went thudding into the belly of the Satanic Goat above the altar. Next second the heavy *prie-dieu* which Richard had swung aloft came crashing down upon the Police-Chief's head.

Rex only paused to see that the banker was completely knocked out, then rushed back to the struggling mass of bodies below the altar steps.

Simon and Marie Lou had managed the little man between them. Almost insane with worry for her child, her thumb nails were dug into his neck and, while he screeched with pain, Simon was lashing his hands behind his back.

Richard was pulling the Duke out from beneath the unconscious *Chef de la Sûreté*'s body. Rex lent a ready hand and then, panting with their exertions, they surveyed the scene of their short but desperate encounter.

'Holy smoke! That's done me a whole heap of good,' Rex grinned at Richard. 'I'm almost feeling like my normal self again.'

'The odds were with us but we owe our escape to Greyeyes' pluck.' Richard looked swiftly at the Duke. 'Let's see that wound, old chap. I hope to God the bullet didn't smash the bone.'

'I don't think so—grazed it though, and the muscle's badly torn.' De Richleau closed his eyes and his face twisted at a stab of pain as they lifted his arm to cut the coat sleeve away.

'I know what you must be feeling,' Simon sympathised. 'I'll never forget the pain of the wound I got that night we discovered the secret of the Forbidden Territory.'

'Don't fuss round me,' muttered the Duke, 'but get that

damned priest's robe off. If these people don't return to the Sûreté more police will come to look for them. We've got to get out of here—quick.'

In frantic haste Marie Lou bandaged the wound while Richard made a sling and the other two wrenched off the clothes of the detective that Rex had knocked out. Simon scrambled into them and, as he snatched up the man's over-coat, the others were already hurrying towards the entrance to the passage at the far end of the temple.

Richard rushed Marie Lou along the dark corridor and they tumbled up the flight of steps. Everything seemed to fade again after those awful moments when they had been so near arrest. She felt the cold air of the wharf-side damp upon her cheeks—they were running down the narrow passage between the high brick walls—back in the gloomy square where the old woman still sat crouched upon the steps near the squalid café. Rex had taken her other arm and, her feet treading the pavements automatically, they were hastening through endless, sordid, fog-bound streets. They crossed the bridge over the Seine and, at last, under the railway arches at Courcel-les, found a taxi. When next she was conscious of her surroundings they were in a little room at the airport and the four men were poring over maps. Snatches of the conversation came to her vaguely.

'Twelve hundred miles—more. Northern Greece. You cannot cross the Alps—make for Vienna, then south to Trieste—no, Vienna-Agram-Fiume. From Agram we can fly down the valley of the River Save; otherwise we should have to cross the Dolomites. That's right! Then follow the coastline of the Adriatic for five hundred miles south-east to Corfu. Yanina is about fifty miles inland from there. You can follow the course of the river Kalamans through the mountains—Shall we be able to land at Yanina, though—yes, look, the map shows that it's on a big lake. The circuit of the shore must be fifteen miles at least. It can't all be precipitous—certain to be sandy stretches along it somewhere—how far do you make it to Metsovo from there?—twenty miles as the crow flies. That means thirty at least in such a mountainous district. The monastery is a few miles beyond, on Mount Peristeri—pretty useful mountain—look. The map gives it as seven thousand five hundred feet—we must abandon the plane at Yanina. If

301

we're lucky we'll get a car as far as Metsova—God knows what the roads will be like—after that we'll have to use horses in any case. How soon do you reckon you can make it, Richard?'

'Fourteen hundred miles. We should be in Vienna by midday. Fiume, say, h lf-past two. I ought to make ʼanina by eight o'clock with Rex taking turn and turn about flying the plane. After that it depends on what fresh transport we can get.'

Next, they were in the plane again—lifting out of fog-bound Paris to a marvellous dawn, which gilded the edges of the clouds and streaked the sky with rose and purple and lemon.

Richard was flying the plane in a kind of trance, yet never for a moment losing sight of important landmarks or the dials by which he adjusted his controls. The others slept.

When Marie Lou roused, the plane was at rest near a long line of hangars dimly glimpsed through another ghostly fog. Someone said 'Stuttgart' an 1 then she saw Simon standing on the ground below her, conversing in German with an airport official.

'A big, grey, private plane,' he was saying urgently. 'The pilot is a short, square-shouldered fellow; the passengers a big, fat, baldheaded man and a little girl.'

Marie Lou leaned forward eagerly but she did not catch the airport man's reply. A moment later Simon was climbing into the plane and saying to the Duke:

'He must be taking the same route, but he's an hour and a half ahead of us. I expect he had his own car in Paris. That would have saved him time while we were hunting for that wretched taxi.'

Rex had taken over the controls and they were in the air once more. Richard was sitting next to Marie Lou, sound asleep. For an endless time they seemed to soar through a cloudless sky of pale, translucent blue. She, too, must have dropped off again, for she was not conscious of their landing at Vienna, only when she woke in the early afternoon that the pilots had changed over and Richard was back at the controls.

'Yet, in some curious way, although she had not actually been aware of their landing, fragments of their conversation must have penetrated her sleep at the time. She knew that there had also been fog at Vienna, and that Mocata had left the airport there only an hour before them, so in the journey from Paris they had managed to gain half an hour on him.

The engine droned on, its deep note soothing their frayed nerves. Richard hardly knew that he was flying, although he used all the skill at his command. It seemed as though some other force was driving the aeroplane on and that he was standing outside it as a spectator. All his faculties were numbed and his anxiety for Fleur deadened by an intense absorption with the question of speed—speed—speed.

At Fiume there was no trace of fog. Glorious sunshine, warm and lifegiving, flooded the aerodrome, making the hangars shimmer in the distance. The Duke crawled out from the couch of rugs and cushions that had been made up in the back of the cabin to accommodate a fifth passenger, and chosen by him as more comfortable for his wounded arm. He questioned the landing-ground officials in fluent Italian, but without success.

'From Vienna Mocata must have taken another route,' he told Richard as he climbed back. 'Perhaps a short cut over the Dinarie Alps or by way of Sarajevo. If so he will have more than made up his half hour lead again. I feared as much when I saw that there was no fog here. I can't explain it but I have an idea that he is able to surround us with it, yet only when we follow him to places where he has been quite recently himself.'

Rex took over for the long lap down the Dalmatian coast above the countless islands that fringe the Yugoslavian main-land and lay beneath them in the sparkling Adriatic Sea.

They slept again, all except Rex who, a crack pilot, was now handling the machine with superb skill.

As he flew the plane half his thoughts were centred about Tanith. He could see her there, lying cold and dead, in the library a thousand miles away at Cardinals Folly. That dream of happiness had been so brief. Never again would he see the sudden smile break out like sunshine rising over mountains on that beautiful, calm face. Never again hear the husky, melodious voice whispering terms of endearment. Never again —never again! But he was on the trail of her murderer and if he died for it he meant to make that inhuman monster pay.

The Adriatic merged into the Ionian Sea. The endless rugged

coastline rushed past below them on their left; its mountains rising steeply to the interior of Albania, and its vales breaking them here and there to run down to little white fishing villages on the seashore. Villages that in Roman times had been great centres of population through the constant passage of merchandise, soldiers, scholars, travellers between Brindisi, upon the heel of Italy, and the Peninsula of Greece.

Then they were over Corfu. Banking steeply, he headed for the mainland and picked up the northern mouth of the River Kalamas. The deep blue of the sea flecked by its tiny white crests vanished behind them. Twisting and turning, the plane drove upwards above desolate valleys where the river trickled, a streak of silver in the evening light. The sun sank behind them into the distant sea. They were heading for the huge chain of mountains, which forms the backbone of Greece.

A mist was rising which obscured the long, empty patches and rare cultivated fields below. The light faded, its last rays lit a great distant snow-capped crest which crowned the watershed.

A lake lay below them, placid and calm in the evening light but glimpsed only through the banks of fog. At its south-western end the white buildings of a town were vaguely discernible now and then as Rex circled slowly, searching for a landing-place. Suddenly, through a gap in the billowing whitishgrey, his eye caught a big plane standing in a level field.

'That's Mocata's machine,' yelled Simon who was in the cockpit beside him.

Rex banked again and, coming into the wind, brought them to earth within fifty yards of it. The others roused and scrambled out.

The mist which Rex had first perceived a quarter of an hour before, from his great altitude, now hemmed them in on every side.

A man came forward from a low, solitary hangar as the plane landed. De Richleau saw him, a vague figure, half obscured by the tenuous veils of mist; went over to him and said, when he rejoined them:

'That fellow is a French mechanic. He tells me Mocata landed only half an hour ago. He came in from Monastir but had trouble in the mountains, which delayed him; nobody but a maniac or a superman would try and get through that

304

way at all. This fellow thinks that he can get us a car; he runs the airport, such as it is, and we're darned lucky to find any facilities here at all.'

Richard had just woken from a long sleep. Before he knew what was happening he found that they were all packed into an ancient open Ford with a tattered hood. Simon was on one side of him and Marie Lou on the other. Rex squatted on the floor of the car at their feet and De Richleau was in front beside the driver.

They could not see more than twenty yards ahead. The lamps made little impression upon the gloom before them. The road was a sandy track, fringed at the sides with coarse grass and boulders. No houses, cottages or white-walled gardens broke the monotony of the way as they rattled and bumped, mounting continuously up long, curved gradients.

De Richleau peered ahead into the murk. Occasional rifts gave him glimpses of the rocky mountains round which they climbed or, upon the other side, a cliff edge falling sheer to a mist-filled valley.

He, too, could only remember episodes from that wild journey; an unendurable weariness had pressed upon him once they had boarded the plane and left Paris. Even *his* powers of endurance had failed at last and he had slept during the greater part of their fourteen hundred mile flight. He was still sleepy now and only half awake as that unknown demon driver, who had hurried them with few words into the rickety Ford, crouched over his wheel and pressed the car, rocketing from hairpin bend to hairpin bend, onwards and upwards.

The last light had been shut out by the lower ranges of mountains behind them as they wound their way through the valleys to the greater peaks which, unseen in the mist and darkness, they knew lay towering to the skies towards the east. Deep ruts in the track, where mountain torrents cut it in the winter cascading downwards to the lower levels, made the way hideously uneven. The car jolted and bounded, skidding violently from time to time, loose shale and pebbles rocketing from its back tyres as it took the dangerous bends.

In the back Richard, Marie Lou and Simon lurched, swayed, and bumped each other as they crouched in silent misery, their teeth chattering with the cold of the chill night that was now about them in those lofty regions. . .

They were in a room, a strange, low-ceilinged, eastern room, with a great, heavy, wooden door, under which they could see the fog wreathing upwards in the light of a solitary oil lamp set upon a rough-hewn table. Bunches of onions and strips of dried meat hung from the low rafters. The earthen floor of the place was cold underfoot. On a deep window recess in a thick wall stood a crude earthenware jug, and a platter with a loaf of coarse bread upon it, which was covered by a bead-edged piece of muslin.

Marie Lou roused to find herself drinking coarse, red wine out of a thick, glass tumbler. She saw Rex sitting on a wooden bench against the wall, staring before him with unseeing eyes at the grimy window. The others stood talking round the lop-sided table. A peasant woman, with a scarf about her head, whose face she could not see, appeared to be arguing with them. Marie Lou had an idea that it was about money, since De Richleau held a small pile of notes in his hand. Then the peasant woman was gone and the others were talking together again. She caught a few words here and there.

'I thought it was a ruin . . . inhabited still . . . they beg us not to go there . . . not of an official order or anything to do with the Greek Church. They look on them as heathens here . . . associates of Mocata's?—— No, more like a community of outlaws who have taken refuge there under the disguise of a religious brotherhood . . . Talisman has affected them, perhaps. Forty or fifty of them. The people here shun the place even in the daytime, and at night none of them would venture near it at any price. . . . You managed to get a driver?—— Yes, of a kind—— What's wrong with him?—— I don't know. The woman didn't seem to trust him, but I had great difficulty in understanding her at all—— Sort of bad man of the village, eh? . . . Have to trust him if no one else will take us.'

De Richleau passed his hand across his eyes. What was it that they had been talking about? He was so tired, so terribly tired. There had been a peasant woman, with whom he had talked of the ruined monastery up in the mountains. She seemed to be filled with horror of the place and had implored him again and again not to go. He began to wonder how they had conversed. He could make himself understood in most European languages, but he had very little knowledge of modern Greek; but that did not matter they must get on—get on. . . .

The others were standing round him like a lot of ghosts in the narrow, fog-filled village street. A little hunchback with bright, sharp eyes was peering at him. The fellow wore a dark sombrero, and a black cloak, covering his malformed body, dangled to his feet; the light from the semi-circular window of the inn was just sufficient to illuminate his face. A great, old-fashioned carriage, with two lean, ill-matched horses harnessed to it, stood waiting.

They piled into it. The musty smell of the straw-filled cushions came strongly to their nostrils. The hunchback gave them one curious, cunning look from his bright eyes, and climbed upon the box. The lumbering vehicle began to rock from side to side. The one-storeyed, flat-topped houses in the village disappeared behind them and were swallowed up in the mist.

They forded a swift but shallow river outside the village, then the roadway gave place to a stony track. Ghostlike and silent, walls of rock loomed up on either side. The horses ceased trotting and fell into a steady, laboured walk, hauling the great, unwieldy barouche from bend to bend up the rock-strewn way into the fastness of the mountains.

Simon's teeth were chattering. That damp, clinging greyness seemed to enter into his very bones. He tried to remember what day it was and at what hour they had left Paris. Was it last night or the night before or the night before that? He could not remember and gave it up.

The way seemed interminable. No one spoke. The carriage jolted on, the hunchback crouched upon his seat, the lean horses pulling gallantly. The curve of the road ahead was always hidden from them and no sooner had they passed it than they lost sight of the curve behind.

At last the carriage halted. The driver climbed down off his box and pointed upwards, as they stumbled out on the track. De Richleau was thrusting money into his hand. He and his aged vehicle disappeared in the shadows. Richard looked back to catch a last glimpse of it and it suddenly struck him then how queer it was that the carriage had no lamps.

The rest were pressing on, stumbling and slithering as they followed the way which had now become no more than a footpath leading upwards between the huge rocks.

After a little, the gloom seemed to lighten and they perceived stars above their heads. Then, rounding a rugged promontory, they saw the age-old monastery standing out against the night sky upon the mountain slope above.

It was huge and dark and silent, with steep walls rising on two sides from a precipice. A great dome, like an inverted bowl, rose in its centre, but a portion of it had fallen in and the jagged edges showed plainly against the deep blue of the starlit night beyond.

With renewed courage they staggered on up the steep rise toward the great semi-circular arch of the entrance. The gates stood open wide, rotted and fallen from their hinges. No sign of life greeted their appearance as they passed through the spacious courtyard.

Instinctively they made for the main building above which curved the broken arc of the ruined Byzantine dome. That must be the Church, and the crypt would lie below it.

They crossed the broken pavements of the forecourt, the Duke leaning heavily on Rex's arm. He nodded towards a few faint lights which came from a row of outbuildings. Rex followed his glance in silence and they hurried on. That was evidently the best-preserved portion of the ruin, in which these so-called monks resided. A gross laugh, followed by the sound of smashing glass and then a hoarse voice cursing, came from that direction, confirming their thought.

All the way up from the inn half-formed fears had been troubling De Richleau that they might fall foul of this ill-omened brotherhood. He assumed them to be little less than robbers under a thin disguise, who probably eked out a miserable existence by levying toll in corn and oil and goats' milk upon the neighbouring peasantry, but this great pile upon the slopes of Mount Peristeri was so much more vast than anything that he had imagined. A matter of fifty men might easily be lost among its rambling courts and buildings.

They advanced through another great courtyard, surrounded by ruined colonnades which were visible only by the faint starlight from above. Built by some early Christian saint, when Byzantium was still an Empire and Western Europe labouring through the semi-barbarous night of the Dark Ages, the colossal ruin must once have housed thousands of earnest men, all engaged day by day in pious study, or various active tasks to provide for that great community. Now it was as dead as those African temples which have been overgrown by jungle, only a small fragment of it occupied by a small band of dissolute uncultured rogues.

In wonder and awe they passed up the broad flight of steps, through the vast portico on which the elaborate carvings, worn and disfigured by time, were just discernible, into the body of the Church.

The starlight, filtering dimly through the great rent in the dome a hundred feet above their heads, was barely sufficient to light their way as they scrambled over broken pillars and heaps of debris round the walls until they found a low door. From it, a flight of steps led down into the Stygian blackness of the volts below.

Marie Lou, stumbling along half-bemused between Simon and Richard, found herself wondering what they could be doing in this ancient ruin, then memory flooded back. It was here, below them, that the Talisman of Set was buried. There had been no fog in the courtyard outside so they must have got there before Mocata after all—but where was Fleur? She was going to die—she felt that she *was* dying—but first she *must* find Fleur.

The others had halted and Richard noticed then that De Richleau was carrying an old-fashioned lantern, which he supposed he had borrowed at the inn. The Duke lit the stump of candle that was inside it and led the way down those time-worn stairs. The others, treading instinctively on tiptoe, now followed him into the stale, musty darkness.

At the bottom of the steps they came out into a low, vaulted crypt which, by the faint light of the lantern, seemed to spread interminably under the flagstones of the Church.

De Richleau turned to the east, judging the altar of the crypt to be situated below the one in the Church above, but when he had traversed twenty yards he halted suddenly. A black, solid mass blocked their path in the centre of the vault.

'Of course,' Marie Lou heard him murmur. 'I forgot that this place was built such centuries ago. Altars were placed in the centre of churches then. This must be it.'

'We've beaten him to it, then,' Rex's voice came with a little note of triumph.

'Perhaps he couldn't get anyone to drive him up from Metsovo at this hour of night,' Richard suggested. 'Our man was supposed to be mad, or something, and they said that no one else would go.'

'Those stones are going to take some shifting.' Rex took the lantern and bent to examine the black slabs of the solid, oblong altar.

'Are you certain that this is the right one?' Richard asked. 'My brain seems to be going. I can't remember things properly any more but I thought when we got the information from Simon in his trance he said something about a side-chapel in the crypt.'

No one answered. While his words were still ringing in their ears each one of them suddenly felt that he was being over-looked from behind.

Rex dropped the lantern, De Richleau swung round, Marie Lou gave a faint cry. A dull light had appeared only ten paces in their rear. Leading to it they saw a short flight of steps. Beyond, a chapel with a smaller altar, from which the right-hand stone had been wrenched. And there, standing before it, was Mocata.

With a bellow of fury, Rex started forward, but the Satanist suddenly raised his left hand. In it he held a small black cigar-shaped thing, which was slightly curved. About it there was a phosphorescent glow, so that, despite the semi-darkness, the very blackness of the thing itself stood out clear and sharp against its surrounding aura of misty light. The rays from it seemed to impinge upon their bodies, instantly checking their advance. They found themselves transfixed—brought to a standstill in a running group—half-way between the central altar and the chapel steps.

Without uttering a word, Mocata came down the steps and slowly walked round them, carrying the thing which they now guessed to be the Talisman aloft in his left hand. A glowing phosphorescent circle appeared on the damp stone flags in his tracks and, as he completed the circuit, they felt their limbs relax.

Again they rushed at him, but were brought up with a jerk. It was impossible to break out of that magic circle in which he had confined them.

With slow steps, the Satanist returned to the chapel and

proceeded to light a row of black candles upon the broken altar there. Then, with a little gasp of unutterable fear, Marie Lou saw that Fleur was crouching in a dark corner near the upturned earth from which the Talisman had been recovered.

'Fleur—darling!' she cried imploringly, stretching out her arms, but the child did not seem to hear. With round eyes she knelt there near the altar, staring out towards the crypt, but apparently seeing nothing.

Mocata lit some incense in a censer and swung it rhythmically before the broken altar, murmuring strange invocations.

He moved so smoothly and silently that he might have been a phantom but for the lisping intonation of his low musical voice. Then Fleur began to cry, and the sobbing of the child had an unmistakable reality which tore at the very fibre of their hearts.

Again and again they tried to break out of the circle, but at last, forced to give up their frantic attempts, they crouched together straining against the invisible barrier, watching with fear-distended eyes as a gradual materialisation began to form in the clouds of incense above the altar stone.

At first it seemed to be the face of Mocata's black familiar that Rex had seen in Simon's house, but it changed and lengthened. A pointed beard appeared on the chin and four great curved horns sprouted from the head. Soon it became definite, clear and solid. That monstrous, shaggy beast that had held court on Salisbury Plain, the veritable Goat of Mendes, glared at them with its red, baleful, slanting eyes, and belched foetid, deathly breaths from its cavernous nostrils.

Mocata raised the Talisman and set it upon the forehead of the Beast, laying it lengthwise upon the flat, bald, bony skull, where it blazed like some magnificent jewel which had a strange black centre. Then he stooped, seized the child and, tearing off her clothes, flung her naked body full length upon the altar beneath the raised fore-hooves of the Goat.

Sick with apprehension and frantic with distress, the prisoners in the circle heard the sorcerer begin to intone the terrible lines of the Black Mass.

Horrified but powerless, they watched the swinging of the censer, the chanting of the blasphemous prayers, and the blessing of the dagger by the Goat, knowing that at the conclusion of the awful ceremony, the perverted maniac playing

311

the part of the devil's priest would rip the child open from throat to groin while offering her soul to Hell.

Half crazy with fear, they saw Mocata pick up the knife and raise his arm above the little body, about to strike.

33

Death of a Man Unknown, From Natural Causes

Rex stood with the sweat pouring down his face. The muscles of his arms jerked convulsively. His whole will was concentrated in an effort to fling himself forward, up the steps; yet, except for the tremors which ran through his body, the invisible power held him motionless in its grip.

De Richleau prayed. Silent but inceasing, his soundless words vibrated on the ether. He knew the futility of any attempt at physical intervention, and doubted now if his supplications could avail when pitted against such a terrible manifestation of evil as the Goat of Mendes.

Richard crouched near him, his face white and bloodless, his eyes staring. His arms were stretched out, as though to snatch Fleur away or in an appeal for mercy, but he could not move them.

Marie Lou had one hand resting on his shoulder. She was past fear for herself, past all thought of that terrible end which might come to them in a few moments, past even the horror of losing Richard should they all be blotted out in some awful final darkness.

She did not pray or strive to dash towards her child. The pulsing of her heart seemed to be temporarily suspended. Her brain was working with that strange clarity which only comes upon those rare occasions when danger appears to be so overwhelming that there is no possible escape. Into her mind there came a clear-cut picture of herself as she had been in her dream, holding what De Richleau said was the great Red Book of Appin. Her fingers could feel the very cover again with its soft hairy skin.

Simon dropped to his knees between the Duke and Rex. He

312

made an effort to cast himself forward but rocked very slightly from side to side, stricken with an agony of misery and remorse. It was his folly which had led his friends into this terrible pass and now he did the only thing he could to make atonement. His brain no longer clouded, but with full knowledge of the enormity of the thing, he offered himself silently to the Power of Darkness if Fleur might be spared.

Mocata paused for a moment, the knife still poised above the body of the child, to turn and look at him. The thought vibration had been so strong that he had caught it, but he had already drawn all that he needed out of Simon. Slowly his pale lips crumpled in a cruel smile. He shook his head in rejection of the offer and raised the knife again.

The Duke's hand jerked up in a frantic effort to stay the blow by the sign of the cross, but it was struck down to his side by one of the rays from the Talisman, just as though some powerful physical force had hit it.

Richard's jaws opened as though about to shout but no sound issued from them.

With a supreme effort Rex lowered his head to charge, but the invisible weight of twenty men seemed to force back his shoulders.

Before the mental eyes of Marie Lou the Red Book of Appin lay open. Again she saw the stained vellum page and the faded writing in strange characters upon it. And once more as in her dream she could understand the one sentence: *'They only who Love without Desire shall have power granted to them in the Darkest Hour.'*

Then her lips opened. With no knowledge of its meaning, and a certainty that she had never seen it written or heard it pronounced before, she spoke a strange word—having five syllables.

The effect was instantaneous. The whole chamber rocked as though shaken by an earthquake. The walls receded, the floor began to spin. The crypt gyrated with such terrifying speed that the occupants of the circle clutched frantically at each other to save themselves from falling. The altar candles swayed and danced before their distended eyes. The Talisman of Set was swept from between the horns of the monstrous Goat, and bouncing down the steps of the chapel, came to rest on the stone flags at De Richleau's feet.

Mocata staggered back. The Goat reared up on its hind legs above him. A terrible neighing sound came from its nostrils and the slanting eyes swivelled in their sockets; their baleful light flashing round the chamber. The Beast seemed to grow and expand until it was towering above them all as they crouched, petrified with fear. The stench of its fœtid breath poured from between the bared teeth until they were retching with nausea. Mocata's knife clattered upon the stones as he raised his arms in frantic terror to defend himself. The awful thing which he had called up out of the Pit gave a final screaming neigh and struck with one of its great fore-hooves. He was thrown with frightful force to the floor, where he lay sprawled head downmost on the chapel steps.

There was a thunderous crash as though the heavens were opening. The crypt ceased to rock and spin. The Satanic figure dissolved in upon itself. For a fraction of time the watchers in the circle saw the black human face of the Malagasy, distorted with pain and rage, where that of the Goat had been before. Then that too disappeared behind a veil of curling smoke.

The black candles on the altar flickered and went out. The chamber remained lit only by the phosphorescent glow from the Talisman. De Richleau had snatched it from the floor and held it in his open hand. By its faint light they saw Fleur sit up. She gave a little wail and slid from the low altar stone to the ground; then she stood gaping towards her mother, yet her eyes were round and sightless like those of one who walks in her sleep.

Suddenly an utter silence beyond human understanding descended like a cloak and closed in from the shadows that were all about them.

Almost imperceptibly a faint unearthly music, coming from some immense distance, reached their ears. At first it sounded like the splashing of spring water in a rock-bound cave, but gradually it grew in volume, and swelled into a strange chant rendered by boys' voices of unimaginable purity. All fear had gone from them as, one by one, they fell upon their knees and listened entranced to the wonder and the beauty of that litany of praise. Yet all their eyes were riveted on Fleur.

The child walked very slowly forward but, as she advanced, some extraordinary change was taking place about her. The little body, naked a moment before, became clothed in a

314

golden mist. Her shoulders broadened and she grew in height. Her features became partially obscured, then they lost their infant roundness and took on the bony structure of an adult. The diaphanous cloud of light gradually materialised into the graceful folds of a long, yellow, silken robe. The dark curls on the head disappeared leaving a high, beautifully proportioned skull.

As the chant ceased on a great note of exultation all semblance to the child had vanished. In her place a full-grown man stood before them. From his dress he had the appearance of a Thibetan Lama, but his æsthetic face was as much Aryan as Mongolian, blending the highest characteristics of the two; and just as it seemed that he had passed the barriers of race, so he also appeared to have cast off the shackles of worldly time. His countenance showed all the health and vigour of a man in the great years when he has come to full physical development, and yet it had the added beauty which is only seen in that of a frail, scholarly divine who has devoted a whole lifetime to the search for wisdom. The grave eyes which were bent upon them held Strength, Knowledge, and Power, together with an infinite tenderness and angelic compassion unknown to mortal man.

The apparition did not speak by word of mouth. Yet each one of the kneeling group heard the low, silver, bell-like voice with perfect clearness.

'I am a Lord of Light nearing perfection after many lives. It is wrong that you should draw me from my meditations in the Hidden Valley—yet I pardon you because your need was great. One here has imperilled the flame of Life by seeking to use hidden mysteries for an evil purpose; another also, who lies beyond the waters, has been stricken in her earthly body for that same reason. The love you bear each other has been a barrier and protection, yet would it have availed you nothing had it not been for She who is the Mother. The Preserver harkens ever to the prayer which goes forth innocent of all self-desire and so, for a moment, I am permitted to appear to you through the medium of this child whose thoughts know no impurity. The Adversary has been driven back to the dark Halls of Shaitan and shall trouble you no more. Live out the days of your allotted span. Peace be upon you and about you. Sleep and Return.'

315

For a moment it seemed that they had been ripped right out of the crypt and were looking down into it. The circle had become a flaming sun. Their bodies were dark shadows grouped in its centre. The peace and silence of death surged over them in great saturating waves. They were above the monastery. The great ruin became a black speck in the distance. Then everything faded.

Time ceased, and it seemed that for a thousand thousand years they floated, atoms of radiant matter in an immense immeasurable void—circling, for ever circling in the soundless stratosphere—beings shut off from every feeling and sensation, as though travelling with effortless impulse five hundred fathoms deep, below the current levels of some uncharted sea.

Then, after a passage of eons in human time they saw Cardinals Folly again infinitely far beneath them, their bodies lying in the pentacle—and that darkened room. In an utter eerie silence the dust of centuries was falling . . . falling. Softly, impalpably, like infinitely tiny particles of swansdown it seemed to cover them, the room, and all that was in it, with a fine grey powder.

* * * * *

De Richleau raised his head. It seemed to him that he had been on a long journey and then slept for many days. He passed his hand across his eyes and saw the familiar bookshelves in the semi-darkened library. The bulbs above the cornice flickered and the lights came full on.

He saw that Simon's eyes were free from that terrible maniacal glare, but that he still lay bound in the centre of the pentacle.

As he bent forward and hastily began to untie Simon's turning they saw him. Tall—haggard—distraught—a dark fondling her and murmuring. 'We're safe, darling—safe.'

'She—she's not dead—is she?' It was Rex's voice, and turning they saw him. Tall—haggard—distraught—a dark silhouette against the early morning light which filtered in through the french-windows—bearing Tanith's body in his arms.

Marie Lou sprang up with a little wailing cry. With Richard behind her she raced across the room and through the door in the wall which concealed the staircase to the nursery.

The Duke hurried over to Rex. Simon kicked his feet free

and stood up, exclaiming: 'I've had a most extraordinary dream.'

'About all of us going to Paris?' asked De Richleau, as the three of them lowered Tanith's body to the floor, 'and then on to a ruined monastery in northern Greece?'

'That's it—but how—did you know?'

'Because I had the same myself—*if it was a dream!*'

An hysterical laugh came from the stairway and next moment Marie Lou was beside them, great tears streaming down her face, but Fleur clutched safely in her arms.

The child, freshly woken from her sleep, gazed at them with wide, blue eyes, and then she said: 'Fleur wants to go to Simon.'

The Duke was examining Tanith. Simon rose from beside him. His eyes held all the love that surged in the great heart which beat between his narrow shoulders. He covered his short-sighted eyes with his hands for a second then backed away. 'No, Fleur, darling—I've been—I'm still ill you know.'

'Nonsense—that's all over,' Richard cried quickly, 'go on—for God's sake take her—Marie Lou's going to faint.'

'Oh, Richard! Richard!' As Simon grabbed the child, Marie Lou swayed towards her husband, and leaning on him drew her fingers softly down his face. 'I will be all right in a moment —but it was a dream—wasn't it?'

'She's alive!' exclaimed the Duke suddenly, his hand pressed below Tanith's heart. 'Quick, Rex—some brandy.'

'Of course, dearest,' Richard was comforting Marie Lou. 'We've never been out of this room—look, except Rex, we are still in pyjamas.'

'Why, yes—I thought—— Oh, but look at this poor girl.' She slipped from his arms and knelt beside Tanith.

Rex came crashing back with a decanter and a glass. De Richleau snatched the brandy from him. Marie Lou pillowed Tanith's head upon her knees and Richard held her chin. Between them they succeeded in getting a little of the spirit down her throat; a spasm crossed her face and then her eyes opened.

'Thank God!' breathed Rex. 'Thank God.'

She smiled and whispered his name, as the natural colour flooded back into her face.

'Never—never have I had such a terrible nightmare!' exclaimed Marie Lou. 'We were in a crypt—and that awful man was there. He . . .'

'So you dreamed it too!' Simon interrupted. 'About you finding me at that warehouse in Asnières and the Paris police?'

'That's it,' said Richard. 'It's amazing that we should all have dreamed the same thing but there's no other explanation for it. None of us can possibly have left this house since we settled down in the pentacle—— Yes, last night!'

'Then I've certainly been dreaming too.' Rex lifted his eyes for a moment from Tanith's face. 'It must have started with me when I fell asleep at the inn—or earlier, for I'd have sworn De Richleau and I were out all the night before careering around half of England to stop some devilry.'

'We were,' said the Duke slowly. 'Tanith's presence here proves that, but she was never dead except in our dream, and that started when you arrived here with her in your arms. The Satanists at Simon's house, our visit there afterwards, and the Sabbat were all facts. It was only last night, while our bodies slept, that our subconscious selves were drawn out of them to continue the struggle with Mocata on another plane.'

'Mocata!' Simon echoed. 'But—but if we've been dreaming he is still alive.'

'No, he is dead.' The quiet, sure statement came from Tanith as she sat up, and taking Rex's hand scrambled to her feet.

'How is it you're so certain?' he asked huskily.

'I can see him. He is not far from here—lying head downwards on some steps.'

'That's how we saw him in the dream,' said Richard, but she shook her head.

'No, I had no dream. I remember nothing after Mocata entered my room at the inn and forced me to sleep—but you will find him—somewhere quite near the house—out there.'

'The age-old law,' De Richleau murmured. 'A life for a life and a soul for a soul. Yes, since you have been restored to us I am quite certain that he will have paid the penalty.'

Simon nodded. 'Then we're really free of this nightmare at last?'

'Yes. Dream or no dream, the Lord of Light who appeared to us drove back the Power of Darkness, and promised that we should all live unmolested by it to the end of our allotted span. Come, Richard,' the Duke took his host's arm, 'let us find our coats and take a look round the garden—then we shall have done with this horrible business.'

As they moved away Tanith smiled up at Rex. 'Did you really mean what you said last night?'

'Did I mean it!' he cried, seizing both her hands. 'Just you let me show you how!'

'Simon,' said Marie Lou pointedly, 'that child will catch her death of cold in nothing but her nightie—do take her back to the nursery while I get the servants to hurry forward breakfast.' And the old familiar happy smile parted his wide mouth as Fleur took a flying leap into his arms.

Tanith's face grew a little wistful as Rex drew her to him. 'My darling,' she hesitated, 'you know that it will be only for a little time, about eight months—no more.'

'Nonsense!' he laughed. 'You were certainly dead to all of us last night, so your prophecy's been fulfilled and the evil lifted—we're both going to live together for a hundred years.'

She hid her face against his shoulder, not quite believing yet, but a new hope dawning in her heart, from his certainty that she had passed through the Valley of the Shadow and come out again upon the other side. Her happiness, and his, demanded that she accept his view and act henceforth as though the danger to her life was past.

'Then if you want them, my days are yours,' she murmured, 'whatever their number may be.'

There was no trace of fog and a fair, true dawn was breaking when, outside the library windows, De Richleau and Richard found Mocata's body. It lay on the stone steps which led up to the terrace, sprawling head downwards, in the early light of the May morning.

'The coroner will find no difficulty in bringing in a verdict,' the Duke observed after one glance at the face. 'They'll say it is heart, of course. It is best not to touch the body, presently we will telephone the police. None of us need say we have ever seen him before if you tell Malin to keep quiet about his visit yesterday afternoon. You may be certain that his friends will not come forward to mention his acquaintance with Simon or the girl.'

Richard nodded. 'Yes. "Death of a Man Unknown, from Natural Causes," will be the only epilogue to this strange story.'

319

'Not quite, but this must be between us, Richard. I prefer that the others should not know. Take me to your boiler-house.'

'The boiler-house—whatever for?'

'I'll tell you in a minute.'

'All right!' With a puzzled look Richard led the Duke along the terrace, round by the kitchen quarters and into a small building where a furnace gave a subdued roar.

De Richleau lifted the latch and the door swung back, disclosing the glowing coke within. Then he extended his right fist and slowly opened it.

'Good God!' exclaimed Richard. 'However did you come by that?'

In De Richleau's palm lay a shrunken, mummified phallus, measuring no more than the length of a little finger, hard, dry, and almost black with age. It was the Talisman of Set, just as they had seen it in their recent dream adorning the brow of the monstrous Goat.

'I found myself clutching it when I awoke,' he answered softly.

'But—but that thing must have come from somewhere!'

'Perhaps it is a concrete symbol of the evil that we have fought, which has been given over into our hands for destruction.'

As the Duke finished speaking he cast the Talisman into the glowing furnace where they watched it until it was utterly consumed.

'If we were only dreaming how can you possibly explain it?' Richard insisted.

'I cannot.' De Richleau shrugged a little wearily. 'Even the greatest seekers after Truth have done little more than lift the corner of the veil which hides the vast Unknown, but it is my belief that during the period of our dream journey we have been living in what the moderns call the fourth dimension—divorced from time.'